THE
SPELL-BOUND
SCHOLAR

CHRISTOPHER
STASHEFF

ACE BOOKS, NEW YORK

THE SPELL-BOUND SCHOLAR

An Ace Book / published by arrangement with
the author

PRINTING HISTORY
Ace edition / August 1999

The Penguin Putnam Inc. World Wide Web site address is
http://www.penguinputnam.com

Check out the ACE Science Fiction & Fantasy newsletter
and much more on the internet at Club PPI!

ISBN: 0-441-00636-1

ACE®
Ace Books are published
by The Berkley Publishing Group,
a division of Penguin Putnam Inc.,
375 Hudson Street, New York, New York 10014.
ACE and the "A" design are trademarks
belonging to Penguin Putnam Inc.

PRINTED IN THE UNITED STATES OF AMERICA

10 9 8 7 6 5 4 3 2 1

With thanks to
Finister's advocate,
Genevieve Stasheff,
who thought Finister could
be reformed

NOTE TO THE READER

The author is very much aware that the events in this book are extremely unlikely, if not downright impossible. Nonetheless, science fiction has always been the domain of the Worlds of If, and it is legitimate for an SF book to say, "If only . . . "

Besides, this book is really science *fantasy*, and fantasy has always dealt with magic bringing about things that can't really happen.

PROLOGUE

Twenty-five years ago, a secret agent named Rod Gallowglass landed on the lost colony planet of Gramarye, determined to turn it into a democracy. That was the purpose of his organization, SCENT, the Society for the Conversion of Extraterrestrial Nascent Totalitarianisms—to sniff out the lost colonies and bring all the colonial planets back within the umbrella of the interstellar democracy that had begun on Earth. But Rod discovered that Gramarye wasn't your average lost colony—about one out of ten people was a telepath, telekinetic, and/or other form of esper. That was much, much higher than the average in the rest of the Terran Sphere—but still rare on Gramarye, and since the planet was medieval, the rest of the people thought the espers were witches. Rod, though, knew that they would be the perfect solution to the communication problems that were beginning to trouble the interstellar democracy for which he worked.

He wasn't the only one to realize Gramarye's value, though—so did the totalitarians and anarchists from the future, who had failed to overthrow the interstellar democracy because of the "interference" of the descendants of Gramarye's "witches." They sent secret agents back to the past— Rod's present—to try to overthrow the monarchy and take over the planet before it could develop a democratic government of its own and join the interstellar democratic federation.

With the help of an attractive witch named Gwendylon, Rod managed to fight off the futurians. Then he achieved the even more remarkable (to him) feat of marrying Gwendylon. He was equally amazed by his four children. Rod and Gwen had their share of trials, but between them, they managed to raise all four (and each other) to maturity.

1

Christopher Stasheff

Not that the futurians gave up, of course. They kept trying to overthrow the government, and when Rod and his family foiled them at every turn, they changed their goal into overthrowing the Gallowglasses, preferably by killing them. When that didn't work either, they changed their tactics: They raised Gramarye witch-orphans to become fanatical totalitarians or anarchists and set them to neutralizing the Gallowglass threat. The only one to be even marginally successful was Finister, a very powerful (and beautiful) young projective esper—she was able to make those around her see in her an appearance completely different from her natural one, and with a talent that amounted to instant hypnotism, was even able to make others see themselves as having changed form—say, into toads. She managed to give the eldest Gallowglass child, Magnus, enough harrowing near-sexual experiences to make him lose all interest in sex (thereby assuring that he wouldn't have any descendants to interfere with the future anarchists) and leave Gramarye, to go wandering around the Terran Sphere overthrowing oppressive governments.

On the strength of that success (and her ability to influence, then assassinate, her top boss), she became Chief Agent of the anarchists of Gramarye. She then set about thwarting Cordelia's romances by becoming her rival to both her suitors. Prince Alain, however, loved Cordelia so much that he was able to resist Finister's blandishments and, after a crash course in being romantic (provided by Cordelia's younger brother Geoffrey), wooed and won the Gallowglass daughter.

Smarting from defeat, Finister tried to recoup her self-esteem by attempting to snare and marry the third Gallowglass child, Geoffrey; she would, of course, make sure he did not reproduce. However, she ran into tough and unexpected competition—a spectacular female bandit who called herself Quicksilver.

Finister disguised herself as Moraga, a plain young witch whose heart had been broken by a greedy knight who had wooed and won her, used her to make him a fortune, then spurned her. Finister discovered this, had Moraga kidnapped and imprisoned, then assumed her appearance by use of projective telepathy. As Moraga, she challenged the local knight,

2

shire-reeve, and count by conquering a few villages on their respective domains. The elves, who had always liked Moraga, were alarmed by her personality change and her probable fate (death, for a traitor and rebel). They asked Geoffrey Gallow-glass to intervene, and he did.

Thus Moraga fought Geoffrey and Quicksilver as a plain, lumpen witch. They talked her into surrendering to them, promising her a fair trial and the chance of justice, by bringing the men who had wronged her to trial with her. She joined the party, and her background did indeed inspire pity in Geoffrey. Once near him, though, Finister exercised her shape-changing abilities, gradually becoming beautiful, voluptuous, and seductive. Geoffrey, however, had already fallen head over heels in love with Quicksilver.

Geoffrey called in his little brother Gregory to help escort Quicksilver and Moraga to Castle Loguire for trial. Finister tried to work her wiles on Gregory but found that he was totally indifferent to sex or, indeed, anything having to do with emotion. Finally, Geoffrey left it to Gregory to defend "Moraga" in her trial before his old friend Duke Diarmid and his parents, Their Majesties Tuan and Catherine. She was pardoned but sentenced to see if she wanted to join the Royal Coven, and sent to Runnymede with Gregory as escort. Geoffrey, on the other hand, defended Quicksilver and managed to have her punishment limited to wandering the countryside with him looking for wrongs to right—whereupon he proposed, and she accepted.

Finister was still determined to steal Geoffrey away from Quicksilver and Alain from Cordelia, but as long as she was on her way to Runnymede and away from the opportunity to do some serious fiancé-stealing, she thought she might as well seize the chance to romantically enslave Gregory and kill him or, at least, his interest in sex and women. Since the latter was pretty low anyway, it wouldn't take much killing.

CHAPTER

-1-

Duke Diarmid pronounced sentence and the witch Moraga rode away toward the north with no more guardian than the wizard Gregory.

The morning was beautiful, and so was Moraga, Gregory noted in a detached, clinical way. Either she improved upon acquaintance or her attractiveness was subtle—she had looked quite plain, even dumpy, when his brother had first met her fighting a knight and his men single-handedly.

Moraga chattered and smiled. "The day is so beautiful, is it not, Master Gregory? I do so love the early morning! The day is crisp and new, the air so fresh as never again in the day! If only it could remain thus forever!"

"It is indeed lovely," Gregory replied. He was bored with the conversation before it had begun but knew enough of manners to attempt to converse. He forced himself to look about him with a smile.

A small smile, Moraga noted. Everything about him was small—his height, his hands, his muscles, his whole body! Or at least what she could see of it. His heart must have been small, too, for his anger was only irritation, his delight only appreciation, his disgust only disapproval. That hussy Quicksilver had stolen that bulk of muscle and appetite Geoffrey from her, leaving her only this wraith! She was tempted to tie him to his saddle so that he wouldn't blow away.

No matter how brightly she chattered, she was seething inside. Her goal was to make sure none of the Gallowglass children reproduced, and she was only managing one out of four at the moment. Magnus she had effectively gelded, in emotions if not in body, but when she had tried to neutralize Cordelia by captivating her suitor, Crown Prince Alain, that grinning hulk Geoffrey had interfered and taught the royal idiot how to woo a lady, and his sister Cordelia was now engaged! To make it worse, Geoffrey was engaged himself to the female bandit Quicksilver, and she was left with this scrap of a man, this Gregory! Why, he seemed no more than a boy, a fuzz-cheeked stripling!

On the other hand, he certainly wasn't going to be much of a problem. He was clearly the weakest of the four younger Gallowglasses, seeming almost fragile and far too bookish to be much of a fighter. Certainly she'd seen absolutely no sign of his being a lover; after all, she was in a position to know, and would have liked nothing better than setting brother against brother in jealousy over her—but Gregory had shown not the slightest reaction to her charms. She wondered whether it were his interest in study that had kept him from girls or his fear of women that had driven him to seek refuge in books. She had to admit he had shown as little fear as he had lust, though. Still, that was no doubt a matter of hiding both well. Finister did not doubt that Gregory would fall very hard for the first willing beauty to come along—though she might have to be a bit more than willing.

Enough of planning; time for action. She adjusted her projection of her physical appearance, making the face and body a bit thinner in the right places, the eyes a bit larger, the lips a bit more full, the nose a little shorter. Then she turned to him with a lazy, inviting smile and said, "The day grows warm and the road long, Sir Gregory. Might we not dismount and rest awhile?" She made the word "rest" as suggestive as possible.

Gregory registered that not at all, only turned to incline his head politely. "There is only an hour or two of daylight left, damsel. Let us remain in our saddles a while longer; then we shall camp for the night." He turned back to the road before them, his lips in a slight smile, his gaze becoming abstracted again.

Irritated but shrewd, Moraga kept her smile in place, making it even more sultry. "As you please, my lord."

The lunk didn't even react to her emphasis on the word "please!" Really, he was useless as a man, a stick, a stone, nothing more! If she hadn't been assigned to slay or geld him, she would have ridden away and never bothered with him again.

But he was her assignment, and she had already failed with his brother and sister. In fact, she had only partially succeeded with Magnus! He still lived, and the Green Witch had halfway undone all her work; Finister had locked Magnus's heart in a box of gold, but the vixen had let him know there was a key! If she couldn't at least maim his youngest brother, the weakest of the four, she would indeed be a poor excuse for a *femme fatale*. It was a matter of professional pride, a challenge that had to be met.

Finister didn't acknowledge that it was very much a matter of personal pride, too.

That didn't mean she wouldn't have to be careful. On the way to Castle Loguire, she had learned that Gregory's magic more than made up for the strength his body lacked. Still, she knew her own forte to be projective telepathy and that her talent was so powerful that she was able to hypnotize people into seeing her in whatever form was convenient, from sultry temptress to baleful hag—even into believing they themselves were no longer human. She was one of the few who could change a prince into a frog, at least in his own eyes, and had even spellbound the High Warlock's redoubtable eldest, the wizard Magnus, into believing he was a snake.

Of course, most men had such raging sex drives that they were eager to believe whatever she cast upon them. It would be interesting to see if she could rouse enough lust in Gregory to make him succumb to her hypnotic charms, even as his brother had. So far she was doing well—he didn't seem to question her being the plain, lumpen witch Moraga. She wondered idly if the elves had found what was left of the real Moraga yet—not that it made much difference. If she could captivate Gregory, all the warnings in the world would do him no good.

If.

She rallied her wiles for another attempt. "There is no need

7

for us to hurry, sir wizard. The royal witches will not expect us on any definite day."

"That is true." Gregory came back out of the clouds instantly, turning to her politely—but not completely; she could see in his eyes that he was still turning over a mathematical problem in the back of his mind. "Accordingly, if I discover the presence of that for which I seek, I shall beg your leave to turn aside and investigate."

That startled her; then it angered her. Even if she had only been Moraga, she would have been an esper powerful enough to be his sole concern on this journey, and as the assassin who had maimed his eldest brother and attempted to kill both his other brother and his sister, she certainly was worth his undivided attention. "What do you seek?" She kept her voice level, even managed to sound mildly interested. "What is it that is so vital as to be deserving of your time?"

The sarcasm was lost on Gregory; he answered gravely, "A site of power, a place in the land that resonates so strongly with my mind as to enhance my natural abilities."

Moraga had seen some of his natural abilities. The idea of their being enhanced turned her spine into an icicle. "What . . . what would you do if you found such a place?"

"Settle for twenty years or so to study aspects of psi 'magic' that no one else has investigated."

Moraga simply stared at him in disbelief. For a wizard of such ability to find a means of multiplying his power, then use it for no other purpose than research? Unthinkable!

But not for this bookworm. Moraga smiled with relief. "What a splendid task! And how delightful, to be able to do nothing but think and discover for so long!"

"Do you truly think so?" Gregory looked at her with interest, the first interest he had shown.

That gave Moraga an idea. She broadened her smile and let her eyelids droop, saying, "Of course. Who would not wish such a retirement from the world if they could have it?"

"Even so!" Gregory said, pleased. Then, though, his eyes seemed to glaze and his gaze drifted away, as though a new thought had come into his mind.

Moraga stifled a shout of frustration. The man was impossible, so completely removed from the world that he seemed scarcely human! She turned to face the road again, hoping that the gentle swaying of her horse would calm her, but it did not. Site of power indeed! Gregory was not only a milk-sop with more brains than sense, he was also a credulous and superstitious fool as well as a virtual eunuch! What would she have to do to capture and maintain his interest—a complete seductive striptease?

The idea was worth considering—but she suspected that she would have to spike his food with an aphrodisiac before even that would work.

She closed her eyes in concentration a moment, mentally "listening" for Gregory's thoughts. The probe yielded nothing, as had her earlier attempts, only an impervious sense of nothingness inside Gregory's mind—he was psionically invisible. If she hadn't seen his intelligence and the strength of his psi powers for herself, she would have thought him a mental vegetable, even more insensitive than an ordinary human being. Knowing he was a powerful esper, though, she suspected that his psychic invisibility was quite deliberate, an excellently wrought shield.

Perhaps she was wasting her time, perhaps her assignment was in vain—as far as she could tell, Gregory didn't *have* a sex drive! But she had to make sure, had to be absolutely certain he could not reproduce—though she couldn't for the life of her think of any woman who would want him.

Besides, there was always the chance of an opportunity to kill him. When they stopped for the night, she would see about gathering hemlock or perhaps some belladonna.

Of course, there was always the possibility of crawling into his bed in the middle of the night—but Gregory made even that impossible. They pitched camp and ate dinner, making idle talk—or at least Moraga made idle talk. Gregory listened politely, giving her his complete attention—well, almost complete—and asking the occasional question to keep her talking. She willingly told him of Moraga's past—it was real enough, after all, and her telling of it was calculated to tenderize the hardest of hearts. Gregory, however, only listened, smiling with sympathy and making occasional comforting noises.

Moraga inched her way around the campfire, closer and closer to him as she told the tale, remodelling her face and form inch by inch until Moraga was really quite attractive, certainly voluptuous, and the telling was so masterful that she actually began to weep at the end of it. Any real man would have taken her in his arms to comfort her, and she could have turned the comforting into a kiss and the embrace into caressing—but Gregory only slipped a handkerchief from his sleeve and offered it to her, saying, "Let the tears flow, damsel. They will hurt nothing, but will lighten your heart. Certainly it has cause to be heavy, for you have been most abominably used."

The phrase conjured up a brief vision from her own adolescence, but Finister clamped down on it instantly, shoving it back into the depths of her mind—one did not dare think openly in the presence of a skilled telepath. She took the square of silk, throttling her frustration, and sniffed, dabbing at her eyes in her most becoming pose. "I—I thank you, Sir Gregory. I had not meant to burden you with my sorrows."

"A burden shared makes a lighter heart and a brighter future, damsel," Gregory assured her. "If I can make amends for some of the wrongs done by my sex, be sure that I shall."

So appealing to him because of her own abuse had been exactly the wrong approach to take; bound and determined not to put her through even a reminder of such a violation again, Gregory forbore to lie down. When she had dried her tears, he said, "Sleep now, and let your dreams heal your heart, for you go to a place where your gifts shall be valued, and you shall have true friends among others of your own kind. Indeed, you shall discover for the first time that you have a kind, that you are not alone. Nay, lie down, damsel, and let slumber bear you away into sweet oblivion."

Moraga felt a moment's panic, for she knew what she would have meant by such a phrase—but she reminded herself that it was the weakling Gregory who spoke, not herself or any of her fellow assassins, and lay down planning to stay awake until he was under his own blanket and more vulnerable than ever to the warmth of a woman seeking comfort.

But what was this? Gregory did not lie down—he stayed

sitting by the campfire, back straight, legs crossed, hands palm upward on his knees, gazing off into the night with a dreamy, absent look.

"My—my lord?" Moraga asked, trying to sound timid instead of indignant. "Will you not sleep?"

"I shall not, damsel." His voice was remote, like a distant call carried on the wind. "Someone must keep watch in case a bear or wolf should come, or even to keep the fire from burning down."

Moraga sat up. "Then I shall take the first watch!" She would abandon it, too, as soon as Gregory was lying down.

"Thank you, but no. I shall spend the night in a trance that will restore me quite as much as sleep would, but that shall let me remain vigilant. Do take your rest; there is no need for any sentry other than myself."

"If . . . if you say so, my lord." Defeated for the moment, Moraga lay down again. She actually tried to sleep—it didn't seem there was much point in anything else, now—but found she could not; she was seething at this latest obstacle, and it brought to mind again the Gallowglasses's defeat of her plans. She thrashed about, trying to banish them all from her mind, trying to forget Magnus's return from the Green Witch's healing, Cordelia standing triumphant with Alain's hands in hers, Geoffrey kneeling to propose to Quicksilver there before all the court at the end of her trial, and the memories of the thwarting of her plans whipped up such a fury in her that she began to shake. She took slow, deep breaths, remembering the ritual for calming that her martial arts teacher had shown her, and gradually managed to let her anger fade, her harmony return to bury the feelings of hurt and outrage that were always there in the depths of her heart, waiting to spring out and betray her whenever she most needed to think clearly. After a few minutes, drowsiness came with a suddenness that surprised her. She was grateful for it and let it sweep over her, bearing her away into a deep and calming sleep, and if dreams of her triumphs surfaced, then submerged as she slept, all the better to restore her confidence in her struggle against this emotionless boy who watched over her slumber.

The dreams, of course, were not entirely the product of an

angry and frustrated mind, nor were the memories of her defeats at the hands of the Gallowglass family. Warned by anomalies in her behavior during their trip to Loguire, Gregory suspected that he had an enemy in his keeping, not an innocent victim who had talents the crown badly needed. The suspicion was strong enough to warrant a breach of the esper's ethics he had been taught, so he inserted key images into Moraga's seething mind that made her remember her various crimes against the family and her defeats. Then he projected a soothing, calming drowsiness, and when she had drifted into sleep, he slipped other key ideas into her mind and paid close attention to the memories they evoked. He witnessed each of the three assassinations she had carried out, even as she had been assigned to do—first winning the man's trust, or at least relaxation of his vigilance, by the sexual magnetism she projected, then slipping a knife between his ribs as he slept, or poison in his food as he ate. He was surprised to discover that she thought herself plain and unattractive but had an amazing amount of confidence in her telepathic ability to convince her victims that she was intensely desirable. He even witnessed her latest and unassigned murder—that of the former Chief Agent, making sure that he left a letter appointing her Chief Agent in his stead.

So, then. He dealt not only with the witch who had mangled his brother's emotions and striven to murder Cordelia, Alain, and Geoffrey, but also with the Chief Agent of the anarchists of Gramarye—not only his family's personal nemesis, but a public enemy, too.

What would she do? He could not say, but he knew the thrust of it would be to kill him or twist his emotions toward a solitary life that would not result in reproduction. He smiled, amused—that last would require no effort at all, would require only that she leave him alone, for he had seen the emotional cripple that Magnus had become, had watched Geoffrey waste an immense amount of time dallying with wenches, and had resolved himself to avoid women as anything but friends and to sublimate his sex drive into research. Moraga had already given him an impulse that should result in a conceptual breakthrough, for though he had been careful not to show it, her flirtations had been most stimulating. He needed the night's meditation badly; he had a great deal of sublimating to do.

He began it by constructing an automatic defense system. He had learned enough about computers from the horse's mouth—the horse being Fess, his father's computer-brained robot charger—so that he knew how to weave a response program into his own mind, conditioning himself to respond to telepathic aggression by reflecting any hostile energy back to its source. Then he relaxed, sure that, though he would not himself take any offensive action against Moraga, anything she tried to do to him would instantly be done to her instead.

Of course, he would still take her to Runnymede, Their Majesties' capital, would still escort her to meet the royal witches—not to apply for membership, but for trial.

He recited a mantra and relaxed into his trance, letting images of quanta rise into his mind—but they kept being overlaid with images of the real and natural Finister as she saw herself in her mirror, a sight that she found repulsive but whose beauty Gregory could only admire. With it came a sensing—only that, a vague mental perception, not even a hunch or a clear thought coming to the surface of her mind and certainly not images, only glimpses of tattered ghosts— but he suspected that there were qualities in Finister that she fought to deny and ignore, a tenderness and ability to empathize, a caring for others that she had been taught to regard as vulnerability and weakness and had consequently suppressed, hardening herself in denial. She had been instructed to use her sensitivity to others' feelings as a means of finding their weaknesses, had been taught that her natural sensuality meant she was born to be a slut and had worth only as a sexual being. Her teachers had told her she could rise above whoredom by using her sexuality as a weapon and becoming an expert assassin, both emotionally and physically.

Gregory's heart wrung with sympathy for the sweet, loving child of whom he gained such furtive glimpses; he was strongly tempted to probe more deeply in an attempt to learn more, perhaps even to cure—but even the ethical penetration

of an enemy's mind had its limits, and Finister had not yet
shown evidence of being so dangerous as to justify such an
invasion—at least, not very dangerous to himself.

Besides, Gregory was afraid of causing more trauma than
he might cure. Firmly putting temptation behind him, he
turned his mind away from Moraga and concentrated on his
favorite mantra, the reconciliation of general relativity with
quantum mechanics and the search for an equation that would
unite the two.

Moraga woke before dawn, amazed that she had slept so
deeply and so well. She stretched, then remembered her current mission and sat up, stretching again as luxuriously as
possible, chin up, back arched, arms reaching backward. She
glanced at Gregory out of the corner of her eye but saw him
in profile, glassy eyes gazing steadfastly ahead. If he had seen
her at all, it was only out of the corner of his eye.

Piqued, she pulled her robe on over her shift, a shift far
more clinging than any true peasant would have worn—after
all, it had been made with artificial fibers spun by a very
advanced technology—and went off into the bushes to perform her morning ablutions. When she came back, she found
Gregory as she had left him and reflected that she really need
not have risked a poison ivy rash—she had only needed to
step around behind his back.

That thought made her toy with the notion of giving herself
a sponge bath where she had slept, at the corner of his eye—
but no, Moraga was supposed to be modest, if not truly innocent. That would have to wait.

On the other hand, Moraga was no virgin and, being a
normal, healthy young woman, might very well have normal,
healthy appetites—perhaps even more than normal. She stood
eyeing Gregory, letting her face and form adjust a little farther
toward their natural state. She might feel herself heavy and
distasteful, but she knew by experience that men thought just
the opposite, no doubt because of the sensuality she projected
into their minds. Besides, she had to admit that her natural
figure was voluptuous and her mane of blond hair was her
glory. Her face she would have characterized as goggle-eyed,

snub-nosed, fat-lipped, and frog-mouthed, but she had learned that men wished to kiss those fat lips and lose themselves in those goggling eyes. She didn't understand it, really, but she knew how to make use of it.

She advanced on Gregory with the intention of doing exactly that.

CHAPTER
-2-

Moraga knelt at Gregory's side, put her lips next to his ear, and breathed, "Waken, Sir Knight. A damsel awaits you, famished and eager to satisfy her hunger ere the night ends."

Gregory sat, mute and immobile, eyes still gazing off into the lightening woods.

Irritated, Moraga moved toward the front and into Gregory's line of sight, bending toward him and wishing she had chosen a low-cut gown, though it would have been out of character. She could, however, undo the topmost button, and she did. "Come, sir! Would you keep a woman waiting? That is most ungentlemanly of you! Cease your vigil and celebrate life with me!"

Still Gregory gazed ahead unmoving, as though she had not even been there.

Moraga passed beyond irritation into outright anger. He would notice her, he would pay attention, she would distract him! She sat back on her heels, tossing her head so that her hair fell forward, its color lightened from the real Moraga's mousy brown to a rich, vibrant red. She smiled secretively, letting her eyelids droop and her lips moisten, then sat directly before Gregory, fingering the second button and purring, "Wake, sir, for the day will be upon us soon! Then we must be on our way, with no more excuse for . . . dalliance. . . ." She let her voice trail off suggestively, leaving the nature of the dalliance to his imagination.

It would seem he had none. His eyes remained glazed, his posture rigidly upright, his expression unvarying.

"Oh, you might as well be made of wood!" she cried, and leaped to her feet. "This is like talking to a wall! Could a woman be more unfortunate than to be cursed with a man

17

whose body is there but whose heart is not? Nay, sit in your trance, then, and may you have joy of your loneliness!" She turned on her heel and strode off into the trees, seething with rage.

Long she paced the wood, letting the anger crest, then subside. How could she begin to seduce a man who scarcely noticed her? How, if his mind was so absent that she could not gain his attention? And not only his mind, either—she found herself wondering if there was also something missing in his body.

Finally she calmed, her course of action becoming clear, her resolution hardening. She sat on a fallen log, letting her mind clear and emotions fall away, then thought, with clear precision and with all her strength,

> *Storks shall flock*
> *Unto the crane*
> *As seven-league boots*
> *Rise Anselm's bane.*

She was very much aware that Gregory could be listening, of course, or any other esper loyal to the Queen. It was an old problem for the anarchists of SPITE, the Society for the Prevention of Integration of Telepathic Entities, one they had solved by developing a code that sounded much like children's nonsense verses. In this case it meant, "All home agents come to the Chief on the High Road twenty-one miles north of Castle Loguire."

She rose from her log with malicious satisfaction. Soon she would begin the ending of this farce, and the Gallowglasses' interference with SPITE's plans.

Gregory came up from his trance striving to fight down the thrill of Moraga's breath in his ear, the memory of her leaning close and the hint of voluptuous contours beneath her sacklike dress, the longing to discover what undoing that second button might disclose. She was quite right, of course—it was time to have breakfast, for the false dawn would not last long, and they should be on their way as the sun rose. He stood, stretching, and called, "Your pardon, damsel, but rising from my trance takes some little time."

He waited a few minutes for her reply, then frowned when there was no answer. He had watched her go off into the trees, but surely she could not have gone very far. "I do not truly scorn your hunger," he called. "Do you blow the coals aflame, and I shall fetch journeybread from my pack and . . ."

His voice trailed off as Moraga failed to reappear. He waited several minutes, but no voice replied to his. He frowned, eyes losing focus, the clearing about him becoming less real than the world of the mind as he listened for responding thoughts—but there were only the sharp sensations of small predators on the hunt, the fear of their prey, some child reciting a nonsense rhyme in her head, and more distantly, the grumbling thoughts of farmers as they stumbled about their morning tasks, cursing their lack of sleep.

Gregory frowned—what could have upset the damsel so that she would have gone so far away? Certainly it was rude of him not to answer when she spoke to him, but when he explained that it took a while for him to surface from his meditations, she would understand, would she not? It was scarcely a calculated insult. She was herself an esper and should understand the requirements of the mental powers that passed for magic on this world. Why should she be irritated if his reply were delayed?

Well, there was no accounting for it. He would simply have to seek her. He turned to saddle his horse, then realized that she had left her own.

Somehow, that struck him more sharply than her mere absence. She had rejected the palfrey that Duke Diarmid had provided. Gregory knew it was ridiculous to feel that by doing so, she had rejected his company as well—but he did.

Of course, if she viewed him as her jailer, she might well reject him or, more to the point, believe that she had escaped him. Gregory sighed and tightened the girth. He would have to seek her out, for jailer or not, he was responsible for escorting her, and for seeing to it that she went to Runnymede and the Royal Coven. He mounted, took her palfrey by the reins, and rode into the wood with the palfrey following.

By the time Moraga reached the marker for the twenty-first mile, she was beginning to wish she had taken that palfrey, or at the very least, picked out a good, stout, dead branch for flying. The quarter mile had not seemed long enough to bother, but as she came up to the milestone, she saw that the men, having teleported, were already waiting. The first of the women came in for a landing as she arrived and the other two were in the sky.

"Good day, Chief Agent," said Mercu. He was a tall, broad-shouldered man of middle years who fought to hide his indignation at taking orders from a chit half his age.

"Good day," Finister replied. She surveyed her male lieutenants with satisfaction, for although she cast no glamour into their minds and they saw her with her natural form and face, she could feel their hunger for her. It was conditioning, no doubt—the residue of the sensuality she had projected into their minds, ever so discreetly, in months past. Like Mercu, Coyle and Lork might resent her rank as Chief Agent, but their hunger for her kept them subservient.

She turned to Leiku and Honoria, just dismounting from their broomsticks. Like the men, they resented her being their boss—but they resented her in every other way, too, envious of her power over men (surely it could not have been envy of her physical appearance!) and jealous of the males' attentions.

Resentful or not, they would do her bidding as long as her schemes worked out, for SPITE had enjoyed very little success on this planet in the past twenty years, and Finister's gains, though minor, were at least not total disasters. She studied the line of faces, taking stock of their abilities and merits. They were all home agents, born on Gramarye of the 10 percent who were operative espers. All had grown up as orphans; most were foundlings. Indeed, only Mercu knew who both parents had been, and that they had died when he was six months old.

They were highly skilled in telekinesis, teleportation, projective telepathy, and, of course, telepathy itself. Moreover, the SPITE orphanage had raised them as it had reared Finister herself—as though it were forging weapons, which in some sense it had. Each was single-minded, dedicated, and ruthless, hating the society that had spawned them and fanatically loyal to the organization that had reared them. There wasn't a one of them who would not cheerfully have died to win Gramarye for SPITE.

Except Finister, of course. In her, the early lessons had taken root too well; she knew she could trust no one but herself. It followed, both logically and emotionally, that she dared not let anyone have power over her, which meant that she could only feel safe if she had both wealth and the power it could buy. Her lieutenants might wish to win Gramarye for SPITE; Finister intended to have it for herself—and these were the weapons with which she would win the fight.

"It's time to divide and conquer," she told her lieutenants. "We're going to split the Gallowglasses away from one another, then hit each of them with an armed squad all at the same moment, so that they can't come to help one another."

The lieutenants stared in surprise for a moment. Then they began to grin.

"Smart, Chief," Coyle said. "They'll have a tough time fighting off a physical attack at the same time as a mental one—and if they call for help, they'll just distract each other. Why didn't anybody think of this before?"

Finister suppressed the urge to say, "Because the old Chief Agent wasn't a genius"; she knew the comment would be too revealing. Instead she said, "Because it was too simple. We were looking for elaborate plots that would tear apart the whole kingdom. We missed the fact that the problem is really personal."

The lieutenants nodded with approval; she could see they appreciated her including them in the credit. Of course, they wouldn't want to share the blame if the attack failed. She gave them a cynical smile.

"What about their psi powers, though?" Leiku asked.

"That will be up to the five of you," Finister answered. "Take some extra home agents with you. Mercu, you take the Lord Warlock. Coyle, take Geoffrey. Leiku, your assignment is Lady Gwendylon. Honoria, you get the chit Corde-lia."

"And I?" Lork asked.

"You gather a band of rankers and hold them ready in the forest until I call."

"What are we supposed to be?"

"Bandits," Finister told him.

Lork nodded judiciously. "Shouldn't take much. We're going to take care of Gregory?"

"You'll help—but I'll take care of Gregory," Finister said, "personally." She grinned, adjusting her mental projection so that her lieutenants saw shark's teeth. "Gregory has become a bit of a challenge."

Geoffrey and Alain went out hunting at dawn the next day. They started home about noon, sending their entourage ahead with the day's trophies, so they were riding down the forest path alone when the peasant maiden stepped from the bushes, hair dishevelled, hollow-cheeked, eyes seeming huge in her gauntness, face streaked with tears, skirt ragged where briars had torn it. Her arms were crossed, holding together the tatters of a blouse that had been slashed and burned, "Good knights, pity, I pray you! Pity on all my village, for we are sorely beset!"

Geoffrey reined in, excitement soaring—a good fight was his second favorite pastime, and it was far more fun when it was in defense of the weak. Alain, however, reined in with alarm; then the fierce protectiveness of the rightful king for his subjects came to the fore. "What has struck you, maiden? Bandits?"

"How badly did they harm you?" Geoffrey asked, taking in the state of her blouse and beginning to be angry.

"Only the bruises and cuts that you see, sir, for I ran as soon as I caught sight of the riders. One of them saw me and dashed away from the pack to chase; he even came close enough to slash at me with his sword before the captain called him back. Some cinders blew upon me from the first cottage they burned, but I thank Heaven they charred only my garment!"

Geoffrey could see they had burned her skin, too, even as the sword had left trails of blood—not deep, for they were already drying—but the woman was clearly in shock and did not yet feel the pain. Frowning, he asked again, "Who are these men who have fallen upon your village?"

"Our own baron, sir! Baron Gripardin, impatient that we were slow to pay our taxes! But sir, we could not—we had scarcely enough to hold body and soul together after all he took last year, and the new crop is only half grown!"

"No wonder the poor thing is so gaunt," Geoffrey muttered to Alain.

"Indeed." The prince's face was set in cold anger. "This cannot be the first time he has chastised you, then."

"Indeed not, sir, but it is the first time he has burned more than one hut. Always before, he contented himself with turning out only a single family, taking the wife and daughters to amuse his men and shackling the father and sons with the cattle who turned his gristmill. Now, though, I know he bade his men set fire to two huts, perhaps more!"

"I have not heard of this Gripardin," Alain said to Geoffrey.

But Queen Catherine had. She told them about the man as they sat in the audience chamber, waiting for the young woman to appear in new homespun. "His grandfather was a bandit who grew fat on the plunder of merchants who dared the forest."

King Tuan nodded heavily. "It would seem his grandson lives by the same rules."

"Wherefore was he ennobled, then?" Alain protested.

"Because he carved an estate out of the rim of the Forest Gellorn, my son," the Queen said, "and your grandfather had need to either put him down or grant him the legitimacy he sought. The man had indeed seen to the clearing of farmland and a better life for fugitives who had run off to the greenwood—nay, even given them a way to rejoin the world, and a guarantee they would not turn robber again. Your grandfather thought him reformed and giving of service to the King and the people, so he granted him a patent of nobility."

"His son has been a rough lord," King Tuan said, "but a fair one, by all accounts, and has seen his people prosper, though he has governed them with an iron hand."

"It would seem that the grandson has kept the iron hand," Alain said, "but has lost the prosperity, at least for his people."

"He must be chastised," Catherine said, pale with anger. "No lord may treat his people thus and be safe from the Queen's Justice!"

"Even so," Tuan agreed, "but we must have proof of his misdeeds, for if we move against him without showing that he has broken the law, all other lords will rise in revolt."

"They would not dare!" But it was bluster; Catherine had already faced one such revolt and had put it down only with the help of Tuan, Rod Gallowglass, and the High Witch Gwendylon.

Geoffrey rose with a wolfish grin. "I shall find that proof, sire. I shall go in disguise and witness his misdeeds myself."

"I, too!" Alain was on his feet in the instant, chin firm.

"You shall do no such thing!" Catherine had finally found a target for her anger. "What, sirrah! Shall we risk the heir? What would the land do if you were slain?"

"There is Diarmid. . . ."

"He shall have his hands full with the Duchy of Loguire! Never think of it, my son! You shall stay close at home! Your mother commands it! You shall not go gallivanting over the land like a fox-errant! Your Queen forbids it!"

Then the ladies brought the maiden in, bandaged, cleaned, and groomed, still pale with shock but clad in a light blue homespun bliaut with a black bodice. Both young men stared, for without the streaks of tears and smudges of soot, she was indeed a beauty.

The Queen turned to consoling, reassuring, and discreetly questioning. Geoffrey caught Alain's eye, jerked his head toward the door, then turned to the King and Queen and asked, "Shall we leave, Majesties?"

"Aye, go," Catherine said absently. "We shall have our hands full here."

Both young men bowed, then sidled out the door.

As it closed behind them, Alain exploded. "My mother commands, my Queen forbids! Am I never to ride forth among my people? How shall I fare if I must lead an army in war when I am King?''

"You may notice that the current King did not forbid the expedition,'' Geoffrey pointed out.

"What matter's that? He is King only by marriage! It is my mother who is true monarch!''

"Then let her blister your hide with invective after you have returned in victory,'' Geoffrey said. "Can you not stand her chiding?''

"Of course I can.'' Alain turned to him with a frown.

"Well, when she is done, she shall have to laud you for having protected her people.'' Geoffrey grinned. "Ride with me as far as the wood's edge, Alain—and if you should happen to ride farther, I promise I shall not tell.''

Alain stared at him a moment. Then he began to grin.

The next morning they both mounted, inhaling the chill of the morning air, eyes bright with the lure of adventure.

Cordelia reached up to give Alain the token he had begged—her scarf. "Be mindful, sir. If there is trouble, only think my name, and I shall fly to you!''

"I shall indeed,'' Alain promised, "and the thought of you shall strengthen me throughout the journey.'' He leaned down.

As they kissed, the peasant girl, escorted by a servant woman, came forth from the kitchen door.

Geoffrey smiled down at her. "Will you show us where your village lies, maiden?''

"Gladly, sir.'' Her voice was so low he could scarcely hear her; her eyes were huge, darting from one to the other. Now that the shock had worn off, she was like a rabbit, frightened by the presence of royalty and nobility.

Alain straightened in the saddle and asked the maiden politely, "Will you ride?''

"Of course she will, Highness.'' Geoffrey moved his horse closer to the girl and reached down. "But she shall ride upon my mount. You would not risk your fiancée's wrath, would you?''

Cordelia eyed the peasant, whose beauty was considerable

25

now that she had recovered. "Ride with my brother, lass, but ride warily."

"Surely you wrong me, sister!" Geoffrey swung the young woman up behind him. "Ride behind me, lass, and guide us to your people."

"Surely, sir, as you wish it," the young woman said, her voice still low.

"And what shall I tell your fiancée when she returns from her errand of mercy?" Cordelia asked pointedly.

"Shh!" Geoffrey laid a finger across his grin. "Tell her no more than you have to, or she will come to join in the fun."

His grin was wide, but she saw the anxiety that touched his face and was gone. "She has faced an army, brother," Cordelia said softly. "You need not fear for her safety if she joins you in fighting a jumped-up bandit's grandson and his thugs."

"Ah, but before, she had an army of her own," Geoffrey reminded.

"And if you should be hurt in the fray yourself, brother? Is it fair to her to leave her to worry over you?"

"Worry over me?" The anxiety disappeared completely, and Geoffrey's grin was as wide and cocksure as ever. "Come, Cordelia! You need not deal in fantasy!"

While her henchmen gathered their forces and laid their plans, Finister became a bit more deliberate in her attempts. She ambushed a milkmaid, knocked her out with a bolt of mental force, changed clothes with her, and left her to waken and explain to her swain why she was wearing such unattractive charcoal-gray robes that draped her without any hint of a figure and were eight sizes too large for her in the bargain. To be truthful, Finister didn't even think about the effects her actions might have on the milkmaid; she was intent on finding Gregory again.

She found him wandering disconsolately along a woodland path, eyes downcast, shoulders slumping. Elation filled her—had she had some effect after all? Did he miss her already?

Then common sense cleared her mind. He was probably

depressed only because she had so easily slipped away from him, and disgusted with himself for having failed in his duty. Either that, or he was contemplating one of his endless problems again.

Well, she would end that, at least.

CHAPTER
-3-

Moraga took a moment to adjust her mental screen, projecting a figure even more voluptuous than her own and a face dazzling in its beauty, framed by hair of a rich mahogany. Sure that she would have tempted a eunuch and strained the vows of a monk, she stepped from the underbrush ten feet in front of Gregory's horse, a playful, inviting smile on her lips, eyes heavy-lidded. "Good day, Sir Knight."

"Hmm?" Gregory looked up, startled—as indeed he should have been, for he had been listening to Moraga's thoughts coming closer and closer to him, and if he quailed within at the vengeful tone, no sign of it showed in his face.

But the woman he saw before him bore no resemblance to the dowdy yet sensuous creature he had been escorting. Indeed, the fusty robes had gone, and she wore a blouse, skirt, and bodice that emphasized both the slenderness of her waist and swelling of her hips as well as a spectacular bosom. But the thoughts were Moraga's; he recognized their overtones and emotional color as well as he would recognize a very familiar face. He was startled indeed.

"I fear that I am lost, Sir Knight." Moraga pulled a stalk of grass from the roadside and began to nibble at the tip. "Will you help me find my way in these woods?"

"Why . . . gladly, damsel." Gregory swallowed as a wave of desire rolled over him. He reminded himself that it was only a projection of Moraga's own mind and said bravely, "If you will mount and ride behind, I shall bear you out of this wood."

"I had rather it were you who did mount and ride, sir," the milkmaid purred. "I shall bear you in delight, you may be sure."

Gregory strove to take her words at face value and failed. "I will rise up, if you insist." The milkmaid swayed up to him, raising a hand to rest on his knee. "Still, I would liefer you came down." Her fingers traced upward on his thigh.

Gregory fought for composure and won. He inclined his head gravely. "I thank you for the invitation, maiden . . ."

"I am no maiden, nor do I wish to be," she said, her voice husky. "In truth, my only regret in leaving that virtuous state is that there are so few boys who wish to play my games— or have the stamina to play them well."

"I am not gamesome," Gregory protested.

"Then I shall teach you how to play."

Now Gregory smiled with relief, back on familiar ground. "If only you could! But I have striven to learn through the years, damsel, and cannot. I go through the motions that give others so much delight but feel only boredom."

Her eyes flashed. "You would not be bored with my games, Sir Knight."

"I doubt not," Gregory admitted, "but I would certainly play them with no sense of fun, no sense of joy—for I lack both. Come, damsel—do you truly wish to dally with a man who would study his every move earnestly, paying the game only the gravest of attentions?"

In spite of her goals, Finister shivered with loathing. Gamely, though, she said, "No man can be so tragically serious as that, sir."

"Not many," Gregory agreed. "I had rather be a rare man in other ways, but I must settle for this, since it is what I am. In truth, I doubt not that I would approach the bout as a study, striving to discover which caress could elicit which shiver."

That was too much even for Finister. "Then I wish you joy of your studies, sir, for it is all the joy you shall have!" She turned and flounced away, disappearing into the underbrush in seconds.

Gregory stared after her, his breast a churning of emotions. He was relieved that he had found his prisoner again, but he found himself shaking with the aftermath of the encounter. No matter how cool a face he had presented to Moraga, his emotions were rampant. Never before had he felt such a tidal wave of desire—which was reasonable, considering that he had never met a woman at once so beautiful and so voluptuous. Worse than that, though, the woman was a projective telepath, and the emotion she had projected was raw lust in proportions he had never known, with a frightening intensity.

That intensity had saved him from falling off his horse and into her arms, no doubt—the fear of the power of the emotion itself, even though he knew that if he once confronted that fear, it would yield to a pleasure more extreme than any he had ever known. Part of him longed for it but another part was repelled by the thought of the time that would be wasted, the energy that would be leached from his research. Still, the fear of pleasure had been a good thing, for now that she had gone away, he remembered a far more practical fear—that while he was distracted by passion, she might strike him a mental blow that would stun him long enough for her to drive a dagger through his ribs or, more likely, use the passion itself to catapult him into her projective hypnotic spell, imagining himself to be some loathsome creature who could not stir from its prison, even as she had made his eldest brother believe himself to be a snake doomed forever to crawl around and around the base of a tree.

He sagged, limp with the aftermath of the confrontation, and was astounded to find that his trembling came not from exhaustion but from desire. Lust so intense was a new feeling for him, and he paused to savor its novelty, bemused, studying the phenomenon—and forgetting his ordeal. It was amazing that the woman could generate such an intensity of feeling. Before meeting her, he had always managed to sublimate such feelings into creative energy, which he channelled into research—a far more productive use.

Still, the current situation had its advantages. He had always wondered what compelled other men, such as his brother Geoffrey, to waste so much time with women. He could have understood counselling, teaching, or working with them to find some way to alleviate their poverty—but simply to trade sallies with them over cups of wine? There was nothing accomplished, nothing achieved! Why would an otherwise completely sane fellow be such a spendthrift of his hours?

It seemed he was about to find out.

Gwen looked up at the sound of voices in the hallway. Glancing at her husband, she saw that he had heard it, too; from his desk to the right of the great window, he paused in his writing and looked up at the door. He glanced at her, eyebrows raised in inquiry, mouth curving in amusement, as though to say it was no doubt something minor. Gwen smiled back from her reading chair at the other side of the clerestory, a smile that said she was equally certain it was a minor matter.

Their solar was filled with light; the great window faced south and was filled with color, for the glaziers still had difficulty making clear glass and, as a result, deliberately tinted the panes in various hues. The furniture was sparse, the books many, with a figured rug covering the flagstoned floor and a tapestry over the mantelpiece. It was a warm and cozy room, though it seemed empty now that the children had all gone out into the world. Nominally, they were still at home, but actually spent very few days there, being always out and about the kingdom, caring for the needs of the people and protecting them from the predators that pervaded a medieval society.

The sentry at the door stepped into the room. "Beg pardon, lord and lady."

"Certainly, Trooper Harl." Gwen smiled to put him at ease. Ever since they had rid the castle of its ghosts and taken up residence, there had been a constant stream of poor people coming to their gate for alms. She and Rod had given a dozen of them jobs, that being the most practical way of alleviating their poverty; the number had increased as the children had begun to spend less and less time at home. They now housed a company of guardsmen, none of whom had ever seen military service before, a dozen servants, and three dozen foresters and farmers. Rod had begun by inventing jobs for poor people and had ended making a profit. It had surprised him immensely and allowed them to hire a mason and a carpenter to instruct a dozen apprentices each in renovating the castle.

"The porter brings word, milady, of a young peasant who has come to the gatehouse begging aid."

"Then bring him in and give him food."

"Well, we brought the food out and tossed it to him, milady, for he would not come near us. The aid he asks is healing; he says his whole village has fallen victim to a plague that none has ever seen before."

"A plague!" Gwen stiffened.

Rod rose. "We'll come."

"Indeed not," Gwen said with some asperity and laid her book aside, removing the spectacles Rod had fashioned for her from the prescription provided by his robot horse, Fess. She rose, saying, "If I cannot mend the disease by myself, it is exotic indeed. Continue writing your history, husband—it is at least important for future generations as healing is for this."

"Well, I do have to admit you know a lot more about medicine than I do, especially at the microscopic level." But Rod looked distinctly unhappy about it. "You'll call if you need any help?"

"On the instant," Gwen promised, then turned to tug a bell rope. She told the guard, "When Lanai comes, ask her to bring my medical pack to the broomport in the west tower."

"I shall, milady." The guard gave a small bow as he stood aside. Gwen swept out of the room and off on her errand of mercy.

Rod sat down slowly but glanced anxiously after her before he took up his own reading glasses again. He put them on, then frowned at the door with vague unease.

After all, who else did he have to worry about these days?

Gregory rode the forest paths, disconsolate, hoping he would find Moraga again but very nervous about it, too. His mind was open, though guarded, picking up all sorts of thoughts—faraway peasants at work, nearer ones at play, and a host of animal emotions with the occasional sharp spike that could almost be shaped into words.

Suddenly he stiffened at thoughts of bewilderment and

fright, but also at resolution to brave whatever dangers the forest might present. The aura was feminine, the cast one of hunger for experience, especially romantic adventure. Gregory listened and probed ever so delicately, and by the time he rounded the trunk of a giant oak and saw the young gentlewoman, he was already certain that the thoughts were Moraga's, though carefully disguised by a consummate job of acting, so thorough as to partially deceive even herself. Only in the hard shell beneath the fictitious character was he able to sense the angry and vengeful emotions that were the young witch's signature.

The damsel he saw had a heart-shaped face of excruciating beauty, framed by luxuriant jet-black tresses that fell onto the shoulders of a stout broadcloth travelling gown of a rich blue that complemented the startling azure of her eyes. The gown was fitted so expertly as to leave no doubt that her figure was spectacular. She looked up at him, and a wave of desire rolled out from her to rock him with its intensity. There could be no doubt that she was a virgin and impatient to be rid of her state, a passionate creature who longed to experience the mystery of romance and the ecstasy of lovemaking of which she had heard and read so much but never tasted, thanks to vigilant chaperones and strict parents.

Not that she said so, of course. She shrank back against the trunk of the oak, wary but also filled with longing.

Gregory had to admire the screen of projective telepathy so complete as to convince him that he was looking at a black-haired, hungry, but virginal gentlewoman, as well as the construction of the character—not the real person, of course. It was an artful construct indeed. He reined in his horse and inclined his head in courtesy. "Good day, maiden."

"Good . . . good day, sir," the young woman said warily, but her eyes spoke of curiosity and pleasure at the sight of him.

"I am Gregory Gallowglass, and it is quite unchivalrous of me to ride when a lady must walk. If you will mount, I shall step down and lift you into this horse's saddle."

"I . . . I thank you, sir." The young woman stepped a few feet away from the tree. "I am Lilia, the daughter of Squire and Mistress Hallam—and I have indeed grown weary." Her eyes belied the last statement.

"Then ride you shall." Gregory dismounted, turned, and found himself a foot from Lilia—at least, his face was. His chest was much closer.

Her eyelids drooped, her lips seemed to thicken and moisten of their own accord; she tilted her head to the side as she breathed, "I thank you for your courtesy."

The wave of desire swept out to enfold Gregory, pulling him forward even more strongly than his natural reserve pushed him back, and his lips brushed hers.

It was as though an electric spark jumped from her to him, then welded their lips together. Hers trembled beneath his, then opened, beginning to nibble. With a sigh, she relaxed into his embrace. The tip of her tongue caressed his lower lip, and his whole body stiffened.

At that, alarm won over attraction, and Gregory backed away, gasping for air. "Your . . . your pardon, mistress. I . . . I have no idea what overcame me."

"I have," she whispered, swaying closer again, "and I only wish it would overcome us both."

But Gregory was on his guard now and caught her around the waist with both hands, lifting so that her own momentum helped boost her up to the saddle. Perhaps it was a mistake, for his hands seemed to burn at the feeling of the resilient body beneath the cloth, and he marvelled that his grip could encompass so much of her waist but feel so much more hip beneath them. He let go quite quickly but still found himself staring up at a view even more tantalizing than before as she blinked down at him in surprise.

At least her lips were safely out of reach.

"I . . . I thank you, sir," she said reluctantly.

"And I must thank you, and very deeply." Actually, it had been Gregory's first kiss, and his emotions were as turbulent as a dozen modulated waveforms in constant interference. He recovered his poise by resolutely ignoring his feelings. "But how does a damsel as gentle as yourself come to be alone in such rough woodlands as these?"

"Oh, my parents are impossible!" Lilia burst out. "They

Christopher Stasheff

must ever keep me close at home, and when they do let me
visit a dance or a meeting, they have my old nurse ever at
my shoulder! There is no chance for fun, no chance to taste
the delights that are the right of youth!''

"Indeed," Gregory said, shaken. "But it is quite dangerous
for you to be alone in the greenwood with none to guard
you.''

"I shall chance whatever dangers come!'' Her eyelids
drooped again. "Are you a danger, sir?''

"I? No, never!'' Gregory protested in shock.

"That is unfortunate.'' Lilia leaned forward, lips seeming
to swell and moisten again. "I would you were a danger to
my maiden state.''

Gregory stared, wordless.

Lilia leaned farther forward, then suddenly fell with a little
shriek. Automatically, Gregory reached up and caught her
waist. She fell right against him, he felt her breasts pressing
against his chest, her thighs and hips against his, and his
body's reaction was so embarrassing that he involuntarily
stepped back.

But she stepped with him, still pressed up to him, lips smiling up, parting, eyes dreamy under heavy lids, head tilted to
the side, voice husky as she said, "You are handsome and
gentle and, I doubt not, patient, and likely to touch a woman
with delicacy. I wish very strongly that you were a danger to
my innocence.''

It was the wrong word; Gregory protested in alarm, "Such
a thing would be quite wrong, maiden! That pleasure is and
should be reserved only for those who are wed!''

"Reserved? I think not.'' Smiling lazily, Lilia pressed even
more tightly against him. "I have known many who shared
a bed without benefit of clergy.''

"And were they not shamed before all the world?'' Gregory stammered.

"Not at all, for the lasses had drunk of a potion given them
by a wise woman,'' Lilia said, "as have I. None needed know
of it save the couple themselves.''

Even with his emotions churning, Gregory's mind caught
the logical flaw. "Surely not so, damsel! For if these women

36

were not exposed to public shame, how could you have come to know of them?''

''Servants gossip,'' Lilia breathed, and her breath was heated perfume. ''Servants boast—and no, not the men alone! I have even heard three wantons arguing about who had bedded a handsome plowboy first!''

Gregory found that hard to believe but knew better than to question her veracity. ''But . . . but not people of your class! Servants perhaps, but not young gentlewomen!''

''Pooh!'' Lilia scoffed. ''Why should they have all the fun? Come, sir, explore new delights with me!'' She caught his hand and pressed it to her bosom.

Gregory tried to pull it away, but she held his wrist with surprising strength—or was it his weakness that was surprising?

''Come, sir, a beautiful woman invites you,'' she breathed, ''and if you turn her away, she must suspect that you, too, are a virgin and afraid of real pleasure.''

''That . . . that is so.''

Lilia stared up at him, her hold loosening. ''You feel no shame in saying it? But all men jeer at those who have never known the delights of a woman's embrace! None will admit it!''

''I will.'' Gregory began to feel a little confidence returning. ''I have far greater interest in books than in sport, damsel, and I doubt that I would be a lover of any skill. I know nothing of how to give pleasure to a woman.''

''Then learn with me,'' she breathed, pressing close again. ''Let us learn together. Do you not hunger for experience?''

''Not at all,'' Gregory said quickly. ''My . . . my hunger is only for knowledge!''

''Then this is a whole realm of human knowledge of which you are innocent.'' Lilia's smile broadened again. ''What manner of scholar could you be if you do not truly know what so many books tell? You may have as fine a chance as this again, sir, but never a better—and I am quite willing to risk clumsiness if I can be certain of gentleness!''

''No . . . no one can be certain if a man loses his senses.''

''Nay, with me you shall find your senses, or their true

37

purpose, at least." Her voice was husky again. "Do you think a virgin wishes to marry a man who has no idea how to make love?"

It was the wrong tack; the argument Gregory had learned from monks came to the fore. "I never mean to marry, damsel—but if I did, I doubt not that marriage would badly need the power of that first lovemaking, which can be a bond of great strength between new wife and husband—and surely every such binding is vitally necessary to make a marriage last. The wedded state has need of every bond it can have, for there are so many strains upon it."

Lilia actually drew away an inch in repugnance. "If so, then perhaps that marriage should not endure! What strains are these that you imagine?"

"Why, poverty and bondage, but most of all the pressures of two people living side by side every day—two people trying to live with the fear of losing themselves in the whirlpool of family life, fearing even more to lose freedom, pride, and their ability to govern themselves."

"You mean fear of being dominated or enslaved!" Lilia drew farther away, anger sparking in her eyes.

Gregory shuddered within, for she was at least as beautiful in the one passion as in the other, and caught between the two, as she was at the moment, she was absolutely spectacular.

CHAPTER
-4-

"Even so," Gregory confirmed. "Mind you, I have seen many pass that barrier and forge a solid home in which each of those fears proved illusory, for they gained as much as they lost and more—but the strains were mighty and needed every bond to surmount them."

"Where did you hear of such things?" Lilia demanded.

"From the monks."

"Then to the monks you may go, sir! In truth, their sterile cloister is certainly the dessert of any man who has dispelled a romantic mood as thoroughly as you have! Go to the monks and do penance for the rest of your life, for the chance you have lost this moment!" With that, Lilia turned on her heel and stalked away. In seconds, she was gone around the curve of the road.

Gregory stood rigid for ten minutes more; then, sure she was out of sight and not apt to return, let himself crumple, collapsing to sit on the ground with his back to the oak, head bowed, whole frame trembling with the aftershock of the emotions she had roused in him. He assured himself frantically that the pleasures she promised must be far greater than anything she could actually provide, for her sensuousness was an illusion no doubt far more vivid than the reality could ever be—but his self still doubted, still longed to believe in that glamour.

He was very much aware that the woman was succeeding in rousing desire he had always been able to suppress or sublimate. He tried to be amused by the irony that she had ignited the very interest in sex that she had intended to eradicate in him; left to his own devices, he would probably have become a confirmed and celibate old bachelor, content with the company of his books and always able to quell whatever minor hankering for feminine companionship arose.

Now, though, he wasn't sure. When he had finally managed to deliver Moraga to Runnymede and the judgement of the royal witchforce, when he had finally managed to purge his life of her, he was very much afraid that he would actually fall in love after all, and waste his energy and his intellect in lovemaking and caring for a family, like the tens of thousands of generations of men before him. He consoled himself with the thought that they must surely have been far happier woven into the fabric of their families than they would have been as lone and easily broken threads, but such joys were only rumors to him, the stuff of gossip and fiction, and with no experience of his own to corroborate them, he had difficulty believing.

Quicksilver rode into the courtyard with five warrior women behind her. As a concession to her fiancé, they wore trousers and jerkins of stout brown broadcloth with cuirasses and greaves—Geoffrey had been so worried for her safety that he had threatened to escort her everywhere if she did not wear a little armor, and something to protect her fair skin from thorns and briars. Much though she loved the notion of having him with her wherever she went, Quicksilver loved even more being able to rise and go whenever she wished, so she wore tin clothes to please him. Besides, she would never have admitted it, but trousers did make for more comfortable riding than bare legs.

She dismounted, looking about her with a frown, but saw only Cordelia hurrying up to her. "Where is that gadabout brother of yours?" she demanded, then remembered her manners. "Hail, lady."

"Hail to you, too, lady and captain." Cordelia stopped beside her and drew breath. "Your fiancé has gone with mine— or mine with him, more accurately." She laid a hand on Quicksilver's arm. "Rinse the dust from your face and come into the garden. We shall have a glass of wine while I tell you the manner of it."

Quicksilver frowned, but considered only a moment before

she turned back to her squadron. "Take your ease while you may, ladies. We may ride again ere long."

Fifteen minutes later, with Quicksilver washed, perfumed, and luxuriating in a silken gown, they sat in the walled garden beneath the solar. It was fifty feet square, crowded with curving flower beds on the sides, a fountain surrounded by more flowers in the center, and fruit trees espaliered against the walls. Half a dozen gardeners were at work, still planting new seedlings and dividing bulbs.

The two young women sat sipping spring wine and discussing the perfidies of young knights-errant who go haring off to save the peasantry with no thought to the ladies they leave behind.

"They have both gone gallivanting, then?" Quicksilver asked.

"Aye, to save a damsel in distress."

"Oh, have they indeed?" Quicksilver's eye glittered with jealousy. "And did not wait for me? How rude of them! Was the damsel comely?"

"She was, underneath the dust of her journey and the ashes of her hamlet—but I think they took little notice of that. They were fired with zeal to protect a whole village."

"That, at least, is worthy," Quicksilver admitted. "Still, they were fools not to bid you fly above to watch over them."

"Indeed," Cordelia said, her lips tight.

"Well, I shall rest an hour, then don my armor again and ride after them." Quicksilver tossed off the rest of her glass and refilled it.

"I am not sure that would be the wisest course," Cordelia said slowly.

"Wisest?" Quicksilver frowned. "With a baron and all his men to set about them? Surely they will need every sword they can find!"

"True, but surely Geoffrey can disable or confuse many of them with his magic," Cordelia said, "and there is always the chance that this baron, no matter how unscrupulous he is, will have the wisdom to heed the words of the heir apparent."

"I would say it was more apparent that he would give

Alain the air!'' Quicksilver eyed her future sister-in-law narrowly. "Surely you do not say that simply because they have not asked our help means that we should not give it!''

"I am not truly worried about their health,'' Cordelia said. "Besides, should they be truly outnumbered, Geoffrey can summon me, and I may surely fly there quickly enough. Moreover, Gregory can be by him in an instant.''

"Gregory is bound to escorting that hussy Moraga,'' Quicksilver reminded her, then looked past Cordelia to a gray-haired gardener. "Come, fellow, why choke on your own laughter? Let it out—and while you are about it, share the jest with us.''

Cordelia turned in surprise, then frowned at the man's mirth. "How are you called, fellow?''

"Why, Tom Gardener, milady.'' The man knelt up straight and pulled his cap off his head. Then his face buckled with humor again and he dropped his gaze.

"We must be amusing indeed,'' Quicksilver observed.

"I shall remember what I have said, to divert Their Majesties,'' Cordelia replied with sarcasm, then turned back to Tom Gardener. "Speak, sirrah! Is our concern for our fiancés so amusing as all that?''

The old man managed to choke down his glee long enough to say, "Aye, milady, for I doubt not that the prince and Lord Geoffrey are equal to a country baron's band of thugs. Nevertheless, giving succor to a village is the smallest part of their reason for going there.''

Quicksilver gave him a long stare, then turned back to Cordelia. "We are up against a male plot.'' To Tom Gardener she said, "Explain, viellard! What do the prince and the knight truly plan?''

"Why, naught but what they have said,'' Tom answered, all innocence. "Yet any old man can tell why they have really ridden away.''

"Can he indeed?'' Storm clouds gathered over Quicksilver's brow. "Then the old man can tell the young women, and speedily, if he cares for his backside!''

"Surely, milady.'' Tom couldn't completely throttle his smile. " 'Tis simply and plainly that young men must ever be proving themselves worthy of their ladies, and the more beautiful the ladies, the more the young men must prove themselves."

Quicksilver gave him a long, level look, then turned back to Cordelia. "There might be something in what he says."

"Aye, the dear fools!" Cordelia smiled, her eyes filling. "Then, Tom Gardener, tell us what would hap if we came to their rescue."

"Why, lady, you would prove that they have no worth!"

"How silly!" Quicksilver scoffed. "Any woman can see their virtues!"

"Do you truly?" Tom Gardener challenged. "Would you, if you had to save them from their own folly?" Quicksilver started to answer, but he kept talking. "Even if you protested that you did not think less of them for it, the young men would never believe you. Indeed, rather than prove their worth, you would have proved their lack."

"Men are foolish in their pride," Cordelia reminded Quicksilver.

Tom Gardener started to say something else but choked it down and turned back to his bulbs.

"What had you in mind?" Quicksilver demanded. "Speak, sirrah!"

"Why, only to ask if women have no pride that makes them think themselves worthy of their men." Tom broke into soft whistling as his earth-covered hands deftly parted lily bulbs, set one aside, and began to replant the other.

"I think we shall ignore his temerity and his question with it." Cordelia wondered briefly if the issue was one she should really consider, but set it aside as ridiculous.

"Still, we should not ignore his advice."

"I gave no advice!" Tom Gardener said quickly.

"I suppose that is true, to a lawyer," Cordelia allowed.

"Aye," said Quicksilver. "He did only answer our questions."

"If they could be truly answered," Cordelia added. "Still, the point is worth considering. Give answer again, Tom Gardener—do the boys not truly wish to be free of our presence, of the velvet manacles they perceive us to be?"

Christopher Stasheff

"All young men need some time away from their beloveds now and then," Tom protested, hedging, "to restore the intensity of their loves. Have you never heard that absence makes the heart grow fonder?"

"Aye, fonder of another wench," Quicksilver said darkly.

"Not if they truly love us." Cordelia laid her hand on Quicksilver's, smiling complacently. "Advice or not, what he says is well spoken."

"He might have scored a point or two," Quicksilver reluctantly admitted.

Cordelia nodded. "If what he says is true, we have only to decide whether we can trust our boys." She raised a questioning glance to Quicksilver. "Or do you truly think that, after he has come to know you, no other woman could hold Geoffrey's attention for more than an hour or two?"

"Even one could be an hour too long," Quicksilver said darkly. "Still, he is not apt to dally in the midst of a battle." She gave Cordelia a challenging stare. "What of you, sister-to-be? Are you so sure of your swain as all that?"

"Oh, yes," Cordelia answered with a small, very satisfied smile. "I think I can trust him, whether he likes it or not."

The old gardener turned his back as he studiously grafted a twig onto a rose root.

It was time for the big guns. Moraga had tried being nice, she had tried being inviting, she had tried being romantic, and all she'd had from Gregory was a sermon against premarital sex! As though that mattered. Her teachers had convinced her that what all men really wanted was sex without consequences or commitments, that the woman they most wanted was the one who would spread her sheets for him, then bid him a cheery farewell in the morning, so she set about giving Gregory more than he had ever known he wanted.

She took her time arranging her next projection, fashioning a form straight out of the most extravagant adolescent dream and a face that would have launched eleven hundred ships (she had a notion Helen of Troy had gone in too much for beauty and not enough for the erotic). Sloe-eyed, diapha-

44

nously gowned, and cherry-lipped, she took up her stance just around a bend in the road from Gregory, struck her most voluptuous pose, and waited.

Gregory went around the bend and froze stiff, staring. The horse, not affected by human standards of beauty, sailed straight ahead toward the reef of femininity lying in wait for the frail barque that was Gregory, propelled by a tidal wave of hormones.

"Prithee, kind sir," the vision purred, "come down to rest a while with me."

Gregory tried (and failed) to pull his eyes back into their sockets and stammered, "I thank you, damsel, but I must forge ahead."

"How unfair to go onward!" The fantasy pouted. "I, sir, am Honey, and all the sweetness that a man could crave. Will you not descend and taste of me?"

The blatantness of the invitation rocked Gregory. "I—I have a mission. . . ."

"You will be missing more than your mission could mean."

"It is a trust and a quest," Gregory stammered, "on which I must wend. . . ."

"That you went not with this witch will be a regret you may trust with no question." Honey reached up to stroke his cheek, leaving lines of tingling behind as she drew her fingertips down to his lips. "What else could be so important? Pass an hour with me, sir, and it will sustain you the rest of your life!"

"Sustain . . . I must . . . my burden. . . ."

"A bird in the hand will sustain you far better than travel." Her fingertips trailed down his chest, parting his robe as they went, leaving a trail of fire as they touched his hand.

"I cannot bear . . ."

"Then I shall bear you." Honey tugged gently and his hand followed under the filmy fabric, where she molded it to her, then drew it forward, shuddering with the pleasure of his caress.

But he felt it too keenly; alarm shot through him, waking him from the erotic trance. He remembered who he sought and why, paid attention to the woman's thoughts, not her body, and recognized the characteristic tinge, the signature that let him recognize Finister more clearly than sight.

"Do I seem too good to be true?" the vision asked him. "I assure you, I cannot be accused of goodness! I know my own worth, and this is it: to give pleasure, and seek it." She tugged at his arm. "Not that I have found more than a little. I seek a man who can send me whirling to the heights of ecstasy, not the mere release that is all any have given."

"I . . . I know not that road, and could be of little use."

"Trust me to know your use," Honey said, "and be sure I know the road. No man will love me lifelong, this I know, so I seek whatever bond I can find with any man, and you are the fortunate one who has met me this day."

Even through the whirl of emotions, Gregory recognized the kernel of truth around which Finister had wrapped this particular lie. She believed herself to be of no real worth, especially of no lasting worth to any man, that males would value her only for her sexual attraction and not for the person inside the body.

Every instinct within him cried foul. He had grown up with a mother and a sister, neither saintly but both very dear, and could not believe that any woman was nothing but a body. Mind and soul were too precious to him. It was the person who mattered to him, not the gender, and several young women had made it clear to him that this was a failing, for he could not relate to them as he could to another man.

"Come down from your high horse, O Favored of Fate," Honey breathed. "Come lay me down, that I may lift you up to heights you can only imagine—for that is what I do best; indeed, it is all that I do well."

"Never think it!" Gregory said sternly, and indignation gave him the strength to sit up straight, clasping the reins with both hands. "Never believe you cannot love and be loved! This is the true worth of every being, to labor for the happiness of another!"

"Make me happy," she said, stretching her arms up to him and arching her back. "Happily make me, and bring me to labor."

Under the sultry words, though, Gregory sensed a secret longing, secret perhaps even from Finister herself—a yearning for love and for someone who would be so much in love with her that he would never leave her, no matter how unpleasant a companion she might be—and he was beginning to realize that Finister knew herself to be unpleasant indeed. She had, in fact, so low an opinion of herself that she didn't believe anyone else could like her. After all, *she* didn't.

"If I should choose your company," he told her, "it would be because you were a pleasant and trustworthy companion, not because of your beauty."

Honey stared with surprise; then her eyes flashed with scorn, but she kept them lidded, kept the sensuous curve of her mouth as she said, "No man chooses a woman for anything else."

"Try me," Gregory challenged. "Ride with me a week and do not invite my caresses. See if I reach out to you with my hands then, or only with my words. See if you would choose *me* as a companion for more than a night!"

"You are surely not more than a knight, nor even as much!" Honey shook with anger. "Do you think I wish a man whose hands are turned only to craft and never to me? What use would you be to me then?" Suddenly she relaxed, her body undulated again, and she stretched out a hand, beckoning as she backed away. "Come, sir, and you shall have no regrets. If you wish my companionship by day, your nights are my price."

Now Gregory was truly tempted, for she no longer pretended to be offering only but showed some sign of demanding. Still, he realized he must make her believe that one man somewhere might value her for more than her body alone. He would not reap the rewards of a loving nature that believed in itself, but some other man somewhere might, and certainly she would. "I thank you, no," he said. "I own I am lonely and would appreciate laughter and conversation, but I wish them for more than a night."

"Do you fear me, then?" Honey taunted. "Are you afraid I would suck you dry?"

"Why, how could that be?" Gregory asked with a self-deprecating laugh. "If you are truly as hungry as you say, so slight a man as I would scarcely be a morsel."

"Slight indeed!" She saw his self-control was back, saw he had slipped her grasp yet again, and let her temper flare. "A mere scrap of a man, one who could scarcely be a mat underfoot, let alone a mattress beneath my body! Go your ways, wanderer, and mourn the day you left me!" She spun on her heel and ran away. Gregory caught the sound of a sob.

That was almost his undoing. He nearly turned his horse, nearly rode after to take her in his arms and offer comfort—but he had at least the good sense to realize it was too late, that he had let the moment pass.

Now Gregory could no longer deny how deeply Finister attracted him. He had always thought that his one big weakness had been his ability to sympathize and empathize—indeed, his unwitting inclination; he had never been able to hear weeping without instinctively feeling the person's pain and, if he learned its cause, mourning their aching as though it were his own. He had worked long and hard to contain that impulse for, although the thoughts he heard from those in anguish might demand comfort, the people were not always willing to accept it—and so he thought it might be in this case. He could only guess, though, for "Honey's" thoughts had disappeared the instant she had turned and fled, leaving only the mental shield that seemed to come so readily with Finister's frustration or anger. Oh, he could read the dire, raging thoughts that came from it, as light reflected from a mirrored ball, but he could not detect the true thoughts or feelings within.

He was amazed to realize how much he desired to do so. It unnerved him to realize that Finister's projective telepathy had reached him, though not in the way she had intended. True, her sexuality had aroused a maelstrom of emotions in him, but it was her angst that had played upon those feelings, not her seductiveness. Sensibilities sharpened by a sudden rush of hormones had induced his empathy to emerge from its shielding, bringing him to sympathize with her and search for the natural good qualities in her that must have been twisted into making her the murderous vampire she had become.

Not that he thought Finister a maligned innocent; far from it. He knew quite well how poisonous she was but couldn't help sensing an underlying sweetness and vulnerability, both rigidly controlled and hidden inside an emotional shell that was virtual plate armor. He was attracted to her deeply and sharply, there was no denying it, but that attraction owed more to sympathy and empathy than to lust. Simply put, his own generosity of spirit had put him perilously close to falling in love with her.

Finister stalked through the woodlands, seething with fury, trembling with rage. Her most blatant invitations, her finest voluptuous form, and the man came away as unshaken as a plaster statue! Oh, she knew she had punched through his reserve, had grasped his nerves, that she'd had him by the glands for a few minutes there. How had he managed to recover his poise? How had he managed to refuse?

How had he managed to escape?!

Well, there was no point in any further attempt. The man had the potential for lust, but he had quashed it so firmly that there was nothing but potential left! He was a eunuch, not a man, and there was nowhere to catch him!

It would have been so much simpler if he had been as susceptible as the rest of his sex. She could have married him, enthralled him, warped him to her so thoroughly that he would not even have dreamed of protest when she failed to conceive. She could have guaranteed that he would father no children—though she might have given him one sired by another man; she was curious about the experience of pregnancy and birth. And in addition, she would have been a lady by marriage, a noblewoman of a family close to the throne, where she could take steps to ensure that the royal bloodline would end with Alain, that Cordelia would never carry a baby to term, that Quicksilver would never conceive!

It would have been so easy, so convenient—but that shell of a man had defeated her hopes! She would have her revenge, revenge on all the Gallowglasses, and when Cordelia was dead, she would encounter Alain again. This time, without interference or competition, she would win him and wed him and make sure he never fathered a son.

Best of all, when his mother died, she would be Queen!

She burst into a clearing and found a log where she could sit, working to compose herself, to let her churning emotions calm enough to project her coded thoughts out to her lieutenants. They all knew what the message meant—that they should fall upon the enemy at noon.

One by one, they replied, their thoughts appearing in her mind as her own did, but with different flavors, the overtones of their personalities. When each had confirmed receiving the message and set about his or her task, she sat still awhile, gathering her scattered energies and gloating at the victory to come. In one instant she would be revenged for all the humiliations these Gallowglasses had heaped upon her!

But one most of all, and that revenge would be the most personal. She would see Gregory racked with agony, as he deserved for having scorned her.

CHAPTER
-5-

There was one way in which Gregory still might be vulnerable, one possible Achilles' heel. Since it didn't necessarily lead to bedding and marriage, Finister had ignored it. Now, though, it was certainly worth trying—now, when all she needed was to come close enough to him to slip a knife between his ribs, or to induce him into lowering his guard so she could plant a mental bomb in his brain. She doubted it would do much good, for Gregory certainly seemed to have little of the knight-errant about him, but the damsel in distress might wring sympathy even from such a stone as he.

Accordingly, she retailored her physical projection to be modest but still alluring (why waste a chance, no matter how slender?). The body's contours were scarcely spectacular and the face was pretty, but neither was striking or fascinating. The gown was modest and serviceable, a green broadcloth with yellow bodice and kirtle. She indulged her dramatic streak and chose a black veil.

Then she sent coded mental instructions to Lork, who, ever faithful, was indeed not far away. That done, she took up her station farther along the road where it opened out into a meadow. She found a boulder for her seat, rolled a log to its foot, and tied her ankle to it with three feet of rope, then bowed her head in grief and despair, thinking of the horrible fate in store for her, concentrating on it until it seemed real, until she felt the tears welling up in her eyes. She held them there, listening with her mind, waiting for Gregory's approach.

Gregory rode alert, mind open to receive, though his shields were still in place. He detected the thoughts of despair, sensed the sobbing, but also recognized Moraga's mental signature. Doubly wary, he rode through the leafy arch into the meadow and beheld a most touching tableau.

On a boulder in the middle of the meadow sat a damsel in green and yellow, head bowed in distress, sobbing piteously. Her auburn hair fell unbound behind her face, making her skin seem to glow even more than was natural. She was the very picture of Beauty in Distress, a portrait to wring the heart of any knight-errant and inflate his protective instincts, vulnerable femininity to perfection.

In fact, too perfect. Gregory eyed her askance, then decided that the wisest course was to fall in with the situation she had devised and watch how she made it develop.

His mind may have known it, but his heart did not. As he rode up to her, the alarm, concern, and sympathy wrung from his masculine nature by her pose and her weeping welled up. For once, he let them show—a little. He dismounted and knelt by her, asking, "Damsel, what grieves you so?"

She recoiled, gasping and staring at him; then, seeing it was only a clean-favored youth, relaxed, burying her face in her hands as her sobs redoubled.

"What horror could affright you so?" The anxiety in his tone was quite real; he almost forgot that this was the predator who stalked his family; only a remote part of his mind remembered it, staying vigilant. "Maiden, what is it? Tell me, I beg of you!"

"Call me not maiden, for I am that no longer, and therein lies my plight!" she sobbed.

Gregory frowned, feeling an edge of sternness arise, anger at a man unseen. "Is it a false love who has used you and left you? The fault is his, not yours!"

"Nay, sir—well, it is that surely, but I suffer only shame for that. Now, because of it, I am likely to suffer much more." She raised a tear-streaked face to him.

It was a lovely face, even reddened by tears—a heart-shaped face with rosebud lips and large dark eyes. Gregory stared, freezing as he felt the wave of her erotic projection roll over him, rocking him. He held still, only gazing on that lovely face as he waited for the wave to crest and begin to level off, and it was all he could do to keep himself from reaching out to take her into his arms. Then he asked, "What affliction is this that can hurt you worse than a true love turned false?"

"Bandits, sir! Here I sit, a sacrifice to them, a victim to their rapaciousness! They have despoiled my people's village these five years, and only by giving them what they seek can my people save themselves from pillage and slaughter."

Gregory scowled, a black mood coming on him. "And you are what they seek?"

"Every fall they come to take half of the harvest," the damsel told him, "and every spring they come to take a young woman for their pleasure." She shuddered at the thought. "To have been seduced, then left, has been like being plunged from Heaven into Purgatory—but to be the toy of a score must be a descent into Hell!"

"It shall not happen," Gregory said, his tone iron. "But you must be a squire's daughter, not a peasant! How durst your villagers turn you out?"

"My people decide who will next be offered to the wild men by discovering who allowed herself to be seduced in the year past, for, say they, 'twould be a shame to send a virgin— so our girls tend to be very circumspect."

"Do not tell me that your swain boasted of his conquest ere he spurned you!"

Her shoulders slumped and her gaze fell. "How else would any but we two have known?"

"But your father, the squire of the village! Could he let his daughter be thrown to the wolves thus?"

"My father, and my mother, too, have cast me out in shame," the young woman said. "These past five years, everyone in the village has become most self-righteous, for those who always inveighed against the sins of the flesh cry that these bandits are Heaven's retribution."

"What a horrid malediction is this!" Gregory said. He stood, looking down at the young woman, and laid a hand gently on her shoulder, but she flinched, and he drew his hand away. "Be calm, damsel," he told her. "They shall not touch

53

you. But if I am to ward you from these bandits, may I not know your name?"

"Why . . . surely, sir." Hope sprang in her eyes. "I am called Peregrine. But how can you, one man alone, stop twenty?"

"By magic," Gregory answered. "I am a wizard."

The spark of hope flared alive in Peregrine's eyes and she clung to his hand, staring up at him, lips parting in wonder.

Gregory wondered, too. What kind of magic could give him, a slender and peaceful man, victory over twenty hardened robbers?

Any, the remote part of his mind answered, for it remembered that Peregrine was, after all, really Finister.

The disease hadn't been much, as epidemics went—only an old virus that had mutated into a new one—but the peasants of that village had had no immunity to it. Left to itself, it could have spread into a plague that swept the whole island. Gwen reflected on the episode as she flew home, amazed to realize that fifteen years ago she would have had no idea how to cope with the outbreak. Her sojourn in the interstellar civilization of the twenty-second century had given her the opportunity to learn advanced physics, chemistry, and a host of other sciences, including microbiology—all direct from the minds of scientists and engineers themselves. Not that she had eavesdropped—she had simply asked questions and *really* listened to the answers.

Fortunately it had been a relatively simple virus, and she had retailored a few specimens into antigens. They had propagated at the usual speed, neutralizing all the rest. She had left the epidemic well on its way to curing.

She idly noticed the hawk circling above her, as she noticed everything in the air when she was flying, but paid it no particular attention until it folded its wings and pounced on her.

With a cry of anger, she batted it away. The bird went spinning head over heels, and her broomstick, ignored for the moment, slipped to the left and started to dive. That saved her life, for the blaster bolt sizzled by a foot over her head.

Fear seared through her, but anger came hot in its wake. She spared a thought for the broomstick, bringing it up and around in an erratic zigzag as her mind probed for the gunner below. Instead she found another telepath, and the disorder and chaos in his mind sent a wave of dizziness through her. For a few seconds earth and sky reeled about her; for a few seconds, she was cut off from the outside world.

The broomstick, left to itself, promptly fell, and her with it.

Two blaster bolts sizzled overhead.

Then the enemy telepath's mind cleared with elation and Gwen's mind cleared with it. She saw treetops rushing up before her—but she saw her hands, too, clutching the broomstick white-knuckled as though they could pull it up and out of its tailspin by sheer strength. She poured the power of her mind into them, and the broomstick sheered off at the last second, though her shoes clipped leaves from the branches as she passed.

Then the hawk pounced again. She saw it coming a second before it struck and swerved to avoid it. A blaster bolt sizzled past and the hawk squawked in protest, sheering off. Smoke curled from the tips of its tail feathers.

Gwen threw her broomstick into a dance, erratic, chaotic. The enemy telepath's mind swept hers with a wave of hatred that made her recoil in shock—but she used the energy of the recoil to strike back, filling the foe's mind with an anger so hot that she felt the other lose consciousness. She withdrew from that mind immediately, rolled aside as a blaster bolt snarled past her, and sought for the minds of the gunners.

There were three of them. She struck with a sudden wave of self-hatred, and the first turned her own rifle on herself. Gwen withdrew the self-contempt quickly, and the gunner realized what she was doing. With a cry of terror, she threw the rifle from her.

But Gwen's mind was already moving to the second, making the rifle buck in his hands, twisting and turning. The man wrestled with it, and Gwen pulled hard, trying to yank the gun out of his hands. He clung desperately, and she reversed; the rifle jumped backward, striking the sniper in the forehead.

He slumped to the ground unconscious, and Gwen dove on general principles.

Not a moment too soon; her distraction had been long enough for the third sniper to aim. The straws of her broomstick burst into flame. Even so, the hawk struck again; claws bit into her shoulder, and she cried out with pain, her broomstick dropping like a stone.

The bird loosed its hold, tearing away; another blaster bolt missed it narrowly. Gwen pulled her broomstick out of its dive but felt another mind pulsing with dread, then relief, and recognized a second enemy telepath, one much weaker than the first.

Strong enough to control the hawk, though. His mind reached out to the bird's, making it circle and swoop again.

Gwen concentrated and took control of the hawk. Its trajectory swerved; it struck at the last sniper, who screamed with rage and swung his rifle around toward the raptor. But Gwen made the bird swoop aside at the last second and the blaster bolt sizzled harmlessly through the air. Gwen saw the sniper's position now, high in an oak. She sent the hawk striking. It was too close for the sniper to shoot; he fell back—and fell indeed, with a howl of fright. He dropped the rifle and caught at another branch—caught, and held.

Gwen reached out with her mind and made the branch whip back and forth through the air. The sniper bellowed in fear as his hold broke and he fell again. He landed crosswise on a lower bough; pain shot through him as his abdomen folded over the limb.

Gwen made a nearby limb swing and strike. A single bright pain filled the sniper's mind before darkness claimed it.

The hawk, though, was circling high to swoop again. Gwen took control of it once more and made it follow the thought that reached out for it frantically. The hawk plunged through the leaves, screaming as its claws tore at the face of its master. Somehow the falconer caught it, but the claws still scrabbled at his face. He stumbled backward, holding the writhing bird at arm's length, shouting commands at it. Gwen adjusted his path, and the man slammed backward into a tree. He slumped to the ground, unconscious, and the bird flew away, dazed and disoriented.

Now Gwen could take a deep breath, regain control of her broomstick, and send out a call for the royal witches to come arrest the assassins. Then, by sheer habit born of many sleepless nights listening for a sick child's breathing, she reached out to touch the minds of each of her family.

They were all under attack.

Geoffrey and Alain had dressed themselves up as common teamsters and had harnessed their chargers to a cart they had rented at an exorbitant sum. No one could see the swords slung across their backs under their cloaks.

They drove into the hamlet beneath Baron Gripadin's castle, a collection of a dozen very run-down cottages—in fact, so run-down that if the peasant girl hadn't told them otherwise, they would have thought the place abandoned. Nonetheless, they drove the cart in, having a fine old time with some very amateurish playacting.

"Well, Daw, what think 'ee?" Alain mimicked the accent of the peasants who served in the castle. "Ought we draw in the horses and buy summat to eat?"

"I see no inn," Geoffrey answered in a similar accent. "What could these people cook that would be worth a brass farthing?" Then, under his breath in his own accent, "Is this your village, maiden?"

"It is, sir." The young woman trembled beside him. "Pray the soldiers do not come!"

"We will pray that they do," Alain whispered grimly, his eyes bright with battle-lust.

"I must warn my family to stay indoors!" The young woman slipped down from the cart before they could stop her and ran for the door of a hut that opened just before she reached it.

For some reason, that rang Geoffrey's mental alarm. He opened his mind to listen and caught a host of angry, bloodthirsty thoughts. "To horse, Alain! On guard!"

He caught up his buckler from the cartbed and sprang onto his charger, drawing his sword and cutting the harness with two strokes. Alain blinked at him, taken by surprise; then he heard the roar of many throats as a dozen men burst from the doorways of the ruined cottages. He reached down, caught up his buckler, and vaulted onto the back of his warhorse, drawing his sword and cutting the straps as Geoffrey had done. "For the people and the right!" he shouted and turned at bay.

The assassins struck, the front rank slashing at him with swords, the back rank stabbing up with spears. Alain ducked to catch the blades on his buckler; one sliced his calf. He bellowed with anger and swung his blade, cutting off two spearheads.

Geoffrey faced a similar double rank and had to admit that this rabble had a commander who had some sense. He raised his buckler to deflect the spearheads while his mind wrenched at the swords. But another mind wrenched them back, cancelling his telekinesis and leaving the swordsmen free to chop at Geoffrey's ankles. He realized he was up against more than he had thought and called, "Up, stout fellow!" His horse reared, screaming, and struck at the footmen with its forelegs. They shouted in surprise and backed away.

The battle-rage was on Alain now, for these foes had come in secrecy, even decoyed him to their ambush with a false damsel in distress. They deserved no mercy, especially since they would probably give none. He bent low to stab at the swordsman who had wounded him, feinting, slashing high, then suddenly circling his blade to stab through the other's defenses as he caught a second man's sword on his buckler. Even then, the first attacker was almost too fast; he managed to parry, but Alain's blade sank into his shoulder, and the man dropped his sword with a shout of pain. He fell back to let two mates take his place.

His charger set his feet back on the earth, and Geoffrey backed him away. The assassins came after with a shout. Geoffrey reversed course and charged then, swinging his sword in an arc right in front of them, bending low to slash. The swordsmen leaped back with shouts of alarm—and collided with the spearmen. All stumbled, and Geoffrey turned his horse back to ride over them. They saw the beast coming and scattered, shouting warnings to one another. Geoffrey turned to cut down the one nearest him.

An invisible hand imprisoned his sword; it slowed, straining against a telekinetic bond. Geoffrey shouted with exasperation and kicked the swordsman in the jaw. Then he sent his mind arrowing after his telepathic foe. He felt the mind thrust coming from a tumbledown cottage off to his left, so he sent a thought bolt that excited the atoms of its thatch, and its roof burst into flames. The bind on his sword ceased abruptly as alarm filled his head, along with an assortment of curses. Geoffrey ignored them and spurred his charger toward the nearest spearman.

Alain had disabled four of his attackers, but the other two ranged themselves on either side of him. If he turned to strike one, the other would run at his back.

Then the spearman pulled a strange sort of short-handled hammer from beneath his tunic and pointed it at Alain.

Alain knew a weapon when he saw one. He kicked out of the stirrup and threw himself off the far side of his mount. As he landed, he heard the creature scream, smelled the sickening stench of charred horsehair, and his battle-lust turned to white rage. He knew without looking that his horse was dead, a good and faithful beast who had always protected his master and fought far more bravely than this mob of cravens. But Alain wasted no time in turning on the man with the exotic weapon—he charged the fellow's mate, thinking the man would not dare shoot at his own.

He met the swordsman sword to buckler, each one's blade clanging on the other's shield. Alain circled around him quickly, putting him between himself and the wielder of the strange weapon. A trail of blue-white light sizzled where Alain had just been. His skin crawled, but he mastered the dread and blocked his foe's sword, feinting low with his own blade. The other man dropped his buckler to meet the blow— and Alain reversed his stroke, swinging high and stepping in to slam his hilt into the other man's chin.

The swordsman hadn't been expecting a fist. He slumped, his eyes rolling up, and Alain caught him in a one-armed hug, holding him tight as he sidestepped and zigzagged in a grotesque parody of a dance, calling, "He still lives! Would you slay your comrade?"

The weapon wielder hesitated. Alain took a huge chance and threw his sword with more hope than skill. Startled, the man swung his weapon up to fire at it, and Alain dropped his living shield to charge the man.

The exotic weapon swung down, but Alain threw his buckler at the man. It struck the arm that held the hammer; the man shouted with pain and spun away, dropping the fell thing. He spun back in time to see Alain's fist just before it smashed into his face.

Alain stood panting, gazing around the wreck of the village, still quivering with battle-lust. All their attackers were down, but Geoffrey was riding toward a hut whose roof burned. The peasant girl who had brought them came running out, and Geoffrey turned his horse to chase. She whirled about to face him, and stones shot from the very ground toward his head.

That told Alain all he needed. He ran quickly and threw his arms about the girl. She struggled, screaming curses that almost made him let go. He held on grimly, though, until she suddenly slumped in his arms, eyes closing.

Alain stared at the limp bundle he was holding, horrified. "Geoffrey . . . you have not . . ."

"No. She only sleeps." Geoffrey dismounted, pulled rope from his saddlebag, and strode over, his face hard. "Many thanks for distracting her, for she is so powerful a witch that I doubt I could have sent her into unconsciousness without your aid." He whipped the rope about the young woman, tying her hand and foot. "This was an ambush skillfully planned, Alain."

"It was indeed," the prince agreed, "though I must needs ask me what has become of Baron Gripardin."

"Perhaps he is alive and well, and only a deserted village on his estate has any guilt." Geoffrey stood, hefting the unconscious woman over his shoulder. "Let us bind their wounds and pile them in the cart. It was a good thought of yours to bring it."

He turned away, but Alain caught his arm. "Geoffrey—that weapon . . . it shoots lightning. . . ."

"So I see." Geoffrey scowled at the ugly thing lying there on the ground. "Ask me not, Alain. I am forbidden to speak of such things."

"Forbidden?" Alain's hand tightened on his arm. "I shall be King of this land someday, and you are forbidden to tell me what endangers it?"

Geoffrey glanced at his face, but could not meet his eyes and looked away.

CHAPTER
-6-

Alain lifted his chin and squared his shoulders, looking very much the king he would one day be. "Who could command you to withhold knowledge from the heir apparent? Only the Crown has such authority! Did my mother or father forbid you to speak with me of this?"

"No—my own father, and the monks of St. Vidicon."

"The monks?" Alain exploded. "What right have they to say what the prince shall or shall not know?"

Geoffrey looked away. "There is reason . . ."

"Then you had better tell it me." Alain lightened his hold and took on the persuasive tone Geoffrey had told him worked well with women. "Come, my friend—no one can now accuse you of having revealed the thing's existence. The cat is out of the bag, so surely you may tell me its markings and how many kits it has."

Geoffrey stood, irresolute.

Alain pushed a little harder. "You are the friend of my childhood and my youth, and I shall someday be your king. Should I not know all things that imperil this land?"

Geoffrey caved in. "You should. My father shall have to live with the exposure. I shall tell you all I can, Alain—but first, let us load these villains into our cart."

The windows of Rod's study were tilted open to let in the fragrant spring air. He sat at the desk, brow furrowed as he set down his latest guesses about the origin and development of the Gramarye espers—a major book that he only thought of as a working agent's notes on his mission. He scowled as he wrote down the latest rumors he'd heard about Father

Marco Ricci's appearances after his death; they had to be there as part of the record, but Rod disliked recording gossip. To appease his own conscience, he wrote very clearly that these were only rumors.

It never occurred to him to be on his guard. After all, his study was on the second floor of the keep, above the great hall with its twenty-foot ceiling—and the keep was well away from the curtain wall and its battlements. Besides, he had a dozen guards on duty—so he never expected the burly young man who climbed in through the window and crept silently up behind him, pulling a garrote from his sleeve.

" 'Ware!" cried a small voice from the baseboard.

"Where?" Rod cried, spinning about. He saw the young man's expression turn from satisfaction to anger as he threw himself forward.

Rod wasn't as quick, but he was a lot more experienced. He pushed his chair away from the desk, and the young man went sprawling across its top. Rod wrenched his arm around in a wrestling hold, pinning him down, calling, "Guards! Guards!"

"Guard yourself," snarled a voice behind him, and he whirled just in time for the truncheon aimed at his head to strike his shoulder instead. Rod shouted with pain and kicked, catching the grizzled attacker behind the knees. The man went down with a shout, but a third assassin leaped in through the other window levelling a blaster, and the first young man shoved himself up from the desk with blood in his eye.

Rod dove for his knees, catching him in a perfect tackle. The young man bellowed and fell on top of Rod, but not fast enough—the blaster bolt caught him in midshout.

"Fiend! You have slain him!" the third attacker cried. He ran forward, reaching down to wrench the dead body off Rod—and Rod turned with it, slamming a fist into the attacker's jaw.

The grizzled man was still trying to get to his feet, but his legs wouldn't work. He hobbled toward Rod on his knees, swinging his truncheon up again.

The guards burst through the door and caught the man, one

seizing each arm. "My lord!" cried one, horrified. "Are you hurt?"

"I don't think so." Rod touched his shoulder and winced. He'd have to check and make sure it wasn't broken. "But I wouldn't be feeling much of anything by now if a busybody brownie hadn't been watching over me." Rod pushed himself to his feet, dusting off his clothes, and called, "Thank you, Wee Folk!"

" 'Twas our pleasure, Lord Warlock," three high-pitched voices answered.

The guards went pale. They still hadn't adjusted to living with elves.

Rod stood still, mind searching for his family out of habit. He encountered Gwen's probe instantly and the two merged thoughts for a minute, calming each other, merging in an instant's caress, and rejoicing that they both lived. Then each mind quested farther—and found their children under attack.

Quicksilver was dressed in more luxurious attire now—a gown of silken rose with an overrobe of burgundy. She and Cordelia strolled about the gardens, chatting.

"You have taken your sentence well," Cordelia told her future sister-in-law.

"Well, I did slay more than a few men," Quicksilver acknowledged, "and once it became a matter of warfare, I would have been as hard put to prove it self-defense as any general would. I cannot complain, milady, since the Queen was so generous. Years spent roaming the countryside looking for peasants to protect is far better than the noose, or even years in gaol. Besides"—she grinned—"our sovereign did sentence me to most agreeable company."

"Would that agreeable company were here," Cordelia sighed, "and his companion my fiancé with him."

"It would be well," said a deep old voice.

Cordelia turned to frown at Tom Gardener. Behind him, his assistants were rising from their knees, lifting hoes and brandishing pruning hooks. A vein of fear opened in Cordelia, but she told herself she was being ridiculous. "It is most discourteous of you, Tom Gardener, to intrude on ladies' conversations.''

"It is indeed," Quicksilver agreed, hands on hips. "Remember your place, sirrah."

"You are neither of you better than I, nor any other," Tom Gardener growled, "and your place is six feet deep." He swung his spade high.

Quicksilver reached under her robe and drew sword and dagger.

But thought was quicker than action, and Cordelia arrested the spade with a telekinetic push. Some other mind pushed harder, though, and the spade began to move again, then faster and faster, and Tom Gardener grinned wickedly.

Quicksilver's sword darted past Cordelia, into Tom's shoulder.

The old man dropped the spade with a howl, clutching at his shoulder, but his assistants ran forward, swinging their tools, and Cordelia suddenly realized how much a pruning hook was like a halberd. She reached out with her mind and wrenched at the nearest.

Tom Gardener grunted, though, and she felt his mind wrench against her own. For a moment the pruning hook hung poised, wavering between their two forces, and the man holding it perforce stopped with it. Others still ran toward them, though, and Tom let go of his shoulder and smashed a fist into Cordelia's face.

Sparks shot through Cordelia's vision; darkness moved in. She felt the ground jar against her knees, heard Quicksilver's scream of rage, then Tom Gardener's shout of pain. Another man screamed. She shook her head, managing to banish the fog that tried to claim her, saw the spade at her feet, managed to grasp it and use it as a cane to help push her upright.

"Against my back! Press hard!" Quicksilver cried.

Cordelia didn't understand but had sense enough to comply. She pressed her own back against Quicksilver's. Then she saw a youth swinging a hoe at her. Her father's training took over and she raised the spade to block without even thinking about it, because she was thinking instead of the grass, how slippery it was, how the youth's feet must slide. . . .

Slide they did, shooting out from under him. He gave a wail of surprise but finished his swing anyway. It bounced off Cordelia's spade without much force. She pushed it with her mind, pushed hard, and the handle shot back to crack against his head. He went limp.

Suddenly there was peace, suddenly the only sound was groaning. She dared a quick look about, saw Tom Gardener lying unconscious with blood spreading from the wound in his shoulder and another in his thigh, and the youth near him, also unconscious. She glanced behind her and saw Quicksilver breathing hard, her gown torn to show a bright red gash, bruises already darkening on brow and cheek, but four men lay on the ground before her, out cold. She kicked Tom Gardener, shouting, "Caitiff! Traitor! Coward, to set upon two weak women with six brawny men! Waken, cat's meat! Come to thy senses, thou pox-faced whoreson offal! Up on thy feet, thou decaying heap of rancid haggis!"

"Why, sister," Cordelia said, panting, "why do you revile him so?'

"For that he will not wake up and keep fighting, so that I might slay him! I cannot kill an unconscious man, after all!"

" 'Tis his good fortune that he lost so roundly, then." Cordelia caught her breath. "I thank you, bandits' chieftain, for I've taken my life from you this day."

"And I mine from you," Quicksilver replied, gasping. Her voice still shook with anger. "I could best the four of them, but not six, especially if their master was a warlock."

"A warlock and a traitor!" Cordelia flared, the anger surging in reaction. "What a coward's ambush was this?"

"One well planned," Quicksilver answered, "and I can only wonder how long ago these men came into your service, knowing this day would come. Only think, sister—we would not have been here if Tom Gardener had not counselled us to stay at home and let the boys prove their valor by themselves!"

Understanding burst in Cordelia's mind. "We would not have been here to suffer their attack indeed—and would have been with our fiancés to defend them!"

"Defend!" Quicksilver cried, aghast. "Quickly, Cordelia! How fare they?"

The bandits burst from the woods on three sides of the meadow, running at Gregory and brandishing weapons. He turned to face them, remembering his father's lessons and staying alert for footsteps behind him while with his mind he loosened the earth in a half circle twenty feet from him. The bandits stumbled into it and sank up to their knees with cries of surprise and anger.

Then the damsel cried "Beware!" and the footsteps came at his back indeed, a hard arm encircled his neck and pulled back, but Gregory was already kicking with his heel. He struck the man's knee; the attacker howled and fell, taking Gregory with him. Fear roared up inside him as the arm tightened about his throat and the world grew dark, for Gregory had never had to fight before, not really, only in practice— but training took over, and almost of its own accord, his elbow struck hard as he twisted. The man grunted with pain, his hold loosening, and Gregory twisted free, rolling and rising even as he had in practice. The bandit struggled to climb to his feet even as he fought to start breathing again, but Gregory thrust a hand at him, thinking of molecules dancing in frenzy, of light and heat, and fire exploded from his palm into the bandit's face. The man fell back with a howl, slapping at his smoldering beard. Gregory stepped in, turning, and hurled the man across his hip. The bandit went tumbling with a wail, then scrambled up, running back toward the trees.

But his fellows were wading out of the sudden slough and lumbering into action again, howling for blood and swinging their weapons.

Gregory needed maximum effect with minimum damage. He thought again of excited molecules, of flames sudden and huge, and a line of fire exploded all along the bandits' line. They skidded to a halt with screams of terror. Then the flames shot up into manlike forms, towering over them, reaching down with hands that shed sparks while thunder boomed overhead and lightning stabbed again and again, first in front of one bandit, then another and another.

One bandit gave a wail of terror and turned tail. The others saw him and followed. In seconds the whole band was running, fleeing back into the woods.

For good measure, Gregory made the firemen stalk after them, reaching out hands of flame with streams of small fireballs shooting from their fingertips.

Squalling and clapping a hand over a posterior burn, the last of the bandits disappeared among the trees. Gregory let the firemen snuff out and stood staring after the bandits, feeling a fierce elation, the first real thrill of victory in his life. It made him feel huge, swollen, superhuman. He stood still, letting the intoxication fill him, letting his lips spread into a huge grin, waiting until the feeling crested and began to ebb. Then, when he was sure he could control himself again, he turned back to Peregrine and was shocked to find her shrinking away from him, eyes wide with terror, hand to her mouth as though stifling a scream.

For a moment, Gregory was totally confused. She knew he had been protecting her. Why, then, should she fear him?

Because thunder, lightning, and fire are frightening whether they protect you or pursue you, of course. Gregory realized he had to reassure her, and quickly. He smiled gently, forcing the aura of triumph to drain away. "The danger is past, damsel. Fear not."

Peregrine was frightened indeed, for the Finister she really was knew that the "bandits" were her own agents and had been ordered to give Gregory just enough of a fight to make him feel manly and protective before they turned tail and ran. She had only expected to boost his testosterone level to the point at which he would be instantly vulnerable to her erotic projections; she had never suspected that this seeming milksop would really be capable of putting up a fight, let alone display the capacity for utter mayhem that his fireworks had shown.

Gregory spread his arms, hands open, as though to demonstrate his vulnerability. "They are gone, they are fled like the cowards such bullyboys are. They shall not trouble you again, for they will fear the shield I have shown them."

Of course—his shield. Gregory's form of "fighting"

wasn't actually aggressive, just a show of strength meant to scare off the bandits—which it had done all too genuinely. Small wonder that it had terrified Finister, too. She had known the Gallowglasses were broadband psis, that in them the rules of sex-linked powers seemed to have been waived, but she had never dreamed that Gregory could be a pyrotic, a fire-maker, as well as a telekinetic.

"You are free," Gregory said. "You may go where you will."

Once again he looked as inoffensive as a doormouse, and if the battle had whipped up passion in him, he showed no sign of it. Finister felt the sharp bite of angry frustration again but fought it down, remembering the purpose of this whole charade—to come close to Gregory with his defenses lowered.

"Go?" she stammered. "Go where? I cannot go back to my village now, and if I wander away into the forest, I shall most surely be set upon—perhaps not by these bandits, but by ones every bit as bad! Would you condemn me to loneliness and abuse, sir?"

"Certainly not!" Gregory said, shocked. "Come, I shall escort you to a safe haven."

"Come I shall." Peregrine stepped forward, only inches from him. "The only haven I wish is here, in your arms. Oh, sir, how may I thank you for such gallant rescue?"

Still he stood with his arms outspread like a scarecrow, face foolish with surprise. "Why, by finding a village where you may live your life in peace!"

She needed to push harder. Peregrine began to tremble; tears rolled down her cheeks. "Oh, when I think what those men might have done—what other woods runners will surely do if they can! Alas, that I was born a woman and weak, prey to every whim of brutal men!" The trembling grew into shivering.

By reflex, Gregory's arms closed around her, gathering her head to his shoulder. "There now, you should not weep! There is no need, damsel, believe me, for though the world may seem harsh now and then, there are more good people than bad in it, and you shall find that your life grows wonderful again.''

"How, if no man will have me?'' Peregrine wailed, burrowing her head into his shoulder—and pressing her body against his. "None will wish to wed a damsel debauched! All will turn in disgust from the bandits' leavings!''

"It is you who have spurned them, not them you.'' Gregory stroked her back, voice a murmur. "Let them out, the fear and the horror—let them out, I say, let them be gone, and let the hardness they have given your body go with them. Let the tenseness be gone from your arms and back, for there is no longer a need to brace yourself against a cruel fate.''

As he said this, Peregrine let herself relax even more, letting her body soften and meld to his—and felt all of him tense in response. She let sobs join her tears, and wept softly but audibly.

Dazed, Gregory stroked her and kept up the flow of soothing murmurs, amazed at the feel of a woman's body against his, mind swimming in a hormonal haze, astounded that a woman could cling to him seeking strength and that he should actually feel he had such strength to give. Confused but delighted, he revelled in sensation, and when her face turned up to his, when the lovely eyes fluttered closed as the moist rosebud lips parted, to brush them with his own was so natural that he did not even think of anything else—and as those lips trembled, then melted under his, they became all there was in the world, and as the kiss deepened, his whole existence became the sweetness of her mouth and the unbelievable thrill of the touch of lip and tongue and teeth. His telepath's nature took over and his mind opened even as his heart and his mouth had, sensing the wealth of emotion in her, the boiling confusion of fear and relief and desire, a tidal wave that swamped him.

Then the sun exploded in his mind and there was no sensation but its heat and its searing light. He clung to the woman in his arms, terrified for her, horrified that the explosion might hurt her.

The afterimage faded from his mind and he felt her in his arms again but not her mouth against his. Wind cooled his cheek, and finally sight returned. But fear paralyzed him, for the woman in his arms was limp, her eyes closed, her mind empty, and she was not Peregrine or Moraga but a stranger, a flaxen-haired beauty with an unbelievably voluptuous figure. Grief overwhelmed Gregory as he realized what had happened. It was Finister he held, as he had known in the back of his mind—Finister in her true form, for when he was lost in her kiss and his mind was wide open to her, she had gathered all her strength to hit him with a mind bolt, one with enough power to have burned out his brain. But the automatic defense system he had constructed had come into play, reflecting the bolt back into her own mind and serving her as she would have served him.

She had meant to kill him, he knew that, but her final spell of desire had done its work too well, and Gregory wept with grief as he knelt to lay her body gently on the ground—wept with grief, and felt the pall of despair descend as he felt for the pulse that he knew could not be there, for surely she had meant to kill.

CHAPTER
-7-

Queen Catherine was livid. Even as the guards hauled the assassins away to the dungeons of Castle Gallowglass, the Queen, alerted by a royal witch, paced the flags of her solar, fuming, "How dare they rise against my son? How dare they strike at his Cordelia? I shall flay them within an inch of their lives! I shall make them howl and gibber and beg for death!"

"They will be fortunate that you do not punish them as harshly as they deserve," King Tuan said with a completely straight face.

"They shall indeed!"

"Nonetheless, my love, before the torturers have reduced them to babbling husks, might we not ask them a few pertinent questions?"

Catherine halted, pivoting to glare at him, beginning to feel the slightest bit abashed. "What questions are these?"

"Why," King Tuan said, "who sent them, why they wished to slay Alain and Geoffrey and Cordelia and Quicksilver, and most importantly of all, how they managed to penetrate Castle Gallowglass even to Lady Gwendylon's private garden."

Catherine gave him a long and steely glare beneath which fury simmered, warring with common sense. At last she said, "You have the right of it in this. Set the investigation in train, husband, an it please you."

In those very gardens, Cordelia and Quicksilver watched the guards haul away the last of the assistant gardeners, or gardening assistant assassins, whichever they truly were.

"Why did they set upon us?" Quicksilver demanded. "I know your family has no shortage of enemies, Cordelia, but

even here? Which ones are these, and why did they set upon
you?''

"They are likely agents sent by a government yet unborn.''
Cordelia took a deep breath and explained to Quicksilver
about the futurians who were trying to sabotage the government of Gramarye in order to win control of the planet in
centuries to come, and why. She had expected to have to
wheedle and work her way around disgusted disbelief, but
Quicksilver only listened with narrowed eyes, nodding every
now and then as points connected to make her kind of sense.
When Cordelia had finished, she asked only, "So you think
these fools were of those who seek to abolish all government?''

"I do,'' Cordelia said. "Assassination is more their sort of
work. The totalitarians prefer to foment rebellion, setting the
peasants to slay the aristocrats.''

"There is reason enough for that, surely!'' said the woman
who had been driven into outlawry by a rapacious lord. "Still,
from what I have seen of how your family manages their
estates, your peasants would not be among those rebelling.''

"I would hope not,'' Cordelia said with a grateful smile.
"But the most recent of these futurians, sister-to-be, is the
one who sought to seduce Alain from my side, then under a
different disguise, to woo Geoffrey from yours.''

"You do not say it! That caitiff Moraga?''

"That was neither her true name nor her true form,'' Cordelia said. "No one knows what they may be. She appeared
to my eldest brother Magnus in four separate shapes to drag
him into heart's torture and devastating humiliation.''

"As a result of which, he will never trust women again.''
Quicksilver nodded heavily, her face stormy. "So you think
it is she who sent these backstabbers?''

"She, or the one who commands her.''

Quicksilver's scowl darkened even more. "But you say this
witch Moraga is only one of her disguises. Was not she dis-
patched to Runnymede under guard of your little brother
Gregory?''

"She was,'' Cordelia replied. Then she caught the implication and her eyes widened in horror. "Dear lord! Gentle

Gregory! If she could so mangle our great towering Magnus, what has she done to my sweet, mild lad?''

"A question well asked," Quicksilver replied, "and I think you had better answer it as quickly as you may."

Cordelia's eyes lost focus as she paid more attention to the world of thought than to the world of the senses. Abruptly they sharpened again with horror. "He is alive, but his whole soul is filled with mourning—and with thoughts of death! Your pardon, Lady Quicksilver! I must go to him!''

"With all speed!" Quicksilver cried. "I shall follow with all the haste four hooves can muster!''

Minutes later, Cordelia spiralled up from the garden on her broomstick and shot off toward the south.

She landed in a meadow, looking about her in alarm. The vista was peaceful, a grassy carpet adorned with wildflowers and surrounded by murmuring trees, set off by the roughness of a boulder in its midst.

The boulder! By it knelt her brother, and he was weeping! Cordelia ran to him, heart hammering in panic.

She slowed as she came near him, almost embarrassed, uncertain how to begin. His gaze was fixed on the face of a sleeping woman, one whose beauty shocked Cordelia and filled her with instant envy even as anger rose in her, for she recognized the witch, and she was as far from the dumpy Moraga she had seen at Castle Loguire as Terra was from Gramarye.

Silent tears rolled down Gregory's cheeks "Good afternoon, sister. It was good of you to come—though I cannot say what good you may do here."

"Whatever happens, you shall not face it alone." Cordelia sent a quick probe into the woman's mind and found it sleeping, but alive. "Gregory . . ." She broke off in confusion.

"You wonder why I weep," Gregory said, his tone leaden, "but who would not weep at the death of beauty?"

"Death?" Cordelia darted another quick look at the sleeping woman but saw her breast rise and fall. She smiled with fond condescension, relieved that his grief was mistaken. "She is not dead, poor lad—only sleeping." She dropped to her knees beside him and caught his hands. "Gregory—she means you harm! No matter how beautiful she is, her heart is hideous! It is she who maimed Magnus and who sought to slay Alain! I do not doubt that she means to slay you, too!"

"I am quite sure of it," Gregory said, but his gaze stayed on the sleeping woman. "She has already made the attempt, but I had forged a mental shield that reflected her own assault back at her, and this is the result—save that the reflection must have scattered the energies, if she only sleeps."

Cordelia stared down at the unconscious woman, appalled. "Why, the vile witch! But if you know she sought to kill you, why do you weep for her?" She guessed the answer, though, and her heart sank.

"Because I have fallen in love with her." Geoffrey's whisper confirmed her fear.

Blind rage struck and Cordelia knelt rigid, waiting for it to pass. It would not help her brother for her to slay the sleeping woman out of hand. In fact, such a deed would lose him forever. But the fury ebbed, leaving her panting. She had not the slightest doubt that the creature had manipulated Gregory's emotions shamelessly—and had made him fall in love for the first time! The very first! And with such betrayal and such hurt for so sensitive a young man's first, he might very well never be strong enough to love again! "Gregory—you cannot think to woo her. . . ."

"I do not," Gregory said in a flat, lifeless tone. "Be assured, sister, that I have tested her goodwill and found it lacking. Greatly though I desire her, I know that if I reached out to her, she would try again to kill me, and again and again. Therefore must I never touch her." The tears rolled down his cheeks with renewed force.

Cordelia searched for words of comfort and found some—of a sort. "It is not you alone she has sought to slay, but all of us, even Quicksilver and Alain. She has even plotted to kill the King and Queen!"

"Do you not think I know?" Gregory's tone became utterly devoid of emotion. "If I had not known it before, I certainly do now, for I saw it in her mind when, in panic, I sought to discover if she lived. Therefore must I execute her."

"Execute!" Cordelia cried, appalled. Striking the woman down in self-defense she could have understood, but not this, not cold and emotionless killing! "Gregory, you must not!"

"Conspiring to regicide is a capital crime," the lifeless voice answered. "So is attempting to murder the heir apparent. Both are high treason—and I assure you, sister, that I have seen three successful murders in her memory, done for her own personal reasons, not for her Cause. The woman is a murderer, and the law demands that she die."

"Then leave it to the law! Leave it to a judge and a jury!"

"Wherefore?" Finally Gregory turned to her. His tears had dried and his eyes become like chips of ice. "I know her guilt from the evidence of my siblings. If more were needed, she stands convicted by her own memories."

"But . . . but you love her!"

"I do." The words seemed wrenched from his heart; then his tone deadened again. "It is wrong for me to let my own feelings sway me from the path of justice. I know her guilt; I must execute her." He turned back to the sleeping witch. "Best to stop dithering and be done with it. Logic forbids any other course." His gaze sharpened.

With a shock, Cordelia realized he had begun to concentrate on slowing Moraga's breathing. She seized his arm to distract him and cried, "Then a pox upon logic! Emotion, too, is a part of truth!"

"When that emotion is the product of scheming and manipulation?" Gregory shook his head. "There is no truth in that—and when you have done with emotion, what is left but logic?"

"Intuition!" Cordelia cried. "The back of the mind assembling a host of facts to present a thought that will then stand the test of reason—and my intuition tells me that this is wrong, that by slaying her you would do grave harm to yourself!"

Gregory's eyes lit with a furtive gleam of hope. "If to myself, then perhaps to others. I pray you, sweet sister, dredge those facts up from the back of your mind to the front. Tell them me, so that my logic may yield."

Cordelia breathed a massive sigh of relief, then realized

that she was trembling. She hid it by clenching her fists and stiffening her body, summoning the self-possession she would need to persuade this gentle brother who had suddenly turned into a remorseless killer. Well, not remorseless, perhaps—indeed, he would feel remorse for the rest of his life. But he would nonetheless kill her.

She took a deep breath and said, "I am appalled that I should have need. You yourself, brother—have you no heart, no conscience that may tell you what mine do?"

"Aye, I have," he returned, "but if reason contradicts the impulse of conscience, I must choose the course of reason. Even now Conscience tells me not to strike a woman in cold blood, but Reason shows me that she merits death and, moreover, will find a way to strike at us again if I let her live."

"But you cannot know that!" Cordelia cried. "She might become sincerely penitent, might truly become your loyal friend!"

Gregory frowned at his big sister. "Do you truly think she does not merit death?"

Then he saw in her eyes that it was not what the woman deserved that concerned Cordelia, but her sudden fear of what her little brother had become. Gregory gazed at her, sadness weighing down his heart. "I am nothing more than I ever have been, sister," he said softly. "It is only this occasion that has made you see it."

The trembling took her again. "The Gregory I have known would always seek the course of mercy! Why death, Gregory? Why not some lesser punishment?" Then a happy thought struck her, and her hand tightened on his arm. "Would it not suffice for her to dwell forever in a prison from which she could not escape?"

"Aye, it would." Gregory gave her a sad smile. "But this is a woman of commanding presence, Cordelia, or she would never have risen to authority among her own band. Come, you know how intelligent and resourceful she is, and how unscrupulous. Do you truly think there is a jailer whom she could not bend to her will or a prison from which she could not escape?"

Cordelia stared at the ground, fists clenched, thinking frantically. Surely the woman was a snake and a backstabber, surely she deserved to suffer, but death? Surely not, surely it would be evil to deprive her of life, especially when she was so young, had so much of life left, so many joys to come. . . .

Inspiration struck, and she smiled at her brother in triumph. "Aye, she could escape from any prison—save one in which she wished to stay."

Gregory stared. Then he frowned and said slowly, "She deserves to suffer for what she has done—but aye, I would be content if you could invent a prison that gave her so much joy that she wished to dwell there forever. How could you craft such a thing?"

"I cannot build a prison, but I can craft witch-moss," Cordelia said. "Let us find a huge mass of that fungus and fashion from it Moraga's ideal man."

Gregory frowned, searching her face, not understanding. Then comprehension dawned and his eyes widened. "Of course! If we search her mind to discover all she wants in a man, then make a construct that embodies those qualities, even all its contradictions and paradoxes, she might become so besotted with him that she would be content to stay with him all her days!"

"Even so," Cordelia said, beaming. "Of course, we would plant it in his mind to take her away to some hidden valley where they might celebrate their love forever . . ." She stopped at the twist of pain in her brother's face.

It smoothed instantly, though, and he said, "Continue. This scheme might march, and a human life is worth the trouble."

And the pain, Cordelia thought, and her heart flowed with love and pity for the lad. She did continue, though. "We would, of course, enclose that valley with an enchanted, invisible wall and ask the elves to set sentries about it night and day."

"In case she does discover her imprisonment? But if she does, elves or no elves, she will one day escape."

"I doubt that highly," said Cordelia, "but I doubt even more that she would ever realize that wall existed. If the construct were truly her ideal mate, she would never tire of her dalliance with him and would never wish to stray far from his side.''

Hope warred with hurt in Gregory's heart. Reason told him that after the novelty of being in love wore off, Finister would take up where she had left off. He warned his sister, ''Ideal or not, she would tire of him and manage to escape, though she might come back. What damage could she do while she were loose, Cordelia? Surely she would strive to achieve the anarchists' goals and, even more certainly, her own. She would continue to disturb the peace, seek to assassinate the monarch, slay people whenever they were in her way or could not be controlled, and generally wreak havoc.''

Despite his words, though, Cordelia could see that hope drowned out reason, and the pain of seeing Finister with another man would be far less than living with the guilt of executing her. ''There might be some way to purge her of those desires.''

Hope ebbed; Gregory gave her a sad and weary smile. ''How might we do that? We speak of impulses inculcated throughout childhood, perhaps even inborn, probably so deeply ingrained that she is not fully aware of them. How can we purge her of such as that?''

Grasping at straws, Cordelia protested, ''There must be some way! If telepaths cannot do it, who could? It only remains to learn more of the workings of the mind!''

Gregory stared, scandalized. ''Do you speak of reaching into her mind to cure all the mental deformities that have made this damsel a ruthless killer?''

Cordelia looked down, abashed. ''I know it goes against every telepath's rule of right and wrong—that we must never peer into others minds against their wishes, unless they are enemies and the danger they present is immediate—and that we may never meddle with their minds unless they attack and we act in self-defense.'' Her head snapped up; she glared into her little brother's eyes. ''But Gregory, she *is* an enemy, and though the danger she presents is no longer immediate, it is sure and drastic! As to meddling with her mind to cure her homicidal ways, surely that is self-defense! There is no question that she will attack—only a doubt of when!''

Gregory showed not the slightest sign of scandal or disgust; he only looked thoughtful. "Such an outcome is most surely desirable, and I have been tempted to try it once myself."

Cordelia's hopes soared. "Why did you withhold?"

"Why, because of the very ethics of which you have spoken," Gregory said, "but more out of concern that I might make things worse instead of better, for I know so little of the mind."

"You know so little of the mind?" Cordelia stared. "You who have studied it all your life?"

"I have studied psi powers," Gregory clarified. "I know a great deal about that, though never enough. Of the rest of the mind's workings, I am ignorant."

Cordelia knew that Gregory had immense knowledge of people and the twists and turns of their thinking, but she could understand his feelings of incompetence—the mind was an amazingly complicated thing, after all. Nonetheless, she seized on his uncertainty. "Then it is only a matter of how to cure her, not of its rightness."

Gregory took his time answering that one. "True—but that 'how' is so complex as to make the task impossible, or at least too chancy to risk—is it not?"

"But it is only a matter of how, not of rightness!" Cordelia insisted. "You do not doubt that if we could cure her instead of killing her, we should!"

Again, Gregory was slow to answer. "We should if we could, that is true—but what if our efforts fail? What if she seems to be cured but is not?"

"We may still let her dwell in that prison she will not wish to leave! Between the two, it should be safe to let her live!"

"Perhaps," Gregory mused, "but if we could so cure Moraga, ought we not to spare every convicted murderer in like fashion?"

"We should," Cordelia agreed, "but I think medieval justice will be a long time accepting the idea. This Moraga, however, has not been given into the hands of that justice yet. She is our prisoner still, and if it was right of you to execute her without regard to the Queen's Justice, then it is surely our right to cure her instead!"

"Only if we can be sure she will be rendered as harmless as the dead." Gregory raised a palm to forestall his sister. "I know, I know—on this planet, the dead are not always harmless. Still, we can be sure of the rightness of our merciful course only if she becomes no more dangerous than a ghost. After all, dear sister, there may be some people who can never be cured, whose wickedness is born into them, or so deeply bred that they live for it and will never willingly leave off."

"That is possible," Cordelia allowed, "but I doubt that this Moraga is one of them. We know she is an agent of our bitter enemies, after all, and young enough so that she was probably raised by them, reared and trained to be a traitor and assassin. Is that not as much as to say she was warped and twisted in her growing?"

"Most likely," Gregory said with immense relief. "You have argued well, Cordelia. If we can cure her, we shall—and cure her or not, we shall do all we can to consign her to the happy prison of her ideal man, at least until we are sure it cannot hold her."

Cordelia breathed a massive sigh of relief. For a moment she swayed, almost unable to stand.

Gregory's arm steadied her. She looked up at him and was astounded to see his face woeful and gaunt with yearning. "But Cordelia—must we consign her to a witch-moss construct? Could I not become her ideal man as easily as some mind-built toy?"

CHAPTER
-8-

That gave Cordelia pause, for all her instincts protested against the idea of letting her little brother remake himself to suit some she-wolf's whims. "There is danger in that, Gregory. Surely it is wrong for anyone to yield their identity to another person's will—wrong and impossible, for you are what you are, and no matter how you try to hide it and pretend to be otherwise, sooner or later it shall burst out in outrage."

"True," Gregory said, pleading, "but I do not speak of changing myself, only of learning what she truly wants and needs of a man, so that I can provide it to her."

"Surely you do not mean to make yourself her willing slave, to be ever at her beck and call, pathetically eager for her slightest nod of pleasure! No woman wants a man who so abases himself!"

"You see?" Gregory said. "Already you have told me one thing that women do not want in a man. You could tell me more, sister, and her mind could tell me the rest if we seek among her memories. It is only a matter of technique, of learning how to speak to her, how to woo—for surely I have never learned anything about courting a woman!"

"You think it is purely a matter of skill, as the song says?" Cordelia asked. "There is more, Gregory. It is not enough to act the part for her—either you are in essence what she wants in a man or you are not; there is no other way about it."

"True, I cannot be anybody but myself," Gregory agreed, "and to try would be only a living lie. But surely I can learn to become all that I can be and to discover how to let it show forth. Where is the wrongness in that, sister? After all, if I am not to her liking, we can still forge the artificial construct, her ideal man.''

Cordelia barely managed to bite back the retort that all ideal men were indeed only artificial constructs, but she put it aside; her brother's need was more immediate. He was so forlorn, his face so beseeching, that Cordelia found herself saying, ''Let us discover what her ideal man is. Perhaps you are already he.''

Gregory gave a mirthless, sardonic laugh. ''I am scarcely a warrior bold!''

''It may be that she is not either, in her heart,'' Cordelia pointed out. ''It may be that she is by nature a shy and retiring creature whom her tyrannical employers fashioned into a weapon as she grew.'' She shrugged. ''Who can say?'' Then she stepped back, surveying her little brother with a critical eye. ''I shall tell you this, though—if you would become any woman's ideal man, you shall have to gain great brawn on that skinny frame, for most women do like a bit of muscle on a man.''

Gregory's jaw firmed. ''If that is what she shall want in me, I shall do it!''

''If you would do it at all, you must do it quickly,'' Cordelia warned, ''and there may be great pain when 'tis done in a matter of days, no matter the magic that aids it.''

''I can withstand it,'' Gregory said stoutly. ''Who knows the doing of such things?''

''Whom should we call to heal the lass's mind?'' Cordelia countered.

''Mother,'' Gregory replied.

It was handy being related to the wisest witch in the land. He closed his eyes for a second, sending out a silent appeal, then was surprised to feel an overwhelming sense of relief in answer.

So did Cordelia. They stared at one another, eyes widening; then she hastened to reassure her mother that she, too, was alive and well. Gwen informed them of the attacks on herself, Geoffrey, Alain, and their father, then told them that she would be with them straightaway.

Cordelia boiled over with wrath, pacing the grass. ''The

gall of them, the duplicity, the malice! To separate us and strike at us all at the same minute, so that we could not come to aid one another! Whoever their captain is, he deserves to be hanged! We must seek him out, we must rake him over hot coals, we must see him drawn and quartered!''

'' 'Twas not a man,'' Gregory said in a small voice. ''It was Finister. I read that in her mind.''

Cordelia whirled, staring, emotions churning in confusion. She had convicted the woman by her own tongue. She glanced down at Finister, seeming so innocent, so helpless, so vulnerable in her sleep, and found that even knowing the woman had meant to slay her whole family only a few minutes past, she still could not bring herself to become her executioner. ''Gregory . . . I spoke in haste, in the heat of anger.''

''I know, sister,'' Gregory said gently, ''but I did not. Your intentions may be excused, but what of mine?''

There was no ready answer to that. Cordelia tried, and found none.

''If we let her live,'' Gregory said, his voice low, gazing at the sleeping woman, ''will she ever forgive me?''

Cordelia said quickly, ''There is no need for her to know.''

''There is every reason for her to know,'' Gregory countered, ''if I am to hope for her love.''

''There is some truth in that,'' Cordelia allowed, ''but not if your love is all that keeps her alive.''

Gregory frowned, thinking that one over. ''Love cannot endure if it is founded on deceit.''

''I have known of many loves that did,'' Cordelia said sourly.

Thus it went, back and forth, argument and counterargument, and Cordelia began to enjoy it thoroughly—it was the first time her brother had shown any interest in relationships outside his own family. She was almost sorry when their mother swooped out of the sky, skimming her broomstick low over the meadow, then hopping off beside them. She stared at the sleeping woman, frowning, puzzled. ''Who is this wench, and how has she need of me?''

Cordelia and Gregory exchanged glances, each waiting for

the other to begin. At last Gregory said, "I have fallen in love with her, Mother."

"In love!" Gwen spun to him in surprise, then smiled broadly and embraced her youngest—only for a few seconds; then she held him off at arm's length. "It has been long in coming, my son. I rejoice for you."

"Do not," Gregory said, his voice hollow, "for this is the woman who even now commanded her henchmen to strike at our family."

Gwen spun, staring down at the slender, frail-seeming blonde in shock. Then the storm clouds began to gather.

Gregory tried to stave off disaster by telling her the worst at the outset. "She is also the witch who tormented Magnus and sought to steal Alain from Cordelia and Geoffrey from Quicksilver."

"The witch Moraga?" Gwen demanded, face turning stony.

"That was but one more disguise," Cordelia told her, "wrought by projecting into our minds the appearance she wished us to see."

"If that is so, she is an extremely powerful projective." Gwen turned slowly to Gregory and spoke with compassion. "Therefore, my son, you have not truly fallen in love with her, only fallen victim to the compulsion she laid upon you."

"Is the love any the less real for that?" Gregory asked, caught between hope and trepidation.

Gwen started to answer, then hesitated.

"Many women have gained love by glamour and allure, Mother," Cordelia reminded.

"Only infatuation," Gwen cautioned her. "If it grew into love, it was rooted in likeness and liking."

"Might she not have been like to me if she had been reared by a mother like you?" Gregory asked. "If her heart and soul had not been twisted by evil folk seeking to use her for their own purposes, might we not have liked one another for goodness and intelligence more than for appearance?"

Gwen took a long, slow look at the sleeping woman. "It is vain to ask what might have been, Gregory. The plain fact is that she was raised as she was and is what she is. Can you love a woman who might stab you in your sleep?''

''I do not need to sleep,'' Gregory said instantly, ''and in my trances, I can watch well enough to protect myself.''

''That avoids my question,'' Gwen said, ''and does not answer it.''

''We think it may be possible to cure her, Mother,'' Cordelia said softly.

Gwen stood motionless.

''I had thought I must execute her,'' Gregory said, ''but Cordelia has thought of a prison she could not escape because she would wish to stay in it—a valley where she might dwell alone with a witch-moss construct, a stock who was her ideal man.''

''We would hem it about with an invisible wall and elves to watch,'' Cordelia said quickly, ''in case she might become bored and seek to leave.''

''That is not enough,'' Gwen said, her tone unyielding. ''If we cannot erase her desire to hurt, she will always be a threat and may yet destroy us all.''

''Cannot that desire be erased?'' Cordelia asked.

Again, Gwen stood mute.

''I am too clumsy to essay it myself,'' Gregory said, ''and I know too little of such aspects of the mind. Indeed, I know little save the use of psionic talents.''

''I know somewhat more of feelings and reasons for deeds,'' Cordelia said, ''but surely not enough.''

''Nor do I,'' Gwen said at last.

Silence held the clearing.

Then Gregory's shoulders sagged. ''There is no hope, then.'' He stepped up to Moraga, face tragic, but his gaze sharpened, and they could feel the power of his concentration as the rise and fall of the woman's breast slowed.

''No, Gregory!'' Gwen cried, appalled. ''You must not slay her if she does not threaten your safety!''

''But she does, Mother.'' Gregory looked up, tears in his eyes. ''We have spoken it again even now—that while she lives, we are all in peril, we Gallowglasses. Nor is it we alone who are in peril—there are also the King and Queen, Alain and Diarmid, and all the folk of this isle of Gramarye. If she has her way, Chaos shall be loosed upon the land, Anarchy shall cry 'Havoc!' and each man's hand shall be turned against his neighbor.''

"The danger is not immediate!" Gwen protested.

"It is not present," her son agreed, but went on with inexorable logic, "yet it is inevitable. Only death will forestall it." He turned to focus his will on Moraga again.

"There must be another way!" Gwen cried. "I did not raise my son to be an executioner!"

"What did you raise me to be, then?" Gregory stared at her with such intensity that his eyes seemed to pierce her soul with the icicles of logic, and for a moment even his own mother was afraid.

Silliness! she told herself. *Ridiculousness! He lay in my arms, he suckled at my breast!* The image evoked gave her the answer to his question. "I reared you to be a whole person, Gregory, one who knew mercy as well as justice, who felt emotions as keenly as the delights of reason, who prized intuition as the capstone of both and was capable of turning it to action. I reared you to love and laugh and sing as well as to analyze, to nurture as well to protect, and above all, to devote yourself to the happiness of your fellow folk, for only thus can you gain happiness for yourself.''

The intensity of Gregory's gaze slackened into brooding. He nodded slowly, not speaking. Finally he said, "It is well spoken, Mother, and a noble cause—but I have fallen somewhat short of the mark before this. Now, though, I have at last learned to love someone other than my kin and understand how much more vast can be the love for a mate. Can you say truly that you have reared me to this and not do all you can to save my love?''

Gwen sighed, capitulating. "As you shall have it, my son. I shall essay it." Then she frowned, becoming stern. "Yet by what right would you have me meddle in her thoughts, dig deeply into her most private memories, and have the temerity to meddle in the workings of another's mind?''

Gregory's gaze did not waver, and he spoke with the certainty of a judge pronouncing sentence. "She lost the esper's right to the privacy of her mind by using its powers to commit murder and torture the hearts of others, for she thus became the concern of the people, who are the nation. The state must know her heart to judge her guilt and decide her fate—justice or mercy; either slay her out of hand, or invade and remake her mind." For a brief moment he lapsed into a smile. "I think she would choose the path of life."

Gwen stood stiffly, staring at her youngest as the realization flooded through her, the shattering discovery of how deeply he had fallen in love. For a moment she had to fight down blind rage and the urge to tear the sleeping woman to bits for having manipulated her son's affections so callously.

The vixen had put her in a devil of a predicament. Even if she turned the witch over to the Queen's Justice, Gregory would be heartbroken by her death—but if she let the woman go free, she would twist and warp his heart until he could no longer love. The only course of action that would not hurt Gregory deeply was curing Finister completely so that she could become a worthy mate for her son, if she had it in her, or be compassionate enough to turn him down gently if she did not fall in love with him.

"I shall cure her, Gregory," she promised. "I shall find a way."

The lad folded. The tenseness went out of him so suddenly that he stumbled, almost falling, and Cordelia dashed to embrace him, hiding the need to prop him up. "Beware, my brother. For all our mother's good intentions, even she may not be able to work so great a spell."

Gregory straightened again, his face settling into lines of resolution. "I shall brace myself for it—but it is kill or cure, and I shall accept what Fate brings."

That was a new title for her, Gwen thought sardonically— Fate. Then she realized that every mother was just that, her children's fate, or at least the greatest single factor in the making of their destinies. No wonder the Fates were pictured as women!

She pushed the thought aside, recognizing it as the refuge and the procrastination it was. She turned to the unconscious woman, kneeling and reaching out to touch her temple. Her eyes glazed and the sunlit meadow blurred and ceased to register on her senses as an avalanche of emotion swept her, anger and bitterness, fear and discord, pathetic yearning and despair all mingled together as the events of the woman's life cascaded through her mind in a shattering kaleidoscope.

Moraga's own reflected mind stroke felled her, memory faded to the blankness of unconsciousness, and Gwen withdrew her hand with a shudder.

"Is it so bad as that, Mother?"

Turning, Gwen saw Cordelia at her side, hands on Gwen's arm, holding her up, and wondered if she had cried aloud, and what the words had been, if any. She said nothing of it though, only nodded. "She would indeed prefer the course of life, even if I remake her memories so vastly that she does not recognize herself, and will be long rediscovering herself, learning that she has still the same identity. Indeed, I find a yearning there, and I think it is for nothing so much as a humble but joyous life. Let us attempt it."

"How are we to begin?" Cordelia asked, intimidated by the magnitude of the task she had proposed.

"More to the point, how are we to end?" Gwen asked tartly. She turned to her son. "As I understand it, this plan of yours depends on you yourself becoming her ideal man, not some stock made of witch-moss."

Gregory blushed and lowered his gaze.

"That . . . that was our notion," Cordelia said with misgiving.

"What will you offer her when she awakens, then?" Gwen challenged. "What qualities will you gain that will make you a fit mate for so beautiful and talented a woman?"

"Have I no talents of my own?" Gregory returned.

"Great talents," Gwen answered, and let a brief smile of pride show. "But you have only cultivated the gifts of the mind, Gregory, and those are only part of what an intelligent and sensitive woman needs. What else have you to offer?"

"A loving heart," Gregory said simply.

"And how shall she know that?" Gwen demanded. "Are you a poet, that you can spin a spangled net of images and resonances in which to catch her fancy?"

"I shall become so," Gregory averred.

"Well begun," said Gwen, "but only begun. Can you also become a romantic, ever thinking of ingenious gestures to express your love, weaving always about her the magical web of romance?"

"I shall learn it if I must read every romance ever written!"

"A better beginning, but there are many more books you must read if you would know enough of women's thoughts to entice her." Gwen smiled, amused. "I need not ask her if you can read her mind, as every woman wishes, for that is the saving grace of the male telepath—but can you understand the desires that you read therein, so that you will fulfill their spirit, not their form alone?"

"If you will tell me what her desires are, I may succeed," Gregory said.

"That she must do," Gwen told him, "even as she sleeps—in fact, most assuredly while she sleeps. Come, sit in my place." She rose in a single fluid motion, gesturing at the place where she had sat. "Touch her temples and read her thoughts. Some will appall you, some will disgust you, but you must know her as she is to understand what she may become, and the cavernous yearning that underlies her needs."

Gregory sat promptly, saying, "I shall give her all that she wishes!"

"Do not," Gwen said. "Give her what she needs—and fulfill only her greatest wishes. Now study her mind, and learn to tell the one from the other." She stepped back, surveying him with a critical eye.

Gregory stiffened in surprise but withstood her inspection.

"There is also the matter of physical attributes."

Gregory sighed with weary patience. "I know, Mother—you were ever telling me that I should have exercised more."

"The hour for telling is past," Gwen said.

Cordelia intervened. "We have spoken of this, Mother, and we shall summon Geoffrey to see to the building of his body. We shall do it by telekinesis as well as exercise, of course."

"You will wish you had heeded me and done this over the years," Gwen warned her son. "Bringing it about in a matter of days will be torture."

"It will, at least, be honest and open," Gregory said stubbornly. "If Magnus could withstand the tormenting of his heart, I can surely endure the agony of the flesh."

Gwen wasn't sure Magnus had really withstood that torture, but he had at least survived it. For a moment she had second thoughts about curing his torturer and saving her life, but she consoled herself with the thought that if she succeeded, Finister would scarcely be the same person as the one who had mangled her son. She would become her true self, shedding layers of bartered affection and frustrated striving for approval, of denigration and insult, of frustration and abasement. Perhaps the core of her identity would blaze with beauty and goodness—or perhaps, when all Gwen's efforts were done, she would still be the same homicidal vampire she had been before.

Gwen put aside the possibility; it was extremely unlikely that Finister had been born a sadist and assassin. "If I succeed in this salvage," she told her son, "the woman will emerge with a heart that is quite fragile for some months. She will try you in every way she can imagine before she risks giving you her trust; she will attempt to drive you away again and again before she lets herself begin to believe you will stay. She will need a man of infinite patience, of extreme empathy, and of great emotional strength to support her through those perilous first days."

"Empathy?" Gregory asked in surprise. "I have always thought my ability to feel what others felt was my curse, for even before I uttered a syllable, I began to imagine how my words might sting others' feelings!"

"So that is why you have spoken less and less as you grew older," Cordelia said thoughtfully.

"Is not such empathy so extreme as to be a weakness?" Gregory demanded. "Do I not feel others' pain out of all proportion to good sense?"

"You must allay sympathy with judgement, of course," Gwen said slowly, "but I would hate to think caring to be weakness."

"He always was the gentlest of us four," Cordelia admitted.

"But you learned to hide those qualities as you grew, Gregory," Gwen interpreted. "Did they make you prey to others' petty cruelties?"

Gregory flushed and looked away. So did Cordelia, though her expression was guilty.

"Shame upon those who played upon your kindness!" Gwen said with a severe glance at her daughter. "Do you now fear that this Finister shall do so, too?"

"She already has, Mother," Cordelia said, "for as she has projected her allure, has she not exploited his instinct to care for others?"

"Do you ask if she has used desire to induce your brother to search for her natural virtues, even though they may not be there?"

"But they are, Mother!" Gregory burst out. "I have felt them, though I have not probed deeply enough to discover memories of infancy. I have sensed good qualities in her that have been twisted into making her the treacherous assassin she has become!"

"We are answered, Mother," Cordelia said softly.

CHAPTER

-9-

"Why, what villainy is this," Gwen said, voice low and trembling, "to use a man's love to strike at him?!"

"It is only as she was taught," Gregory said stubbornly. "There is great sweetness underlying the shell of malice she has grown, Mother!" Then he broke off, staring from mother to sister and back. "What have I said? What makes you so intent?"

"The clarity of your love for her," Gwen said. "It is not that you have been duped into loving a viper, but that you have seen the loving babe she was 'ere the sorcerer transformed her."

"This love, at least, is not blind," Cordelia agreed, "though at first I thought it was."

Gwen shook off the mood and spoke. "If your love sees truly, I shall have to be extraordinarily wise and skillful to peel away that shell of scars to reveal the sweet and gentle child beneath—if that child has not died."

"She has not! Oh, Mother, she is still there and alive! I know it, I feel it!"

"How is this, then?" Gwen said with a rueful smile. "Do you love the child, or the woman she grew to be?"

Gregory stared, more into himself than outside, then said slowly, "Neither. I love the woman that child could have grown into and that may yet be—a Woman of If."

"Then let us see if we can make of her a Woman That Is," said Gwen. "I shall go to learn what I may of the human heart and mind. Whiles I am gone, do you submit yourself to the less-than-gentle ministrations of your brother, and when he lets you rest, read the sleeping mind of this woman in depth. Come to know her needs, delights, and secret fears, that you may fulfill the first and avoid the last.''

Gregory nodded, huge-eyed. "I shall, Mother."

"You shall also have to acquire a sense of fun and play,"
Gwen said grimly. "I know you have never truly done so,
but few women would wish a man who can never be gamesome." She turned to her daughter. "Tease him unmercifully,
Cordelia, until he has learned to recognize it and enjoy it."

Cordelia looked dubious. "I shall try, Mother, though
Heaven knows I did enough of that when we were young,
and he always mistook it for cruelty."

"I shall learn it now," Gregory assured her.

"Betimes engage him in contests of wit," Gwen counselled. She turned back to Gregory. "Therein, at least, you may
discover pleasure in the game itself. Once you do, you can
enlarge that to other play."

Now Gregory looked uncertain, but he said, "I shall do all
that I can to achieve it."

"There is something more you shall need to know," Gwen
told him. "Geoffrey shall teach it to you, mind to mind."

Gregory blushed even at the thought.

Cordelia smiled wickedly. "He shall listen with a beet-red
face, Mother."

Gregory turned to her with a frown but saw his mother's
smile of amusement. "Oh! I see. This is some of that 'teasing'
of which you spoke. Well, if I must learn lovemaking, I shall,
even if it must be with a purple face—but it shall also be
with dogged determination."

"I would rather it would be with delight and wonder,"
Gwen sighed, "but I will take what I may."

Gregory glanced at her uncertainly, then glanced away.
"Mother—do you truly believe I can become all these
things?"

"What have I told you of your ability to learn, Gregory?"
his mother demanded.

"Why, that I could learn anything I wished. . . . Oh. I see."
Gregory tried to smile. "At last I wish to learn it, is that what
you mean?"

"Exactly," Gwen told him. "I will say now what I said
then, my son—you can learn anything you truly wish to learn.

It is simply that, before this, you have never seen any sense in it.''

Gregory frowned, looking inward again. "Am I truly being a devoted lover, Mother, or am I seeking to remake myself in slavery to a woman's whims?''

Cordelia looked quite worried, but Gwen let the question roll over her and took her time phrasing the answer. "You are setting yourself to realizing your full potential, my son, with which you never would have bothered if this Finister had not spurred you to it.''

"To become her ideal male, and to cure her of her urge to maim and kill,'' Gregory whispered, daunted. "Surely only magic can bring about either one!''

"Then I shall go and learn that magic,'' Gwen promised him. She turned to Cordelia. "Be sure she stays asleep.''

The trip took Gwen the rest of that day and most of the next, for she had to fly half the length of Gramarye, and even at airspeed and with a favorable wind, that took time. She stayed the night at an inn, then went on to her goal at sunrise and came in sight of the convent early in the morning of the third day. She brought her broomstick down in a clearing so as not to frighten the holy women and walked the rest of the way.

When she came out of the trees, though, Gwen stopped, staring, wondering if she were in the right place. A mob of children was running about outside the walls, some playing with a ball, some whirling tops, others playing an intricate game involving small hoops, and some simply standing about and chatting. Gwen watched, rather startled—on her last visit, she'd had the impression that the nuns isolated themselves from the neighboring villages. That had to have been a mistake, of course—they were healers; patients must come to them in a regular procession. Her last visit had been in the Christmas season; no doubt the children had been home with their families.

But what were they doing here?

A nun came out of the convent gate and clapped her hands. The children immediately quieted and formed concentric cir-

Christopher Stasheff

cles, the oldest on the outside, the youngest and shortest on the inside. The nun nodded, satisfied, and said, "Good morn, my pupils."

A chorus of voices answered, "Good morn, Sister Elizabeth!"

"Let us ask God's blessing on our day's work." The nun knelt and the children imitated her. She began to pray aloud, and Gwen watched, scarcely able to believe what she saw. Was this truly a school for peasant children? In a land where only the nobility and the clergy learned to read and write?

But never women. No, Sister Elizabeth must have been there to teach them only religion.

The prayer done, they stood. One of the smallest raised his hand.

"Yes, Lawrence?"

"Must we go inside, Sister?" the little boy asked, his voice plaintive. " 'Tis so warm and so sunny outside!"

Sister Elizabeth cast a knowing smile at the oldest children, one or two of whom had the grace to blush and look down; they had put the child up to asking but hadn't fooled Sister for a minute.

"Nay, I think not," Sister said. " 'Tis indeed beauteous, and like to be one of the last warm days of autumn. We shall stay out of doors."

The children cheered. Sister Elizabeth smiled and waved for them to quiet down. As their noise subsided, she said, "Sit, now, and take out your slates."

The younger generation disposed itself on the grass, not without a bit of chatter. Sister Elizabeth clapped her hands. "Pay heed, an't please you! Senior students—write out an answer to this question: 'How could Christ be both fully man and fully God?' "

The older teenagers bent over their slates, frowning. One or two began writing immediately.

Gwen stared. Peasant children, writing?

Sister Elizabeth was going on. "Junior students—are those we call witches truly evil magicians devoted to Satan, or people like any other, but with talents few of us have? Judge by their works, good or evil. Then say if your answer could be true anywhere but on this Isle of Gramarye. As you write out your answer, bear in mind the three parts of an essay.''

The younger teenagers frowned at her, puzzled, then looked down at their slates, growing thoughtful.

Gwen was astounded, not only by the fact that these youngsters could write and therefore presumably read, but also at the nun's application of religion to a problem that was, for anyone on Gramarye, an issue of daily life.

''Older children, come near this tree!'' Sister Elizabeth took a sheet of parchment from her sleeve and tacked it to a tree trunk. It was covered with arithmetic problems. ''Solve these on your slates,'' Sister said as she glanced back at the senior students—then glanced again. ''Garrard! Your eyes on your slate, young man! Truly, one of your age should be above letting your eyes wander without purpose!''

There was a smothered snicker from the teenagers, and one of the boys snapped his gaze back to his slate. The girl at whom he had been gazing glanced at him out of the corner of her eye, then back at her slate with a covert smile.

Sister Elizabeth turned to the youngest children. ''Now, then! Let us recite the alphabet!'' She held up a hand, but glanced back at the older children and snapped, ''Matthew!''

One of the boys looked up, startled and guilty.

Sister Elizabeth stepped over to him and held out her hand. ''School is for slates and chalk, naught else. Give me your reed, young man.''

In sullen silence, the boy pulled a narrow tube out of his sleeve and gave it to her.

''You may keep the beans,'' Sister said, ''so long as you do not use them. If you are well behaved the remainder of the day, you shall have this reed again.'' She didn't say what would happen if he didn't; apparently everyone knew. She turned to go back to the youngest students but stopped short as a girl quickly covered her slate with her sleeve. Sister levelled a forefinger. ''Ciphering only, Cynthia. I wish to see naught but numbers on your slate.''

Other students craned their necks, trying to see what Cynthia had been drawing or writing.

''Eyes on your own slates,'' Sister reminded them, and

they all whipped their gazes back to their work. Sister sighed and shook her head as she returned to the youngest—and Cynthia took out a scrap of cloth to erase her slate. "Now," said Sister, "the alphabet."

The children began to chant with her.

Gwen moved on, shaking her head with amazement. A school for peasant children was unheard of! Still, now that she knew of it, it made a great deal of sense—an order dedicated to the health of the mind would naturally wish to develop those minds as fully as possible.

She was also amazed at the woman's patience. A few days of that would have reduced her to a screaming scold—or a gibbering idiot. She wouldn't blame the nuns if they changed teachers every few days—but from the children's air of familiarity, it was evident Sister Elizabeth was with them constantly. A truly amazing woman, indeed.

The novice at the gate started looking frightened as soon as she realized that Gwen wasn't just an accidental passerby, but she held her ground and stammered, "What would you, milady?"

"Speech with your Mother Superior," Gwen answered. "Good day to you, lass."

"G-good day." The girl's eyes were huge. "Who shall I say wishes speech with her?"

"The Lady Gwendolyn Gallowglass."

The girl swallowed heavily, nodded, and stammered, "Y-yes, your ladyship." Then she turned and scrambled away, leaving Gwen to wonder why they bothered with a gate when the wall was so low—or, for that matter, why they bothered with having a porter.

She took the opportunity to study the layout of the convent. It was very obviously a homemade affair, built with the willing labor of the local peasants—Gwen had a momentary vision of fathers and brothers hauling blocks of stone for the curtain wall and wattle and daub for the buildings. The structures were only larger versions of peasant huts—considerably larger, since several of them were double-storied. But regardless of their construction, their layout adhered to the time-

honored ground plan of convent and monastery alike—
dormitory, refectory, cloister, and chapel—though the cloister's pillars were wooden and the chapel was of painted boards. Not for the first time, Gwen wondered if the sisters were wise to try to keep themselves secret from the monks, who would surely have aided them with funds and labor had they known.

Of course, they also might have wished to establish their authority over the women's Order, as the nuns feared. That didn't seem terribly likely to Gwen, but she did think there was a definite chance that the Abbot might have forbidden the Order to form.

Her speculation was cut short by the advent of the Mother Superior, hurrying across the grounds so quickly her brown robe snapped about her ankles. The novice trailed along in her wake, still looking scared.

The older nun came up to the gate and curtsied in greeting. "Good day, Lady Gallowglass! You honor our house!"

" 'Tis a house of God, Mother, and 'tis my honor to be herein," Gwen returned.

"Only 'Sister,' an't please you," the nun reminded her gently. "We hold no official ranks past our final vows; 'tis simply my sisters' regard that doth give me precedence. I am only Sister Paterna Testa, like to any among us."

"Your pardon, Sister." Gwen inclined her head. "I come seeking wisdom."

The nun laughed. "You, the wisest witch in the Isle of Gramarye? What wisdom might I offer you?"

"Knowledge of healing," Gwen returned. "I had cause to see, when last I journeyed here, that you and your sisters know far more than I of the healing of the mind."

" 'Tis gracious of you to say so." The nun turned serious with compassion ready in her eyes. "Has your husband gained worse hurts?"

"None new, I think," Gwen answered. " 'Tis not one of my own I seek to cure, but an enemy who might cease to be a foe if she were healed."

"What an amazingly Christian deed!" the novice exclaimed, round-eyed, then clapped her hand over her mouth, appalled at her own temerity.

Gwen smiled with gentle amusement. " 'Tis not true charity if we wish to spare ourselves trouble thereby.''

"But it is true charity when the headsman's ax would be simpler and far quicker," Sister Paterna Testa said, her gaze probing and speculative.

"There are even better reasons than that," Gwen admitted, "though I do not wish to speak of them. Canst tell, Sister, why the wounds of the body heal with time and harden with greater protection of the softer flesh within, while those of the mind fester and grow worse?"

"For that they have not been well tended," the nun said promptly. She held out a hand, turning back toward the interior of the convent.

Gwen accepted the invitation, stepping through the gate with her and toward the main hall.

"You know," said Sister Paterna Testa, "that if a soldier is struck by an arrow but does not die, the barb must be cut out and the wound anointed with healing balms, then bandaged with a poultice."

"Aye, certes."

"Then will the cut flesh grow together once more and the skin seam itself over. Even thus in the mind, the barb must also be drawn out and the balm and poultice given."

Gwen looked up, frowning. "I have given what balm I may."

"Yet we may know of others," Sister assured her, "and there is yet the matter of the barb."

"Why, even so," Gwen said slowly. "Yet how can one draw out that which one cannot see?"

"Or even know is there?" The nun nodded. " 'Tis that which we may tell you of, milady—but anon. For the present, you have journeyed far and are surely wearied and a-hungered. Will you dine with us, thereafter to take your ease in our guest house?"

The refectory was a long hall, with cream-colored walls, a crucifix at the far end, and a picture of two women in peasant dress, one holding a baby, one with a face that would have turned plums into prunes if the smile on it hadn't been so warm and welcoming. There was no other decoration, but the cleanliness of the hall and the huge open windows that filled it with light made it cheerful and refreshing.

Sister Paterna Testa said grace, her sisters said "Amen," and immediately broke into happy conversation. Two of the nuns and two novices rose from their places and went out of the room. They came back moments later carrying trays laden with hearty, but very plain, food.

"I trust you shall not find our company burdensome, milady," Sister Paterna Testa said as she dipped her spoon into her soup.

"I feel peace suffusing my soul already, simply from being within your house," Gwen rejoined. "But who are those dames pictured on the wall? Surely the one is not meant to be the Blessed Virgin."

"You have it; she is not." Mother Superior (for so Gwen thought of her, regardless of her claims) smiled. "She was only a peasant woman, milady, alone and forsaken with her babe—though she was far younger than she is pictured while her daughter was yet an infant."

Gwen began to understand. "Yet she was one of your founders?"

"Aye—the mother or our compassion, much as the other, Clothilda—blessed be her name!—was the mother of our strength." Sister Paterna Testa settled down to tell Gwen the story of the founders of her Order.

Morning started with a bang, one loud enough to bring Gregory out of his trance. He turned his head slowly, feeling his metabolism rise but not yet trusting it enough to leap up—and saw there was no need, for the explosion had simply been the burst of air compressed outward as his brother's body had suddenly filled the space where it had been.

The knight-errant strode up to him, grinning. "Good morn to you, brother!"

"And to you, brother," Gregory returned. "I thank you for coming to aid me."

"Though somewhat tardily," Cordelia said, rising from her bedroll. "Good morn, brother, even though you could not afford us the benefit of your company sooner."

"Ah, but if I had, I should have left Quicksilver to languish," Geoffrey said, "and you would castigate me for a careless suitor."

There was truth in that, but Cordelia wasn't about to admit it, especially since she was quite sure how Quicksilver had benefitted from Geoffrey's company and he from hers. She kept her expression of severity but said, "How say you, Geoffrey? Shall we make a lover of our ascetic brother?"

"Let me see if the game is worth the candle." Geoffrey stepped up beside the sleeping Finister and looked down. His eyes widened and he gave a long, appreciative whistle. "This is her natural semblance, yet she chose to go in disguise?"

"She has low self-esteem," Cordelia explained.

"It must be low indeed, not to know the power of such a face and form!"

"She thought the power came from her projective talents," Cordelia said, "that men loved her not for what she was but for how she could hypnotize them into feeling."

"Not without reason." Geoffrey turned to his brother. "Even you, who pride yourself on the cold and emotionless clarity of your mind, have fallen under her spell."

"I cannot altogether deny it," Gregory admitted, "but I can at least claim not to have fallen in love with the form, for I saw her in so many disguises that I knew not which one was real."

"So it would seem," Geoffrey said. "What do you think of the true shape?"

"Far more beautiful than any image she has worn!"

Geoffrey raised his eyebrows at the emphatic tone. "So speaks a man who indeed loves the mind and heart—but how can you, if she is a treacherous murderer?"

"Because I can feel beneath the roil of confusion, anger, and hatred to the forlorn child beneath, the heart of hearts, and it is beautiful indeed."

"That deuced empathy of yours!" Geoffrey exclaimed in exasperation. "Did I not say it would prove your undoing?"

"Then rejoice that you are proven wrong," Gregory said, looking steadily into his eyes, "for it shall prove instead the making of me."

Geoffrey gave him a long, weighing look, then said, "Perhaps. It shall, at least, give you reason to make yourself into a more conventional notion of manliness." He did not say whether that convention was wise or foolish, but only asked, "Have you dined?"

"Why . . . I have not," Gregory answered, surprised by the question.

"So I thought." Geoffrey took a packet from his wallet and held it out, unwrapping it. "A gift from Cook to you, my lad, and freshly and expertly grilled it is!"

Gregory looked down at the huge slab of steak and blanched. "Meat!"

"I know the stuff is alien to you," Geoffrey said, "but you shall become quite attached to it, and it to you."

"But—for breakfast?!!"

"And lunch, and dinner, and belike for elevenses and tea, too," Geoffrey said, grinning but remorseless. " 'Tis high time you were introduced to a high-protein diet. Steak," he said, looking down at the slab of meat, "this is Gregory. Gregory, this is beefsteak. Come now, embrace it and make it yours."

Gregory took the steak warily. "*This* will make me more attractive to a woman?"

"No," said Cordelia, "but the muscles it builds within you shall." She looked at the huge slab and wrinkled her nose in disgust but said, "Eat it, Gregory. Tell yourself it is medicine."

"Well, if I must, I shall," Gregory sighed, and drew his dagger to begin cutting.

"Clothilda it was who first built a dwelling in this place, though 'twas only a cottage, and a poor one at that. It had but two rooms, in one of which her chickens roosted."

Gwen frowned. "Why did she dwell alone in the forest?"

"Her parents were dead and she had no husband, having been born poor and unusually . . . plain. . . ."

"Aye." Gwen nodded, glancing at the picture. The woman was not merely plain but downright ugly. "Yet I have seen plain women married afore, if their natures were sweet."

"Hers was not. She was a termagant and a scold, with a sharp tongue and no pity—for she bore a grudge 'gainst all the folk of her village."

"Against the men, because none did want her?"

"Aye—because none was strong enough to stand against the vinegar of her tongue, nor wise enough to see the treasure of the spirit within her. And she hated all the women for sneering at her."

Again, Gwen nodded. It was a common enough story; people always seemed to need to have someone at the bottom of the social heap, and in a medieval society, the women determined that by who was married and who was not. Then, among the spinsters, they determined rank according to who was liked and who wasn't. "She does not seem the sort of woman who would have borne such treatment with patience."

"She was not. She railed against the other women, scolded the men, and became quite the terror of the village."

"Such folk begin to pride themselves on their loathsomeness, or seem to."

"And so did she."

Gwen nodded. "That could not endure. They would oust her soon or late."

"So they did. Someone unnamed denounced her to the priest, charging her with witchcraft. None spoke in her defense; indeed, all were quick to cry that she must needs be a sorceress. They drove her out with bell, book, and candle, and she fled here to this hillock, where the rock beneath the ground made a small clearing. Here she built a hut, then went back to steal a hen and a cockerel and scraped out a lean and meager existence with a garden and chickens, and nuts and berries to gather."

"Hard enough," Gwen murmured.

"Aye; but her true diet was her own heart. She nurtured herself on bitterness and hatred, on thoughts of revenge and plans for dire deeds."

"I have met such as she—yet they commonly become the

village wise women, learning the virtue of each herb and simple.''

''Clothilda did not; she swore she would never do good to her folk, only ill to those who had cast her out. Yet she did learn the powers of the herbs, but to harm, not to heal.''

Gwen shuddered. ''How could such an one endure?''

Mother Superior shrugged. ''Given time, she might have sought to wreak havoc on one person or more and been burned at the stake—but ere she could fulfill her desires, she was distracted.''

''By what?''

''By a baby's cry.''

CHAPTER
-10-

"It was not the common, lusty bawling of a babe a-hungered," said Sister Paterna Testa, "but the tearing bleat of one in true distress. Sour as she might think herself, there was some mother's instinct in her naetheless, and she followed the sound—only from boredom, as she told herself. There under an oak, seeking shelter in a hollow 'twixt great roots, sat a lass not yet twenty, gaunt with hunger, trying to give suck to a babe wasted almost as badly as herself. . . ."

"Why, what a parcel's this?" Clothilde snapped, instantly furious on the young girl's behalf. "You cannot give, child, when you have no substance yourself! Nay, come to my cottage and we'll find food for you."

The girl looked up, startled and frightened, then saw another woman and began to weep with relief. "Oh, praise Heaven! Thank the kind God! I had feared I would die alone!"

"Heaven has taken little pity on you, child, and the male God whom you praise has left you to die! Nay, come up on your feet and we'll take you to better shelter than this—though not greatly so, I fear." She bent down to take the girl's arm, and the baby squalled. A flow of gentleness sprang up in Clothilde from she knew not where, and she took the babe gently from the mother, crooning and rocking it. "There, there, little one, we'll find you gruel at least, soon enough. . . . Why, 'tis scarcely aged a month!"

The girl nodded in misery. "I hid away in the kitchens and pretended to fatness—but I could not hide the child's coming."

"Nay, I warrant not. Up with you, now." She caught the

109

girl's arm and lifted. The lass tried to rise, then fell back with a small cry. "I cannot!"

Clothilde was instantly concerned. "Nay, you are wasted worse than I feared! Bide in patience, child—I'll take the babe to feed, then bring back soup for you!"

She turned away, the girl's strangled thanks filling her ears, and strode as quickly as she could to her cottage. The babe pawed at her breast, seeking to nurse, and something brimmed and broke open within Clothilde, something that she had not known endured. To cloak it, she filled the babe's ears with savage denunciations of the father who had left it to die.

In her cottage, she ladled soup from the kettle where it always simmered, cooled and thinned it with water, then fashioned a teat from a scrap of cloth and trickled the broth into it, that the babe might suck. So she held the child against her breast and fed it as best she might, and her feelings were so tender that she had to breathe maledictions against all the male race as she did it. She knew better than to let the babe have its fill, so she had to endure its wailing whiles she carried it, and a crock of soup, back to the mother, fearing she would find the lass fled to Heaven whiles she had been gone—and she was aghast to see the young woman slumped against the oak with her eyes closed. But at the sound of her coming, the girl stirred and opened her eyes. Then for the first time in a year, Clothilde breathed the name of God in aught but a curse, though she quickly denied it to herself, and gave the lass spoonfuls of soup while she cautioned her not to eat too quickly. The lass could not heed, of course, but gobbled every drop Clothilde gave her—and the older woman was glad she'd had the foresight to bring only a small crock of the soup. Then she gave the babe back to the lass and bade her rest, and both dropped off to sleep. Clothilde watched over them, and her thoughts 'gainst men were murderous.

When they woke, Clothilde fetched more soup, feeding the babe even as she had done before; then the lass found the strength to come to her feet and, leaning on Clothilde and pausing oft to gasp and rest, stumbled toward the hut. Time and again she would have lain down to sleep and likely never rise, but Clothilde urged her on, for night was falling fast.

They came at last to the hut and Clothilde lowered her onto her own poor heap of straw, saying, "What is your name, child?"

The lass murmured, "Meryl," and slept instantly, and the babe was too weak to stir far, so Clothilde laid it in Meryl's arm and shooed the chickens within before the fox could come, then latched the door and blew the coals on the hearth to flame.

Thus they endured some days, the lass ever eating more soup and more, till her milk came again and the babe could have its proper nourishment. All that time, Clothilde nursed babe and mother alike, cutting up her spare apron to make linen for the child, linen that she washed as soon as it was soiled. She grumbled at the work, but secretly rejoiced, as she told us years later. . . .

"So secretly," asked Gwen, "that even she did not know it?"

"Mayhap. And whiles the lass gained strength, they talked."

It began when Clothilde saw Meryl waken that first night and came to feed her again, grumbling, "A curse upon that foul churl who got you with child and abandoned you!"

"Oh, speak not so!" the lass cried, "for he was my one true love and would have wed me—had he lived!"

That gave Clothilde pause. She recalled what the lass had said of her labor and said, "You did speak of hiding in the kitchens."

"Aye."

"You were a scullery maid in the manor, then."

"Aye."

"And the squire espied you."

"Oh, nay! 'Twas his son."

"As I thought." Clothilde's mouth settled into a grim, straight line. "So he deflowered you, then cast you away with no thought for you or your babe, eh?"

"Nay, nothing o' the sort! He did love me, aye, and we did meet in secret for nigh onto a year—but never once did he press me for more than a kiss, and that upon the hand! 'Twas I had to raise his hopes higher.'' She giggled at the memory. ''He was so clumsy in that, yet so graceful in all else! And he asked me to wed him, yet I did hesitate, knowing the difference in our stations.''

''Wise,'' Clothilde sniffed.

''Yet he did woo me and court me, and assured me that he would leave his inheritance if he had to, to wed me.''

''You would not wish that,'' Clothilde scoffed.

''Nay. I wished not to make a rift betwixt himself and his family, so told him I would wed him only if he could gain his parents' blessing—and I could gain mine.''

''Aye. Your mother and father had you matched with some village swain, did they not?''

''With three, and would have rejoiced at my choosing any of them. Yet my father groaned under the squire's rule and spoke often against him—so I determined in my heart that if I could but gain my mother's blessing in secret, it would suffice.''

''Men care so little for us!''

''Nay, say not so.'' Meryl smiled with fond memory. ''Tostig cared so greatly for me that he went with the lord's army, leading a troop of men off to the war, that he might gain some money of his own and enough of his parents' pride to outshine their contempt of my station.''

''A pretty fool was he! What manner of caring is this, to risk dying and leaving you lorn?''

Meryl's face saddened. ''Aye, 'twas foolish, but a man in love will do many foolish things, will he not? As will a woman.''

Clothilde stared at her, not understanding. Then she realized the implications of Meryl's words, and her eyes went round as saucers, mouth springing open for a jibe that she bit back just in time.

''Aye.'' Meryl bowed her head. ''I could not let him go without giving him my fullest pledge of love—and being sure I would have something of him left, if he were slain.''

''As he was! And left you with child!''

''Aye.'' Meryl lifted her face, tears rolling down her

cheeks. "Who could I tell? My ma and da would have been outraged at my foolishness, and the squire would have disowned me as an imposter."

"As they both did, when your babe was born!"

"Aye." Meryl bowed her head, the tears falling faster. "The squire's wife cast me out of her kitchens, claiming that she would not have a lying slut to serve her. My own folk did turn me from their door in shame, and the folk of the village drove me out with stones and gibes. I have lived on roots and berries this last fortnight and lived in fear of wild beasts till you did find me."

"The wolves and bears are yet to be feared, child." Clothilde welcomed the change of subject. "We must see to making this cottage stronger." Somehow the matter seemed more important now that she had a baby living with her, and a girl not far out of childhood herself.

"Aye." Gwen smiled, amused. "Children give one a greater stake in life."

"I would not know; what your children are to you, the folk of the villages hereabout must needs be to myself and to my sisters—though I will own, the care of these women doth give me cause to be glad in life, even had I not my God to love." Mother Superior looked up at the nuns around the table, who were all listening to the tale as raptly as though they had never heard it before. Gwen wasn't surprised; Mother Superior was a good storyteller. "They lived together, then, and reared the child?"

"Aye, though it seemed they would not, that first year—for the winter was hard and the wolves became hungry. They were glad they had made the hut stronger, Meryl and Clothilde, though they feared they had not made it strong enough."

"Were they not hungry themselves?"

"Most assuredly so, and Famine lurked at their doorstep."

Clothilde's garden had yielded a goodly crop of tubers and vegetables that could be stored for the winter, but she had planted for one, not two. They set snares for hares, but those remained empty—the foxes and ferrets had accounted for the small game. They sought the squirrels' hordes, but a handful of nuts goes only so far. They began to eat as lightly as they could, and even then, Clothilde later confessed she had taken less than her share, that Meryl and the babe might eat. It was a lean Christmas and a gaunt Epiphany, and by Lent they were so hungry that they could not see clearly. The babe wasted away until it had scarce strength enough to cry.

Then, weakened, Meryl fell ill. Her cough grew worse and worse, and though Clothilde tended her with hot cloths and every herb she knew, the lass waned daily, slipping down toward death. When she began to murmur her beloved's name, Clothilde lost her temper.

"Do not dare to seek him!" she railed at the lass. "Do not dare! What has he ever done for you, except to leave you with child, and alone? Yet I have given you care with mine every minute! How dare you leave me for the shade of him? How dare you leave your babe without a mother?" And on she railed, louder and louder, growing weaker but feverish in her own right and, when she had done railing against Meryl's lack of faith, began on God's. "How can you be a good God," quoth she, "if you will let a blameless babe die of cold and hunger, and a lass whose only fault was to love in folly? Nay, you must needs be a most cruel God indeed, for even your deer and hares do starve, and your lilies of the field lie dead beneath the snow! Let me die if you will, I can see the justice in that, for I am a sour and bitter woman, but this sweet child has never lusted for anyone's hurt, though she had cause, good cause indeed! You are the God of the hawk and the wolf, of the owl and the vulture, and no God of loving creatures!"

She would have gone on, but a strong voice cried outside the hut, "Who doth speak against the Lord?"

Clothilde froze, for to her mind, any man might sooner seek to reive them of what little life they had left than to aid them. She pulled herself to the knothole in the door and looked.

She saw a friar standing in the clearing, frowning about him, then calling, "Was it you in the hut who did rail against God? Nay, if it was you, have the courage to admit to what you said!"

He wore but a simple friar's robe, said Clothilde later, and sandals only, yet his feet were not reddened with the chill, nor did he shiver with the cold, though it was bitter. Clothilde considered, watching him, then resolved that there was small enough harm he could do them, for quick death would have been more merciful than slow—and he might have carried food. She unbarred the door and showed herself, crying, " 'Tis I have spoken 'gainst God! And can you truly tell me I should not?"

He turned and saw her, and his face was stern. "That I can. Wherefore should you think to rail 'gainst your Maker?"

"Why, for that I've a child in here sick of the cold and starving, and a smaller child who will die without her! Is that not cause?"

" 'Tis a cause that many have known down through the ages," the monk returned, "and their souls have been tried full sore. Naetheless, those of them that clung to the love of the Lord even to death, they bask in His eternal light and live with joy in Him."

Clothilde would have given him a right sharp rejoinder, but the words stuck in her throat as her knees gave way, dark spots filled her vision and swelled into night, and the weakness of hunger claimed her, for she had spent her last strength in railing against God and His monk.

When she woke, the fire was higher and much warmer, and she lay on her own pile of bracken, warmed by the monk's robe. Looking up, she saw him naked save for girded loins, and she assures us there was no beauty in his body, for it was gaunt and scarred from wrist to wrist across his shoulders and breastbone, yet still with the strength of leather. He held the babe in his arm, soothing it. Clothilde stirred herself and said curtly, "Naught will comfort her save food."

"Why, that have I given her," the monk returned, "and have more for you. Do you hold the babe awhile." And he laid it on her breast. Then he put aside the cup from which the babe had drunk and gave Clothilde broth from the pot he had set steaming over the fire. She knew she must eat sparingly, yet drank greedily, as much as he would give her. The flavor, though, was new to her. " 'Tis meat!"

The monk nodded. "I carry salt beef with me, and journeybread. That last is softened now, enough that you may partake of it." And he spooned a small biscuit into her mouth.

She ate of it thankfully, then asked, "What of the child?"

"The mother? I have given her a small amount of medicine and she sleeps with greater peace than she has in a fortnight, I warrant."

Panic clutched Clothilde's breast, that the 'medicine' might have sent Meryl down into the depths she sought; but a racking cough sounded from behind the monk, and she relaxed. "Can you do no more for her?"

"Not if you do not tell me of her illness."

" 'Tis only a cough, but it has worsened and worsened in spite of all my herbs."

The monk nodded. "So I had feared. Her lungs are filled with fluid and she has hard work to breathe even a little."

"Can you not save her!"

"I shall attempt it." The monk turned in the firelight and laid his hand over Meryl's forehead.

Then, as Clothilde told it, a most sweet change came about that was so amazing she thought it a miracle—for in minutes, Meryl's breathing deepened, becoming more even, and color returned to her face. She coughed again and again, but each time more lightly, till at last she coughed no more but only slept the deep and dreamless sleep of exhaustion.

The monk took his hand away; it trembled, and his face was pale.

"Why," whispered Clothilde, "what witchcraft's this?"

"No witchcraft, but the gift of God," the monk answered, though his voice was strained with weariness.

"Gift! To whom?"

"To this child, through me. I have had this talent for as long as I remember, though it took me years to come to use it for people's welfare instead of their hurt."

"You are a witch!" Clothilde breathed, eyes wide.

"I was born as what you term a witch," the monk agreed, "yet my soul was heated in the forge and put against the anvil, whereupon I came to see that I might yet worship God and serve my fellow mortals. I have looked inside this woman's body, see you, yet 'twas not with the eyes in my face, but with some other sense that shows me the inside of each muscle and vein, and the ugly monsters, too small for gross vision, that swim through her blood and cluster in her lungs. I have taught her body to fashion other creatures to fight them—watchdogs 'gainst wolves, if you will—and to make more and more of them. 'Twas the heat of their battle caused her fever, and I have given aid and comfort to the watchdogs, sealing their triumph over the wolves.''

''Where have you learned this?'' Clothilde whispered.

''From an older monk than I, somewhat, but most from the doing of it, and the knowledge God has given me as I have striven to aid the sick. Then I taught her body how to take the fluid from her lungs, turning some of it to air, and the rest to small bits and pieces, wafted throughout her body by her blood.''

A lust kindled within Clothilde—or a hunger for knowledge; she said it might be likened to either. ''You must teach me the way of it! For she and the child may fall ill again!''

The monk turned to look at her and she swore his eyes pierced through her flesh so that they saw her soul naked. Then he touched her hand, feather-light, but it burned, and she knew fear and outrage, for she felt that he read every most secret thought she had ever hidden. But he took his hand away and shook his head. ''I have read only your intentions toward other folk, woman, naught more. There is bitterness and lust for revenge in you, but I think it may pass.''

Looking within herself, Clothilde was astonished to discover that his saying was true; revenge mattered less to her now than the welfare of Meryl and the babe. She wondered if she had spewed all her poison at God, or if the monk had somehow cast a spell on her—though she cared not which at that moment. She only knew that the villagers and the hurts they had given no longer seemed quite so vital as they had. ''Must I swear that I will never use the knowledge you give me to hurt another person?''

''You must give me your word for it, aye.''

Clothilde stared into his eyes, and the rage and lust for

vengeance burned up in her again—but only briefly; she found it within her to forgo them, for the hurts she'd borne seemed small against the delight of this newfound knowledge. She nodded. "I swear by Almighty God—"

The monk put out a hand to stop her. "I did not ask for an oath."

Again, Clothilde stared into his eyes, reflecting that, considering what he had heard her saying against God, he was wise not to trust an oath in His Name—though she would have meant the words she would have sworn; she found it within her to forgive even God, now.

Gwen stared.

Mother Superior smiled, amused. "Aye. There is no limit to our self-conceit, is there?"

Yet Clothilde did as the monk asked and said only, "I give you my most solemn word that I shall never use this knowledge to harm people, save in defense of me or mine. Nay, I may even seek to aid folk that I know not."

"Well enough, then." The monk sat down, swept a patch of the earthen floor smooth with his hand, took a twig from the firesticks, and began to draw scant pictures that would make his words more clear. Clothilde watched, listened, and marvelled within as he explained to her how different substances may join to make new ones or divide to make pure ones, and how the blood doth flow and what 'tis made of, and of the host of small creatures, too tiny for the eye to see but perceptible by the mind, that dwell within the body. All the rest of that day did he teach, and she learned fiercely, asking a hundred questions and more. All through the night he taught, pausing now and again to feed her, Meryl, and the babe from the pot that seemed never to grow empty, though he himself ate not at all. When the sun rose, he sighed and took back his robe, belted it around himself again, and took up his staff.

"You will not leave me!" Clothilde cried. "There is so much more to know!"

"You know enough now to puzzle out the remainder," the

monk assured her, "and I must leave you, for you shall thrive without me. 'Twould take years to teach you all I know, good woman, and I cannot tarry so long."

Clothilde stared, amazed almost as much by the magnitude of the knowledge he indicated as by someone actually calling her a good woman.

"There are many other souls in need of my aid in this Isle of Gramarye," the monk explained, "and where I am needed to heal, there must I go—for there is a power in this universe, one called Entropy, that doth continually seek to make things go awry, pushing ever toward that final Chaos that is the undoing of us all and brings grief and misery to all souls. Illness is one aspect of it, for in illness the body's natural order is upset, and Disorder seeks to claim the whole of the mortal clay. Therefore must we strive to preserve Order within it, that human suffering may be eased."

Clothilde frowned, trying to understand. "Do you tell me that, if I wish to fight illness and stave off death, I, too, must have Order within me?"

"Within, and without." The monk touched her shoulder. "I charge you with the forming of such Order, and will give you the first rules upon which it will rest."

Clothilde gasped and clutched at his hand, for it felt as though lightning lanced through her, probing downward into her heart and upward into her brain. But she could not touch his hand; her own hovered an inch from his, and his eyes held hers.

CHAPTER
-11-

Then the current ceased, he took his hand away, and, looking within herself, Clothilde found that all bitterness and hatred were gone. She remembered the slights and injuries the villagers had given her, but they seemed remote now, almost as things that had happened to another person, and brought no renewal of hurt with them.

The monk asked her, "Do you wish these rules?"

"Aye," she whispered, "with all mine heart." And she bent her knees, seeking to kneel to him—but he upheld her, protesting, "I am only a man, sister in Christ; you must not kneel to me. I am only a man who tries to be good and to do good but does not always succeed."

"You have done a world of good to me and mine," Clothilde whispered.

"Then do for others as I have done for you. That is the first of the rules of Order for healing: that you will use this knowledge only to aid folk, save in defense of yourself or those in your care—and you will find that, even then, you can betimes turn attack by giving aid."

"I shall," Clothilde breathed.

"This is well enough, but I shall require more of you— that you will use this knowledge to aid any who are ill who may come your way, and will never turn away from a person who is sick."

Now Clothilde frowned, and 'twas she who sought as she gazed into his eyes, wondering at his reasons for asking that promise of her. At last, "I shall live by those rules," Clothilde promised, "and shall do all I may to raise an Order in living by it."

"Stout heart!" The monk smiled at last, a full and brilliant smile, then of a sudden frowned and looked aside. "I feel another's pain—great pain, and I must go to heal it as quickly as I may. I shall come again if I can, to give your Order a name. Godspeed to your work!"

"Where do you go?"

"Wheresoever I am needed. Farewell!"

The door closed behind him, and Clothilde pushed herself up from her pallet, tottered to the portal, and wrenched it open—but he was nowhere to be seen, nor was there sign of him in the falling snow.

" 'Twas a miracle," one of the nuns whispered.

"It may have been." But Mother Superior's tones were cautious. "Still, he may have been only a monk like any other. We have learned that the friars at the monastery are ever searching for new knowledge of the uses of these strange powers with which some folk are born . . ."

Gwen thought of telling them that very few outside the planet of Gramarye were born with psi powers, but decided against it.

". . . and he may have been one such monk, abroad on a mission for the Abbot. Surely we have found that there is naught miraculous in the cure he worked, for we have learned the manner of it ourselves; and the pot that never emptied may simply have been a large one, and the portions small."

"Yet there was the scar," one of the older ones noted.

"Aye—the mark of burning from wrist to wrist, up his arms and across his chest." Mother Superior nodded. "He may have been cruelly hurted when young, and known from his own pain the need for forgiveness of which he spoke."

"Or . . . ?" Gwen knew Mother Superior was only trying to provide a rational explanation for something her nuns saw as miraculous—and Mother didn't answer her question. She sat back and waited, and an older nun reminded Gwen, "The saintly Father Vidicon was burned in such a manner by lightning, which wrought his death."

Gwen lifted her head in surprise. Father Vidicon had taken hold of two high-voltage wires, knowing the electricity would kill him. In this culture, they would think of that as lightning.

She was about to point out that the burn would have been interior with no scars except those on his hands, but decided against it. People need their illusions. "You do, then, believe your convent was begun by a visitation of the sainted Father Vidicon himself?"

" 'Tis possible," Mother Superior allowed, "though there is no good reason to believe it, save our own desire."

Most of the nuns bowed their heads, and the few who didn't fought down smiles, but their eyes were lively.

Privately, Gwen agreed with what Mother Superior had said, though obviously did not want to believe—that the monk had been only a man, though obviously a highly skilled esper. "Do you know this monk's semblance? Is there any image of him?"

"Aye, for Meryl witnessed this conversation, nodding in and out of sleep, and was skilled with the brush." The Mother Superior rose. "An you will come to our chapel, I shall show you his portrait."

To Gwen, it seemed an odd place for a picture of the founder, but she dutifully rose with the rest of the nuns. Mother Superior bowed her head and said a short prayer before she dismissed her charges and took Gwen out through the cloister to the chapel.

"Another bite! Another! Aye, there's a man! Chew that beef! Gulp it down! Well done! Only two more bites, now! Masticate! Macerate! Chew, engorge! Finish it all!"

"Geoffrey," said Cordelia, "I think he might prove able to eat the whole steak even without such enthusiastic encouragement."

"Aye, but it is so much fun to watch him force it." Geoffrey grinned as Gregory closed his eyes and compelled himself to swallow the last bite. "Well done, my lad! How do you feel?"

"Absolutely bloated," Gregory said in a thick voice.

"Well, we cannot have that. Here, I have fetched a pillow. Lie down, my lad, and let Cordelia's mind work on your muscle cells."

Gregory lay down with a sigh of resignation. "What shall you do, sister?"

"Yes, what shall I do?" Cordelia asked, puzzled.

"Speed up his digestion, sister, and direct the protein to flow into his muscle fibers—first, his left biceps."

Cordelia frowned, concentrating. The clearing grew silent as she accelerated natural processes. Gregory studied the actions of her mind and his cells so that he might accomplish this on his own—somehow he was sure it would be a lifelong undertaking.

Then Cordelia told him, "Flex your arm."

Frowning, Gregory did, and Geoffrey deliberately pulled against the motion with his mind as Cordelia packed new muscle cells into Gregory's biceps. He cried out in surprise at the pain.

"Do you wish me to do it or not?" she challenged.

"Do . . . I shall rise above it. . . ." Gregory panted.

"Then flex your leg."

Gregory did, and clenched his teeth against the agony.

Cordelia read it in his face and bit her lip, but forced herself to go on. "Your other leg . . . your left arm . . . Now sit up."

White-faced and gritting his teeth with determination, Gregory complied. His heart grew faint at the pain he sustained, but he glanced at the sleeping face of the woman he had come to know as Moraga and forced himself to sit up, straining against the load his brother dragged on him.

The chapel was very small, as churches went—at the most, it might have held a hundred people. Gwen looked around. "How have you Mass?"

"The pastor of the nearest village comes each Sunday." Mother smiled. "None has ever felt the need to say aught about us to their brethren of the monastery."

Gwen could understand how loyalty to the people nearby could prove more pressing than fidelity to an abbot far off in the south, the more so as there was a certain resentment between the parish clergy and the cloistered monks akin to the old rivalry between engineers and physicists. There was also probable recognition of the importance of the work the sisters were doing—and considerable pressure from the peasants of the countryside, perhaps even from the lords. No, quite probably from the lords.

Gwen looked around at the church, reflecting that it needed to hold no more than its hundred, for there were only a few dozen nuns. There was a large crucifix above the altar and a statue of the Blessed Virgin at one side, with one of Joseph against the other. The style of sculpture seemed quite distinct from those Gwen had seen in other churches. "Whence came these statues, Sister Testa?"

"All works you see within were made by our nuns themselves, milady." She led Gwen to the north wall. "Yon is the monk who did appear to Clothilde."

Gwen looked, and the picture slapped her in the face—at least it felt as though it had, for she recognized the visage. It was Father Marco Ricci, the Terran priest who had founded the Gramarye chapter of the Order of St. Vidicon—and one of the very few of the original colonists who had been able to keep his memories of an advanced civilization, perhaps the only one. She felt her heart twist within her and was giddy for a moment, for she had known Father Marco herself, when she and her husband had been kidnapped into the past many years before. It was a strange and disturbing sensation to look at an icon of the man she had known and confront the fact that he had been dead for four centuries and more. But when had he discovered he was an esper? And how had he come by that horrible scar?

Of course, she had never seen him unclothed; he might have had it even when she had known him—but she found room to doubt it.

"You seem disturbed." The Mother Superior's interest kindled. "Have you seen this face before?"

Gwen realized that she was in an excellent position to destroy all the Order's illusions but firmly rejected the opportunity; confronting them with reality was not her task. Instead, she "answered" a question with another. "When did Clothilde and Meryl live, Sister Paterna?"

"Four hundred fifty-six years ago, milady. Our convent has kept exacting records."

Four hundred fifty-six years! That would have made Father

Marco a very old man—but it was just barely possible. Gwen determined that she would have to go to the monastery and search their records, to find out if Father Marco had gone abroad much in his later years.

Still, the picture was not that of an old man, but of one in his middle years. . . .

"What you think, milady?" Mother Superior asked, her voice low.

"You may have had just such a visitation as you think." Gwen carefully did not say by whom. She turned away. "May we turn to the matter of healing, Sister?"

The nun frowned slightly but respected her wishes and turned aside, leaving Gwen to ruminate over the idea that the convent had just as strong a right to exist as did the monastery, if the monk had indeed been Father Marco. "Did he come again, as he had promised?"

"He did not promise—yet he did come again, years later, when a score of devoted women had come to share the hermitage of Clothilde and Meryl, and the babe Moira had grown to womanhood. Clothilde began to try her newfound knowledge on injured animals and discovered, to her delight, that she had the power the monk had shown her. She taught it to Meryl, who seemed also to have the healer's talent, and the two of them began to jest that she was in truth the witch the village folk had thought her to be. A passing woodcutter must have heard them, for one day a farmer came to their clearing with a listless hen who had lost most of her feathers. Clothilde felt her old resentment return but thrust it aside; she had promised the monk to aid any who needed healing, and though this was not a person, she knew the spirit of her promise should encourage her to examine the hen. But Meryl of the soft heart anticipated her; she cried, "Oh! The poor, wretched thing!" and hurried to lay her hand upon it. Then she mused a while and the hen became once more healthy. The farmer stammered his thanks and fumbled forth a coin, but Meryl returned it sternly. "We do not heal for pay," quoth she, thereby creating another Rule of our Order. The farmer thanked them and went away—but the next day, his daughter came with a healthy cockerel, a gift from her father, and stayed to ask the manner of their healing. Clothilde taught

her the basis of it and found the girl had the talent. She came
again the next week, leading a farmer with an ailing pig.
'Twas Clothilde who healed it this time and again refused
payment, saying only, "Belike we shall be in need of your
aid someday, neighbor." He looked startled and stammered
that she should have any help he could give. He was as good
as his word, for when the haying was done, he and a score
of villagers came with saws and hammers and builded them
a stouter cabin that would turn away any wolf. The women
thanked them, though they had been healing a constant stream
of animals, perfecting their skills and learning more; and the
workmen were still there when the peasant folk brought a
woman who was like to die of fever, carrying her on a pallet.
Clothilde came hurrying to meet them, scolding them for
having moved one so ill when they could have come to fetch
herself or Meryl (and the peasant folk looked amazed to hear
it). Then Clothilde laid a hand on the woman, realized the
depth of her illness, and told the folk they had done right, for
the woman might not have endured the extra time it took to
fetch her. Clothilde did her best, and the fever lightened but
did not cease, so she called Meryl to come and aid.

Together they made great inroads on the fever, yet it per-
sisted. Then the farmer's daughter, who had come so frequently to learn from her, knelt down to aid, but Clothilde
took her aside and explained that if she were to show her own
power of healing, the folk of the village would like as not
cast her out as a witch. The lass considered, and while she
did, felt the call of God powerfully within her and said there
was little to keep her in the village. So together they cured the
woman, who walked home well two days later, but the farmer
was now wary of his daughter and made no argument when she
told him she wished to remain with the healers. Yet he came
weekly with provisions for them, and to build and mend for
them, and she learned from another patient that he boasted of
her in the village and was honored for being her father.

"So more ill folk had begun to come?"

"More and more, till there was scarcely a day that one was
not at their doorstep."

"And if the villagers honored the father whose daughter had joined the healers, would not others have sought to join them, too?"

"Aye, though few wished to stay when they came to see they would have to give up home and hearth. Yet there came also women who had conceived out of wedlock, to be 'healed' of their babes. Clothilde rebuked them sharply, telling them she sought to save lives, not to end them—and one challenged her then to keep the babe for her. Clothilde promised she would, and the lass dwelt with them till her babe was born, then left it with Clothilde and went back to her village, claiming that she had not the vocation to abandon motherhood and wifehood for devotion to healing; yet she came often in after years to visit and bring food, and watch how her babe grew."

"And others did as she had, I doubt not. The babes also grew up to become women of the Order?"

"Some aye, some not. Meryl's babe, though, chose to stay, and proved to be the most powerful healer of them all. Moira she was named, and Clothilde appointed her to succeed to the rule of the Order upon her own death."

"Then the monk did not come again whiles Clothilde did live?"

Mother Superior shook her head. "He had not promised, but only said he would try. When Moira was aged, though, a monk did come to their gate—for they had a wall by then, you see, and all the buildings we have now, save the cloister. This monk asked a night's lodging and was kept in the guest house, where Moira visited him with two of her women— they did not yet think of themselves as nuns. The monk proclaimed their convent a wonder and asked to see the hospital. They were glad enough to show him and let him watch as they healed a feverish lad, one who had turned were, and needed many healings. . . ."

"Were! You can heal one of being a werewolf?"

"The kind who are wolf-men, aye," Mother Superior told her, "not the kind that change their whole forms. But we can heal the ones who have only begun to behave like wolves, for they are not truly were, only victims of a disease that ends in fear of water and the urge to fall upon anything that moves.''

The monk watched such a cure, and marvelled. The next morn, he said Mass for them all and, upon his departure, gave Moira a box that was long and flat, neither metal nor wood, and fitted within another box.

"Touch your fingers here and here," he told her, "and you shall hear a voice telling you marvels of healing."

She stared, not knowing what to say, but he gave it to her with a smile. " 'Tis called a 'cassette,' said he. "It should be the emblem of your Order, for henceforth you shall be the Order of Cassettes."

Moira essayed a smile that faltered ere she found her voice. "I thank you, Father. . . ." Yet she could not bring herself to say 'twas none of his affair what name they took—which was well, for she yet struggled to comprehend the meaning of his visit. As she grappled with the paradox of his seeming arrogance coupled with his humble manner, he strode away into the wood. Then she sighed, shook her head, and went to the church, that blessed influence might reassure her as she tried the virtues of his gift. And lo! The magic box told her what may go awry inside the brain of one who becomes mad, and showed her ways to cure such maladies, and Moire knew then that "cassette" must be the shortened form of the old words *casse tête*, which do mean "broken head."

Gwen knew otherwise, but forbore to say so. "It was, then, a monk of the monastery who had heard of them, and brought them that which they needed to better fulfill their mission."

"Mayhap." The Mother Superior smiled. "But when Moira looked up at her mother's picture of the monk who had saved her life so long before, she felt a shock, for surely this was most strangely like to their guest of the night."

Gwen paced onward, thinking that one over. Yes, definitely when she was through here and Finister healed of the twistings done to her mind, she would have to go to the monastery and ask for historian's privilege.

For now, she only looked up at the Mother Superior and asked, "May I hear that cassette?"

"Gladly, yet I think that first we should go on to the hospital. There is a case that I believe you would wish to see, and treatment cannot be put off."

"Nor should it! But what is this case, that I might find it to be of interest, Moth . . . Sister Testa?"

"A werewolf," Mother Superior said, "much as I told you of before."

"Well enough—you may rest," Geoffrey said with regal condescension.

Gregory sagged against the nearest tree trunk, panting and red-faced. His chest, arms, and legs seemed sickly pale by contrast, for he had taken off his robe to exercise, both of which he rarely did. Gasping for air, he asked, "Wherefore must I perform so silly a ritual when we are increasing my body by telekinesis?"

"Because it is not enough to build up bigger muscles—you must also exercise them, for they will change your balance, the proportion of effort for each action, and the speed and timing of your movements," Geoffrey explained. "Many adolescents are quite clumsy when they suddenly shoot up like young willows, because the greater length of limb and the strength that goes with it change such patterns. They can adjust their coordination over months, but you have not that luxury. You must learn the adjustment quickly, and not all at once either. That is one reason why you must exercise after each increment of gain in your muscles."

"One?" Gregory gulped down air. "Why else?"

"Because you must tone the muscles as they grow, not all at once. Then, too, you must develop endurance, which comes only with practice, not with the gain of muscle only, for you must adjust your breathing and learn to pace your flow of energy."

"I am not a warrior," Gregory protested. "Wherefore should I need endurance to love a lady?"

Geoffrey only gave him a long look, weighing his words, then decided to let them sink. "Trust me—with this wench, you shall need all the endurance you can muster. To the calisthenics, then! The Salute to the Sun, now! Right sole against left knee! Balance on one foot! Arms up straight! Now bend slowly from the waist."

Off to their right, Moraga stirred restlessly, muttering; her eyelids fluttered. Cordelia looked up in alarm and probed her mind, finding her dangerously close to the surface of consciousness. With a gentle, lulling thought, she slowed pulse and rate of breathing and turned off synapses. Moraga sank back into sleep and began to dream again.

Cordelia read just enough of those dreams to shudder before she turned her attention away.

CHAPTER
-12-

Sister Paterna Testa led Gwen out across the courtyard into a long, low building with many windows, the last two of which were barred. Gwen wondered at that but was answered very quickly, for when they came into the hospital they passed directly by the rows of beds with straw mattresses, many filled by patients who were surprisingly cheerful—perhaps not surprising when the room itself, though spartan and with only a few religious pictures on the walls, was filled with light, reflecting off its cream-colored walls, and fragrant with flowers. They passed directly through it, though, to a stout oaken door, double-barred and guarded by two nuns who sat saying their rosaries, but with their eyes ever aware of what went on about them. They came to their feet as Mother Superior came up to them and ducked their heads in greeting. "Good day, Sister Paterna Testa!"

"Good day, Sisters. We must enter to see to the were-wolf."

The women nodded, obviously expecting it, and turned to unbar the door. They went through into a short hallway with four doors opening off it. One of the nuns checked though the small barred window in the farthest door, then unlocked it and stepped aside. Inside the room, two stout peasants sat on either side of a narrow bed, sweating profusely. A third man was bound to that bed with many ropes—if you could call him a man. His face was covered with a wild, unkempt beard, his eyes were red-rimmed and furious, and saliva drooled from his mouth, foaming. The fury and hatred in his face were horrifying. His hands, bound to the sides of the bunk, bore cracked, chipped fingernails grown far too long, and his tunic was so ripped and filthy as to scarcely exist.

When he saw the women enter, he howled in rage, his whole body convulsing as he struggled to leap up and get at them. The men stiffened and stepped in, one swinging up a cudgel, but Sister Paterna waved them back and came closer to the bed. Gwen followed, amazed at the woman's courage.

"These two men and four others brought him in this morning, milady," Sister Paterna said, so calmly that she might have been discussing a joint of beef. "He was bound hand and foot with many ropes, and even then it took all six of them to bring him, for he has become monstrously strong."

"Is he not dangerous, Sister Paterna?"

"Most horribly dangerous, not only because he would rend us limb from limb if he could but also because he would delight in biting us and giving us this same disease that doth make him to seem to be half wolf."

"He was bitten by a wolf," one of the men contributed, "a hateful one, that did foam at the mouth."

"Did you see it?"

"Nay, Mother, but all do know that is how werewolves are made."

Mother Superior glanced at Gwen, and the look was as much as to say that she knew, as well as Gwen, that the villain could just as easily have been a hare or a squirrel; the germs did not restrict themselves to people and wolves.

"Yet we have some protection," Sister Paterna said and, stepping over to a little table at the side of the room, poured some water from a pitcher into a bowl. The man shrank away with a howl of rage. "He is half crazed with thirst," Mother explained, "but the mere sight of water induces such painful throat contractions that he dreads the sight of it."

"Hydrophobia," Gwen breathed. She had learned enough of modern medicine to recognize rabies.

"So is it called," Mother Superior said, "but not all have that fear—only some."

"How can you cure it?"

" 'Tis all due to seeds of illness, small, voracious creatures I have told thee of, likening them to wolves too small to see. We must transform them or slay them and aid the body in making watchdogs to harry them." Sister Paterna stepped around behind the man's head, drew up a straight wooden chair, and sat. Knowing she was there, he writhed against his ropes and howled, striving to reach her. " 'Tis to be regretted," she said, "but we must touch him, which he will loathe—and most carefully, too, so that he will not lunge and twist to bite us." Carefully, she laid a single fingertip against the man's forehead. He contorted his whole body, twisting his head to try to snap at her, but she moved with him, her face tightening in concentration. The patient's movements slowed; then his eyelids grew heavy and finally closed. Sister stayed intent, frowning in concentration, until his breathing eased and deepened. Then the nun relaxed with a smile. "I have but put him to sleep; 'tis a necessary precaution and will allow me greater room to mind what I must do inside his blood. Do you join with me, Lady Gwendylon, that you may study what I do."

Gwen was quite glad to accept the invitation. She came around behind the bed, and one of the men was quick to pull up the other chair for her. She thanked him with a smile, sat, placed one hand on the "werewolf's" head, and bent her mind toward observing what Sister Paterna did within him. The room grew dim, and the inside of the man's body seemed to appear through his flesh, growing larger. Sister Paterna directed her attention toward the festering wound near his ankle—far lower than was likely for a wolf—and made it seem to swell, filling all of their communal field of view. It kept on swelling till Gwen saw only the tube of an artery, then only the blood within it; then, without actually seeing them, she became aware of the microscopic organisms that thronged the infection and the vastly outnumbered crew of white blood cells that fought them.

The white blood cells began to increase in number.

Amazed, Gwen watched as Mother Superior caused them to split, grow, split again, and keep on multiplying till they outnumbered the rabies germs. Then, incredibly, the germs themselves began to change, withering and drying up. Sister Paterna was withdrawing the fluid from them, and the white blood cells swarmed in to absorb what was left.

It was only a beginning, of course. The germs had spread

throughout the man's body, and Sister Paterna had to follow the main arteries to the heart, then sit in concentration while the blood circulated, killing the germs as they approached the ventricles.

Finally the germs were dead and the infection had ceased to fester. Mother Superior withdrew her concentration from the inside of the man's body with a sigh. Gwen followed suit, dazed by the magnitude of the woman's accomplishment. She looked up to see that the shadows had lengthened and the light in the room had taken on the ruddy glow of sunset. She turned to Mother Superior. "That was amazing, Sister Paterna!"

"Gramercy." Mother Superior gave her a weary smile. "Though 'twas more in the magnitude of the task than in the nature of it that the accomplishment lies."

The two peasants were staring at their fellow in disbelief. "Is he truly cured, Mother?"

"He will live," Mother Superior answered, "but his mind is still filled with hatred and rage. It will take a while for the poisons to ebb from it—and I must teach him how to think like a well man again."

"Like a man of any sort," the other peasant said, his voice low. " 'Twas a miracle, Mother."

" 'Twas nothing of the sort!" Mother Superior said indignantly. " 'Twas naught but the skill of one who can heal with the mind. There was no magic in it and certainly no miracle, for miracles come from God alone, and I am not saintly enough to serve as a channel of His grace!"

The looks the peasants gave her clearly denied the claim, but they didn't argue. Mother Superior sighed and gathered herself together. "They wait upon us for the evening meal. Lady Gallowglass, will you come?"

"Aye, Sister, and right gladly."

When they had gone out of the hospital, Gwen asked, "How is't you allowed those men to call you 'Mother' when you deny the title?"

"The poor folk would not understand the distinction, Lady Gallowglass, and would think there is no head to this Order. And, too, they have a need to look up to others who do not seek to oppress them. I would rather they called me only 'Sister Paterna,' as you do, but I am past arguing the matter with them—they will agree with all I say, then turn and call me 'Mother' again.'' She looked up at the crescent of the rising moon. "We should retire early this night. Tomorrow will be long."

It was an all-day process, starting early in the morning, dining and resting for two hours in the middle of the day, then laboring inside the man's mind till evening. Gwen followed Mother Superior's movements in silent wonder, watching as she stimulated production of new brain cells to replace those destroyed by the disease, increased resistance in a host of synapses, and lowered the neural blocks in others. In the afternoon, she moved inside the sleeping mind to banish memories of attack by opposing them with symbols of forgiveness and self-assurance—usually saints. Then, with images of other saints moving in the man's subconscious to show him the virtues of charity and compassion, she taught him to be human once again.

They returned to the refectory at sunset, Gwen still marvelling at the techniques Mother Superior had used. "Can you thus heal the minds of those who are mad, but not from disease, Sister Paterna?"

"Many of those we think to be 'mad' truly suffer from a disorder of the body, Lady Gallowglass. The body must be set to rights within before we can teach them to think again as they were before their illnesses manifested."

"The point is well taken." It helped confirm what Gwen had suspected. "Yet what of those in whom the body is not awry? Of those who are not truly mad in their own minds but whom others have twisted in their rearing, or who have suffered mightily at the hands of their fellows and cannot believe in goodness any longer?"

"We can aid, but only if the patient is willing—for in the end, look you, all we do is to teach them how they may heal their own minds."

Gwen nodded slowly. "I think that will suffice."

•   •   •

The "werewolf," no longer rabid, went home the next morning, albeit with considerable help from the other two peasants; he was very weak. Gwen left not long after, coming out of the refectory right after breakfast.

"I hope you will visit us again, Lady Gallowglass," Mother Superior said. "There are many questions I wish to ask, much that I believe you may teach me."

"I shall be delighted, Sister, when this current trouble is ended—though I think you may know more of healing than any in Gramarye."

"Nay," Mother Superior said quite seriously. "There is thyself, and an holy hermit who doth dwell by the Northern Sea, and a witch in the West who doth dwell by a lake"—a shadow crossed her face—"though I am not certain I can approve the means by which she effects her cures. Still, she is the foremost in disorders of the mind that stem from the heart. . . . Well, God speed thy journey."

Gwen hesitated at the gate, then turned back. "One last favor, if I may."

"Ask it," said Mother Superior with the hint of a smile.

"May I see this cassette from which thine Order doth derive its name?"

The smile grew and broadened. "I feared you had forgot."

Mother Superior led Gwen to a small room adjacent to the solar. It was little more than a closet with a reproduction of the picture of Father Marco on the wall and a flat box with two indentations on its top and sitting on a small table.

"Place thine index and middle fingers in the hollows," Mother Superior said.

"Naught more?"

"Naught."

Gwen placed her fingers in the two indentations, guessing that the computer within the box would recognize human skin temperature and texture and would feed its signal through her neurons.

She was right; her head seemed to fill with a voice saying, "Introduction to Neurology: Lesson One." Then a schematic diagram of the human body appeared in front of her, superimposed over the walls of the room, and the voice began to describe the nervous system. As it enumerated each component, that element appeared in blue on the schematic—first the brain, then the spinal cord, then the nerve trunks and the plexi. Gwen stood entranced, forgetting the cassette itself and caught up in the wonder of new knowledge. She stood transfixed through all ten lessons until the voice finally said, "That is the end of this recording. Please insert Cassette Two."

Then the room was back and the voice was silent.

Fatigue hit, and Gwen swayed on her feet. A strong arm reached out to brace her and she found herself looking into the smiling face of a middle-aged nun. "I am Sister Cecilia," the woman informed her. "Mother saw that you did not wish to leave the cassette and asked that I watch over you, which I have been glad to do. Come, let us go to her."

Dazed, Gwen went where she was led. "I—remark that you do term the cassette only that, Sister, a cassette."

"What else should we call it—a relic?"

"I would not have been surprised," Gwen said slowly, "or at least 'holy' or 'blessed.' "

Sister Cecilia shook her head. "Mother Moira was most firm upon the point—that it is only an artifact, a thing made by human hands, and not holy in itself. Any holiness about it would attach only from our Benefactor, and we have no knowledge that he was a saint."

No, they hadn't—but Gwen was beginning to think a case could be made.

Sister Cecilia steered her into the solar, which was fortunately right next door, and Mother Superior looked up from several pages of parchment upon a table before her. "Ah! She is done, then. I thank you, Sister Cecilia."

"It was my honor, Sister Paterna." The nun inclined her head, then went out.

"Have you learned much, then?" asked Mother Superior with a twinkle in her eye.

"A great deal that I knew not. Are there . . . more of these cassettes, Sister Paterna?"

"Alas, no. The good monk gave us but the one, though the hint of a second will forever tantalize us."

Gwen knew then that she really was going to have to go to the monastery and that the trip could not be put off.

Geoffrey stood back and eyed his brother's near-naked form narrowly. "What think you, sister? Will he do?"

Cordelia looked Gregory up and down, trying to imagine him as a stranger come a-courting. The face was familiar, but from the neck down he might indeed have been someone she had never met. His body rippled with muscle now, shoulders, arms, and chest become baulks of beef, legs shapely pillars, not the sticks she had seen when last he went swimming with the family—though admittedly, that had been four years ago and more; he had not revealed his body since Magnus left home.

"Walk," she directed Gregory. "Walk over to Moraga."

Gregory gave a martyred sigh and turned, striding with feline grace to the sleeping woman. He looked down at her, and his face stilled with the effort of holding his emotions in check—not quite successfully, for something of the besotted moon calf still showed through. She had to admit, though, that he was quite restrained, and wondered how long he could hold the expression.

"Come back," she said.

Gregory returned, treading like a roebuck poised to leap.

"His body will do," she told Geoffrey. "Whether he has learned to court a lady, I cannot say."

"There, too, he must have exercise," Geoffrey sighed, "and I fear he shall have only this one damsel for practice."

"Scarcely a difficulty," Cordelia said dryly, "since she is so various in her appearances."

"A good point," Geoffrey said. "Who was she when last you knew her, Gregory?"

"A damsel named Peregrine," Gregory said, "who had been left as an offering to a troop of bandits because she had allowed herself to be seduced."

Cordelia made a sound of disgust, but Geoffrey frowned, considering. "That sort of censure has the ring of something from her own past."

"It is men laying the blame for their own lechery onto their victims!" Cordelia blazed.

"As I say, a sign of her own past," Geoffrey said.

Gregory stared at him in surprise. "Such perception is rare in you, brother."

"Not in this regard; there are some aspects of women I do know and understand," Geoffrey told him. "I also see that her choice of name flaunts her deception in your face, for a peregrine is a kind of falcon, a bird of prey."

"The thought had occurred to me," Gregory admitted. "I kept my shields up almost long enough."

"You may need to keep them up a while longer," Cordelia said, eyeing the sleeping woman.

Gregory glanced at Finister, troubled. "Sooner or later, a lover must begin to trust."

"The question, though, is 'when?' " Cordelia said quickly.

"We shall leave that to Mother," Geoffrey said briskly. "She has not returned, though, and there is little more we can do to prepare Gregory to be a suitor."

"I had thought of that," Cordelia admitted, "and we should not leave Moraga asleep much longer, or her body will begin to lose muscle tone."

Geoffrey nodded. "The obvious course, then, is to wake her and let her test the new model Gregory."

Gregory looked suddenly nervous. "I am not ready!"

"You shall never be ready," Geoffrey agreed, "but you shall have to deal with her anyway. Do not think of yourself as a suitor, brother—only a most considerate jailor."

Cordelia looked up at him in surprise, then slowly nodded. "A good thought. You were her warden when she fell asleep; if she woke to find you a lover, she would suspect a ruse. Aye, do as Geoffrey says—be her jailor, and little by little, begin to compliment her, bring her the odd flower for her hair, find a gem to adorn her."

"After all, you may claim she should wear it to honor Their Majesties when she enters their presence," Geoffrey pointed out. "But never be the moon calf in her presence, never gaze upon her with fawnlike doting. Be the man of the world who becomes intrigued, who knows himself to be her equal in

141

attraction and begins to enjoy the game of flirtation.''

"Man of the world?" Gregory bleated. "Could any man be less of the world? I have no experience, no appeal, no faith in myself as a lover!"

"I have downloaded a thorough knowledge of the sport into your brain," Geoffrey said, but admitted, "though it is true you will need a round or two of play before you begin to believe you have the skill."

"I can only be what I am," Gregory protested.

"Then be so." Cordelia's eyes gleamed. "Be the scholar distracted bit by bit from his studies; let her think she teaches you the game for her own purposes."

"An excellent stroke!" Geoffrey cried. "Then when you are sure of your skill, you can turn the tables on her and outplay her with her own hand!"

Gregory still looked very nervous. "It is a pretty metaphor, but I am unsure what it means in practice."

"So shall you be until you have that practice," Geoffrey told him. "Come, you must essay it some time, little brother. Fear not that she might overwhelm you or slip a knife between your ribs, for Cordelia and I will stay within half a mile of you, and you have but to squawk to have me by you, and her with us only minutes later."

"You must essay it sooner or later, Gregory," Cordelia repeated gently, "or leave her asleep for the rest of her days, and that were as unkind as slaying."

Gregory turned away to pick up his robe and don it, then turned back, face frightened but resolute. "Well enough, then. Wake her."

"No, that you must do, brother," Cordelia said firmly, "for 'tis your spell that plunged her into sleep, and 'tis your face she must see when she wakes."

Gregory looked still more frightened. "Must I wake her with a kiss?"

"Definitely not!" Geoffrey exclaimed. "This must be a chase, brother, not an ambush!"

"Aye, but before it becomes a chase, it must be a tracking," Cordelia said. "After all, she has been raised to be a hunter, so pursuit itself may incline her to entangle her emotions in yours.''

Geoffrey stepped backward toward the trees. ''Let us retire, and when we have passed from sight, do you kneel by her and quicken her sleeping mind.''

He and Cordelia disappeared into the greenery. Gregory raised a hand to call them back, but fear rose up to clog his throat and prevent him. Slowly he lowered his hand, turning to Moraga with resolution. He swallowed and forced himself to kneel by her side.

Even sleeping and with her erotic projections dormant, the woman's beauty hit him like a tidal wave, arousing awareness of his own sexuality all over again, a sexuality so intense that he froze, frightened by the strength of his own reactions. But as he knelt entranced, the fear receded and he began to grow accustomed to the stimulation. He could have sworn it to be more intense than it had been a week earlier, before his siblings had begun his crash course in romance.

The panic ebbed and he bent to his task, accelerating Moraga's pulse and metabolism slowly while he brought her mind up from the depths of sleep.

CHAPTER
-13-

The sight of a woman at the gate of the monastery was rare, to say the least. Still, it was not unknown, and when the woman in question presented herself as the Lady Gwendolyn Gallowglass, the effect was salutary. The monk on portal duty bowed, mumbled some apology about keeping her waiting, assured her he'd be back as soon as possible, and stepped a dozen paces inside the compound. There he flagged down a passing novice and said a few words to him, gesturing toward the gate. The youth looked up, startled—almost, Gwen might have thought, even frightened—and hurried away across the courtyard. As soon as he could, he started running.

The porter came back. "Now, milady, if you will enter our guest house, I shall fetch you summat with which to refresh yourself."

"I thank you." Gwen followed him into the little house beside the gate. She knew she could not have been the only woman in the history of the monastery who had needed to claim its sanctuary—and from the look of the sitting room in the guest house, one of the previous occupants had stayed a considerable while. The furnishings and decoration definitely showed a woman's touch, though the maintenance looked to be rather spartan.

The monk asked her to be seated, then went out and returned with a tray bearing wine, cheese, and wafers of hard bread. Gwen thanked him, took a little of the wine, then sat and waited. Looking around, she noticed a picture on the wall, a portrait—then stared, riveted, recognizing Father Marco Ricci again. It was a different portrait, done in a more realistic style at a younger age and in a different pose, but it was undeniably the same face.

There was a commotion at the door, quickly stilled; then the young Abbot of the Order stepped in. His face lit with pleasure as he hurried over to clasp her hand and bow. "Lady Gallowglass! What a pleasure to see you again!"

"And you, milord Abbot." She smiled and proffered her hand.

He pressed it briefly, then released it and asked, "Has Brother Dobro offered you refreshment? Ah, I see he has! I trust your wait was not fatiguing."

"Scarcely a wait at all, and one with interest, for I find that portrait on the wall to be intriguing."

"Portrait?" The Abbot turned and looked. "Ah, Father Marco Ricci! 'Twas he who did found this abbey, Lady Gallowglass."

"Indeed," she said. "He was of the original colonists, was he not?"

The Abbot took his time about turning back to her, keeping his smile carefully in place. "I should have known that you, too, would know the full history of Gramarye. Aye, he was."

"And lived in this monastery until his death?"

"Ah, no. He had frequently to ride abroad on missions of mercy, or to remonstrate with dukes or earls or, aye, even with the King. 'Twas he who established the foundation of our strength, for he made the King and the nobles accept the immunity of the clergy; they were too much needed by all the folk to become pawns in the barons' games."

Gwen nodded. "Yet he always did return and was Abbot till his death?"

"Nay, though 'tis odd you should mention it. He was prudent and yielded his seat to a younger monk, one native-born—I suspect he did wish to assure himself that the monastery would continue under stable rule when he died. Yet he did not linger to watch, fearing that his presence would hobble his successor; no, he left the cloister to become a mendicant, wandering about over the face of Gramarye."

"And was never seen again." Gwen's pulse quickened; the stories coincided.

But, "Not so," said the Abbot. "To tell truth, some ten years later a mania for burning witches swept the isle and

Father Marco appeared again from obscurity, to preach against the silly superstition of thinking true witches could live—for why should Satan give power to a person who had already set himself on the road to Hell by seeking to sell his soul? Nor doth God permit real magic that would break His laws; only He may so suspend the principles of the Universe, and such events we term 'miracles.' "

"Ah," Gwen breathed. "Father Marco knew even then of our psi powers."

The Abbot nodded. "His journal shows that he had begun to suspect such."

"And he did defend us by putting down the witch-hunts."

"Aye, but in the doing of it, he was slain. Yet even his death served his fellow folk, for those who had slain him abandoned the witch-hunt in guilt and remorse and saw to it that all others did likewise."

"Bless him," Gwen breathed.

"We trust he is blessed indeed. We hope, now that we are once again in communication with the Vatican, that we shall be able to present Father Marco's case to His Holiness the Pope and have his name added to the Canon as one of the saints of God—but it will be a long and tedious process."

"I wish your enterprise success." Indeed Gwen did, for she had begun to see a way for the convent to be officially recognized as separate and independent and for the monks to gain an account of a miracle to bolster their case; she suspected they did not have very many.

That, however, was for the future. It would wait, having waited five centuries already. There were more urgent matters at hand.

" 'Tis polite of you to inquire and allow me to speak of our founder," said the Abbot with a smile, "when you must needs truly wish to speak of the matter which brought you hither. Enough of Father Marco—now for the Lady Gallowglass. I trust you are well, you and all your family?"

"Not entirely, milord Abbot." Gwen smiled. "And I thank you for coming so quickly to the matter that concerns me."

The young man still smiled but with obvious curiosity.

"Your Order, Lord Abbot, is known to study the mind."

"Only by such as your husband, yourself, and Their Majesties," the monk said. "Yet we work only with those mental gifts that seem more than natural; we do not seek to understand the mind itself."

"The one must necessarily lead you to the other, must it not?"

The young man nodded, his eyes glowing. "I had known you to be quick of wit. Aye, milady, we do know something of the order of the normal mind, order and disorder—but we cannot claim to be expert in it."

"Yet I think there is that among you which does."

The Abbot lost his smile. "Of what do you speak?"

Gwen looked away and her gaze fell on the picture of Father Marco. " 'Twould be a thing of metal, Lord Abbot—metal and plastic, that substance which—"

"I know of it."

Gwen turned back to him with a smile. "I know that our ancestors came from distant Terra, milord, and that they came in a huge metal ship. Moreover, I know that there were brains in that ship made of metal and glass and plastic, things that could not truly think but that could quite well simulate the operations of our minds."

"How do you name these metal brains?"

"They were called computers."

The Abbot expelled a long hiss of breath. "You have learned much with your husband, have you not, Lady Gwendolyn?"

"We are wedded, after all, Lord Abbot. Do you think he would keep secret from me the natures of mine own children?"

The Abbot grinned broadly. "Nay, though I would conjecture God has kept the fullness of their natures secret from both of you—and all of us."

Gwen gave back a rueful smile. "There's some truth in that."

"You do ask if we have still among us those metal brains, do you not?"

"More." Gwen looked down at her fingers, plucking at her skirt. "I note that your monastery stands in a valley, Lord

Abbot, but is on a hill in the center of that valley.''

"Aye.''

Gwen looked directly into his eyes. "I could find it in me to wonder what lies beneath the earth of this hill.''

The Abbot's eyes twinkled. "If any in the Isle of Gramarye should have a right to go therein, milady, it would be you. Come.'' He rose and took a yard-wide square of lace from a peg. "I will ask you to veil your face, for your beauty is still such as to distract our monks from their labors of the mind and from their devotions.''

Gwen rose, surprised to find that she still could blush. "I thank you for the gallantry, milord.''

" 'Twas ever my pleasure to speak truth.'' He handed her the mantilla. "Then, milady, if you will accompany me, I shall take you down into our cellars.''

They went across the cloistered garden to the main hall— this monastery was as much castle as church—and went down a wide, curving stair. Gwen glanced about her at huge kegs and barrels, but the stair went farther—and farther, and farther. Finally a landing opened out before a simple wooden door. A monk knelt by it on a prie-dieu, reading his Office. He looked up in surprise.

"We must enter, Brother Milton,'' the Abbot said softly.

The monk cast a startled glance at the veiled figure beside the Abbot, then leaped up to haul open the door, protesting, "Milord. . . . this is highly irregular. . . .''

"Even so. Therefore you will accompany us, Brother Milton, to still the tongue of Rumor.''

"But milord—it will not speak to me!'' Then Brother Milton realized what he had said and in whose presence and clapped a hand over his mouth, appalled.

"Be more cautious in the future,'' the Abbot admonished him, "but be not chagrined today. The lady has already guessed what lies beneath our cloister.''

Brother Milton stared at Gwen, amazed, but was silent as he lit a lamp, handed it to the Abbot, and followed them through the simple oaken door, closing it behind them.

The flickering flame illuminated a small room perhaps six feet square—with a curving floor that rang softly underfoot.

Gwen looked down at the gleam of metal. Brother Milton bent to catch a handle and lifted it. A circle of metal swung back, and Gwen looked down into a lightless hole.

"Be of stout heart, milady," the Abbot said softly. "Nothing within will give hurt to any of us—though it will not speak to me, either. It has not spoken to anyone since Father Ricci left our monastery—or at least, it has spoken only to say it will not speak."

Gwen fought off a wave of apprehension and stepped through the circle, bending to catch hold of the edge. Her feet found narrow steps where she had expected the rungs of a ladder; a bright and sourceless light sprang up, and she descended with a bit more confidence.

She stepped down onto softness. Looking about her, Gwen saw that she had descended into the twenty-sixth century. She was in a ship's companionway, its carpet faded, its chrome dulled, but unquestionably modern—at least in terms of the off-planet civilization she knew. She stood looking about her, trying to accustom herself to an environment that was at once both familiar and alien.

Brother Milton stepped past her, beckoning. "Follow, milady, if you will." His eyes were wide and his face glistened; she realized he wasn't all that tranquil about this expedition either. The sight of his nervousness lent her calm; she knew there was nothing to be afraid of. This ship and its computer had been made to protect people, not to harm them. She followed Brother Milton down the companionway, the Abbot close behind her.

Brother Milton entered an elevator, whites showing all around his irises. Gwen and the abbot followed; Brother Milton pressed the top button, and the car rose. He swallowed heavily.

" 'Tis not a spell," Gwen murmured. "I would know if 'twere."

Brother Milton nodded. "I know that with my mind, milady, but not with my heart."

The car stopped, the doors opened—and Gwen found herself on the bridge. The captain's couch and console stood in the center, facing four huge screens. Between them stood the consoles and couches for the other ship's officers.

"Sit in the central chair," the Abbot advised. "It will speak to you there."

But Gwen shook her head. "I have not the right of command over such a ship as this, and the computer would know it." She moved over to the observer's couch and sat down, aware of the two monks' startled stares.

Nothing happened.

"It will not speak to any save they who sit in the central chair," Brother Milton protested.

"Small wonder that it would challenge any who sat there." Gwen frowned, thinking, then called out, "Starship's computer! An you do hear me, answer!"

"I receive and am attentive," a resonant voice answered.

The two monks started and glanced at one another wide-eyed, then back at Gwen.

"I am a descendant of the colonists of this planet," Gwen said.

"Acknowledged. Classified information is denied to all except those of administrative rank. All other information is freely available."

The Abbot watched keenly; he had come this far before. So had Brother Milton.

"I require information regarding neurology and psychiatry."

"I regret to inform you that your request must be denied without authorization."

Gwen bit her lip in disappointment. "I am worthy of such authorization."

"Valid authorization must be issued by the captain or his representative."

"The captain and his officers are long dead," Gwen explained.

"I acknowledge this datum. However, there may be those among his descendants who may function as his representative."

Gwen's mind raced. "What is the purpose of such restriction of information?"

"To avoid cultural contamination," the computer answered. "The colonists of this planet were quite insistent on preventing any knowledge of modern technology becoming widespread."

Gwen thought it through. "Then you may provide information to those who are already aware of contemporary technology and events in the Terran Sphere beyond this planet."

The computer was silent. The two monks exchanged glances, then turned back to watch, frowning.

"That is reasonable," the computer finally said. "Any person already containing such knowledge is either committing cultural contamination or is wisely refraining from doing so. Under such circumstances, my furnishing of knowledge would not contribute to further aggravation of the condition."

Gwen heaved a sigh of relief. She had made it past the first hurdle.

The two monks watched her in amazement.

"However," said the computer, "you must demonstrate such knowledge."

"Then ask questions and I shall answer."

"More is required," the computer countered. "Many such questions can be answered by deduction and conjecture. I require that you yourself pose questions demonstrating such knowledge."

Gwen frowned, searched for a question, and found one. As she opened her mouth to ask it, the computer intoned, "Such questions would constitute a breach of security. Unauthorized personnel might memorize the answers and present them as proof of right to know. Please hold while security measures are instituted."

"What manner of measures?" Gwen asked, alarmed, but a blue light lanced down from the ceiling, enveloping her in a transparent cone.

The two monks' mouths opened in a shout of alarm and they came plunging toward her—but she could not hear them.

The blue cone winked out. "Session will be terminated if security precautions are not observed," the computer said.

The Abbot reached her first. "Are you well, Lady Gallowglass?"

"I am unhurt, Lord Abbot." Gwen smiled. "It is but the

computer's means of assuring that our conversation shall not be overheard. I will ask you to bide in patience—and to pardon me for excluding yourself and Brother Milton from this event.''

Brother Milton looked uncertain; so, for that matter, did the Abbot—but he stepped back, nodding, though doubtfully. '' 'Tis not you who do exclude us, but the machine. Well, we must abide it—but if you are in the slightest distress, Lady Gallowglass, you have but to beckon.''

''The subject will not be harmed,'' the computer assured him. ''Please withdraw from the area in question.''

Reluctantly, the two monks stepped back, and the blue cone sprang into being again.

''Please ask a question demonstrating knowledge of the modern world,'' the computer said. ''The gentlemen who accompany you will hear neither your voice nor my own.''

''Well enough.'' Gwen pondered. ''Art you conversant with events occurring in the Terran Sphere since this planet was colonized?''

''Yes. A courier from Terra supplied me with an FTL transmitter and receiver, contemporary data storage facilities, and additional memory capacity.''

Gwen nodded. ''That would have been Father Aloysius Uwell, twenty years past.''

''That is an accurate observation,'' the computer confirmed, ''but one that could be the product of conjecture coupled with knowledge of local events.''

The two monks could only watch anxiously.

''You are now continually in communication with Terra,'' Gwen inferred.

''I am. My data banks are regularly updated.''

''Then you are aware of the existence of the Society for the Conversion of Extraterrestrial Nascent Totalitarianisms.''

''I am. It is a quasi-military body officially operated by altruistic private enterprises so that blame for its actions cannot accrue to the government of the Terran Sphere.''

Gwen nodded. ''My husband is an agent of that society and has spoken with me of what he knows.''

The computer was silent, digesting the information. Then

it said, "I have heard the gentlemen nearby addressing you as Lady Gallowglass, and the SCENT agent's local alias is Rod Gallowglass."

"Even so," Gwen said. "He was born Rodney d'Armand, though he has also some twenty middle names with which I shall not trouble you."

"They are unnecessary," the computer agreed.

"Now must you ask your question," Gwen said.

"What is the current government of the Terran Sphere?"

"The Decentralized Democratic Tribunal, which is the product of centuries of effort by an organization founded by one Charles Barman. Now to technology: Your link with Terra is accomplished by audio and video signals modulated onto waves that speed faster than light, is it not?"

"It is." The computer countered with another question. "What is the medium for these waves?"

"Tachyons, which are particles that cannot go more slowly than the speed of light. Why cannot anything made of matter accelerate to that speed?"

"Because mass increases with velocity. Accordingly, it can always approach more closely to light-speed but cannot attain it."

"Like to Achilles and the tortoise," Gwen said. "There is an old conundrum that tells of a race between Achilles, the greatest soldier of the Greeks of old, and a tortoise. If Achilles did let the tortoise come halfway to the goal, then began to run, and if, in the first ten seconds, he did cut the distance between the starting point and the turtle by half, then in the next five seconds did halve it again, and in the next two seconds did halve it yet again, and in each time period did halve the distance again and again, he might approach the turtle but would never reach it."

"An exact analogy," the computer agreed. "But in the real world, such a riddle is meaningless; it is obvious that the runner would soon pass the turtle."

"Aye, but only because he would not travel at a relativistic speed. If his velocity did approach that of the speed of light, he would indeed never attain the tortoise's position—which is analogous to light-speed."

"I am satisfied of your knowledge of modern physics," the computer answered, "yet the fields in which you requested information were neurology and psychiatry. Have you any knowledge of those areas?"

Gwen expelled an explosive sigh. "I have."

"What is the central nervous system?"

"The brain and the spinal chord." Gwen blessed the Order of Cassettes and Father Ricci for the information.

Then she began to wonder if she was doing this entirely on her own.

No, of course she wasn't. Thousands of human beings had contributed to this knowledge down through the centuries. No human endeavor could really be said to be accomplished by one single person, could it? Certainly not.

It was her turn to ask a question. "Are the psychodynamic theories of Sigmund Freud valid?"

"It is impossible to know," said the computer, "since most of them, by their very nature, cannot be tested. What is a synapse?"

And so it went for a dozen questions more. Gwen grew more and more tense; the answers and the unfamiliar words began to spin in her brain until she wondered if she were making sense. Panic seized her; she visualized Gregory and the woman who slept by him and felt renewed determination. Her thoughts stopped whirling as she clamped down on them with rigid control and answered yet another question. "The time machine was invented by Dr. Angus McAran in 1952."

The computer was silent for a far longer time than usual. Then it said, "That information is under the most restricted classification; not even my former captain knew it. How did you learn of it?"

"I travelled in time and met Dr. McAran," Gwen answered.

"I am satisfied of your right to know," the computer said. "What information do you require?"

CHAPTER
-14-

Finister woke as she always did—carefully. For a few minutes after consciousness returned, she forced her body to stay relaxed while she probed her environment, first with her mind, then with her senses.

Her mind met the usual plethora of small and wild thoughts—sharp hunger from predators, contented feeding from earthworms, anxious concern from parent birds, voracious competition from their hatchlings as a beak came in view with a tasty grub. But there was a hole in this background, a psychic vacuum that puzzled her until she recognized it as Gregory's mind. This time, though, that dark spot seemed to radiate anxiety and concern. For a moment, she was astounded to realize his concern was for her. Then her familiar cynicism came back, bearing the thought that he was, after all, entrusted with bringing her alive to Runnymede and was no doubt concerned that he fulfill his mission.

She let her eyelids flutter open, frowning as though puzzled as she looked about her, and heard Gregory's sigh of relief above. "Afternoon . . ." she said, not looking at him.

"It is indeed," he answered. "You have slept long."

"Why . . . ?" Then she remembered the burst of light, her own mind-bomb reflected back at her, and fought to keep her expression confused while she trembled with anger. The swine, to strike at her so! The viper, to have seemed so enamored of her, so overcome with desire, but still be alert to attack!

"You are cold," Gregory said, and whipped his cloak from his shoulders to tuck about her.

Whom did he think he was deceiving? A master telepath certainly could not have mistaken the reason for her trembling! Then she realized that she had felt no mind probe, that he had only listened to such thoughts as she had chosen to let escape, which was to say only a sense of confusion. The more fool he, to let himself be so duped! Yet he seemed to have done so again and again—his foolish ethics, when anyone could see that the only ethic was to win!

But doubt crept in as quickly as anger had come. He had outtricked her before and might do so again. Was he truly ethical or only seeming to be so? Certainly he was never off his guard! She would have to ward herself very carefully from now on.

And dissemble even more carefully. "What . . . why . . ."

"Bandits came," Gregory told her. "When the fighting and the outlaws sped, you most suddenly collapsed."

Again—whom did he think he was deceiving? Did he truly think she did not remember, never would? Or could it be that his defenses had been so completely automatic, so unconscious, that he had never even realized she had attacked?

She liked the sound of that, liked it very much and embraced it—but with a reserve of caution. Still, it would do no harm to let him think her completely taken in.

What persona had she been using? Oh, yes—the village girl, seduced and abandoned as a sacrifice to the outlaws . . . Peregrine! That had been her name! What now, though? Peregrine had only been designed to last until the bandits' attack, and Gregory's lowering his guard enough for *her* assault. What now?

There, that was it! "What . . . now . . ." She murmured, then buried her face in the crook of her arm and wept.

She could feel the wave of Gregory's distress wash over her. "Damsel . . . be not so saddened. You are well, you are alive—and free!"

"And homeless," she sobbed. "My village will not take me back for fear of the bandits. I have no family, no husband, no home, no wealth. Where shall I go now?"

Gregory was silent a moment, then said hesitantly, "Travel with me. You shall not be alone, you shall not want for food or drink. Travel with me until we can find you shelter!"

Yes, such as the Royal Coven, she thought with her old

cynicism. If he had pierced her disguise, he might quite easily and amicably take her to imprisonment, for surely the royal witches would know her for what she was!

But he sounded so shy and so timid that there was a chance he might be sincere, might not know her for who she was—or might not care. She felt a thrill of victory and promptly quashed it out of caution; she would need proof before she let herself take a higher hand with him. She kept those thoughts internal and unvoiced, let only her distress and a wild thread of hope escape to be read—but it seemed that Gregory read her thoughts anyway, for he spoke a little more boldly. "You need not fear to be alone with me. I seek a witch named Moraga who was supposed to travel under my protection. If we encounter her again, we shall journey as a threesome."

Too auspicious, too appropriately said! But if he thought she believed his charade, his guard would be down a little. Peregrine sat up, wiping her eyes on her sleeve and sniffling—and realizing that she was playing a game of bluffs and hidden knowledge, of "He didn't know that she knew he knew what she knew . . ." And on and on in a circle, till one of them took action and the other revealed what he or she truly did know! But the game was worth the candle, so she said in a choked voice, "I thank you, sir. If you do not mind being encumbered, I shall gladly travel with you."

"Encumbered? I shall rejoice in your company!" Then, quickly, as though he had revealed too much, "The road grows lonely, after all, and a companion is much to be prized."

"I shall certainly find it so," she said softly, head bowed, looking up at him through her lashes.

He reached down to help her rise; she took his hand and stood, stumbling to lean against him. He braced her a moment and she clung to make it last, alarmed that the stumble had been real—how long had she lain unconscious, anyway? But she might as well turn the accident to good effect, so she turned to press against him—and my, he seemed to be much more substantial than he had been! Perhaps she had been so intent on slaying him that she had not noticed—though that was very much unlike her. . . .

With an effort, she pulled her thoughts back to her masquerade, saying, "Your pardon, sir. I seem to be still weakened."

She looked up at him, eyes wide and innocent, and heard his muffled gasp with vindictive satisfaction. He stared down into her eyes, amazed, so she lowered them and pushed away, tottering a little, then standing firmly. "There now, I seem to be recovered. I can walk." She took an unsteady step.

"You shall not have to." Gregory guided her to a horse, a palfrey who turned to watch her with gentle eyes. Beyond it stood his own mount.

He had managed to hold on to their horses! Or to call them again. Now that Finister thought of it, that shouldn't have been hard for a telepath. She wondered why she hadn't considered it herself.

"You have only to cling tightly enough so that you shall not fall off," Gregory assured her, "and I shall ride closely enough so that I may catch you if you grow faint."

With any other man, his motives would have been suspect, but Finister was all too much afraid that Gregory meant what he said—so she was shocked when his hands closed about her waist, more surprised to find that they actually met. "Sir!"

"Your pardon, damsel," Gregory said, his face turning impassive. "Are you ready to mount?"

That impassivity was surely cloaking a thrill of pleasure at touching her. Again Finister suppressed a smile of triumph and said faintly, "As . . . as you wish, sir. But I have not ridden much."

"You have only to hook one knee over the sidehorn. Ready? Up you go!"

She did indeed, seeming to float through the air to land gently on the saddle. She stared down at him, amazed that so bookish a man had such strength. Then she blushed becomingly and looked away, hooking her knee over the sidehorn, spreading her skirts to cover it, and taking up the reins. "I—I think I can ride, sir."

"I shall be beside you in seconds," Gregory promised and turned away to mount. He brought his horse around beside hers, saying, "Let us be off!"

They rode away into the forest along the northward trail. Finister consoled herself with the thought that she still had several hundred miles to work on him.

She was quite surprised to find that Gregory, so taciturn earlier, had become quite the conversationalist. When she had asked questions before, he had either answered in very few words or had given her lectures, always managing to avoid talking about himself and switching the topic to science or philosophy. Now, though, he replied with tales from his own experience, then asked a question of her in turn. At first she was quite pleased to find him opening up, even a little, but soon began to grow suspicious, even though his questions were about her opinions or tastes or village life versus city life, and not about her politics or her past. Several times she had to bite back a revealing comment and decided that he had only resolved on a different and more effective method of learning her criminal history. She never did quite realize that they had reversed positions, she talking about impersonal topics and he becoming quite convivial.

When they camped for the night, she resolved to see if his attitudes toward physical intimacy had changed, too, though she doubted it—he might have decided to work at being more human and better company, but she was sure he had his limits.

Sure enough, when they had scoured their plates and stored them, he gave her a friendly smile and said, "Sleep well, maiden. You need not trouble yourself about keeping watch; I shall hold vigil."

As always, Finister thought, but as Peregrine, she said anxiously, "Are you certain, my lord? Surely you shall grow weary, if not tonight, then tomorrow!"

"My vigil will refresh me as much as your sleep," Gregory assured her.

How well Finister knew that! But the day had given her such hopes of actually generating interest in herself as a woman that she was loathe to give up the golden hope of persuading Gregory to hold her while she slept, whereupon Nature might actually take its course—so she protested, "Surely there is no need for you to forgo your rest, good sir! The bandits are schooled; I am sure they will not trouble us further." Being their boss, she was sure of it indeed. "Without their threat, this is not a very dangerous area—there is no wild beast larger than a fox nor any lesser outlaws, since all who were not of that robber band fled for fear of them. Stretch your length on the greensward, do!"

"The bandits might rally and seek to recover their pride by attacking me," Gregory explained, "and one never knows when a bear or wolf may wander into a new part of the forest. I thank you for your concern, damsel, but I must stay on guard."

"You must sleep some time!" Peregrine protested.

"Perhaps, in a week or so," Gregory said judiciously, "but certainly not in a day. My vigil is meditation and renews my body as much as ten hours' sleep."

Finister did indeed know the restorative powers of Gregory's trances—and how impregnable they were! Still, she had never made any but the most casual effort to distract him. Why not give it a good, solid try? Accordingly she sighed and said, "Good night to you then, sir—but if you grow weary, do wake me for my turn!"

"I shall," Gregory promised, "though I doubt I'll have need. Dream sweetly, damsel."

Finister closed her eyes but had no trouble staying awake— her whole body thrummed with the excitement of the chase. He might have been immune to the distractions of talk and a light touch or two, but surely he could not resist extended caressing!

She waited half an hour until she was sure he was too deeply entranced to surface quickly enough to push her away. If she played upon his body as surely as she knew she could, by the time he returned to his senses he would be far too much aroused to be able to resist her!

When his breathing had slowed and lightened so much that she was no longer certain he was alive, she rose from her pallet and stalked him on hands and knees like the wildcat she felt herself to be. Her pulse sped faster and faster with the excitement of the chase; she felt the glow of warmth within, felt her heart pounding within her breast, and knew she had taken on the glow that no male eye could resist.

Except Gregory's.

She made sure she was within his direct vision, but he showed not the slightest sign of recognition. Piqued, she nestled up beside him and reached out to stroke his arm.

It was like rubbing wood.

Unable to believe her senses, she pulled up his sleeve and tried to pinch his forearm, but his flesh had grown so hard that she could gain no purchase. Seeking softer flesh, she pulled his sleeve all the way up—and stared at the huge bulge of his biceps. Unbelieving, she probed his underarm and found the triceps equally swollen. An excitement of a kind she had rarely felt tingled within her, for though she projected sexuality, she rarely felt any percolating of pleasure herself except the thrill of the chase. Only Gregory's brothers had been well enough formed to kindle any inner sensation—they, and one or two others. Surely she had never expected it of this retiring scholar! But he, too, seemed able to inflame her. Whether it was the challenge, or the surprising swell of his muscles coupled with the handsomeness, almost beauty, of his face, she knew not, but the excitement was there and could not be denied.

The muscles may have bulged, but so did a burl in a stick of wood, and that was exactly how it felt. Unbelieving, she yanked open his robe and stared at the swelling pectorals and the layers of muscle revealed between neck and shoulders, and felt a stirring inside her that made her very impatient indeed. She reached out to caress but found those pectorals oaken. She reached for flesh that she knew should be delicate, his minuscule nipples, which she had found to be sensitive even in men—but his felt like those of a statue.

Peregrine knelt directly in front of Gregory, bending forward to make sure she exposed her cleavage thoroughly, and glaring into his eyes, she tried a telepathic probe. It proved informative but worthless; she learned only that he had set his mind to register outside stimuli but ignore them as un-important—unless, of course, they were threatening. That he managed to keep ignoring her meant that he must have had more sexual experience than she had thought, for if he was the total innocent he'd seemed, surely he would have inter-preted her advances as threats, or at least something to fear! There was no sign of such fright, though, no response at all to her presence other than a mere noting and setting aside of her actions. Most of his mind was in a strange sort of ecstasy, contemplating the union of the four major forces of the uni-verse, mathematical equations springing into life and flashing past, merging one into another too quickly to follow, though her masters had trained her in modern physics. She couldn't probe deeper than the surface of his mind, of course, but that was certainly enough—how dare he find nuclear forces and gravity more interesting than herself! What kind of man was he, if the interplay of mathematical functions intoxicated him more than a woman's caresses? Was he really a man at all?

With an imprecation, she pushed him as hard as she could; if he toppled, surely he would waken. But he didn't even rock—his folded legs gave him a damnably secure seat!

Seething with frustration but not daring to curse for fear he should hear, somewhere inside that wooden facade, Fin-ister went back to her pallet and lay down—but her night's sally had left her every bit as agitated as she had wished him to be.

Relentlessly aroused, she passed a very restless night.

Sunlight made the world turn scarlet, and Finister squinted, then realized she was awake. That meant she had finally slept—but if the sun's rays had penetrated this grove, how late was it?

She forced her eyes open, squinting against the light, and saw that execrable Gregory sitting by a fire and a steaming kettle, looking as fresh as the dew and as tranquil as a sated lover.

He saw her movement and smiled at her. "Good morn, damsel."

An acerbic retort sprang to her lips, but she bit it back and forced a smile that she managed to turn sweet. "Good morn, sir." She glanced upward, saw that the sun was halfway to the zenith, and gasped. "You have let me sleep far too long!"

"You have been through an ordeal that would have exhausted a man of iron," Gregory said with ready compassion. "I trusted your body's wisdom."

Her body had been anything but wise, Finister reflected sourly. She lowered her gaze modestly and said, "Forgive me if I step away from you some little while, sir. No damsel would wish a gentleman to look upon her while she is disheveled from sleep."

"And no gentleman would!" Gregory said in consternation. He turned away. "Your pardon, damsel!"

"Given," she assured him. "Whatever you are brewing, sir, it smells heavenly, and I shall return to sip with you in minutes."

When she stepped out of the underbrush again, her hair was coifed and her dress without a stain or a wrinkle; it was amazing what telekinesis could do with fibers. Smiling bashfully, she came to fold herself gracefully next to Gregory and accept the mug he proffered.

They chatted idly for perhaps half an hour while he fried oatcakes for her and they sipped the herbal tea he had brewed. She was amazed all over again at his skill in conversation, his ability to make her laugh with his small talk.

Then they mounted again and rode off down the forest trail. Before she knew it, Peregrine found herself doing most of the talking and narrowly escaped telling Gregory her real feelings about what women wanted from men. He would scarcely have found them attractive.

When the sun was a little past the zenith, Peregrine spied a lovely stream that pushed the forest back into a delightful little glade as it curved around a great boulder that screened it from the trail. It struck her as the ideal romantic dell. Accordingly, she let her shoulders droop, fluttered her eyelids as though with fatigue, lost her smile, and hollowed her cheeks to make her face look drawn and pale.

Gregory surprised her with the quickness of his perception.

"You are weary, damsel; surely the fright of these past few days still weakens you. Let us dismount and pitch camp for the night."

"I—I am certain I can hold to the saddle some while longer, sir," Peregrine said in faltering tones. "Let us at least ride till twilight."

"There is no call," Gregory protested. "We have no great need for haste, after all. Let us dismount and rest by the stream."

"If . . . if that would please you, sir," Peregrine said, her relief plain to hear.

They dismounted and tied their horses to a spreading yew bush. Gregory took off their saddles and bridles and made sure their tethers were long enough to allow them ample room to graze. Then he kindled a fire and set his leather kettle to boil.

"We must not tarry long," Peregrine protested in faint and faltering tones. "I would be loathe to delay you."

"I have ample time," Gregory assured her. "I journey to Runnymede, after all, and so great a city will not wander away while we travel. You are bound for the nearest town that will grant you shelter, and surely it shall not stray any more than the Queen's castle."

"That is true," Peregrine said, lowering her gaze demurely.

Gregory felt the upwelling of grief and watched closely. He saw the first tear fall and clasped her hand to reassure. "Damsel, damsel! Do not mourn, for if one life has ended, surely a better and brighter has begun!"

"If only that were true!" Peregrine's voice broke on a sob.

"Surely it is," Gregory said, taking her hand in both of his. "You are young and beautiful with decades of joy before you! Who knows what delights await you? Perhaps a warm and friendly town eager to welcome you, with a handsome young merchant who will fall in love at first sight of you!"

"Or perhaps a cold and unfeeling village who will despise me for being a fallen woman," Peregrine said, and gasped as the tears rolled down her cheeks.

"Surely not!"

Peregrine shook her head with miserable certainty. "No

man wishes to have a wanton to wife, sir. I have only two paths open to me through this life—the one a road of deception, convincing some stalwart young man that I am a virgin in heart if not in body, or the primrose path of harlotry and a bitter, lonely life as a forest recluse after!''

''No, not a bit!'' Gregory cried. ''There are many men who would understand a woman deceived—for many of them have been just such deceivers!''

''And therefore feel nothing but contempt for the woman who lets herself be so beguiled,'' Peregrine said bitterly, and broke into racking sobs.

Gregory gathered her into his arms, cradling her against his chest. ''Damsel, damsel! Not all men are such beasts! There are many men who have fallen in love with women who thought them wealthy, then spurned them when they discovered that they were truly only disinherited apprentices! There are men who will recognize your pain as their own and will cleave unto you because of it!''

''Are you one so deceived?'' Peregrine said with wild hope. She stared up into his eyes, her own still limpid with tears, and Gregory caught his breath at her beauty.

She felt his response, felt the tension in every limb, saw the admiration and yearning in his face, and stretched up to meet his lips with her own.

CHAPTER
-15-

Gregory stiffened with the electricity of that kiss and sat frozen in every fiber except his lips, which thawed, then brushed, then parted and met hers with enthusiasm to match her own. Finally he managed to break away, panting, "Damsel . . . this is not seemly. . . ."

"It seems very right to me," she gasped, and pulled his head down again. "It does to you, too, I feel it in your kiss! Oh, sir, take my sweetness and give me your own!"

But Gregory sat stiff-necked, braced against her pulling. "I would not wrong you. . . ."

"Wrong me, despoil me! Only give of yourself to me!" Peregrine panted. "I should blush, but I do not! Oh, sir, I had only lain in love with my Corin half a dozen times, only enough to truly discover ecstasy, when he tired of me and revealed me to the derision of the whole village! My delight was turned to ashes, my joy to bitterness, but you have given both new life! Your kiss inflames me, the press of your body ignites me, I burn with the aching for another taste of the delights I had barely discovered before they were denied me! Do not withhold yourself, I beg of you! Take me, enfold me, lose yourself in me, and give me back the thrill and the wonder I have lost!"

"I . . . I must not," Gregory stammered. "I would wrong you, I would merely leave you as Corin did. . . ."

"I care not!" Peregrine's voice shook with passion. "Tomorrow I may, but tonight I do not, tonight I would only rejoice. This, this is what I want, the caressing and merging and delighting of bodies! Cast me aside tomorrow if you wish, sir, but leave me not lorn tonight!"

"Such union should not be for a single night only, nor even one single year. . . ."

"I shall take what I may! Oh, fie upon me, for I know myself now to be truly a wanton! I will take this pleasure now without let or demand, I crave it so deeply! Do not withhold it, sir, I pray you!"

"There . . . there is more that you wish, far more, whether you know it or not." The agony of desire racked Gregory's voice. "There is no true ecstasy without a union of hearts as well as bodies, and that I cannot give!"

"Love me, then," Peregrine panted. "I care not for how long—only love me for now, delight me for now!"

"I cannot," Gregory said, as though it were torn from the roots of his soul. "A man cannot love others if he does not love himself, and I see too much that is despicable within me."

"Then let me show you what is admirable!"

"There is too much wonderful in you for me to ever be worthy of your touch," Gregory said with total sincerity. "It is not despoiling that you wish, but sanctuary while you wait for the one who is born to love you, born to delight you, born to give you joy to your very core! I know a convent where you can shelter while you wait. Let me escort you there!"

Perigrine froze in his arms. "A convent?"

Instantly she thawed, heated, turned to fire. "How can you speak of barren nuns when I know you burn to make love to me? Do not deny me, for if you do, you deny yourself! Give in to your true nature, as I do! Love me, make love to me, take my surrender, and revel in your triumph!"

"I . . . I am no lover. . . ."

"I know that you are!" Peregrine moved back a little, just enough so that she could gaze up into his eyes squarely and, for the moment, soberly. "If you are not, turn yourself to wood again as you did last night! But I know you cannot, for that wood would burn with the heat of your ardor. Only restore yourself to your vigil and I will cease to importune. Attempt it—but I know you cannot when I am here in your arms!" To prove it, she pressed close, wriggling in a way that he should have found electrifying.

But she had given him the wrong challenge; Gregory stilled, his eyes lost focus, his breathing slowed and lightened, and as she watched in horror, he stilled into immobility, leaving her trapped in arms that had become hard as wood.

Finister stared appalled for a minute. Then in fury she cried, "A murrain upon you!" and pushed herself away— but found those wooden arms held her fast. Enraged, she flailed about, rocking and thrashing, crying, "How dare you! Coward! Eunuch! How can you so spurn a lass who craves you? How can you turn to wood with a wanton warm and burning in your arms? How can you so despise me that you would send a woman in the ripeness of her youth to dwell among dry old relics of nuns?"

No matter how she railed, though, he sat like a statue, arms still folded to embrace her, rigid as timber. In desperation, she pressed herself tight against him and slid, squirming, out of his oaken embrace.

For a moment, she was tempted to ignite a spark within him by telekinesis to see if that wood could burn, but decided it would give too little satisfaction. Instead she snatched the hidden dagger from her kirtle and drove it into him.

The point stuck in his skin; the blade bent, then skidded aside.

With a curse, Finister threw the useless thing on the ground. She stood rigid, fists clenched, glaring into his glazed eyes, trying to think of some way to hurt him, to shock him out of his trance, to make him notice her. She probed his mind but found only the blank reflectiveness of his shield and knew she could press no further, for that shield would only turn her own energies back on her. First she must wake him, bring him out from that shell; then she could touch him again—but unless she could touch him, she could not jar him out of the trance. It was a closed loop, a snake biting its own tail, and she turned away to stalk off into the woods in frustration and anger.

Walk away indeed! her pride said to her. *He cannot stop you! Leave him, go back to command your agents, and find another way to slay him!* But she found she could not; she told herself it was important not to arouse Gregory's suspicions but knew the truth was that she found him too much of a challenge. Since leaving her foster parents' home, she had measured her own worth by her sexual attraction on the one hand and her skill as an assassin on the other; in spite of the chill with which he had rebuffed all her advances and the skill with which he had turned aside her knife (or perhaps because of them), she wasn't yet ready to admit defeat.

Accordingly, she paced the woods for an hour or so to cool off, then returned to find Gregory sitting by the fire and looking very dejected. He looked up and said, "I must apologize for the discourtesy with which I took leave of my senses."

"I am glad to hear it." She glared down at him. "You must fear me mightily to have sent your mind sailing and left me a lifeless statue."

"Perhaps it is fear," Gregory sighed, "but I am determined to treat you with respect."

"Whether I wish it or no? Fie, sir! What manner of man are you who can spurn a lady so?"

"One who cannot resist a challenge, I fear," Gregory lamented.

That struck too deep a chord within Finister. She snapped back, "You certainly should have! Resist your pride, not my favors! I am so embarrassed I shall fear to offer them again ever!"

The scoundrel should have looked appalled, and tried to, but he had the audacity to be relieved beneath it! Sizzling with anger, Finister said, "Well, there is no help for it. I would have made a man of you, but it seems the material is lacking. Come, let us mount, since you will not, and ride where your reason takes us, since you will not be guided by passion!"

"Even so," Gregory sighed, and stood up, reaching for her hand.

She snatched it away and stalked to her horse. She heard him coming quickly behind her but snapped, "You need not aid me to mount, sir!" and set her foot in the stirrup, then sprang up to the saddle, curled her knee about the sidehorn, and shook the reins. The palfrey walked away, and Gregory had to scramble to mount and join her.

Thus it went for the rest of the day, Finister carping, snapping, and shrewish, insulting Gregory in every way she could, but the sheepish fool only rode there, returning meek replies that were neither agreement nor contradiction, and never once during that long afternoon did he show enough spirit to lash back.

She might as well have been made of wood herself! There could be no question about it—he had no real regard for her, did not care enough about her to grow angry. He must have lacked even the male drive to be irritated—either that, or he was sick of her and eager to be rid of her.

So that evening, when once again he sat down by the fire and went into his trance, Finister threw up her hands and stalked off into the forest again, thinking bloody thoughts and determined never more to come near him without overwhelming lethal force at her back.

She had access to the computer and all its data banks! Gwen almost went limp with relief and realized that she hadn't really believed she could win this contest, pass the examination that no monk had managed for five long centuries. But pass it she had, and the opportunity, once gained, had to be exploited. She pulled herself together and phrased her first inquiry very carefully—the question could not be too broad or she would reveal that her knowledge was out of date and lose all she had gained. "What are the most recent findings concerning the mechanisms by which the brain produces hallucinations?"

The computer launched into an explanation of surges of neural currents, activators and inhibitors, and malformations in new brain cells. Gwen hung on its every word, afraid to lose a syllable—and hoping she could come up with just as effective a question about child abuse, mood disorders, paranoia, and insecurity.

She did.

When it was over, she was exhausted, trembling—and understood Moraga far better than she wanted. She found herself

repelled by the tortuous ways in which the foster parents who
had raised the orphan must have deliberately twisted her mind
and ravaged her emotions. "I . . . thank you, computer. I will
strive to make this information benefit as many others as I
may."

"You are welcome—to any information at any time," the
computer responded. "Look upward, please."

Too exhausted to wonder why, Gwen looked up almost
involuntarily. A bright light winked next to the blue one. She
flinched, looked down quickly—and just managed to see the
afterimage as it faded.

"There is no damage to your vision," the computer assured
her, "but I have now recorded your retinal patterns. If at any
future time you wish to consult me, you need only sit in that
chair, look upward, and I will respond."

" 'Tis . . . good to know. Again I thank you."

"And again you are welcome. May you have a pleasant
journey."

The blue light winked off and Gwen started to rise—then
had to grasp at the arm of the chair to avoid falling. Brother
Milton and the Abbot were at her side in an instant. "I thank
thee, gentlemen," she murmured. "I will . . . be well presently."

"Aye, praise Heaven," the Abbot said, "but first you
needs must dine and rest."

"There is a chamber for such uses, only a little way away,"
Brother Milton assured her. "Come, good lady."

Gwen let them steer her toward the elevator, protesting,
"The guest house . . . 'tis quite adequate. . . ."

" 'Tis a long, long climb away, milady, and thou art exhausted," the Abbot said with gentle firmness. "Thou hast
sat in converse with the computer for twelve hours without
pause."

"Twelve hours?" Gwen looked up in disbelief.

The Abbot nodded as he ushered her into the elevator.
" 'Twas amazing."

"Oh! Milord Abbot—I am sorry to so long detain
you. . . ."

"It was mine honor—and my joy, to see one at long last

find a means of speaking with the daunting mechanism. When all is well with you, milady, I may ask you to return and pose certain questions to it."

"I . . . shall be delighted. . . ."

The elevator door opened and they escorted her down the hall. "There is a question of propriety," the Abbot explained, "and I know the abilities of your children and husband. Can you summon one of your kin?"

Gwen considered, clinging to his arm a moment. Rod would be too much alarmed, too solicitous, and she had left Cordelia to watch over Gregory. That left only one. She frowned in concentration a moment; then air boomed, and Geoffrey rushed to support her. "Mother! What have they done to you?"

"Naught. I have done it to myself; they have but cared for me." Gwen gestured at the door ahead. Geoffrey looked up, startled, and ushered her toward it. "I must rest, my son. Do thou stand watch over me."

"With delight!"

"Bless you, my son." Gwen turned back in the doorway, inclining her head toward the Abbot and the friar. "I thank you, gentlemen."

" 'Twas our honor. Good night, milady."

"Good night," Geoffrey seconded. "I thank you, milord— and you, brother." Then he turned to half-carry his mother into the cabin.

Deep in his trance, Gregory watched Peregrine leave with disappointment. He knew that when he emerged from the trance he would be buried under an avalanche of sorrow. His calisthenics, his lessons in Finister's mind, his crash course in lovemaking—all had gone for naught, cancelled by his timidity. Of course, Finister had not yet undergone her own therapy, but as far as Gregory could see, he was no more attractive to her now than he had been before. He had failed, that was the plain and simple truth of it, and when he surfaced, he would know himself for the worm he was.

Still, it had to be faced. He knew Finister quite well now, knew that if he stayed here she would come back with a dozen or more ruthless killers to help her slay him. He was proof against them, of course, but accidents could happen, and he had no wish to kill anyone. He would have to brace himself for a more direct onslaught, preferably by being gone.

Accordingly, he began the process of waking. His muscles softened, his breathing accelerated, and the world began to seem vivid and real again.

The emotions hit.

Sorrow and self-recrimination, knowledge of inadequacy, inferiority, failure—all struck and bore him down. Gregory sat still, trying to relax, trying to let it all wash through him. It did, it passed, but it left him trembling with self-contempt.

Still, if he had failed at human relationships, he knew he could succeed as a wizard—even more, as a researcher who could learn new and varied ways to use psi powers. Resolved to find some way to disable Finister without hurting or killing her, he rose, set and grim, and went to untie his horse, mount, and ride down the woodland path. His first goal must be the nearby village that Finister had claimed was Peregrine's home. Gregory didn't doubt the hamlet was real but was sure the villagers knew nothing of Peregrine and never had. He had to find some way to protect it from the spillover of a psionic battle.

He rode for fifteen minutes, mind open and seeking the village, before he heard its thoughts clearly enough to be sure where it was. He turned his horse off into a deer trail then and rode away from the cluster of huts—its best protection was distance. He pushed aside low-hanging branches, underbrush swiping at his knees.

Then, suddenly, he reined in, stiffening, eyes widening. He had felt it, a resonance, a sort of mental echo, a reverberation and reinforcement of his psionic field. When he was sure the feeling was real and constant, not imaginary, he dismounted, tied his horse, and pushed his way into the forest, through a screen of underbrush, turning a little to his right, then right again around a huge rock, feeling the resonance grow and grow.

Beyond the rock, the land was clear, no shoots or brambles, only emerald grass, thick and soft, cropped low by deer.

Boughs arched high above, the afternoon sun's rays sifting down through a thousand nodding leaf shadows. What lay beneath that turf, Gregory had no idea—perhaps nothing, only a confluence of lines of force, perhaps some strange collection of piezoelectric crystals that reflected his own energies back to him in an endless circle—but whatever it was, it grew stronger and stronger as he paced to the center of the clearing.

Then, suddenly, the feeling thrilled through him from head to toe, rooting him to the spot, filling him, making him feel as though he were swelling, growing ten feet tall, and all his self-doubts fell away as he knew he had found his site of power.

The trance came upon him suddenly, unbidden. He became aware of vast, dim presences, of spirits of a land that had known hundreds of years of telepaths. The forest was rich with witch moss, storing and reflecting their memories, emotions, and knowledge. Bitter and joyful, angry and grateful, vengeful and loving, the paired emotions drove him into a higher and higher state. Dimly he felt the presence of a host of ghosts, women and men flocking to him, attracted by a wizard mind at the site of power. He heard their voices whispering in his ear, confiding the terrors and joys and guilts of their lives, advising him of their successes and failures, their regrets and delights, filling him with the knowledge they had wrung from life, but more often than not, too late.

Now he could see them, dim shades in muted colors, flocking toward him, joining hands, beginning to move in an age-old dance as their advice and experience poured into him. Huge though the site may have made his mind, they filled him—yet he seemed to grow more huge yet. Dazed and awed, knowing but not yet understanding, he let the procession weave about him, sharing thousands of lives with him, he who could focus them and sort them and match them, balancing remorse against a burning and unslaked desire for vengeance, fulfilling regrets—for hurts not returned—with guilty memories, countering joys with sorrows. Through him the restless spirits came each to his or her own resolution, some pairing, many matching, all gaining a sort of peace and filling him with their power in the process. Unheard praises filled his mind, tears of gratitude and unsung tributes, as the specters began to fade, leaving the immensity of their combined experiences, memories, and powers behind—and Gregory knew that he had survived the ordeal, the rite of passage, and become a man grown and a complete human being, truly a wizard in every way.

When they were gone, he thought he must sag, must fall to the ground senseless with the barrage of emotions, thoughts, and memories he had sustained. Instead, he stood straight and tall, vibrant and bursting with power, feeling more alive than ever he had. He let the feeling of exaltation build and peak, then ebb and finally fade, leaving him filled with energy and delighting in existence.

Finally he relaxed with a smile and went off into the forest to bring back armfuls of brush. When he had a pile as high as his waist, he stared at it intently, beginning to move molecules with his mind. When the work was done, he went back to gather more brush, and more. There was much to do and only a few hours left in which to see the task fairly begun.

Alarm thrilled through him, echoes of hatred and shame. He thought another band of ghosts had come to fill him again, but looking up, he saw Finister approaching in her own form, face aflame with passion, with desire and lust for vengeance, and her mind boiled with thoughts of mayhem.

CHAPTER
-16-

Finister was astounded to discover Gregory so near to the place in which she had left him. She was even more astounded, almost shocked, to see him calmly dragging brush to the center of the clearing and staring at it while it shrank in on itself, melding into a single substance and hardening into gleaming off white blocks, very fine-grained, seeming almost translucent, almost to glow with an inner light as they sat there. He had already made a score of them, piling them up by telekinesis, then fusing them together so tightly and making them melt together so that they became one seamless wall. He must have welded their very molecules.

How dare he! Did she mean so little to him that, instead of seeking her, he would cast aside all thought of her and set himself to playing with blocks? How childlike, how feckless, how fickle!

How improbable. The thought gave her pause; he was very deceptive, seeming to have decided on one course of action while he really pursued another. What might it cover, this facade of seemingly aimless play? From hiding, she projected a thought at the blocks, trying to analyze them—and was amazed to find that the cream-colored substance drank up her psionic probe as though it had never been.

So that was it! He was trying to build himself a shelter to protect himself from her! He had feigned desire while he really sought first to trap her, now to wall her out! Blazing with anger, she strode out into the clearing to confront him.

But she was too late for a frontal assault; the wall was already high enough and wide enough to come between them easily. Gregory had only to step behind it to become impervious to any telepathic attack.

That left sex, which hadn't worked, and anger, which she hadn't tried much yet. She advanced on him, crying, "For shame, sir! Would you leave a woman lost and defenseless in so perilous a forest as this?"

Gregory didn't even try pointing out that it was she who had left him—he knew now that emotionally it was the same thing. "Your pardon, lass—but enemies may come and I had need to prepare a shelter."

She noticed he hadn't said whose enemies, or whom the wall was supposed to protect. "And how would you have sheltered me if enemies had fallen on me while you were building here?"

"Indeed, I fear you have the right of it. I should have kept seeking until I found you."

He didn't sound very penitent, though, and her blood boiled at the suggestion that he had indeed searched for her. Of course he had, and of course she had made herself very hard to find. "What manner of guardian are you, sir, who ceases the search so soon? Indeed, if you cared at all for your ward, you would rack the forest for months until you found her!"

"I am a careless escort indeed," Gregory said, striving to seem remorseful—but he was definitely trying and seeming, not being.

"Dare I travel with you more?" Peregrine advanced on him. "How do I know you would not turn and attack me?"

At least he looked genuinely appalled. "Oh, no, sweet lady, I would never do such a thing!"

No, he wouldn't, more was the pity, unless she could make him so angry that he forgot himself. "How can I be sure?" she taunted. "Is it because you are not man enough? Not man enough to search, not man enough to care, not man enough to lust after a woman badly enough to seek her out?"

For a moment, desire flared in his eyes. "So beauteous a creature as yourself could inspire lust in the very stones!" Then the desire doused as quickly as it had come, leaving him as bland and polite as ever. "But I would never act upon it to wrong a damsel."

"Then you cannot care much for her," Peregrine said acidly. How could the maddening boy remain so calm? She had insulted his very manhood! She pushed another button. "Or perhaps you were afraid to seek me, fearful that you might indeed happen upon some cruel, crude woodmen who would fall upon you with cudgels—or some bear or wolf who would rip with fang and claw!"

"Perhaps I am," Gregory said with chagrin but no great conviction.

He was entirely too sure of himself, and for a moment she saw again the fire with which he had frightened away her bandits. Fear rose within her, but she thrust it aside and pressed the attack. The foul insults she had heaped upon him must have stimulated some emotion, no matter how well he hid it! She changed tactics and pressed close, projecting desire and recklessness even as she denounced him. "There, I am within your reach, only inches away! Have you the courage to reach out and take what you say you desire? No, for you are afraid my passion will burn you, sear you from limb to limb, leave you shaking with emotions that tear you asunder!"

Her eyes flashed as she spoke and she saw the shudder run through him as her projections touched him. She felt an uplift of elation, knowing she held him fascinated, and pressed right up against him, hip to hip and breast to chest. "There, you did not even have to reach—I have come to you! Do you dare to grasp what you touch? Dare to enfold me in your arms and taste the sweetness of my mouth?" She hit him with every ounce of attraction she had, both sexual and emotional, eyes glinting with vindictive delight.

Gregory swayed for a moment but steadied himself and straightened, arms rising but not touching. His voice shook with desire as he said, "I dare, but I withhold. You are too precious a gem to debase with the sweat of my hands."

She almost screamed in frustration. She knew his whole body clamored for her! How was he able to resist?

Gregory felt the power rising from the earth to fill him, power to resist, to maintain his integrity. He wanted her, yes, so badly that he ached with the yearning—but he did not want her like this, angry and challenging, eager only for proof of her power over him. If he could not bring her to him out of her own desire for the totality that was Gregory, for himself and only for himself, he would not accept her at all.

The thought tripped him into an analytical mode and he felt his senses sharpen, his reason honed by the power of the earth on which he stood. Why should she be angry and challenging him sexually only because he had not come hotfoot after her? Surely not merely to prove her own power! Her anger must be only another ploy in her game of seduction—but why should she want to seduce him if she were not in love with him? He was immensely flattered that she would go to such lengths and dearly wished to believe she had been moved to boldness simply because he had become more attractive—but with the clarity of the site of power, he knew it could not be true.

Still the idiot boy refused her, refused to grasp what was his for the taking! Could he suspect how she wished to strike at him once she had him mesmerized by desire? No, surely not! But she would never have him transfixed more thoroughly than she did now, and if he would not reach out to consummate his desire, she would! Reaching up, she clasped his face in both hands and pulled it down to her own, kissing him lightly at first, lips nibbling, then with tongue teasing, and as his mouth opened to embrace hers and his arms finally rose about her, she reached out with her mind, pulling his into an erotic dreamland strong enough to make him lose contact with the world.

Gregory knew well what she was doing and why but allowed hope to spiral and carry him away, letting his heart believe what his mind denied—that she was truly in love with him. He remembered everything Geoffrey had taught him about kissing and put it to practice, letting the kiss deepen almost of its own accord as he touched her back, her shoulders, her hips in the places Geoffrey had told him of, and was elated to feel an answering increase in her desire. Overcome with affection and wanting to give her even more pleasure than she gave him, he fed her own eroticism back to her, amplifying it strongly. He felt his own desire feed hers, then felt her tremble as her emotions became rapacious, feeding back into him until he felt he would burst even though he threw his whole heart into the kiss and fed the desire back into her, swollen with love.

Finister's whole body convulsed; dazed, she melted in his arms, and Gregory let himself be lost in her kiss and in the ecstasy she wove about him as the emotions of her desire and his fed upon one another, swelling and spinning them both into a whirlpool of rapture that paralyzed them, so intense as to prevent the very deeds it inspired, until the power of the spell overwhelmed Finister and she broke the kiss, slumping in his arms, unconscious.

Gregory teetered, scarcely able to hold on to consciousness himself, but the power of his site slowly steadied him, and he reached down into her mind with overwhelming love but found there only a sort of rosy haze. With great tenderness his mind groped through that mist, trying to achieve mentally what his body had been denied.

He froze, and his heart turned to ice. Beneath the haze of a very real desire still burned the white, actinic spark of hatred and lust for revenge, the hunger to slay him as soon as he dropped his guard. It was still there, the determination to fulfill her assignment, to enslave or slay him, and the hormonal intoxication of erotic feedback only obscured it, delayed it, but never for a moment cancelled it.

Reaction hit him and he plunged into a despair as great as his intoxication had been only minutes before. He slumped to the ground mourning, holding the unconscious woman in his arms and gazing down at her with yearning and agony, overcome with the realization of his failure. All his efforts had been insufficient. His magic had amplified her desire, yes, but he himself had proved inadequate. His enchantment might have taken the desire she had kindled within him and caught her up in a gyre of emotion—but his body, his face, his personality had all failed to win her love.

Cordelia found him there weeping over the unconscious woman. So deeply immersed in his grief was he that he did not even notice her panicked call for her mother and brother.

Something flickered across the face of the moon; looking up, Cordelia saw her mother's broomstick spiralling down to land—holding not only Gwendylon, but Geoffrey, too! So that was why he had not teleported to her immediately, only sent a thought that he would join her "presently." Her alarm doubled—what had happened to him, how had he damaged himself, that he must fly on a broomstick rather than teleport?

Her concern diminished only a little when Geoffrey said as he dismounted, "Mother, you are not sufficiently recovered to do this!"

He sounded quite anxious. Cordelia cried in alarm, "Recovered? Recovered from what?"

"I have slept well and long, Geoffrey," Gwen assured him. "Be not anxious, my son. For the patient's sake as well as my own, I shall not attempt this healing if I so much as suspect I have not the strength." She turned to her daughter. "Your brother is kind to be so concerned, Cordelia, but I have not suffered anywhere nearly so much as he seems to think."

"No, only exhausted herself, first in a game of riddles with a computer, then with drinking it dry of all its knowledge of the human mind!" Geoffrey protested.

Cordelia stared. "What computer? Where?" And nothing would satisfy her until she heard the whole story or at least a summary of it, at the end of which she-regarded her mother with admiration. "You must tell me how you outguessed a mainframe, Mother, when we have leave—but Geoffrey is right, you must be careful not to strain yourself."

"I shall be cautious, never fear, and if you doubt me, remember my concern for the patient." Gwen touched her hand with a warm smile. "Now, my dear, what is so horribly amiss? . . . Oh!" She stared at her youngest, sitting on the ground before a wall glowing with twilight, head bowed over the beautiful young woman in his arms. Even from ten yards' distance she could see how his shoulders shook. She stepped closer to Cordelia and murmured, "What has happened here?"

"I know not," her daughter answered in the same tone. "I know only what I see; I have feared to inquire without you."

Gwen touched her son's mind and found it in turmoil. "Wisely refrained, Cordelia, when he is so distraught." She stepped forward to kneel by Gregory and asked softly, "Why do you weep, my son?"

"For a love that shall never live, Mother," he answered in a hollow voice.

Gwen studied him for a moment, frowning, then said, "Say that you weep for unrequited love, rather—and if the poor child you hold in your arms has been so wounded in her heart as I think, it is small wonder that she cannot love, neither you nor any man."

Gregory looked up at her with deadened eyes. "There is no hope of healing her heart, then?"

"I have not said that," Gwen answered. "There may be hope indeed. Let me study her mind awhile."

Gregory straightened, his eyes coming alive. He sat very still, cradling Finister in his arms, waiting while his mother probed and sifted through the woman's memories, even the ones she had forgotten, and especially the ones of which she had never been aware. Finally Gwen nodded and said, "I think she can be healed."

Gregory heaved a sigh of relief, going limp, then remembered that he held Finister in his arms and straightened again.

"Before we do, though," Gwen said, her voice suddenly grim, "we must ask whether we should."

Her children stared at her, appalled.

Then Gregory found his voice. "Do you ask if it is right to slay her, Mother? We have threshed out that question already!"

"You have threshed it," Gwen agreed, "but have you found wheat, or chaff?"

Cordelia frowned, looking into her mother's eyes. "What have you found, Mother, that makes you now doubt her right to live?"

"Chiefly that, though her will may have been formed by those who punished her for independence and rewarded her for subservience," Gwen said, "it was nevertheless her own choice to slay and maim. Perhaps I can cure her, perhaps not; perhaps I can bring her true self out clear of the fears and yearnings that shroud it—but she may still choose to murder and steal. Have we the right to cure her and free her if she will become no more human for our efforts?"

The young people were silent, two of them staring at Finister as though they were seeing her as a monster for the first time—but the third still with love. "Surely we have the right to decide it, Mother," Gregory said, "for it is our family that has suffered from her actions more than any other."

"There is some truth in that," Gwen said slowly. "Must we summon your father for a family council, then?"

"Father? No!" Cordelia said instantly, then explained, "There is no need, for we know what he will say—that if she has injured even one of his children, the only mercy she deserves is a quick death."

Geoffrey nodded. "*If* he votes for mercy. I think he might prefer that her death be slow."

"Yes, if he did not have to wreak it," Cordelia returned.

"There is truth in that," Gwen sighed. "He loses reason at thought of hurt to you and myself."

"More pertinent, I think, is the question of what Magnus would say if he were here," Geoffrey offered. "After all, it is he who has suffered most at her hands."

Gwen cast a dubious look at the tormented face of her youngest but agreed, "There is merit in that. Do you truly think Magnus would say we should slay her?"

"Probably not," Geoffrey said in disgust. "You have reared us all to be too merciful."

Thank Heaven for that, Gwen breathed in silent prayer.

"We need not wonder," Gregory said, his voice listless. "I have spoken with my brother every other month or so since he left home."

Gwen turned to gaze at him. "Indeed you have, and have told me of his exploits."

Geoffrey and Cordelia eyed their brother with some envy; his telepathic range far exceeded their own—though, Cordelia had to admit, it might only have been that his desire for contact with Magnus was greater than theirs. He had been very young when his idolized elder brother had left home.

"Well enough, then," Gwen said. "Reach halfway across the galaxy if you must, my son. Let us hear what your brother says."

Gregory's eyes lost focus; his body stilled.

Cordelia stared, then whispered to Geoffrey, "So that is the secret of it! He sends himself into his trance of meditation to reach our brother!"

"No doubt aided by the likeness of genes," Geoffrey agreed, then shook his head decisively. "I should never have the patience for it."

"Nor I," Cordelia agreed. "I have never been able to understand how Gregory can waste so much time in contemplation when he might be out and about doing wonders and celebrating life with others his age."

Geoffrey sighed. "It is his choice, and who are we to criticize?"

"After all," Cordelia said, "he does not criticize us."

"Magnus speaks," Gregory said, his voice remote. "He delights in my thoughts; he greets you all with love."

"Oh, and ours to him!" Cordelia had never been present during one of these conversations.

Neither had Geoffrey. "What foes does he vanquish now?"

"None." Gregory gazed off into space, his voice like the sighing of the wind. "He is aboard his ship, journeying between planets."

"How does he?" Gwen asked anxiously.

Gregory was silent a minute, then said, "Better than at any time except in the heat of battle, Mother. He has a new companion now and she has calmed his inner turmoil considerably."

"She?" Cordelia pounced on the word with delight and jealousy. "What manner of she?"

Gregory paused for an exchange of thoughts again, then

said, "She is a peasant woman named Alea, one who has been as badly hurt as he in her way."

"Is she indeed!" Gwen said, fascinated.

"She is, and Magnus is now intent on healing her."

"Magnus?" Cordelia frowned. "What does he know of healing a woman's heart?"

"Only what his computer Herkimer can tell him, but that seems to be a great deal."

"Does she think of healing him?" Cordelia demanded.

"He cannot say, for he will not, of course, read her thoughts unless there is danger," Gregory said, "but he thinks she may be a telepath, though untrained and so of unknown strength."

"That is hopeful," Gwen said, "and might incline him toward mercy toward this woman whose emotions were exploited and twisted in childhood. Tell him our dilemma, my son, but not of your own feelings toward this Finister."

"I shall try," Gregory said, "though he is skilled, and will no doubt read some of it from my mental overtones." Then he was silent.

His family waited as he told the whole of the tale to his brother, hundreds of light-years away. Gwen wondered how thoughts could bridge a gap that nothing material could. That led her to thinking of the breakdown of simultaneity at near-light speeds and wondered what time, what year it was where Magnus sailed, how old he was now, and if by some magic of H-space he might be no older relative to herself than he would have been if he had stayed on Gramarye.

Then Gregory spoke. "He is horrified at the thought of executing Finister for her injuries to him, but thinks she should suffer in her own turn so that she will not injure others again."

Gwen expelled a sigh of relief and Cordelia clasped her hands. "His heart is still generous!" Then her face darkened. "But I am loathe to hear that he wishes her to suffer."

"Be sure that she has," Gwen told her, "and it has not inclined her toward mercy—but if I cure her, she shall relive those sufferings in such a way as to triumph over them." She turned back to Gregory. "Does Magnus understand that she is a proven murderer?"

"I spoke to him only of his own grievances," Gregory said, his voice still distant. "Shall I make him judge of her other crimes, then?"

Gwen took her time answering and phrased it carefully. "Say rather an advocate, either for or against. Will her murders change his mind? I cannot, after all, be sure of my healing; the mind is ferociously complex. She may yet murder again."

"Surely not!" Cordelia protested, but saw the look on her mother's face and fell silent.

Gregory was silent, too, but his face creased in pain as he mentally recounted Finister's crimes. Then he said, "Magnus says that death is the traditional punishment for murder, but the murderer may be forgiven if she is sincerely intent on not killing again and makes such restitution as she can to the victim's family and to society."

"That would surely take a goodly portion of her life, if not all of it," Geoffrey said.

"A lifetime of public service is not entirely unrewarding," Gwen said as one who knew.

"Magnus mentions an order of mendicant nuns," Gregory sighed, "and says that if she cannot find one, she may start one—perhaps even a lay order."

"Even cured, I cannot see this woman accepting such a life," Geoffrey said. "Yet there is more. Tell Magnus of her attempt to steal Alain and kill Cordelia, and to seduce me away from Quicksilver." He frowned at a thought. "You have told him of our betrothals, have you not?"

"Yes, and of the witch who sought to prevent both," Gregory said, his voice like a distant wind, "but I shall remind him." Again he was silent; then suddenly he winced. "He is angered far more by danger to his siblings than to himself. Now indeed does he advocate the death penalty."

"Give him my fond thanks," Cordelia said with a sentimental smile, "but the threat was to myself and Geoffrey, so surely we may say whether we should risk forgiveness."

"It is our right," Geoffrey said grudgingly, "and I suppose

I shall speak for mercy, if Mother can cure the harpy.''

Cordelia beamed at him and patted his hand. "Well said—and I think Quicksilver would be wroth if you did not.''

Geoffrey turned to her. "Perhaps she should have some say in this, and Alain, too.''

Cordelia shuddered at the thought. "Alain is Crown Prince and would insist on enforcing the law of the land.''

"I shall speak for Quicksilver,'' Geoffrey said, "when I have consulted her mind.''

"But it is so like Magnus to make light of his own hurts, yet be angered by ours,'' Cordelia said with a fond smile.

Gregory began to sway. Geoffrey leaped up to steady him, and Gwen said, "We must be done with this exchange, for your brother is nearly worn out with his emotions. Come, join with me in concert; let us lay our farewells in Gregory's mind, that they may travel to your brother.''

Cordelia and Geoffrey joined hands with her; Geoffrey was already touching Gregory. Their thoughts blended in a fond farewell, modulated onto Gregory's telepathic beam. They all felt the nostalgia-laden burst of yearning and resignation that underlay Magnus's own good-bye. Then he was gone, and Gregory sagged against his brother.

"If he feels like that,'' Cordelia asked, "why does he not come home?''

"I think he is waiting for his own healing,'' Gwen said, "and for his own notion of maturity.''

Cordelia frowned. "He is nearly thirty. What manner of maturity does he seek?''

Her mother could only shrug and shake her head.

Gregory lifted himself away from Geoffrey, saying, "Grammercy, brother. I am restored.''

"Not overmuch,'' Cordelia said with a searching and skeptical stare.

"Enough,'' Gregory assured her, and turned to his mother. "If Magnus has spoken for mercy, surely even Papa would not object.''

Cordelia looked much less certain, but Gwen said firmly, "I shall explain matters to your father. Believe me, he has some notion of redemption and perhaps even more faith in it than any of us."

All three of her children looked puzzled, but Gwen did not feel the need to elaborate. Instead she reached for their hands and said, "Come, lend me your own psionic energy, for this is apt to be a harrowing ordeal."

They came, they formed a circle around Finister's sleeping body and linked hands as Gwen began to work her way into the depths of Finister's mind.

> *Riding up to Boston,*
> *Riding up to Lynn,*
> *You'd better watch out*
> *Or you're going to fall IN!*

Little Finister gave a squeal of surprise and delicious fright as she plummeted between the knees that had been her seat— but Papa's hands still held her waist firmly and bounced her up again, then down to sit on his closed knees once more. She laughed with delight and carolled, "More! More!"

"Now, Papa, you know better than to make a wee one so excited while Maud and Sukey are even now setting the table," Mama reproved.

"Aye, it is naughty of me," Papa said, chuckling, and hoisted the three-year-old off his lap.

Little Finister pouted and demanded, "More!"

"Tomorrow, little one," Papa said. "Into the high chair, now." He turned her around and sent her toward the table with a pat on her bottom.

The table was very long, as it had to be to hold twenty children and two adults—but the keeping room of the old farmhouse was ample. It had once been a whole cottage itself, but Papa and the big boys had built the sleeping wing onto the end—a boys' dormitory and a girls' dormitory, with Mama and Papa's room in between—and a new kitchen, pantry, and scullery onto the other end. The second wing was easily as big as the first, for a farmhouse kitchen had a great deal more to do than preparing meals, especially when it had to take care of twenty-two people.

They sat down to dinner, and Mama and Papa looked around the table, smiling. Gradually the children fell quiet. Then Papa said, "Before we eat, let us pause to remember all the people oppressed by the King and Queen, and how we may work to free them."

Everyone was silent for a minute, staring at his or her plate, except the tiny boy who was even younger than Finister. There was a baby only a few months old, too, but she slept in her cradle by Dory's side.

Then Papa picked up his knife and began to carve the first capon. It was the signal to begin passing the bowls and platters. They went from place to place, the children serving themselves with fork or spoon, the older children helping the ones who were still too young to serve themselves and scolding mildly if they forgot to use their tableware, then passing the dish on to the left. Mama beamed as she watched her adopted brood, saying, "Very neatly done, Angela! That's how a big girl eats. . . . Derek, not so much, now! That pease porridge has six more to serve. . . . Corey, help little Vera with that milk pitcher, it is so very heavy. . . ."

The pitcher, wobbling in thin air, steadied suddenly. With all the affectionate assurance of fourteen, Corey smiled down at eight-year-old Vera. "There, I shall bear its weight with my mind. Do you make it tilt, now—not too much, of course."

Vera studied the pitcher fiercely. It tilted slowly, poured the milk into her mug, then tilted back.

"There, neatly done!" Corey said.

Vera beamed up at her, then turned to glower at the pitcher. It drifted to the left and Essie said, "I have it, Vera. Thank you."

"You're welcome," Vera said, then settled herself rather proudly as her mug lifted off the table to tilt against her lips.

On the boys' side of the table, a turnip floated out of the bowl and toward one of the smaller girls. The older children shouted angrily; one plucked the offending vegetable out of the air.

"Put back that turnip, Jabelle," Papa said sternly. "No,

Robey, do not do it for her—she must undo her own misdeeds. Send it back, Jabelle.''

Jabelle tucked her chin in, glancing about her in fright, then stilled long enough to stare at the turnip balanced on Robey's palm and send it back to the bowl with a thought.

"That's better," Papa said. "If you do it again, though, I shall give your portion to someone else."

The little girl shrank in on herself. The teenager across the table from her smiled down at her, and they could all hear the thought he sent into Jabelle's mind, for the little girl did not yet know how to shield very well. *Never fear hunger, Jabelle: Mama and Papa will see to it there is a serving left for you when the bowl comes around.*

Finny wondered why Dory had to lean over and repeat the message for Mama in a low voice. She found out three years later that Mama and Papa couldn't hear thoughts. She found out even more quickly, though, that she couldn't get away with thinking nasty things at other children or making unheard jokes about Mama and Papa—the older children were quite severe about that.

Plates filled, the girls ate with their hands in their laps. Finny wondered why the boys got to hold their forks and spoons, but the girls had to make them move by thinking at them. Little Lally forgot and picked up her fork, but Mama instantly frowned and said, "Make the fork move itself, Lally. Hands in your lap."

Wide-eyed, Lally dropped the fork and tucked her hands together. "I'm sorry, Mama—I forgot."

"Of course, dear." Mama smiled reassuringly. "See, you manage almost as well with your mind already. Beri, help her."

"I shall if she needs it." Twelve-year-old Beri smiled down at her little foster sister. "But she is doing quite well by herself."

Lally glanced up at her with a shy smile, reddening with pleasure.

Mama and Papa were allowed to hold their utensils. Finny thought this was because they were grown-ups, their privilege as mother and father, but she found out later it was because they couldn't move things with their minds.

"Dory, give the cradle a push, there's a dear," said Mama. "She seems a little restive."

The cradle began to rock again, but Dory assured Mama, "Her body may be restless, Mama, but her mind is still deep in sleep."

Dory was the eldest girl, nearly eighteen and really a young woman. She turned eighteen and disappeared a few months later; Finister still remembered the party, and the sense of loss when she realized Dory was gone. Mama explained to her, though, that Dory had grown up and moved away, for she had adult work to do in saving the people from the King and Queen. Finister wasn't sure what the King and Queen were, but she hated them for taking Dory away from her.

Not that there weren't two other girls to fill Dory's place, nor a new foundling on the doorstep to make their numbers twenty again. Rhea and Orma were really young women, too, as Jason and Donald were really young men. Nonetheless, little Finny still missed Dory, though it helped that she came back to visit now and again. There were always "alumni" coming back to visit, and always new "graduates" leaving.

When they were finished eating, three of the older children went out to the kitchen; the other teenagers made the serving bowls and dirty plates float out to them for stacking and washing. The younger children concentrated fiercely at sending their forks and knives, and those of the bigger children next to them, after the dirty plates. Then Dory came back in, a huge cake floating before her, and the other teenagers began singing in joy:

> With a hey, ho, the wind and the rain,
> For the rain it raineth every day!

"A celebration! But what is the cause, Mama?" Papa asked, but with a twinkle in his eye that said he knew very well.

"For Beri," Mama said. "She has become a woman to-day—a very young one, but a woman nonetheless, for she woke to the beginning of her first period this morning.''

All the children cheered, and little Finny, not understanding, cheered right along with them, banging her spoon on her high-chair tray. The cheering turned into singing:

> *At last she has come to woman's estate,*
> *With a hey, ho, the wind and the rain!*
> *May thieves and knaves never be her fate,*
> *For the rain it raineth every day!*

Bedtime was nice; Rhea gave Finny her bath and made sure she washed behind her ears, then Mama herself tucked the little girl in and told her a bedtime story. Finny looked away, though, frowning.

"What is it, Finny?" Mama asked. "Are some of the other children thinking nasty thoughts again?"

Reluctantly, Finny nodded.

"Everybody does, now and then," Mama assured her. "Even the nicest people have bad days sometimes. Just close your mind to them."

"How do I do that, Mama?"

But Mama only said, "Rhea will tell you how," then leaned down to kiss Finny's forehead and stood up.

Finny wondered why Mama didn't tell it herself.

Rhea sat down at Finny's bedside. "Pay no attention to the angry or spiteful thoughts, Finny."

Finny frowned a moment, then shook her head. "Doesn't work."

"Of course not," Rhea said. "If I tell you not to think of an apple, what's the first thing that comes to mind?"

There it was in her mind's eye, a big, ripe, delicious apple. Finny grinned. "Apple!"

"Of course," Rhea said, smiling, "so instead of thinking about apples, think about pears."

Finny frowned, not understanding, but the ripe, golden pear was there in her mind.

"And while you're thinking about the pear," Rhea explained, "you don't think about the apple, do you?"

Finny stared in surprise, then giggled and shook her head.

Christopher Stasheff

"And while we've been talking about apples and pears, you haven't noticed the nasty thoughts, have you?"

Finny's eyes grew round; so did her mouth.

"That's how you block them out long enough to fall asleep," Rhea explained. "Think about the warm and loving thoughts all around you, think about apples or pears—or sing a song in your head, something you really like, and sing it over and over until you fall asleep."

Finny gazed up at her wide-eyed, thumb in her mouth.

Rhea gently pulled her thumb out. "You're a little too old to need that anymore, dear. Think you can sleep now?"

Finny nodded.

"Good night, then." Rhea kissed her forehead, then stood up and went away.

Finny rolled over on her side and closed her eyes, thumb going back in her mouth again without really thinking about it—because she was already thinking about the rain, with a hey and a ho.

> *When that I was and a little tiny girl,*
> *With a hey, ho, the wind and the rain,*
> *Foolish things were all a-whirl,*
> *And the rain it raineth every day!*

It didn't really rain every day, of course, but even when it did, there was plenty to do indoors, more and more as Finny grew older. The cleaning, canning, and cooking always went on, and there were chores enough in the barn and henhouse—but when chores were done, there was chess and backgammon and whist, all manner of games. The girls weren't allowed to move the pieces with their hands, of course—though the poor, silly boys had to, not being able to move things with their minds. They resented the girls for it but made up for it at games like hide and seek, where they could disappear and appear in another place. The girls showed off on their nighttime broomstick rides to get even. They all had to use their hands for outdoor games with balls and sticks, though. Finny never understood why the girls were allowed to use their hands on some games and not on others. Perhaps it was because some involved sticks. She noticed that if they were supposed to hit the ball with a stick, they had to move that stick with their minds. If there were no sticks, though, they could hit the ball with their hands as well as their minds—in fact, they weren't allowed to use their minds alone.

There were races and wrestling and boxing, too, though after a girl's body started developing curves, she had to stop wrestling and content herself with boxing and karate—or quarterstaves; they all practiced with quarterstaves, though they were allowed to use their minds to strengthen their own blows and weaken their opponents' strikes. They practiced archery, too, of course, directing the arrows with their minds, though it was their arms that had to pull the bows. Finny liked hide and seek best. She was very good at making the others think she was a rock or a stump or even a dog, so good that even her foster brothers and sisters couldn't always see through her disguise. She couldn't understand why—all she had to do was think of the form she wanted to appear to be, then try to think as that form thought (or failed to), and the others took the longest time to find her. Mama and Papa noticed and praised her for it. She changed shapes whenever she could after that, especially when it came to getting out of chores. As she grew older, she had more and more chores to do—but hiding never worked; if she wasn't there when she was needed, she lost her dessert to someone who had worked harder. Sometimes she even had only half portions for dinner.

Another problem with growing was that other people's jealous and petty thoughts began to clamor as loudly as their warm and loving ones. The older girls taught her how to pay attention to thoughts she wanted to hear and ignore ones that she didn't. But impatient thoughts grew more frequent as she grew older and the warm and loving thoughts became more and more rare, especially Mama's. Her fond thoughts seemed to center on the babies—the new foundlings and the toddlers. Finny grew very jealous of the babies, especially since Mama never seemed to tuck her in anymore—she was always rocking or feeding one of the tiny ones. One night when Mama paid her no attention, she couldn't get to sleep for the anger and finally realized that if the baby weren't there, Finny might become more important to Mama again. So she reached out to the baby with her mind to look inside it and see if there were some way she could make it go away. . . .

Sudden, blinding pain seared inside her head, and voices echoed there, stern and scolding.

CHAPTER
-18-

The voice was Beri's with Rhea's and Umi's behind it:

No, Finny! You must never hurt anyone unless Mama tells you to!

Finny cried out in fright—then a bigger fright as a huge, horrible ogre seemed to stalk into her mind. She could see the hag very clearly, huge muscles bulging under dirty blouse and red plaid kilt, dark jowls and little piggy eyes under an unruly thatch of hair, club upraised in her hand, booming, *I am the Hurter! Where's the foolish girl who likes to hurt people?*

Finny shrank down in her blankets, too frightened to cry.

Then the ogre was gone, there was only a pinkish light in her mind, and Dory was beside her, stroking her forehead and saying, "It's just a bad dream, Finny, but that's what you look like inside when you think about hurting one of us. Never even think about it again." And she crooned a lullaby, soothing the five-year-old to sleep.

Finny didn't stop being angry, of course, or stop wanting to hurt the babies who were her rivals—but she never tried to do anything about it again, especially since it was quite clear that when the older girls gave her orders, those orders really came from Mama. But Dory and the other big girls loved the tiny ones, cuddling them and singing to them and playing with them when there was time, and Finny loved Dory and Rhea and the others. She began to feel guilty about hating the babies.

"Don't worry about it, Finny," Agnes assured her as they were hoeing the pea patch. She was an eight-year-old, and

Christopher Stasheff

Finny's favorite playmate. "I hated you when I was five and Mama was making such a fuss over you."

Finny dropped her hoe, turning to stare at the bigger girl. "You hate me? But . . . but I thought . . ."

"Oh, I love you now!" Agnes dropped her hoe, too, and turned to hug the younger girl. "But I didn't when I was only five. I was very angry because Mama was so busy with you that she didn't seem to have much time for me anymore. But as you grew older, you were such a happy and loving little darling that I couldn't stay angry with you, and you wound up being my favorite toy."

"Toy?" Finny stared up at the bigger girl even as she relaxed into her embrace.

"Of course, my toy, 'cause I played with you all the time. Then you got big enough to play back, and now we're playmates. Don't worry, you'll wind up liking the new one, too."

Finny did, but it took a few years and, in the meantime, she didn't want Agnes to be ashamed of her or to have the big girls scold her, so she began to learn how to hide her anger and hatred from them. Every now and then, she slipped; her anger at the babies showed enough for one of the big girls to feel it, and the Hurter would come stomping through her head, making it ache from side to side—so she learned how to hide her feelings more deeply.

At least the punishment told her that the older girls were always paying attention to her. In fact, there was always somebody to play with, somebody to talk to, and somebody to listen to her troubles—but that somebody wasn't Mama, at least not very often. Sometimes she wondered if Mama had forgotten about her and did something naughty where Mama could see. The punishment was quick, but at least she knew Mama was watching.

It worked better when Mama told her to do something; when she did it, Mama would give her a quick hug or a pat on the curls. Most of the time, though, she left Finny to the big girls, and they were even more strict than she was about making sure Finny obeyed.

Then one day when she was churning cream, she stumbled

200

and the churn started to fall. In a panic, she reached out with her mind and pulled it upright.

"Why, Finny, how very clever!"

Finny looked up, heart pounding.

Mama stood there, beaming down at her. "Did you catch the churn with your mind? How deft you've become!" She bent to kiss Finny on the forehead. "There's my wonder girl!"

Finny's heart sang. "I could push the dasher with my mind, too, Mama."

"Yes, you could, but your arms would grow weak," Mama said, still beaming. "Besides, ordinary things like churning aren't so amazing. It's being able to think and act on the spur of the moment that's wonderful." She gave Finny a quick hug. "Extra dessert for you tonight, young lady."

It was the first time Mama had called her a young lady.

From that time onward approval was rarely given, and was generally reserved for psionic feats exceptionally well done. Doing chores was expected and not celebrated, but if she didn't do them, punishment was quick.

The older girls put the younger ones in their places beyond the slightest shred of doubt. Hair would pull itself, skirts would blow up when the boys were near, noses would tweak themselves painfully, sticks would leap up to trip you. The worst was the nightmare in which an older girl would turn into a monster and chase you and chase you, and no matter how hard you tried, you couldn't wake up. Finny learned to obey very quickly, and though Mama and Papa couldn't hear her thoughts, there were always older sisters who could, and who took care of the punishments themselves.

Mama and Papa never knew about that, of course. She tried telling them once, but Mama only looked sad. "What did you do before your hair pulled itself, Finny?"

Finny clasped her hands behind her back and watched her toe while she made it trace circles on the floor.

"The big girls wouldn't have made your hair hurt if you hadn't made them angry," Papa said. "What did you do?"

"Agnes told me to go back along the row and hoe the weeds I'd missed," Finny said grudgingly.

"And did you do it?"

"No," Finny admitted.

"What *did* you do?" asked Papa.

"Told her she wasn't Mama," Finny grumbled.

"Now, that was wrong, Finny," Mama said. "When any of the older girls gives you an order, they're giving it for me—unless they order you to do something you're not supposed to do."

"The older you grow, the more people you can order," Papa agreed.

Finny decided she didn't like order very much.

"Dory gives orders to Rhea and Rhea, gives orders to Orma, and so on down the line," Mama told her. "Any of them can give orders to you, and I expect you to obey them. Do you understand?"

"Yes'm," Finny muttered, still tracing circles with her toe. Inside, a rebellious voice shouted, *It's not fair!*

"Don't worry, little one." Papa patted her on the shoulder. "When you grow to be big, you can give orders, too. For a year, you'll even be the oldest girl in the house, and you'll be able to give orders to any of the other girls!"

That was a nice thought. Finny looked up at Papa with adoring eyes and decided that someday she'd be the person who got to give orders to everybody else.

Little children accept what they're told is the order of the world, but as they grow, they begin to wonder about it. One day when the heat and humidity were oppressive, Finny stopped gathering berries and started to take off her dress. She might have succeeded, but Orma was in the next row and saw her. "Finny! You put that right back on!"

"But it's so much cooler without it," Finny whined.

"You'll get a sunburn without it, too," Orma said, "and it makes my heart ache to hear you crying. Put it back on, Finny."

Finny did, grumbling, "Why do we have to work, anyway?"

"Because if we don't work, we won't have anything to eat," Agnes said, proud of knowing something Finny didn't.

Finny felt a moment of pure hatred for the older girl, then a deep shame, for Agnes had said she loved Finny.

"You should feel ashamed," Orma said. "After all, you know more than the younger children, too—and she's right. If we don't help Papa plow and sow seeds, there won't be any wheat or barley. If we children don't plant potato eyes, there won't be any potatoes."

"But the hens will keep laying!"

"Only if we take care of the hens—and take care of the pigs and the sheep, too, or there won't be any meat to eat. Then we have to salt it and smoke it, and can the fruits and vegetables, or there won't be any food left to eat in the winter."

Understanding burst in Finny's mind. "That's right! We have to put seeds in the ground if we want wheat to reap in the fall!"

"And if we don't reap it and bind it and thresh it, it will rot in the fields." Orma nodded, happy that her little foster sister understood. "And if you don't go to school, you'll never learn enough to help make the King and Queen go away."

Finny had already started school, and learned about all the horrible things the King and Queen did, such as taking people's money and making laws to keep them from doing what they wanted and starting wars. She didn't understand how learning how to add and subtract was going to help get rid of the King and Queen, but she did understand that she had to learn to read if she wanted to know what people long ago had done to try to do away with crowns and how the Kings and Queens had stopped them. Of course, she'd have to learn to write if she wanted to be able to let people who came after her know what she had done for the fight in her own turn.

Somehow getting credit for what she did do seemed more important than letting other people know what didn't work. She liked it when people praised her, and since it didn't happen very often, she was trying to figure out every way she could of winning that praise.

Mama taught them in school that winning was very important, because they all had to try to win against the King and Queen, and that was very hard, because the King and Queen were very rich and had very, very many soldiers. They even had mind readers like Finny and her foster brothers and sisters helping them. Finny hated those other mind readers; they should all have been on the same side. Mama taught her a nice word for those royal mind readers: "traitors."

She also told them never to let the people in town know that they were planning to get rid of the King and Queen. Nobody had ever broken that rule, so the villagers thought Mama and Papa were fine people, generous and caring, because they took in so many unwanted children and taught them to work hard and even to read and write and cipher, which meant they would be able to earn a living without taking jobs away from anyone else.

The villagers didn't seem to have taught that to their own children, though. Finny remembered her first trip to town. She was very excited and could hardly hold still as Dory herself tied her bonnet on. "You have to remember now, Finny," she warned, "don't let those village children get you angry. Promise me that no matter what they say, you won't let them hear your thoughts or try to hurt them, no matter how badly you want to."

That took some of the excitement out of it. Finny stilled, staring up at her big sister round-eyed. "I promise, Dory."

"And you must promise me never, never to let anyone outside the house know that you can read minds or move things with your thoughts."

Finny stared. "Why not?"

"Because most people can't do it, and if they find out we can, they'll grow jealous and even afraid of us, and try to hurt us for it. Promise, now."

"I promise," Finny said, but the day seemed dimmer, somehow. She felt as though she had done something wrong already.

Then they went out and climbed into the wagon, though, and the excitement came back. Finny couldn't keep still; she found herself dancing. Dory laughed with joy to see her and drummed her heels in time to Finny's steps.

• • •

Finny had never seen so many houses so close together, and never any so tall. She clung tightly to Orma's hand as she looked about her, inhaling the mixture of strange fragrances and seeing all the bright and enticing things on the stands under the awnings along the streets. She could tell the lumpy green and yellow things were vegetables and the red and green ones were fruit, but she didn't know what to make of the stiff, colorful bundles in a third stall. "Orma, what's those?" She pointed.

"Those?" Orma followed the pointing finger. "Cloth, Finny. Many different kinds and colors of cloth."

"All that cloth?" Finny stared; it was ever so much prettier than the brown and gray homespun the big children wove at home.

"And look! The cabinetmaker!" Orma pointed and Finny looked, but it wasn't anywhere nearly as exciting—only an old man scraping curls from some sticks with a strange sort of double-handled knife, though she had to admit the chairs and tables about him were much prettier than the ones Papa made.

"Nyah-nyah! Little foundlings!"

Finny turned to stare at the four richly dressed boys who were thumbing their noses at the girls. Orma stood her straightest and turned Finny's head frontward. "Don't look, Finny. Don't pay them any attention at all!"

"Didn't have a father," two of the boys chanted in derisive singsong. "Never knew your mother!"

"If I knew theirs, they'd be in trouble quickly," Orma assured her.

Out of the corner of her eye, Finny saw Rhea and Agnes marching with their eyes stiffly ahead.

"Walk away," two more boys taunted, " 'cause your mommy couldn't stay!"

It was strange, the menace Finny felt from the boys, and the thoughts they were emitting weren't nice at all, almost like a bad smell. There were pictures with them, ugly, naked pictures that made her shiver.

Orma noticed. "Close your mind," she muttered.

Finny thought about apples. It was very hard, with those

horrible thoughts coming out of the boys, but she managed to think only of apples—and maybe a pear or two.

"That's right, don't bother with us," one of the boys called, "just like your mommy didn't bother with you."

Finny felt her face growing hot even though she didn't know why. She glanced up and saw that Orma's and Agnes's faces were red.

"Hey, love child, how about a kiss for me?" one of the boys taunted.

"All right!" Orma cried, and turned toward the boys. "Come on, Agnes!"

Finny stared in surprise as the girls ran at the boys, their lips puckered grotesquely, arms reaching out. The boys made noises of disgust, but their minds leaked fright as they turned and ran.

Finny crowed with delight and clapped her hands.

Orma and Agnes came back red-faced but smiling. "It's a good thing they were young," Orma said, taking Finny's hand again. "Don't ever try that with big boys."

"Why not?" Finny asked.

"Because they might kiss back."

"Ugh!" The thought of kissing somebody with a mind like that made Finny feel sick. She decided never to try it.

"So there you are!"

She looked up and saw Papa and the boys coming toward them, grinning.

"We sold the pigs for a very good price," Papa said, "and made even more on the grain! Come along! Candy for everyone!"

The candy was sweet and the whole family was laughing and joking as the big people drank from cups that foamed while they watched the acrobats performing in the town square. After the acrobats came a puppet show, then a minstrel who sang funny songs that made them all laugh. They had so much fun that Finny almost forgot about the nasty boys.

Almost. But in the wagon on the way home, a tired little Finny sat in Dory's lap and rested her head on her big sister's shoulder. She didn't know how to feel. Town was a wonderful place, the candy had been a rare treat, and everything had been so exciting—but there were the horrible names the town children had called them. "Dory," she asked, "why do they hate us?"

"Because we're not like them, dear," Dory said. "It's us against them, and they know it."

"Maybe they'd like us if we lived in town."

"No," Dory said, "because our real mothers left us on Mama's doorstep. They were too poor to keep us, you see. Then they married rich men in the village and kept the rest of their children. That's why those children jeer at us—it makes them feel better than us."

"It's so hard not to give them tummyaches or headaches!"

"Yes, but you didn't, and I'm proud of you. If you had, the whole village would have come marching out to our farm and tried to hurt us all."

That thought made Finny feel ashamed. "Dory—is there something wrong with being mind readers?"

Dory gave a sharp gasp, then tightened her arms protectively around her little foster sister. "Of course not, darling. Mind readers are special. The others call us 'witches,' but we aren't that at all. We don't really work magic, we just have special gifts—and we certainly don't have anything to do with the Devil!"

" 'Course not," Finny said. "Papa says the Devil is just another prince, and princes always hurt people."

"The Prince of Lies, yes. No, we'd never have anything to do with that. The village people wouldn't believe us, though. Their jealousy is so sharp that it would make them hate us if they knew we were mind readers—hate us so much that they would call us witches and burn us at the stake!"

"Burn us!" Finny sat bolt upright, horrified.

"But they won't, because we won't let them know," Dory said. "Will we, Finny?"

The little girl shook her head, eyes round.

"So all in all, it's better that they call us foundlings and feel that they're better than us, isn't it?"

Finny made an "O" with her lips as she understood.

Dory smiled. "That's right, dear. That's why we just ignore

Christopher Stasheff

them when they call us names and don't try to hurt them—
because there are more unpleasant names they could call us.
There are worse things than being a bastard.''

"Such as a villager," Jason said, and the boys laughed.

Finny didn't laugh, but she snuggled up against Dory again.
All in all, she decided, the farm was much nicer than the rest
of the world.

Forever after, though, she looked at the villagers, and the
rest of the nonpsi world, as strange and threatening, even
though she knew she was better than they were—though deep
in her heart, she would also know that she wasn't even as
good as they were. After all, she was a foundling.

There were many trips to town after that; they went four
times a year, and the biggest girls took turns staying home
with the babies and the toddlers. The town children were always mean to them. The girls would come out wearing their
prettiest dresses right where Finny and her foster sisters
couldn't help see, and talk about how horrible it must be to
be poor. The boys just called them names.

That changed when Finny turned twelve and her body began to change, though.

CHAPTER

-19-

By the time she was fourteen, Finny had begun to take her turn disciplining and teaching the younger children. She had also developed some very pronounced curves and a face that made the town boys whistle when they saw her, but there was still something threatening about them. When they called for kisses, she didn't go chasing them anymore. Instead, she and the other girls scolded them, refusing to be treated with disrespect, but the attention gave her a glow and made her feel special. More than that, it made her feel powerful in a strange way. When that feeling came upon her, the boys stared, then began to talk to her in admiration, and her foster sisters began to be envious—but when the boys crowded close to try to fondle, the girls drove them away with slaps, the power of which was increased by telekinesis.

At home, she would catch her foster brothers watching her with open admiration now and then, though most of the time they only talked with her as they always had—after all, she was only Finny and they'd known her all her life. But there was a new note of respect in their tones now, something notably absent from the town boys' voices, and it kindled that warm, powerful feeling again.

Finister found that remembering that feeling and letting it build made her foster brothers vie with one another to help her with her chores.

"That bucket must be too heavy for you, Finny!"

"Oh, no, Jason. I can manage it easily."

"Nonsense. Here, I'll carry it. Aren't Mama's flowers beautiful this year?"

Then there would be a nice, close conversation that made her feel even more special. Finally she decided to try the effect of that feeling on her foster father. She waited until they were alone in the keeping room at the end of one cold winter day. Papa sat down by the fire and she said, "Here, Papa, let me pull your boots off!" She bent to tug at his boot, then smiled up at him, letting the special feeling grow.

"That's good of you, Finny," he said, then looked at her a second time, staring. "Why, Finny!" he exclaimed, "you're a projective empath!"

"A what?" Finny asked, confused, and the special feeling went away.

"Mama!" Papa leaped to his feet and went to the kitchen door. "Mama, come here! Our little girl is growing into a projective empath!"

"Really?" Mama came bustling out, wiping her hands on her apron. "You must mean Finny! We've known for a long time that she's good at making people think she doesn't look like her real self. You mean she can project emotions, too?"

"Project them and raise them in another person!" Papa turned to her. "Show Mama what you just did, Finny!"

Finny wasn't at all sure she wanted Mama to know how she had charmed Papa—but the older woman was looking at her with such hope that it made her remember the few times Mama had been delighted when she'd been particularly deft with telekinesis and, hoping to receive that kind of approval again, she tried to remember the feeling the boys raised in her. She managed to recall it and let it grow—and grow, and grow.

Orly came in with a load of firewood in his arms. He turned toward the fireplace and saw Finny. The wood clattered on the floor as his jaw dropped.

"Yes, I see." Mama beamed, lit by a glow of her own. "How wonderful, Finny! But I think that's enough now." She looked up at Papa and said, "I think our little girl will go far."

"Even to high places," Papa agreed, one arm around Mama's shoulders. "Congratulations, Finny! An ability like that is rare, very rare indeed!"

"Unfair, too," Orly grumbled as he bent to pick up the wood.

"Oh here, let me help you!" Finny cried, all contrition. She knelt to pick up the logs, but Orly's breath hissed in and she straightened, staring. "I—I'm sorry, Orly."

"Don't be," the teenager said. "It's been a horrible day, but you just made it a good one."

His eyes were warm with admiration, but also with amusement. Finny smiled and helped him finish with the wood.

When they were alone later that night, though, Mama had some very earnest words for her.

"It's a gift with which you must be very careful, Finny. If you make a boy fall in love with you, he could become very angry when you spurn him—and very badly hurt inside. You could do a great deal of damage."

Puzzled, Finny asked, "You mean I shouldn't use that gift?"

"If you can project one emotion, you can project them all," Mama said slowly, "and raising pity or sympathy in somebody, or a sense of responsibility, can do a lot of good. If you fall in love with a boy, of course, you're going to want to try to make him fall in love with you—but strong though they may seem, boys aren't made of steel, you know."

Finny looked doubtful. "You don't mean I could use that gift to hurt a boy, do you? I mean, do real damage."

"You certainly could," Mama said, "and you must be careful not to, unless your commander orders it when you're grown up. If you play with boys' hearts carelessly, you could wreck homes, turn men into thieves, make them kill one another—all sorts of horrible things."

Finny swelled inside with the feeling of power that gave her, even as her heart shrank from the thought of the guilt she would feel if she used her gift in such a way. "I'll be careful, Mama. I promise."

She was, trying very hard not to let the special feeling leak out—though she couldn't keep it from rising whenever one of her foster brothers let slip a glance of admiration. She reminded herself that, when a boy smiled at her that way or whistled or came over to talk, it wasn't her face or figure that had attracted him but the warmth of the emotions that she had let slip out. She knew she was a cheat and a fake, but she couldn't see any way to be anything else. She was born to be a deceiver and would have to live with that nature for the rest of her life.

In town, Finister discovered a new and thoroughly acceptable use for her gift. When five of the girls went shopping and a gang of town boys gathered to heckle them, she let her special feeling grow and projected it. Then the boys began to sweet-talk her and she paid attention first to one, then to another, until she had them arguing over who would have the pleasure of escorting her back to Papa's wagon. Then she projected anger into them as she led her sisters away a step at a time, watching as the boys began to shove one another and shout insults. They forgot the girls as they began to fight in earnest, and Finny and her sisters made their escape. As soon as they were out of sight, they began to laugh at the boys' foolish-ness—but Orma didn't laugh and began to eye Finny with envy. That bothered her.

In fact, her emotional growing pains were becoming strong enough that the schoolroom was something of a refuge. There Mama and Papa took turns teaching the more advanced sub-jects, such as physics, psychology, economics, and history—not just the history of old Earth but also of the whole Terran Sphere. They learned about SPITE, the Society for the Pre-vention of Integration of Telepathic Entities, the selfless and virtuous organization that spanned all the colonized planets and all of civilized time to try to save the people from tyr-anny—especially the tyranny of VETO, the Vigilant Exter-minators of Telepathic Organisms, the totalitarian organization that tried to enslave all common people and make them labor at jobs that dulled the spirit until they be-came virtual robots, all in the name of the State. The ineffi-cient and equivocating democratic governments weren't much better, according to Mama and Papa—they spent so much time vacillating and never making a decision that they left the people victims of Big Business, which was as willing to grind the workers into robots as VETO was, but also poisoned the people with the products it made them buy. Worst of all was the DDT, a democratic government that was trying to subvert the government of Gramarye.

All the children became very angry at the villainous VETO but even more at the sneaky DDT. Mama and Papa told them that if they became really skilled in their use of ESP, they would be allowed to join SPITE when they grew up and become Home Agents. Then they could help rid Gramarye of both VETO and the DDT. Finny began to realize that she could use her special gift to set the men in both organizations fighting each other the way the town boys had. Men were so easy to manipulate, after all.

Now that they were old enough, Mama took the big girls aside and told them how they had probably come to be born—not by parents who wanted them but didn't have money enough to keep them, but by women who had let men seduce them with their lies and charms, get them pregnant, then abandon them. Those women may have wanted to keep their children, but having no husbands, they would have been hard-pressed to make enough money to live. Worse, once they were no longer virgins, few men would be willing to marry them, not without dowries, and they might have to become prostitutes. It was quite possible that several of the children could be half brothers or half sisters, the unwitting by-blows of their mothers' pathetic attempts to make a living—though most of the money they earned would have been taken by their pimps.

Now Finny began to feel the hot, burning anger that would be with her the rest of her life, the urge for revenge upon the man who had seduced her unknown mother or forced her into prostitution. Since she didn't know who the man was, she would spend long years trying to revenge herself on any man who came by.

Except for Orly, but he came later—at least, as something other than a brother.

Mama and Papa knew which of their foster children were more tenderhearted than the others and knew that Finny was among them, so they didn't let her see a chicken beheaded until she was twelve. Even then, they told her to brace herself, described what she would see, and told her to erect her full mental shield so that she would not feel the fowl's death pangs. They did tell her that it would be quick, and it was— but in her case, twelve was still too early; she was naturally a very sensitive and affectionate child, and it gave her nightmares. The next year, they let her start seeing sheep butchered, and at fourteen, pigs. It was horrifying and sent her into fits of tears, but Mama told her gently, "It's the way of the world, Finny. If we want to have chicken for dinner, we have to kill the chicken first—and if we want bacon and pork chops and pigskin to sell, we have to slaughter the pig and clean it. You'll learn to cope with it, dear. We all do, sooner or later."

Finny tried, she tried very hard, though she couldn't stand to eat meat for months after each encounter. As the years went by, though, she managed to repress her horror and become herself a hardened butcher. Papa congratulated her when she beheaded her first chicken, and Mama herself made much of her. They both showered her with approval again when she butchered her first pig, then her first sheep—but when they were alone, Mama gathered Finny's head onto her breast and let the teenager weep. "I know it's hard, Finny, but the world is hard. It's a cruel place, and the only way to live in it is to become capable of cruelty yourself, and to harden your heart to others' pain."

That was hard for a telepathic girl, very hard, but Finny learned how to make her mental shields more dense and managed it.

The older girls started telling her about menstruation well before her courses began, so it was no shock to her, and she had a passage party just as the older girls had had. Afterward, though, Mama took her aside to make sure she understood how women became pregnant and to warn her against men who wanted to use her. Then her older sisters taught her how, even if a man did manage to seduce her, she could use telekinesis to keep from becoming pregnant. Finny listened intently and rehearsed as much of it as she could without a boy on whom to practice. She wasn't apt to remain a virgin forever, after all, though from everything she was hearing and from what she saw in the barnyard, she wasn't terribly interested in sex. Mama had made it quite clear that, since they were foundlings with no family and certainly no dowry, the girls weren't very likely to marry. It might happen, of course, especially if the young woman were really beautiful, but Finny knew she wasn't. She might be able to bewitch a man into thinking she was, but did she really want a husband who fell in love with the illusion she created, not with the real Finny? Maybe Dory could find a husband, or Orma—they were both beautiful, and certainly they were patient and good-natured, even sweet—but not Finny. She accepted the fact that she would never marry, but she was determined not to become an old maid. Old she would one day be, but not a maid. It was only a matter of time.

Then Orly changed, and she decided that time didn't matter.

She was in the middle of her sixteenth year and a few of the village girls her age had already married and were with child. Orly was a year older. She couldn't say how he had changed. Maybe it was that the last signs of baby fat melted from his face under the sun that summer, or maybe it was only that she had never noticed. Certainly when he came in from the fields and stopped by the well to strip off his shirt and sluice away the dust and sweat of the day, she noticed how huge his muscles had become and wondered why she had never noticed before. It started a peculiar feeling in her, like the special feeling that came from boys' admiring glances but stronger, much stronger. The biggest difference came when they talked. Somehow they managed to be alone even if there were others nearby, alone sitting on a bench in the backyard and talking about the stars or the crops or the newest baby talking as they always had, about subjects they had always discussed, but somehow the conversations seemed so much deeper, so much more meaningful; it was as though she were hearing undertones and hidden meanings she'd never known before. Both of them had their mental shields up, as they had all learned to do—the constant storm of others' thoughts could drive you crazy, after all, and you didn't want everybody knowing your personal secrets.

They didn't notice Mama and Papa watching them with

thoughtful faces, then looking at one another and nodding slowly.

It must have been an accident, of course—certainly Mama wouldn't have sent her up to the hayloft if she had known Papa had just sent Orly up there to make sure the hornets hadn't started another nest. He caught Finny kneeling to pet the swollen cat and called, "Why, Finny! Have the kittens come, then?"

"Oh! You startled me!" Finny leaped up, then saw it was Orly and couldn't help letting out some of that special feeling as she gave him a sleepy-eyed smile. "No, they haven't come yet, Orly. But it's late enough that we need to watch her closely."

"We should have been watching her closely two months ago." Orly grinned as he came closer. "It's a little late now."

He was standing a little too close and Finny felt a strange new presence about him, something like her own special feeling, and wondered if Orly were a projective empath, too. She lowered her gaze and looked up from under her lashes. "Puss didn't seem to mind it at the time."

"Yes, but look at her now." Orly frowned, drawing a little away. "There are always consequences."

Finny felt a touch of distress—she had liked him standing close, even liked the hint of danger in it. She let out more of her own special feeling as she said, "There don't have to be. She'd have two litters a year if we let her."

"You mean you stop her from . . . ?" Orly frowned. "Can't be. I've seen her go into heat only a few weeks after one litter's grown."

"Into heat, yes, but we don't let babies start." Finny spared a wink for the cat. "We females have to take care of one another, don't we, Puss?"

Puss purred and stretched, flexing her claws.

"You certainly do!" Orly said in surprise. "I didn't know."

Finny made a face at him. "Boys don't need to know everything."

"Maybe not." Orly grinned and stepped closer again. "We know what really matters, though."

"Oh?" Finny said archly. "And what is that?"

"Ask Puss," Orly said deep in his throat and stepped a little closer, reached out to almost touch her waist, and his face hovered near, so very near, and his breath smelled sweet and musky. She looked deeply into his eyes and felt her special feeling growing; she clamped her shields tight on the instant, but left an opening for him and felt his mind reaching out. For a moment their thoughts mingled, and she shivered—but she realized he wouldn't close that last inch on his own, so she swayed just a little forward.

He swung toward her as though he were iron and she a magnet and their lips brushed, then brushed again. It was a tickling that called deep within her, and her whole body answered with a wave of sensation that frightened her even as she welcomed it. His lips brushed again, then stayed; hers melted against his, her whole body seemed to melt against his, and he was so hard and strong, his chest pressing from the front, his arms holding her fast, and her lips fluttered open. He gasped, and the tip of his tongue touched her lips. She shuddered and opened her mouth wide. For a moment, tongue caressed tongue, and fire coursed through her—for a moment, then another moment and another.

Finally the feeling ebbed; she realized, with surprise and shame, that she had been pressing her hips against his and stepped away, eyes downcast. "Orly . . . we shouldn't—"

"Oh, yes we should," he breathed. "You know it and I know it—but not today."

"Not ever." She spoke sadly, managing to get her hands between them—but that was a mistake, too, because they felt the hardness of his chest and seemed to want to go exploring on their own.

So did his hands, though they didn't stray far from her waist. "Someday, beautiful Finister," he breathed. "Someday."

It was the first time she had ever really liked the sound of her name.

Somehow they met frequently after that, every other day or so, then every day. The first few times, Mama and Papa had

made mistakes again, Mama sending Finny down to the creek
to pull tubers for dinner, Papa sending Orly there to rake the
leaves from it. They would start to talk, not meaning to embrace, but it was as though they couldn't keep apart from one
another. Kissing led to caressing, and caressing to a desire
for more intimate touching. They began to meet in the barn,
in the woodshed, in the grove to explore one another's minds
and bodies—never going as far as they wanted, of course.

They were so wrapped up in one another that they never
stopped to think some of their foster siblings might have noticed, and certainly not that Mama and Papa could be aware
of their meetings, for they would have stopped them at once,
wouldn't they? They both felt guilty about it, but not very—
just enough to add another level of thrill to their secret.

The family always went to the midsummer festival—that
expedition was no surprise—and Papa always told them to
go in three different wagons by three different routes so that
they wouldn't seem so intimidating to the villagers; they
didn't usually all come to town at once. This time, though,
Finister and Orly exchanged a glance, then quickly looked
away. It never occurred to them that their older siblings might
have thought of this before them. They were only delighted
at how easy it was to slip away.

CHAPTER
-20-

Finny and Orly managed to melt into the shadows while Papa and Mama were dividing up the family, letting each of the three groups think they were with the other. They hid until all three wagons had driven out onto the road. Then, secure in the knowledge that they were the only people on the farm that afternoon and evening, they crept out of their hiding places and ran toward the barn.

Finny reached the haymow first. She paced, waiting nervously and fretting, then heard boots on the ladder rungs. She turned and saw Orly stepping off the ladder, silhouetted against the light from the window, big and handsome and muscular and impossibly attractive. He stepped forward, lifting his arms, and the yearning swept from him to engulf her, to sweep her into his arms and wash her up against his chest, his mouth to hers.

The older foster children were well used to blocking out the amorous feelings of the villagers at the midsummer festival, for as the evening darkened and the bonfire was lit, there was dancing and drinking, and many of the young people disappeared from the firelight two by two. The young psis were even used to blocking out the erotic impulses of their foster siblings, which, coming from telepaths, were far stronger than those of the villagers—so even at that festival, when the musky aura of coupling seemed to permeate the atmosphere, they had rarely been aware of one another's misbehavior.

They were stunned when they did feel the aftershocks of orgasm.

The teenagers looked at one another in surprise, then with

desire and longing, for the erotic feelings they had sensed aroused their own yearnings.

Mama might not have been a telepath, but she had eyes, and knowledge enough to draw her own conclusions. "Orma—what is it?"

"Someone has just been having a very good time," Orma gasped, "someone telepathic and projective. If they aren't part of our family, they should be."

"I suspect they are," Mama said darkly. "You and Jason round up the children and take special care of the little ones. Papa and I will see what has been going on." Off she went into the merrymaking crowd, searching for her husband.

When she found him, she said, "We seem to have succeeded better than we knew, Papa."

"We, and they," Papa agreed. "I think we had better go back to the farm at once, Mama, before they decide to have too much of a good thing."

"Or decide that it is indeed a good thing," Mama agreed. "It would never do to have two of our brood desert the Cause to start a family of their own."

Papa winced. "What a waste of time and effort that would be! Well, we'll go quickly, but I don't think there's much to worry about. We've done this often enough before, after all."

They left, driving the wagon through a cloud of hormones, for even the nontelepaths, without knowing why, had begun to feel more amorous toward one another than was usual, even at that festival. It was a midsummer that would become a legend in the village.

They drove up as Orly and Finny were coming out of the barn, still starry-eyed and holding hands. They stopped in the moonlight to kiss.

Papa leaped down from the wagon and strode toward them, seeming to swell with anger. "And just what have you two been doing, I wonder?"

"And out in public, or as good as!" Mama scolded, clutching her skirts and hurrying to catch up. "Your brothers and sisters could feel your lust all the way into town! You might as well have told them all what you were doing before they left!''

Finny blanched and shrank from Mama's anger. Orly tried to stand his ground but turned pale.

''I've never heard of such a thing!'' Mama scolded. ''You're as bad as your birth parents! Really!''

''You could have controlled yourself, Orly,'' Papa snapped. ''Now you've dragged Finny down with you! Couldn't you think of anything but your own pleasure?''

''But . . . but we only—''

''No excuses!'' Papa thundered. ''We've told you how disgusting your parents were! The monks have told you how vile such an act is, in church every Sunday! Don't try to tell me you didn't know it was wrong!''

''Selfish! Depraved! Disgusting!'' Mama ranted, and the two of them went on and on, Papa starting in just as Mama had to pause for breath, then Mama again when he ran out of wind. On and on they went for half an hour without pause, denouncing their errant wards for horribly ungrateful children, born of lustful and morally depraved parents and destined by that birth to be promiscuous themselves. Both were gratified to see Orly drop Finny's hand and to see her bury her fingers in her skirt. Finally Finny's sobs became so deep that she nearly fell. Orly reached out to support her, but she flinched away from him. Mama stopped ranting and gathered Finny in to sob against her bosom. ''All right, now, it's done, and there's no undoing it. But never again with another telepath, you hear?'' She glared at her foster son. ''Go away, Orly, and don't make her look at you again for a month!''

Orly finally bowed his head, shoulders slumping in defeat, and turned away. Papa clasped his shoulder and steered him off toward the creek to wash, and Mama comforted Finny, then took her inside and filled the brass tub with hot water for her.

Finny wept into the soapy water.

''Ashamed, and very right to be,'' Mama told her. Then, generously, ''Well, what's done is done, and the spilt milk cannot be poured back into the jug. We'll promise not to tell your brothers and sisters about this, Finny, as long as you swear never to do it again with one of your own kind!''

"Oh, I swear, Mama," Finny said fervently, and meant it with every drop of blood in her heart.

On the banks of the creek, Papa handed Orly a towel to dry himself, saying magnanimously, "We'll go on just as we always have, then. There's no reason for anybody to know about this except your mother and myself—and Finny, of course. Come now, back into town, or your siblings will count noses and know who wasn't there."

So back to town they went, Finny and Orly riding in the back of the wagon as far from one another as possible with downcast gazes, feeling so depraved that they couldn't even look at one another.

It was the longest ride of Finny's life.

Orly and Finny saw each other after that, of course, but quickly looked away, sheepish and guilty. They didn't speak much to their siblings, either, feeling accusing stares every-where they went. Finny didn't stop to think that she was be-having just as Orma had two years before, or Rhea the year before that, and of course she had been too young to notice when Dory had gone through this same ordeal.

Finally they began to come out of it; finally Finny realized, from the comments about them, that their siblings hadn't counted up and compared the roll call of each of the separate parties. The boys exchanged coarse jokes and jibes that made Orly realize they weren't sure which of their number had done what to whom, and Finny began to understand that the other girls weren't even sure the psionic lovers had been of their family. She made up excuses for her bad mood and started laughing off their expressions of concern. Every now and again she would look up to find Orly gazing at her with yearn-ing, but she quickly looked away, blushing with shame.

The worst of it was that she still wanted him, wanted an-other evening in the hayloft with him. That was how she knew how depraved and disgusting she really was.

She was so ashamed that she never even thought of talking about it with the older girls, or with Dory or any of the other alumnae who came back to visit from time to time. It was hard to talk with them after they had been away, anyway—

they seemed harder somehow, bitter and weary. It made Finny afraid of leaving home—but she couldn't stop time, and she knew the rule well: When you turned eighteen, you had to go out into the world and earn your own living. Papa and Mama weren't rich, after all, and though the farm was productive, it couldn't support more than twenty children at a time. Besides, they were rare assets by the time they were grown—educated people in a land in which most were illiterate—educated, and espers.

Finny never thought to wonder why, if telepaths were so rare, all the children left on Mama's doorstep were espers.

Orly turned eighteen that winter, and his birthday was a mingling of rejoicing and sadness, for everyone knew that when spring came, Orly must go. It was a tortuous year for Finny, with Orly there but untouchable, with the thought of him being so compelling but still so disgusting. Spring did come, though, and when the mud had dried and the trees were in leaf, they held one more sad party and bade Orly good-bye. Off he trudged down the lane to the road. There he turned back, waving one last time, then went slogging away.

Finny couldn't forgive herself for imagining that he had been waving to her.

She didn't see him again, not at the farm, but Mama heard gossip from the alumnae. When Sukey, one of the first foster daughters—she had graduated twelve years before—had come to visit, then gone, Mama took Finny aside and told her, rather severely, what Orly had been doing since he had left. She made it clear that the Chief Agent had ordered him to find a position with the Baronet of Ruddigore's household and to cultivate acquaintance with one of the baroness's maids, but that didn't really excuse his having an affair with her—with several of them, in fact. "I knew he would be just as much of a womanizer as his father must have been," Mama said severely, then turned mournful. "But he was such a sweet little boy!"

For a moment, Finny was afraid that she was going to have to comfort Mama, but the older woman regained her composure and told Finny not to blame Orly too much. After all, once you left the farm, you had to put the past behind you.

Burning with anger and shame, Finny put the past behind her with a vengeance. When the next midsummer's festival came, she felt weighed down with grief as they rode the wagons into town, remembering what had happened the year before. It kindled desire in her at first, then grief, then shame as she remembered Mama shaking with anger and telling her and Orly that they were both no better than their profligate parents. If Mama had been right about Orly, she must have been right about Finny, too, which meant that profligacy was all she was good for. So Finny locked away any compunction or grief she might have felt and took four separate farm boys aside that night. On the way home, she felt horrible, soiled and filled with self-loathing—but she felt a strange satisfaction, too, because she knew she deserved it. And there hadn't been any great, soaring ecstasy, only some tickling and some evanescent, thrilling building to a climax that was only a release, wasn't even much of a pleasure. She never knew those rolling waves of sensation again, for she only coupled with nontelepaths, just as she had sworn to Mama—and just as the Chief Agent assigned her to do.

For her time at the farm was almost done. She turned eighteen in March, passed her final examinations in history, anarchist theory, and psionic manipulation, then applied to join SPITE, and was delighted and relieved when she was accepted. It showed how good Mama and Papa were as teachers, that none of their graduates was ever rejected; SPITE welcomed them all, giving their wastrel lives a purpose.

The family gave her a wonderful going-away party where all the girls cried and hugged her, and Mama wept a bit, too, and gave her one last embrace, then sent her off down the road with Rufus, a young man who had graduated when Finny was ten.

Overcome with loneliness and homesickness, Finny wanted the warmth of human contact very badly that first night and was sorely tempted to entice Rufus into sharing a blanket with her—but she remembered her vow to Mama, that she would never sleep with another telepath, and managed to resist the temptation. Rufus must have sworn such a vow, too, for he only told her "good night" and rolled up in his own bedroll.

Of course, it could have been that without her erotic projection, Finny wasn't very attractive. The more she thought about it, the more certain she became.

Rufus took her to the chapter house in Runnymede. She was amazed at the size of the city and the towering granite houses, most of all by the royal castle on top of the hill in the center of town. Thousands of people thronged the streets, there were stores that sold virtually anything she could want to buy and a great deal more besides, there were musicians who played on street corners and in the public squares where several streets met, musicians and acrobats and puppet showmen and even actors. There were theaters, too, where the actors were a great deal better than in the squares or the inn-yards.

There were also cutpurses and armed robbers and pimps with trains of prostitutes. She learned quickly to be very selective in regard to which thoughts to heed and which to block out.

The Chief Agent's lieutenant assigned her a room and told her when the common room would serve meals, then gave her a moderate amount of money and told her to explore the city, paying particular attention to the houses of the aristocrats, the guardhouses, and all the other government offices. Finister went a little wild exploring, with a young woman several years older who seemed rather cynical but was very friendly. After the first two weeks Finister was assigned marketing trips, then day jobs as a scullery maid—cover, of course, for an opportunity to spy by telepathy. She was surprised at the number of men, young and old, who made advances to her, for she did not consider herself to be at all pretty, and decided to keep a very firm hold on her erotic projections. She managed to deflect all her would-be suitors, though she might not have if any of them had been terribly handsome.

After a month, the Chief Agent himself summoned her. He seemed surprised at her appearance and, for a few seconds, gave her a thorough, searing inspection that made her feel she was being stripped naked. Then he managed to thrust his lust back into safekeeping and assumed an official demeanor as he scanned a paper on his desk. "Home Agent Finister. You're a telepath."

It was a statement of fact, though he could only have known from the paper he was reading. A single light, quick probe showed her that he wasn't a telepath himself. "Yes, sir, and a projective, too. And telekinetic, of course."

"Yes, most of you girls seem to be." The Chief looked up at her with impassive eyes. "I've had good reports of your first month here, Agent. You seem to have become acclimated to the city quickly and have already brought in several useful bits of information from three noble houses."

"Thank you, sir." Finister still felt rather guarded; certainly she had not yet done anything exceptional.

" 'Finister' is an odd name," the Chief Agent said. "Did your foster parents tell you what it meant?"

"Yes, sir—'land's end.' It was pinned to the basket in which they found me and they couldn't understand why my real mother would have given me such an odd name. They thought it might have been the name of my natural father, but there was no one by such a name in the county."

The Chief Agent nodded. "Possibly a sailor; there are families by that name on the coast, where you would expect it. Of course, you could also translate the name as meaning 'the end of the world.' "

Now Finny blushed. "They did give me a nickname that meant 'the end,' sir, but I'm sure that was only an accident."

"Accident or not, Agent Finister, we expect it to be an omen for the aristocrats and civil servants who cross your path," the Chief Agent said. "Destruction of government begins with destruction of governors, and with your particular gifts, you should be able to disable them emotionally even when you can't kill them physically."

His words gave Finny a frightening rush of elation, of a feeling of power—and of despair, because she knew this was all she was good for. Well, then, she would do it well, she vowed to herself—and she was sure her victims would deserve whatever she gave them.

"This is your first major assignment." The Chief Agent took another piece of paper from his desk and handed it to her. "The Marquis of Cromcourt, currently a member of the Queen's Privy Council. He is also an unprincipled scoundrel who has exploited his peasants unmercifully—especially young and attractive women."

Finny stared down at the page, not seeing it, but holding it tightly in both hands, elbows pressed to her body to keep it from shaking. "Am I to assassinate him, sir?"

"First drain his mind of everything he knows about the government's current plans," the Chief Agent said. "Then assassinate him, yes. Revenge his peasants upon him—but leave no signs."

"Yes, sir." Now the paper did shake. Finny's studies had prepared her for this duty, so it did not shock her—but she understood that the only way she would be able to catch the Marquis at a sufficiently vulnerable moment would be to seduce him, or rather, to let him seduce her—which he would surely want to do, if she used her projective power well. She didn't doubt that she would have to submit to his embraces, or even his bed, but since that was all she was good for, what did it matter? It wasn't as though it would be her first time, after all. She felt no compunction about one more such foray. She just hoped he wouldn't be too old or too ugly.

CHAPTER
-21-

Something of her misgivings must have shown in her face because the Chief Agent's voice softened, becoming sympathetic. "Of course you're frightened, Agent Finister—anybody would be. There is some risk involved in killing a nobleman, after all—but very few of our agents have been caught. You're nervous, too, as nervous as a hunter before he shoots his very first deer. But think of it as slaughtering a pig. In some ways that's exactly what you'll be doing. You may be sure he deserves it."

"Oh, I don't doubt that, sir," Finister said. "I've read about the *droit de seigneur* and I was thoroughly disgusted."

"So you're equally disgusted by this nobleman and quite ready to stick a knife between his ribs."

"Yes, sir!" Finister nurtured her anger, nurtured the reserve of rage and bitterness that seemed always to be there now at the core of her being.

"Righteous anger. Good, good." The Chief Agent nodded. "But a knife between the ribs would be very likely to see you arrested and executed, Agent Finister, and we'd rather not lose you. It would be much less suspicious if the Marquis's heart simply stopped beating."

She nodded and tried to keep her stomach from turning over. It was, as he had said, very much like slaughtering a pig, and she remembered how frightened and sick she had been the first time she'd had to do that. She knew she would feel the same way again, her first time killing a man—but she knew she would get used to it.

She carried off the assignment quite well, obtaining a position as chambermaid in the Marquis's household, then blushing prettily at his flattery. He was only middle-aged, fortunately, and still rather good-looking, though with an edge of cruelty that made her quite sure of the rightness of what she was doing. She projected pure sexuality whenever he came near, and sure enough, his flattery became dalliance, furtive kisses and caresses on the back stairs, during which she drank in all the information about the Privy Council's doings. After only two weeks he summoned her to his bed-chamber. It was mortifying, but she knew she wasn't worth anything more; she gritted her teeth and went through with it. That made it all the more satisfying when he yawned and went to sleep—and she reached out for his heart with her thoughts and stopped its beating. Then she dressed and slipped out of his room, letting her humiliation and disgust show in response to the guards' ribald remarks. No one would be surprised if she disappeared from the house that night; the Marquis had a reputation for dismissing women as soon as he'd had his way with them. She wasn't there when they discovered that the Marquis had died in his sleep. Instead, she hurried back to headquarters, unnerved and trembling, for her first experience with human death at close quarters had been as shocking as she had known it would be.

The Chief Agent was sympathetic, assigning her light duties again and assuring her she would grow accustomed to the experience.

She did.

A mélange of similar assignments followed, some lethal, some not, some only for the gathering of information. There were continual attempts to penetrate the royal castle, but the Queen's telepaths soon detected any agents of their own kind; she barely escaped capture twice. By and large, though, her career blossomed, taking her from one assignment to another, each more important than the last.

She met Orly years later, in the line of duty, but they never talked about their past. Some months after that, she met Sukey, and when they talked about the farm, feelings leaked through Sukey's shield—resentment and anger at Mama for having excoriated her so thoroughly when she'd caught her in the barn with one of the boys. Shocked, Finny made a point of finding Dory and holding a similar conversation—

with similar results. She simmered with anger toward Mama and Papa after that—they had made it sound so horrible, as though she and Orly were the two most deplorable people in the world, when it was really something that happened every year! But she couldn't find them and scold them, of course. She didn't dare. After all, they were Mama and Papa, and if they didn't love her, no one did.

Then followed a catalog of atrocities and disillusionment as Finister began to realize that her SPITE superiors were trying to feather their own nests and competing for promotion and rank with all its perquisites, one of which turned out to be her, and several other of the prettiest female agents. Worse, though they still believed in the rightness of their cause, they had lost faith in its eventual triumph.

Finister had not. She resolved to gain both vengeance for her own exploitation and renewed zeal for the Cause by assassinating her superiors and becoming Chief Agent herself. But she had become cynical enough to strive for material luxuries, just as her bosses did, and finally realized that the perfect revenge on the nontelepaths who had persecuted her and her foster siblings, and on the bosses who had betrayed her by their cynicism and exploitation, would be to marry into the nobility, becoming a Duchess or perhaps even Queen (since the Crown Prince was her own age). Besides, in that way she could work to destroy the aristocracy and the government from inside as well as outside.

So when her boss assigned her to either assassinate Magnus Gallowglass or make sure he would not reproduce, she was fired with zeal to achieve both his plans and her own.

"The swine!" Gregory said, pale-faced and trembling. "To use the love of a child as an instrument to warp her soul!"

"Her foster parents will have much to answer for when this curing is finished," Geoffrey promised him grimly.

"The villains!" Cordelia cried. "The caitiff swine!"

"Worse," Gwen said, face contorted with disgust. "They bartered affection, they withheld approval, they bound her to servitude by her own heart and debased her self-esteem systematically."

"They reared her to be a prostitute and a killer!" Geoffrey exclaimed. "That business with teaching her to slaughter animals—'twas all done in such a way as to lead her to slaughtering people!"

"And to encourage her sexuality only to disable it, to twist it in such a way that they could use it, and her, as a weapon!" Cordelia's voice was harsh with bitterness.

"Not to mention the poisoning of her mind," Gwen said, "in teaching her history from only their own biased point of view and excluding all others, let alone facts that might contradict it!"

"People have done that from time immemorial, Mother," Cordelia said angrily.

"Yes, but not so consciously, not with so great an awareness of what they were doing! She has been reared to be a tool, nothing more, and has not been given the slightest chance to develop her own soul, to become an individual in her own right!"

They were all silent for a moment as the words sank in. Then Cordelia ventured, "But we now propose to do so ourselves, do we not? Can you truly cure her, Mother, or only remake her into the image of what we wish her to be?"

Gwen turned to her youngest son. "What say you, earnest lover? Do you wish the woman to become as you dream her to be, or do you wish her to become fully herself and take the risk that she will no longer find you attractive? Perhaps she will even become someone repugnant to you."

Gregory paled again but said firmly, "I wish her to be herself. Then let us discover if I appeal to her, or her to me."

"You might also discover that your great passion has been only illusion," Geoffrey cautioned.

"Then I must know that! I must know the truth so that I can see the world as it really is—and at this moment, she is the world to me! Cure her, Mother, if you can—make her to be her own person and none other's, not even mine!"

"Well said," Gwen told him, and his siblings murmured assent. "I am proud of the son I have reared," she said, then glanced at Geoffrey. "All of them, but never so proud of

Gregory as at this moment. I must have done *some*thing right."

"More than you know," Cordelia said, then suddenly frowned and said reluctantly, "I suppose Finister's foster mother and father did a few things well, too."

"Oh, yes," Gwen said. "They reared her with love and devotion her first few years. Even after that, her home was always a secure refuge—until she was sixteen. But they did so only to assure that she would be able to love, for if she did not, she could not have become so loyal to their cause or have ached so for their approval and feared their censure. Truly the right thing for the wrong reason. They were quite clever in achieving their goals."

Cordelia eyed her with misgiving. "You do not mean they were virtuous people mistaken in their beliefs!"

"Mistaken, aye," Gwen said, "but there is little virtue in corrupting children in the name of a cause. We must confront lies with truth, though. Let me find these two and discover what was truly in their hearts."

Her eyes lost focus and her children were silent, careful not to distract her as her mind sped to the farmhouse Finister remembered—not difficult to find, since she also remembered the route from the farm to Runnymede. They knew Mama was sifting through the memories of the man and woman she found in that house. Cordelia, at least, hoped that her mother would not kill the couple in their sleep, though she did not doubt they deserved it.

Then Gwen's eyes focused again and a grimace of disgust crossed her face. "Their memories show that they lied deliberately and often. Worse, they knew what they were doing, and had even come to enjoy the humiliation and the despair they caused."

"Corrupted by their own goals?" Geoffrey asked.

"No, by the means of achieving those goals—and I cannot say which I deplore more, the means or the goals. Let us see if I can counter the one and overturn the other." She reached out to either side. "Join hands again, children. We have thus far only learned what we must confront; the true labor has yet to begin."

"But how can you cure her, Mother, rather than make her into another form of statue?" Cordelia asked.

"By freeing her from the bonds of her past, from the fetters her foster parents and her commanders placed upon her," Gwen said, "but not replacing them with manacles of my own choosing. I must allow her to remember her past without being enslaved by it, leave her free to decide her fate and her faith for herself. Lend me strength, children."

The three young people fell silent and joined hands, gazing upon the unconscious woman who lay in their midst.

Gwen was silent, too, a while, comparing the structure of Finny's brain to that of the healthy brain, which she had learned well from the computer. Synapses had grown wrongly, whether from birth or from learned responses she could not tell. She regenerated here, straightened a pathway there, lowered some resistances, and raised others until the brain was restored to its original functions.

Then she began to work on Finister's past.

Overcome with jealousy, five-year-old Finny reached out to the baby with her mind, to look inside it and see if there were some way she could make it go away. . . .

Sudden blinding pain racked her head and voices echoed there, stern and scolding, Rhea's voice with Beri's and Umi's behind it:

No, Finny! You must never hurt anyone unless they're trying to hurt you very badly!

Finny cried out in fright—then a bigger fright as a huge, horrible ogre stalked into her mind; she could see the hag very clearly, huge muscles bulging under dirty blouse and red plaid kilt, dark jowls and little piggy eyes under an unruly thatch of hair, a club upraised in her hand, mouth opening. . . .

Suddenly, though, the monster froze in midstride and a beautiful motherly face appeared beside it, a kindly-looking woman whose face showed the first lines of age and whose red hair was shot with silver. She spoke, and Finny heard her reassuring voice inside, where the hag was. *Foolish, is it not?* the lady asked. *Only a bogie to frighten children—but far too much of a fright.*

Suddenly, by some magic she couldn't understand, Finny was standing outside of the scene, the grown-up Finny watching the little girl she had been and the horrible creature inside her head. The hag began to move again, thundering her dire threat, but the motherly woman only smiled at it with amusement. Then Beri took the little girl in her arms, stroking her forehead and saying, "It's just a bad dream, Finny, but that's what you look like inside when you think about hurting one of us. Never even think about it again." And she crooned a lullaby, soothing the five-year-old to sleep.

The kind lady said, *They frightened you far too much, but the rule they told you holds true—that you should not hurt others who are weaker than you.*

The grown-up Finister, powerful now and able to hurt many people in her turn, bridled at the notion that she should hold back. *Why should I not? They cannot hurt me now!*

Someone can, the kind lady warned. *There will always be someone stronger than you. That is why a law that protects the weak will someday also protect you.*

So I must live by that law if I want its protection? Finister frowned. *That is a strange notion.* But she could see the sense in it, for she remembered with a shudder the burst of light in her mind when she had attacked Gregory Gallowglass.

There is that, the kind lady acknowledged, *but look at the little girl you were. Would it be right for someone older and stronger to hurt her for their own amusement simply because they could?*

Finister didn't even have to look—she knew in an instant that it was vile. *You mean that if it was wrong to do it to me, then it was wrong to do it to anyone,* she said slowly.

Even so, the kind lady agreed.

I do not hurt for amusement now, though, Finister protested. *I hurt for revenge—revenge for myself, or for other people who have been injured by the strong.*

Then you do know the rightness of the law.

I do not recognize the rightness of any law! Laws are tools of government, tools of the strong to oppress the weak!

There is no law that cannot be twisted against its original purpose, the kind lady agreed, *no law that the powerful can-*

not corrupt to misuse—but that corruption can be purged, the twists unwound. Without the law, everyone is a victim sooner or later. If we defend the law, it will protect the weak more often than not.

A dozen answers sprang to mind but somehow none seemed adequate, for the kind lady was presenting ideas Finister had not heard before. She wondered how Mama and Papa had missed this thought.

Unwilling to argue when she suddenly doubted all the old answers, she asked instead, *Are you my mother?*

Not the mother who bore you, no, the kind lady answered, *only your guardian while we search your life for this little while, search for the hurts that were done you.*

Why should we do that? Finister demanded, though she knew she had little choice—she recognized power when she saw it and could tell this woman had it, had far more power than she did.

Suddenly she saw the point of her law.

We must right the wrongs that were done you, the kind lady said, *insofar as we may.*

How can we do that?

Simply by seeing them with an adult's eyes and judging them with an adult's knowledge, the kind lady answered, and the tableau before them suddenly blurred into a whorl of colors, whirling, then steadying to show Finister herself, little Finny at seven, telling Mama how the big girls had pulled her hair and pinched her—without using their hands, of course. Mama, looking sad, uncovered Finny's guilt and lectured her on the need for taking orders from the big girls.

"The older you grow, the more people you can order," Papa agreed.

"I give orders to Rhea, and Rhea gives orders to Orma. Orma gives orders to Umi, Umi gives orders to Agnes, and so on down the line," Mama told her. "Any of them can give orders to you and I expect you to obey them. Do you understand?"

"Yes'm," Finny muttered, still tracing circles with her toe. Inside, a rebellious voice shouted, *It's not fair!*

But the kind lady was watching and said, *You are Chief Agent now. Do you still find it unfair?*

Fair or not, it is the way of the world, Finny said bitterly. *It is better to be the one who gives orders than to be the ones who have to take them.*

Then you found nothing wrong with the system, only with your place in it?

Oh, I saw fault enough! Finny retorted. *Wouldn't it be wonderful if no one had to take orders from anyone! But if they did, nothing would ever be done—there would be no way to coordinate groups.*

It is government, the kind lady said.

Of course it is. Finny smiled, secure in her knowledge—the kind lady obviously wasn't the omniscient being she pretended to be. *I have known this paradox for a long time, that only by government within SPITE will we manage to destroy the government of Gramarye. But when we have done that, SPITE's government will wither away.*

Then Papa was patting her shoulder and saying, "Don't worry, little one. When you grow big, you can give orders, too. For a year, you'll even be the oldest girl in the house and able to give orders to any of the other girls!"

Do you truly think SPITE's chain of command will wither away? the kind lady asked. *Before you answer, tell me—do you still work to abolish government because you believe it to be right and admire your leaders, or because you wish to please Mama?*

Before Finny could answer, the scene dissolved into a whirlpool of colors again. When it steadied, she was little Finny once more, stringing beans and trying to do it exactly as Uma had said—but it was Mama sitting beside her, not Uma, Mama smiling and saying, "That's very good, Finny. Break them up into sections an inch long, now. . . . No, you don't need to measure them, just make them about an inch—that one won't make three, so just break it in half. Yes, very good."

But that wasn't how it happened! Finny cried inside. *It was Uma, not Mama, and she found a dozen faults with the way*

I was doing it! Then Mama came and told me Uma was right, that I was doing it wrong!

No more, the kind lady's voice said. *The past may be set in stone, but your view of it is not. Were you doing the task as well as an eight-year-old could?*

Well, yes, but that still wasn't anywhere nearly as well as a fifteen-year-old could. Finny stopped, amazed at her own words. Then anger began to grow, anger at Uma for her fault-finding and at Mama for hers.

A dozen vignettes of memory followed—washing dishes, darning a sock, practice stitches on a sampler, her first effort at baking tea cakes, tending the four-year-old, and every time, Mama or one of the older girls scolded or criticized or corrected. Finally Finny cried inside, *Enough! I can't do it perfectly, you know! I'm only human—and only a child!*

Then she waited, quaking, for Mama's severe scowl, Mama's tongue-lashing, Mama's anger. . . .

Instead, the kind lady's voice said, *True. You were only a child—and only human. They should have applauded your accomplishments, then told you the largest ways in which you could improve.*

But would I ever have learned to do things right?

Over the years? Yes. Of course you would have.

Then the vignettes happened again, only this time Mama supervised Finny herself and only encouraged, then gave advice to better her work. Little Finny glowed with the approval, felt happiness flowering within her, even though she knew this wasn't what had really happened. Still, she knew it was what should have happened, knew that she was a far better person than she had believed at the time, and that was what mattered.

Then the rainbow whirled her away again and she was sitting in the schoolroom, listening to Mama talk about all the horrible things the King and Queen did, such as taking people's money and making laws to keep them from doing what they wanted and starting wars. She told them about SPITE, even though Finister was sure the two lessons had been a year or more apart—SPITE, the selfless and virtuous organization that spanned all the colonized planets and all of civilized time trying to save the people from the tyranny of VETO.

Then the kind lady was there, asking, *Do you still believe the anarchists of SPITE are virtuous and selfless?*

Finny thought of her superiors in the organization whom she had originally admired but who had ordered her to warm their beds, then of the luxuries each had acquired, even the sumptuous quarters of the Chief Agent, of the mission on which she had been assigned to steal some famous paintings from a castle, famous paintings that were not sold but stayed in the house of one of the senior officers. . . . *No.* Then, before the lady could say anything else, *But I most certainly do not believe that the totalitarians or royalists are any better!*

Nor do I, the kind lady agreed. *When ideals wane, self-interest rises. Let me show you pages from books you have not been allowed to see.*

There they were, peasants struggling to guide plows through black earth. Their feet were bound in rags, their tunics were of rough cloth frequently patched, their plows clumsy, heavy constructs of timber and cast iron, their oxen fat and muscular but the people scrawny and malnourished. Their growth was stunted, their faces haggard with weariness, the sores of vitamin deficiencies abundant on their skin.

Finister felt vindication—this was how the peasants lived under the Kings!

But the picture rippled and changed. The peasants drove purring machines now, machines that pulled plows with six plowshares each. They were well dressed in blue garments of stout cloth, unpatched; the feet on the pedals of the machines wore hardy brogans. Their faces were ruddy with health.

The land and machines belong to the State, the kind lady said, *but the people are well fed, well clothed, and healthy.*

It is a lie! Finister cried, though she knew it was not. In feeble protest, she added, *They have few luxuries!*

They have books available, and they all can read, the lady explained. *In their free hours they make their own decorations, cultivate their own gardens, and play music. Do they need more?*

Finister thought of her own early willingness to live without pleasures for the good of the Cause and her disillusionment in seeing the fripperies her superiors had collected. *Yes, they need more! Everyone wants more!*

Like this? the kind lady asked, and the picture rippled again to show people in brightly colored clothing pushing machines over lawns in front of houses that stood all in a row, well apart, along a tree-shaded street. In front of each house sat a strange-looking machine; others passed on the street with people inside, so Finny knew they were carriages. Each house was painted in different colors. Children played with balls on patches of pavements and rode wheeled contrivances. Some of them glided along the pavement with wheeled boots strapped to their feet; others drew on those pavements with colored chalk.

Finister's mind whirled with the richness of it. *Too much! Far too much! No one needs so much!* Then the fault-finding that she had learned so early and so well came to her rescue. *They have so little land!*

True, but they own it themselves, the kind lady said, *though many have borrowed heavily to buy it and must pay those loans back all their lives. They are the citizens of a democracy. There are many who are far more poor than these, but there are some who are even more rich.*

They are enslaved by money, Finister grumbled, but she lacked conviction.

The lady was silent, showing her kindness, for which Finister was grateful. She did not need to have it said out loud that Mama and Papa had lied to her, that SPITE had lied— or at least that they had told her only partial truths and kept her from learning any facts that contradicted the ideas they wanted her to believe.

But if she did not have Mama and Papa, she had nothing at all.

She looked up and found she was still in the schoolroom, though she was much older now, and Mama was telling them that winning was very important, because they all had to try to win against the King and Queen, and that was very hard, because the King and Queen were very rich and had very, very many soldiers.

Winning is not the only goal in life, the kind lady countered.

What else is there, then? Finister asked in surprise. *All life is struggle! Put two people in a room and you have a contest for dominance! If you do not win, you submit!*

Competition is only one of the ways in which people interact, the kind lady contradicted. *There is also cooperation. There are times to compete, surely, but there are times to help one another, too.*

Finister was silent, considering the idea—but in the classroom of memory, Mama was still lecturing, telling them that the King and Queen even had mind readers like Finny and her foster brothers and sisters helping them. Finny hated those other mind readers; they should have all been on the same side. Mama taught her a nice word for those Crown's espers: "traitors."

Thus they sundered you from your fellows, the kind lady told her. *They were not espers themselves, but needed psis to counter those who had accepted the Crown's offer of sanctuary—so they reared you to be weapons.*

Stung, Finister retorted, *Do not the king and queen rear the royal mind readers thus?*

We do not rear them at all, the kind lady said. *We do not take them at birth, but invite them to join when they are grown, or nearly grown.*

Finister noted the "we" with alarm—but listened intently nonetheless.

The royal witchfolk recruit grown espers who wish to be among their own kind and are already loyal to the Crown, the kind lady explained. *Often we must rescue those recruits from the anger and jealousy of their neighbors, or welcome lonely ones who, shunned by the villagers, have gone to seek hermitage in the woods or mountains. These we may try to persuade, and some choose to join us—but we do not take babies and indoctrinate them as they grow.*

Finister was silent, watching the tableau before her, trying to think of an objection. Finally she said, *Then you do not give refuge to foundlings?*

The Crown has many homes for foundlings, the kind lady

protested, *but none take only esper babies. It is not good for them to grow up completely isolated from their neighbors, after all, and there are not so many in any one parish.*

There were always enough to fill Mama and Papa's house! Did you truly think they discovered so many foundlings on their doorstep? the kind lady asked in surprise.

CHAPTER
-22-

Why . . . why, of course, Finister said, taken aback. *Two a year? Surely that is not so many!*

And that is what they told you, the kind lady said with a sigh. *There was little truth in it, I assure you. Those babes were brought from all over Gramarye and smuggled to that farmhouse, and most of them were neither orphans nor castaways.*

Finister went rigid. *What is this you tell me?* she demanded with terrible intensity.

That you are probably neither an orphan nor a foundling, the kind lady said with relentless pity. *Oh, some few were, I am sure—but I have looked into the minds of the anarchists who brought the babes, into the minds of the man and woman who reared you, and found that most of the babes were kidnapped from loving homes when they showed the first signs of psi powers.*

A scream of anger and anguish tore the world apart. It went crazy for a few minutes, becoming a swirl of colors that blinked in and out of darkness. Finally it steadied and Finister, exhausted and panting, realized that the scream had been her own. Gasping for breath, she demanded, *Proof! I must have proof!*

There it was, the world from Mama's eyes, taking a baby from the arms of a man whose breath steamed—winter, then—and who was saying, "Her parents will never miss her. They have a dozen brats already. The youngest is still nursing and this one was trying to push the other away from the breast with her mind."

The surroundings swam, and Finny saw a little cottage, modest but well kept. In a sunlit garden, a mother was picking beans while her baby slumbered in a cradle. The mother looked up at a sudden sound, then went quickly back into the house, leaving the baby alone.

The cradle came closer as the man ran up to it. Two hardened hands lifted the baby out and tucked it in the nook of his elbow. Then the cradle swam away and the road came closer again. The man who was carrying the baby swerved onto the road and ran along it until trees shadowed him on all sides. Then he slowed to a walk as a scream sounded behind him in the distance.

Another night, another baby, another admission of kidnapping—and another and another.

The anger boiled up again, but Finister was too furious to scream. She stared, breast heaving, and in the silence, the vision changed to the street of the village near Mama and Papa's farm, with the boys out to taunt.

"Nyah-nyah! Little foundlings!"

Finny turned to stare at the four richly dressed boys who were thumbing their noses at the girls. Orma stood her straightest and turned Finny's head frontward. "Don't look, Finny. Don't pay them any attention at all!"

"Didn't have a father," two of the boys chanted in derisive singsong. "Never knew your mother!"

Then it was not true? Finister cried. *We need never have suffered that humiliation, none of us?*

One or two, in the time you were growing up, the kind lady told her. *No more.*

Finister's heart twisted with the need to know if she were one of those two—but she knew ways to find out now.

Why did they do it? she cried. *Why couldn't they have at least told us we were orphans?*

Because they wanted you to be loyal only to them, the kind lady explained. *They did not want you thinking that you had family somewhere to whom you could go, or to whom you might owe love or allegiance—and they did not want you becoming fond of the village, beginning to think of it as home or learning to love its people.*

You cannot mean it! They reared us to work for the good of the people!

All the people, yes, the kind lady said, *but not those closest to home. They want you to work for the people only through SPITE. They want you for themselves.*

Finister groaned, sinking in on herself. She searched for an argument but found none—other than to question the kind lady's motives, and with them, her whole argument. When she woke from this dream, she would seek evidence—but she suspected it would only prove the kind lady's tale. There were too many little questions she had ignored as she grew up, too many answers not given.

Then a glaring, horrid memory—the slaughter of a sheep, and herself wielding the knife. The others congratulated her on her courage, though quietly, and when they were alone, Mama gathered Finny's head onto her breast to let the teenager weep. "I know it's hard, Finny, but the world is grim. It's a cruel place, and the only way to live in it is to become capable of cruelty yourself, and to harden your heart to others' pain."

Then she was outside the event again, watching herself weep, and the kind lady was saying, *I disagree. The world can be cruel, yes, but it can also be kind and loving. You must protect yourself against others' pain that you cannot avoid, but if you shut out all feeling, if you truly harden your heart, you shall close yourself off from all that is tender and affectionate.*

Finister frowned, uncertain. *If that were true, why would Mama have said such things?*

The better to make you able to kill human beings, the kind lady said. *That is why they insisted that each of you help in the slaughtering. You were trained to kill; you began with chickens, progressed through sheep and pigs, and ended with men.*

Finister said nothing, only watched her younger self sob in Mama's arms and brooded. It would explain why Mama had given her so much attention on her first slaughtering—to make her wish to please Mama by killing again. It certainly was training for assassination, especially if you learned to block out all the victim's pain and anguish and to ignore your own qualms, the suspicion that killing might be wrong.

Then, suddenly, she saw a succession of all the men and women she had murdered, thirteen deaths by the power of her own mind, by the silent explosion in the brain or the stopping of the heart—deaths that were quick and merciful, but murders nonetheless.

It was not my fault! Finister cried. *You have seen even now how they made me do it!*

That explains your deeds but does not excuse them, the kind lady said. *You might as easily try to excuse your foster parents' actions by saying that they did it for the Cause.*

They did!

Did they hurt you any the less thereby? Is your soul any the less corrupted thereby?

She waited for Finister to answer, but she only stood mute, her mind churning, trying to find some concept that was secure, to rebuild a new understanding of her world.

The damage they did you is still done, no matter what the reasons were, the kind lady said. *Only by acknowledging their responsibility, by telling you that what they did was wrong, could they begin to heal the wounds they made.*

They do not see that they have done anything wrong, Finister said in sullen tones, *nor do I!*

I think that you do, the kind lady contradicted. *If you wish to regain control of your own life, to win back your soul, you must accept the blame you have earned and the damage it has done. They may have reared you to it, but it was nonetheless your mind that struck the fatal blow.*

The world whirled again, making Finister dizzy, but before she could cry out in protest it steadied again and the words froze on her tongue, for she was looking at the hayloft of her parents' barn with a sixteen-year-old Finny coming up the ladder to make sure the barn cat had not yet started to labor. She went over to Puss's corner and parted the hay to look down at the swollen-tummied feline, who lifted her head and parted her eyelids to purr at Finny—but behind her, Orly's head appeared on the ladder, then all of him, and he swung off, grinning.

"Why, Finny! Have the kittens come, then?"

"Oh! You startled me!" Finny leaped up, then saw it was

Orly and couldn't help letting out some of that special feeling as she gave him a sleepy-eyed smile. "No, they haven't come yet, Orly. But it's late enough that we need to watch her closely. Why are you here?"

"Papa sent me to knock down the old hornets' nests so the bee-sties wouldn't come back," Orly said, then looked at Puss. "Watch her closely now? We should have been watching her closely two months ago!" Orly grinned as he came nearer. "It's a little late."

He was standing a little too close, and Finny felt a strange new presence about him, something like her own special feeling, and wondered if Orly were a projective, too. They talked, some inane chatter about Puss, when all the while they only wanted to talk about one another. Then Orly stepped a little closer, reached out to touch her waist, to almost touch her waist, and his face hovered near, so very near, and the adult Finister watching remembered how his breath had smelled sweet and musky, remembered how she had felt her special feeling growing as she looked deeply into his eyes, the delightful shivering sensation all through her body as their thoughts mingled and she swayed just a little forward and their lips brushed, brushed again, and stayed. She watched her younger self melt against Orly, pressing and grinding against him. She remembered that she hadn't known she was doing that while it happened, had only been aware of her whole body melting against his as that fatal first real kiss had deepened into sensations that set her whole body on fire.

For a moment, adult Finister longed to be back in Orly's arms, longed for that sweetness, that yearning again. Then the kind lady's face appeared beside the young lovers, smiling fondly at them and saying, *How fortunate that you both came to this loft at the same moment, or this adventure would never have begun.*

Even now, Finister's face grew hot with embarrassment, and she protested, *It must have been an accident. Surely Mama would never have sent me to the hayloft if she had known Papa had just sent Orly up.*

Would she not? the kind lady asked. *You learned later that all the other graduates of the farm had encounters that began as secret assignations like this—that led to sexual initiation and this same early bliss. Could they really have all been accidental?*

She had put Finister's own covert suspicions into words. Afraid to confront them, Finister lashed out. *You're saying they arranged that private meeting, that they wanted me to have that first tryst with Orly. Impossible! They told us it was wrong! Why would they have maneuvered us into doing something that disgusted them?*

Because they did not really think it wrong, the kind lady said, *only useful. Remember!*

A haze seemed to spread over the hayloft. When it cleared, the hay was lit only by moonbeams that managed to find a way through the chinks in the wall, to illuminate cast-aside clothing, and two young lovers separating to stare into one another's eyes, panting and both alarmed yet exalted by the emotional and sensational explosion they had just experienced. Then they rolled back together, kissing fervently, deeply, trying to raise that ecstasy again. The haze rose over them, and Finister was aware of her own pulse hammering. She started to protest, but the haze cleared, showing her younger self just climbing down to the barn floor, with Orly a step behind her. Laughing, they ran lightly out the door . . .

. . . and froze to see Mama and Papa striding toward them, their faces red with wrath.

Even now, Finister shrank from this most horrible of all memories, from the intensity of her foster parents' rage, from the humiliation, guilt, and shame they had heaped upon her and Orly—but their lips moved without sound, and the kind lady's face appeared between her and them. *It was wrongly done, and they knew it, and at a moment when you were both most vulnerable. They linked your first sexual experience with shame and guilt, and by doing so, they deliberately destroyed your ability to ever enjoy it again, or even to remember this first experience without pain. They publicized something intimate instead of teaching you how to keep it private even in your most ecstatic moments. They contaminated something pure; they desecrated the part of the experience that was spiritual, convinced you it did not exist, that there was only physical sensation and nothing of true joy—and did all this purposely.*

Purposely? Deliberately? You talk nonsense! Finister cried, all the more angrily because it resonated with her own unspoken fears. *Why would they have done such a thing?*

To debase your self-esteem and convince you that you were fit only for prostitution, the kind lady said, *the better to make you a tool for their use. They destroyed the core of your sexuality and left you only the husk and the techniques of seduction, the better to make you a more effective agent and assassin in ways that only women can be.*

The shriek started deep inside and burgeoned upward and outward into a wild scream of rage that went on and on as Finister took hold of the picture of Mama and Papa ranting and whirled it about and about with her mind, circling it over her head as though on a rope, swinging it again and again as the scream echoed on and on, deep and ugly and shrill and raw until she finally let the picture go to fly away, sailing farther and farther over the farmyard and house, over the trees, over the horizon, and out, far away from Finny's world.

With them, the farm disappeared, leaving a void of darkness, and Finister collapsed in on herself, panting and heaving with exertion, stunned and dizzy and frightened by the magnitude of her own anger. Panic clawed up in her at the thought of losing Mama and Papa, of the farm and her foster siblings.

Then she regained self-awareness with a shock of alarm. *I cannot hate them! Without them I have nothing, am nothing!*

Only without them can you truly be yourself, the kind lady's voice said sternly. *You must cast off the chains with which they bound you and discover yourself as you truly are, as you might have been without the devastation they wreaked upon your mind and heart and soul.*

Finny longed to believe the words but still felt the numbing fear of being alone. *It is all right,* she assured herself frantically, *I still have SPITE.*

Then she froze, suddenly realizing why she had clung so frantically to SPITE, no matter how foul the tasks her superiors ordered her to execute.

Yes, said the kind lady. *Your foster parents made sure that, deep within, you saw SPITE as an extension of the farm, as a home away from home, as a place where you might feel secure when you had to go out into the world.*

It is that for which they trained me, Finister protested. *It is my purpose in living.*

It was they who made it so, not you, the kind lady reminded. *They never even suggested you might have a choice.*

Choice? The concept burst upon Finister like an explosion of light, leaving her numb. *But—what else could I do?*

You have risen to be Chief Agent by your own strength and intelligence, the kind lady reminded her. *SPITE is nothing without you now, but you have no real need of them—only the illusion of such need. Step out of the shadow they have cast over you, put behind you the fears and self-contempt they inculcated in you. Discover your own virtue, your own worthiness, for if you are the most potent of the anarchists' tools, you can also be the most outstanding woman of your generation—aye, in virtue and wisdom as well as in strength and intelligence.*

But I am nothing! I am corrupted!

Suddenly she was thrashing her arms and legs, though they struck nothing. She lay against something soft but secure and, looking up, saw a blur of a face framed by touseled hair matted with the sweat of labor, a face that sweetened as a smile of delight and amazement lit its features. "She is beautiful! I shall call her Allouette."

Then it was gone, and Finister stood alone, crying, *What was that? Who? What name?*

Your earliest memory, the kind lady said, *dredged by magic from the depths of your mind. She was your mother, and the name she gave you is your true one.*

It cannot be! It is a trick, a deception!

Memories can deceive, the kind lady agreed, *but this one does not. Allouette is the skylark, whose music charms, and you are a woman of power and great magic who can move a world—this world.*

I cannot be! They would have told me! But Finister knew that was not so.

That is why they needed to shackle you, the kind lady corrected. *Burst your fetters, stand free, and grow into your true self. If you were a valued tool, you can be of ten times greater value as a woman.*

Finister tottered in the void, wanting to believe but afraid. Then she felt a wind at her back, a wind that rose, strengthening to a gale, and it was all she could do to hold her place against its push.

It is the wind of Destiny, the kind lady said. *Have the courage to rise without broom or wing and ride it. Trust your destiny, trust your own talent and intelligence, your own immense worth, and see where they all may take you.*

A vision of a castle sprang up in Finister's mind, but with shock and amazement she heard herself saying, *What use is a castle?*

None, unless it shelters people from attack, the kind lady said, *or serves as a storehouse for food to feed them when famine comes, and medicines to heal them when they are ill. You who were reared to serve the people—can you make a castle that will truly do so?*

Yes! Finister's soul shouted, but she withheld the words from her lips, shocked and frightened by her own essence.

Go and do it, then, the kind lady's voice said, and the darkness seemed to deepen around Finister; she stood naked in the void, the tatters of the illusion in which her foster parents had wrapped her drifting away, drifting thin, fading, extinguishing themselves. At last she stood bare and shivering in the cold wind, still not quite daring to trust it to bear her away, to trust herself to ride it, to fly, but the kind lady's voice echoed around her, saying, *Rise and go. Explore your soul, sound your own depths, then rise and grow and become all you can.*

That last word rang and echoed and built into a whirlwind of sound that surrounded Finister and dazed her to distraction, vibrating all about her, within her, making her one with it. With glad relief, she realized her consciousness had joined with it and was dissipating, and surrendered herself to harmony and to the Void.

•   •   •

Gwen went limp, shudders racking her every limb. Geoffrey and Cordelia instantly caught her between them.

"You have exhausted yourself, Mama!" Cordelia cried in alarm.

"I shall . . . revive. . . ." Gwen gasped. "What of . . . yourselves?"

Cordelia paused a moment to take stock; in her concern for her mother, she hadn't noticed her own depletion. "I am wearied, but far less so than yourself."

"I, too," Geoffrey said. He glared daggers at Gregory. "This lass of yours had better be worth such a wasting of our mother's strength."

"I need only . . . rest," Gwen said, beginning to catch her breath. "Then I shall be . . . stronger than ever." With an effort, she straightened. "As to Allouette . . ."

"Who?" Cordelia and Geoffrey asked together, but Gregory protested, "Is she not truly Finister?"

"She is not," Gwen said. "I unearthed a buried memory, her very first after birth. She has used it as a *nom de guerre* several times but never used any other more than once. It is her true name, that which her mother gave her at birth."

"Allouette," Gregory said, wondering, then again and again, tasting the word, making it a part of himself. "Allouette . . . Allouette . . ."

"Je te plumerai," Geoffrey said bitterly, "and her plumes were most definitely plucked."

"So that she could not fly freely," Cordelia agreed, then said, remembering, "Allouette—skylark."

"You must never call her that without her permission," Gwen said sternly. "You must not let her know that you have heard of it until she tells you."

"Then why did you tell us, Mother?" Cordelia asked.

"Because Gregory must know it is her true name," Gwen said, "not merely another she has invented."

"I shall take that to heart, even as I forget the name," Gregory promised.

"That is well," Gwen said. "Be sure that she shall be well worth your love and my labor—if my attempt at healing has indeed succeeded."

"But what of Gregory's labor?" asked Cordelia. "For surely there shall be a great deal of constant work needed to woo and win this lass, then more to bond her to him."

"That is true of all romances," Gwen told her. "The effort never ceases. You must win one another's love again and again, all your life long, and work at the bonding as surely as any mason building a castle."

"But it will shelter you all your days."

Gregory nodded. "I expected nothing less."

Nor did any of them. They had all watched Gwen's lifelong struggle to keep Rod believing he was good enough for her. Only Cordelia, though, had noticed his constant effort to convince Gwen that he was good enough for her, too, and looking back to her toddling days, she suspected there had been several times when her mother had doubted that rather strongly.

" 'Tis well," Gwen said, satisfied. "Be mindful, though, that this Al . . . this Finister will have all the self-doubts and uncertainties of a lass of fourteen, though she has the memories and experience and skills of her twenty-four years."

"A difficult combination." Gregory frowned. "Will she, then, struggle with the guilt of those years, too?"

Cordelia looked up, startled by his insight.

"She will," Gwen confirmed, "and will have a greater need to prove that you love her for herself, not for her body. Why do you love her, my son?"

"I cannot pretend to be immune to her beauty," Gregory admitted, "though I have seen it in so many forms that I begin to doubt it enough to cancel its force. I also cannot claim indifference to the allure she projects, though I know it to be only a skill of the mind, like to my ability to reason. But I am most attracted by the fire of her spirit, by her intelligence, her ingenuity in solving a problem, and her tenacity, her refusal to give up when solution after solution proves inadequate."

"The problem being yourself," Cordelia said darkly, "or at least, the enslaving of you by her erotic charms."

Gregory made an impatient gesture, waving the comment away. "The problem matters little; the intelligence and the tenacity do."

Geoffrey smiled, amused. "How like you to be attracted by such turns of the mind!"

"How like me indeed," Gregory agreed, "and I feel no need to apologize for what I am."

Geoffrey's smile disappeared. "Nor do I." He seemed to bristle.

Gwen interposed smoothly. "The question, then, is not her worthiness of my effort, but whether the healing will succeed."

Gregory shrugged. "Only experience will tell."

"Yes, but if this healing has failed, the proof will be your death or enslavement," Geoffrey said grimly. "Guard yourself well, my brother."

"That is one lesson the youngest learns well." At last Gregory smiled. "Fear not for me, my sib." Then he frowned again. "But how if there is no improvement in her?"

"Then you must summon me," Gwen said, "and we must confer as to the meting out of justice again."

"Justice." Cordelia looked down at the unconscious woman. "How if she is cured, Mother? How many has she slain?"

"Thirteen," Gwen said, "though only one was of her own choice—her former commander."

"Then is it justice to let her go free when she has slain so many?" Geoffrey asked.

"Justice must be tempered by mercy," Gregory said quickly.

"Do not underestimate the agony of the ordeal through which I have guided her," Gwen said, "and the pains of the humiliations that have gone before. Still, if she devotes the rest of her life to aiding people in need, can we not say there is at least some measure of justice served?"

"*If* she so dedicates her life," Geoffrey said, his skepticism clear upon his face.

"Perhaps that will be the measure of her healing," Cordelia suggested.

"A life for a life," Gregory said, musing. "If she saves thirteen, will that not be justice?"

"Ask the families of those she has slain, brother."

"It will be hard enough for us to say that she has earned mercy," Gwen said. "What will be hardest of all is for her to forgive herself. You must be very patient, my son, while she struggles to believe she is worthy of love—indeed, that she is worthy of life."

"I shall rival Job!" Gregory said fervently.

"She has been your companion in your search for this Site of Power you have found," Gwen mused. "Is it not right, then, that you accompany her on her quest to discover how she may make reparations and forgive herself?"

"She had little choice about his company," Geoffrey reminded her, "and her motives were scarcely helpful."

"Her motives may have been sinister," Gwen said, "but you may be sure she had every choice. She might not have been able to escape our Gregory, but she did not know that."

"The woman has no difficulty believing in her own abilities, that is true," Cordelia said.

"No, only in her own worth." Gwen laid a hand on her youngest's shoulder. "Go wisely and warily, my son—but remember that in this instance, it is wise to follow your heart. Only use your knowledge and caution to ward it."

"I shall, Mother," Gregory promised.

Gwen turned, leaning on Cordelia's arm. "I believe I shall ride with you, daughter."

"Cling tightly to your own broomstick nevertheless," Cordelia said nervously, and the two brooms rose together to make a seat and a handgrip for Gwen.

The young men watched the women rise into the predawn sky. Then Geoffrey turned to his little brother, made an abortive gesture with his hands, and said, "Fare you well, my sib. Good fortune attend you."

"And you, bigger brother," Gregory said with a smile.

They clasped hands, Geoffrey frowning earnestly into Gregory's eyes, perhaps remembering the two-year-old who had toddled after him once. Earnestly he said, "Patience is all, brother—patience and enticement. The reward is well worth the effort."

Gregory understood that he was speaking of more than

making love. "I thank you, brother," he said. "I assure you your teachings shall not go in vain."

"Fare well, then! Remember to block with your left and test each coin!" Geoffrey took two steps back, squared his shoulders, and disappeared with a bang.

Gregory stood staring at the space where he had been for some minutes, musing and pondering. Then he looked down at the woman who slept at his feet, looked down and knelt down. Taking her hand, he settled himself to wait for the dawn and her awakening.

CHAPTER

-23-

From the depths of sleep, she heard the lark heralding the dawn. The song drew her upward, away from the refuge of unconsciousness. She resisted bitterly, fighting the compulsion—until she remembered that she was the lark now, Allouette, and it was her namesake calling

Up from the womb of sleep she rose. Even then, fully conscious, she lay with her eyes closed, willing sleep to return, but it held aloof. Finally and with massive regret, she opened her eyes.

Slight though the light was, it hurt, and she squinted against it, looking upward, seeking the lark—but she found the boy instead, the callow youth whom she had been set, and set herself, to enslave or slay.

Massive remorse overwhelmed her, and the sight of his face blurred. She blinked away the tears angrily—how foolish they were, when she needed to see the world clearly! She knew with a certainty that reached to the roots of her soul that she would never again kill any human creature unless it were trying to kill her. Even then . . .

She became aware that she was sitting up, that an arm supported her, encircling her shoulders. She flinched, moving a little forward, away from the touch, and looked up into the face beside hers, the deep and aching concern in his eyes. *Poor fool, he is still under my spell,* she thought, and withdrew any vestige of projection to free him.

The look of concern stayed, the arm still hovering an inch from her back.

Alarm seized her. Was he so thoroughly bewitched that she could not free him? Then her old cynicism came to her rescue—perhaps he was only concerned for another fellow crea-

Christopher Stasheff

ture. After all, only in that last embrace had she felt his desire, and had followed it back to . . .

She winced, sheering away from the memory of that attempt to slay—but it drew all the memories of her earlier murders, and the tears came so hot and fast that she could not stanch them.

Gregory gathered her in against his chest, murmuring, "They are only tears, sweet lady, and the natural overflow of a heart filled with emotion. Let them fall."

His voice was so tender, so reassuring, that for a moment she gave in and relaxed into his embrace. Then she remembered that he, too, had been one of her intended victims and stiffened, pushing away from him, angrily dashing her tears to the ground, trying to stop their flow. She sought for a thought to distract, anything to take her mind from this crushing burden of guilt—and his even more crushing sympathy. "The kind lady," she gasped, "the woman who led me through my dream quest. Where is she?"

"I know not, for I have not seen your dream," Gregory told her, "but I believe it was my mother, the Lady Gwendylon, for it is she who sat beside you and labored to heal the rifts in your mind and heart."

"Lady Gwendylon!" Allouette cried, aghast. "My enemy, and wife of my greatest enemy? The mother of those I sought to butcher? *Your* mother?"

"Even so," Gregory told her. "She saw great worth in you and labored to save you therefore."

The tears sprang afresh, but Allouette twisted angrily away when Gregory reached out to comfort. How could she accept his solace when she had sought to slay him? How could she accept this healing when she had sought to slay or spay her healer's children?

Long experience in argument brought the excuse to her lips: "She sought to save me for you! It was your desire, not hers, that healed me!"

"There is truth to that," Gregory admitted, "but she would not want to see me victim of a *femme fatale*. Nay, she would not even have attempted such a work if she had not seen great goodness buried within you."

"It cannot be! I am corrupted, I am wicked!"

"But you know the truth of that now," Gregory said quietly, "and there is none."

"There is a great deal! I have slain thirteen, mangled one, and sought to slay or warp—yourself! Your brother! Your sister!"

"It was my sister herself who bade me spare you," Gregory told her.

Allouette whirled, staring at him in amazement—then saw something more in his eyes. "You would have slain me! You would have executed me for my crimes! You must have decided that, for it was the only just and reasonable course!"

"Then favor Cordelia for showing me that mercy is as important as justice," Gregory said, "and emotion as vital as reason."

"She took my part only because killing me would have rent your heart for all time!"

"It would indeed." Gregory looked directly and deeply into her eyes. "Your death by any hand would have caused me agony—but I should never have recovered if that hand had been my own."

Witting or not, the wave of emotion swept out from him to engulf her, a wave so powerful that it made her shiver. Then it swept back and was gone—he had realized he was projecting and stopped—but the force of his love left her trembling. In defense, she accused, "Your emotion comes only from the desire I cast and raised in you!"

"It does not," Gregory told her, "for I held on to reason against the most intense of your projections and knew them for what they were, only tricks of your own mind."

"Indeed! Then how did I win your heart?"

"By your intelligence and tenacity," Gregory said, "by the fire of your spirit and your craving for life. It was that which made me fall in love—though when I saw your true face and form, I was bound past withdrawing."

"My true face and form?" Allouette stared at him, astounded. "I am plain, I am lacking!"

"You are beautiful," Gregory said, voice reverberating with emotion. "Your face is enchanting, your body voluptuous.'' Then the emotion dwindled as though he had dammed a stream, and he sat back on his heels a little. ''Mind you, I could have withstood the desire your loveliness aroused in me if I had not already become besotted with your mind and your character.''

''I have no character!''

''But you do not deny your mind.'' Gregory smiled with amused affection.

She blushed. Allouette actually felt her face grow hot for the first time in eight years. She turned away, pushing herself to her feet. ''Enough of such nonsense! We have a journey to complete.''

Gregory rose with her, a slight smile still on his lips, a glow still in his eyes.

She glanced at him, then glanced away. Seeking to change the subject, she said, ''Where is this mother of yours who has been my guide?''

''Gone to rest,'' Gregory said, ''for even with all our energies to draw upon, she is most thoroughly wearied.''

''All!'' Allouette turned to stare at him. ''Who is 'all'?''

''Myself,'' Gregory said, ''and Cordelia and Geoffrey.''

Allouette barely stifled a wail of despair. To be saved by her enemies! Grasping at straws, she said acidly, ''But your eldest brother had no part in this.''

''He could not, since he is most distant, journeying among the stars,'' Gregory said, ''but even he spoke for mercy toward you. I doubt not he would have lent his strength if he had been here.''

Allouette bit her lip to keep from crying out. It was too poignant, too humiliating, to have all of them forgiving her! She bowed her head, squeezing her eyes shut, but the tears came anyway. ''I have wronged you, I have wronged you all! However may I make amends, however can I repay this kindness to cease its tearing at me?''

''By aiding others,'' Gregory said simply. ''Let kindness pass from person to person in a stream that never ends and it will grow most amazingly on the way.''

Allouette stared at him in astonishment. Then she said

softly, "I am having a most amazing number of revelations today."

She turned away to hide her face from him. "How you must despise me, all of you!"

"We do not," Gregory said, "for we all realize that your spirit was twisted quite deliberately, that you were trained and molded to be an assassin and traitor, warped by lies and by coercion of which you were unaware. We despise those who have done this to you, but not you yourself."

"How can you not," Allouette said, "when you know what I have done?"

"Because I have seen the great goodness in you that was buried by your rearing, and my mother confirmed it when she had read your memories." Gregory frowned. "She did say, though, that your greatest difficulty will be forgiving yourself."

"Indeed." Allouette turned to glare at him, angered by the feeling of truth the statement raised in her. "What else did she say?"

"That since you accompanied me in finding my Site of Power, it is only right that I accompany you on your quest to discover your true nature."

"True nature? I know my true nature! I am a slut and murderess!"

"That is what people have made you, not the essence of yourself. Already you begin to seek ways to make reparations for your past conduct so that you may forgive yourself."

"Reparations?" Allouette gave him a thin and bitter smile. "So you are to help me find a punishment drastic enough to satisfy even myself, is that it?"

"Perhaps," Gregory allowed. "I do not think we shall know your nature until we have found it."

"Yet you claim to know it already!"

"Of course." Gregory beamed upon her. "You are sweetness and tenderness, intelligence and quickness of wit, tenacity and diligence."

Allouette felt her face growing hot again and turned away quickly. "You are mistaken, sir."

"Let us see." Gregory glanced at the horses; their reins

untied themselves from the tree limbs to which they'd been bound. The two beasts looked up, then came plodding over to them. "Mount," Gregory invited, "and seek. Find your true nature and prove me wrong."

"A dare?" Allouette's eyes kindled; she was much more at home with competition. She stepped up to her palfrey, but Gregory caught her around the waist and lifted her up. She lost her smile and settled in the saddle rather indignantly, though she was surprised all over again by his strength. "I shall mount by myself in future, sir, if you do not mind!"

"If it pleases you, I shall refrain," Gregory said in mock penitence. He mounted and turned his horse's head toward the forest trail. "Where shall we travel?"

"Must you not still take me to Runnymede?"

"Aye, but there are many roads that lead there, and some are longer than others. Which would you choose?"

Allouette eyed him narrowly and said, "That depends on our goal. What do you think we seek?"

Gregory shrugged. "Perhaps you will discover that you wish to spend the rest of your life trying to aid the poor and the relatives of your victims." She bridled, and he added hastily, "Other than my family. Perhaps you will find some greater work that will benefit everyone indirectly, such as a cure for poverty or war."

"You develop fantasies, sir!"

"Of such dreams are better worlds made." Gregory shrugged. "Or perhaps your penance will take some form that I cannot imagine, but that you can and will."

"Then we go we know not where, to seek we know not what," Allouette interpreted.

"Why, just so." Gregory flashed her a grin. "This much I know, however—that once you have set yourself upon this quest, you shall not stop until you have found what you seek."

"If it exists."

"Even if it does not."

"You have more faith in me than I have, sir," she said darkly.

"I have indeed," Gregory agreed. "Shall we ride?" Not

waiting for an answer, he thumped his heels against his horse's sides and guided it down the forest trail.

Allouette watched him go, resenting his confidence, resenting his belief in her. But when all was said and done, where else had she to go? Searching her heart, she found she had purged it completely of any desire to follow the path set for her by her foster parents and their organization. With a sigh, she shook the reins and told her horse to follow Gregory's.

As they rode away from the pale wall he had been building, Gregory glanced at Allouette with concern; she was very subdued, and he wondered at her brooding, hoping that she would be able to absorb and cope with all the new information she had gained. For a moment, he wished that the old seductive Finister would reappear. He realized, though, that the image was only that, an image, deliberately fashioned and the result of methodical exploitation, so he retreated into his old reserve, becoming again the soul of politeness.

They pitched camp at sunset. Gregory brewed a stew of salt beef and roots; Allouette asked how he knew which to choose, and he showed her. He was tempted to caution her about the ones that were poisonous but had second thoughts. Then he had third thoughts—if she still could not be trusted, he preferred to know it at once. Besides, he honestly believed she had really put all that behind her. He told her which plants were unhealthy or inedible as he seasoned the stew with wild herbs and parsley.

"This is women's knowledge," Allouette said as they ate, "or monks' knowledge. How came you to learn it?"

"I have a hunger to learn everything I can." Gregory smiled. "You are scarcely the first to tell me that I think like a monk."

"Why do you seek it?" Allouette demanded. "Riches? Power?"

"Simply for the joy of learning," Gregory answered. "If there is a use for the knowledge, I will discover that someday, too. All I really care about, though, is the learning."

Allouette studied him for a few minutes, chewing, then swallowed and delivered her verdict. "If that is so, you are a fool."

"It is not the first time I have been told that, either," Gregory said wryly.

Allouette made no apologies but was silent for the rest of the meal, and very thoughtful.

When she was done, she joined him in scouring their bowls and spoons, then said, "I am most amazingly wearied."

"Scarcely amazing," Gregory said. "You may have slept a night and a day, but that sleep was filled with a year's effort."

Allouette blinked in surprise. "That long?" Then, quickly, "Also, my head throbs with an ache. I shall lay me down to sleep, an it please you."

"Do so, of course," Gregory said. "I shall keep watch."

As usual, Allouette thought, but did not say it. He was perfectly understanding, which irritated her, but she knew that resentment was irrational and lay down on her bed of bracken. She had been lying about the headache, but she had been quite truthful about exhaustion and felt her eyes closing almost of their own accord. At the last second, though, she saw Gregory settling into his trance, sitting cross-legged, hands on his knees, gazing off into the forest, seeing more of his inner landscape than the outer. Resentment sparked again and she determined to learn how he did it.

But not now. Now all she cared was that the warm darkness beckoned, and for a few hours at least, she did not have to worry about the cares and struggles of life.

He still sat unmoving when the birds woke her. Somehow that bothered her. She stretched, stretched her whole body as sensuously as possible, but he reacted no more than any wood. She considered trying to wake him from his trance by tickles and husky words, then realized why the thought had come—she was still convinced that only sexuality could gain a man's attention. She scolded herself—she did not really need attention, and certainly not the kind that her well-practiced allure would bring. Still, she found Gregory's meditation insulting, for he seemed to ignore her.

A dilemma, and a pretty one. She wished his attention, but not as the result of her erotic projection. How could she achieve it?

Fight fire with fire, of course. If he would ignore her, she would ignore him—but for just as good a reason. She decided that she should study his form of meditation. Besides, sharing his trance might win his attention when nothing else did.

Ridiculous! she told herself. *How can he pay attention to you when that trance ignores the whole world?*

Still, it was an idea worth developing. She set about fanning the coals and setting the kettle over the fire to boil.

These signs of morning and waking cued Gregory to rouse from his trance when her self-display had not; he began to stir, a turn of the wrist here, a deeper breath there, then rose slowly, stretching and inhaling the aroma of the morning. Then he looked down at Allouette with a smile. "Good morrow."

"Good day," she returned. "You must teach me how to do that."

"What?" Gregory asked, staring. "To stretch? But you know that already."

So he *had* noticed. With a little self-satisfied smile, she said, "Yes, but I do not know your trick of waking sleep. How do you do it?"

Gregory sat down and began to tell her. She frowned with skepticism but attempted the first stage of meditation, sitting cross-legged with back straight and hands in her lap. She was amazed to find a feeling of tranquillity stealing over her as her breathing slowed and her pulse began to beat in her ears. The forest before her eyes began to seem removed, as though it were something seen through a thick pane of glass.

"Rise, now," Gregory said softly. "A step a day is enough. It is best learned slowly."

Her heart began to beat more quickly, her breathing grew deeper and faster, and the world became closer, more immediate. She felt the transition back to her ordinary state very clearly and turned to stare at Gregory. "Amazing!"

Gregory nodded, smiling, eyes glowing. "It is no mere trick."

"No, I can see that." Allouette turned away, a little shaken because she realized the implication: The trance could increase the effectiveness of her psi powers amazingly. Even more remarkably, she realized that she could still be totally aware and prepared to defend herself. "Will I remain cognizant of the real world if I learn the deeper trance?"

"You will," Gregory assured her, "but it must be learned slowly, for it requires skill as well as knowledge. Also, there are dangers on that road; you must learn it from someone who has travelled it already."

She gave him an arch glance. "Whom did you have in mind?"

Gregory only smiled in answer and explained, "You shall have to practice."

She did. As the days passed and her trances deepened, she was amazed to discover how much she noticed that she had never registered before, even beginning to understand ecological interactions—then began to see parallels between them and the ways in which people related to one another. Little by little she began to suspect the existence of something greater than individual human beings, perhaps even greater than political organizations.

But that came slowly, over weeks. For the rest of that day she helped break camp and rode on into the forest with Gregory.

They spoke with one another now and then as they rode, until Allouette grew bored, gave in to habit and temptation, and began to work double entendres into the conversation in hopes of seeing Gregory blush. Instead, he turned the topic to the ribald deeds of the old Greek gods and soon had her laughing at the variety of their liaisons with mortals.

Thus in high good humor, they rode out of the forest to see a large house before them, and behind it, a castle on a hill. As they came closer, though, they saw two mounted men come riding around the side of the house, driving a woman and children before them.

CHAPTER
-24-

"How dare they!" Allouette exploded. "Will the government never cease exploiting the weak?"

"If that woman lived in that house, I think she may be more a member of what you call the government than one of the downtrodden," Gregory said. "See—her gown is damask, and her children wear good leather boots, not peasants' buskins."

"No matter what they wear, she is oppressed at this moment! What, sir, will you see her suffer and not raise a hand to defend her?"

One of the soldiers swung his arm up for a backhanded slap at the woman. Allouette cried out in anger and kicked her horse into a canter, shouting, "Now I bid you *hold*!"

The man's arm froze in midair. He looked up at it in alarm; then his face twisted with effort, but his arm stayed high.

Smiling, eyes glowing, Gregory rode after Allouette. If this were not a test of her newfound love of virtue, nothing would be.

Allouette cantered past the soldier, snatching his pike from his nerveless hand. "Flee, woman!" Then she turned her horse and walked it in until the point touched the man's throat.

His comrade shouted and spurred his horse, reaching out to yank Allouette off her mount—but a fat blue spark jumped from her shoulder to his hand. He shrieked and reined in, blowing on his fingers.

Allouette gave Gregory an angry glance. "I shall fight my own battles, thank you." Only a glance; she kept her gaze fixed on the first soldier.

"Witch!" the second soldier howled.

267

"Aye, and one too hot for you."

With a yell, a third soldier came riding around the corner of the house, lowering his pike. Allouette spared him one disgusted glance, and the pike wilted. He swerved wide around her, staring at the limp pole.

"You had best begone ere other staves turn incapable of stiffness," Allouette told him.

All three soldiers stared at her in horror, then turned their horses and rode. A hundred feet away, the one with the elevated arm pulled up and turned to call, "We shall be back with a dozen more behind us!"

"It had better be a score," Allouette informed him, and his arm jerked straight up in the air. He shouted with pain, then the limb went limp. He raised his hand, staring in amazement as he rippled his fingers.

"Aye, as good as ever," Allouette called. "If you wish to keep it that way, wait till I have gone before you come this way again."

The soldier blanched and kicked his horse into a gallop, riding hard after his mates.

Allouette watched them go with a curled lip, then turned back to Gregory. "Where went our wounded bird?"

Gregory nodded toward the forest. "In among the leaves. That was quite well done, beauteous lady."

"It was not," Allouette said, riding past him toward the woods. "I have had too much practice at that sort of thing." She wondered at his compliment, though.

She drew up near the underbrush. "Come forth, dame. None shall hurt you now. Come forth, and tell us the reason for this bullying."

She heard a child crying and the mother's lulling voice; then the woman came out, clutching a child against each leg, and Allouette saw that Gregory had been right: Her clothing marked her as a gentlewoman, the wife of a squire at least and perhaps of a knight.

"I thank you for your protection, kind lady." But the woman looked rather nervous, knowing she was addressing a witch.

"It is gladly given," Allouette told her. "I have many debts to pay, and this is a beginning."

"Debts!" the woman's face crumpled. "I, too, have many debts and cannot pay them! Alas, if my Herschel had only lived!"

"Your husband?" Allouette frowned. "That is why you lost this house?"

"Indeed," the woman acknowledged. "I am Nora—Nora Musgrave, kind lady."

"Then your husband was Squire Musgrave."

"Indeed. He left us a little money, but it lasted only a month. Sir Hector was patient, he allowed us six months, but when we could not pay the rent, he appointed a new squire and sent his soldiers to rid the house of us."

"Poor dame!" Allouette said, and was about to launch into a diatribe against the wealthy when Gregory came up beside her, saying, "Then if you could pay, he might let you have back your house?"

"What matter?" the mother lamented. "We have no money, nor any prospect of it! My husband's father hid a small fortune somewhere on the land and on his deathbed told Herschel where to find it, but what use is that?"

"Did not your husband tell you where it was?" Allouette demanded, seething.

"Aye—that it is buried at the top of the shadow the old oak cast on Midsummer's Eve." She turned, pointing to a broad, low stump. "There it stands, or what is left of it. Since we had no need of money at the time, Herschel thought it best to let the treasure lie—but lightning struck that tree a month later and he despaired of discovering where its shadow might have fallen. Mind you, he probed the earth all about the stump, but found nothing."

"A buried treasure?" Allouette frowned at the stump. "Wizard, have you any skill as a douser?"

The children looked up at Gregory in alarm and huddled against their mother, who clutched them tight, staring at the wizard with wide and frightened eyes.

"Stuff and nonsense!" Allouette told them. "A wizard is

a blessing if he is on your side. How say you, man of magic?''

Gregory shook his head. "I could cast such a spell, but it would be quicker to calculate the lay of the shadow."

"Calculate?" Allouette turned to him, brow furrowed. "How would you do that? Pythagoras's theorem? But we know not the length of any side!"

"True." Gregory smiled at her, eyes glowing. "But as you have seen, the tree and its shadow form two legs of a triangle. If we can learn its height and the position of the sun on Midsummer's Eve, we can learn the angle of the line between the top of the tree and the top of the shadow."

"By what method?"

"The answer," Gregory said, "lies in geometry."

"Geometry? What is that?"

Gregory's eyes widened in surprise. "You know algebra but do not know geometry?"

"Have I not but now said it?" Allouette demanded. "You know for which tasks I was trained. They did not require geometry."

"I shall demonstrate it, then, if we can discover where the sun rose on Midsummer's Eve."

"I can tell you that, sir," Dame Musgrave said. "Herschel remarked upon it every year, for it reminded him of the treasure he could no longer find."

"Where, then?" Gregory asked. too mildly. Allouette glanced at him, recognizing the sign of interest. She could not blame him; the puzzle intrigued her, too.

"Yon." Dame Musgrave pointed. "Just over the northern tower of the gatehouse."

Gregory gazed at the structure, pursing his lips. "Good, good. Now for the height of the tree."

"Let us measure the thickness of the stump," Allouette suggested, "then find three other oaks of the same thickness and learn their heights."

"Figure the average?" Gregory nodded, smiling with pleasure. "That will give us a good estimate of the old oak's height. Come, let us set about it!"

Allouette soon had the average height of three forty-inch-thick oaks.

Gregory said, "We must wait until the sun is even with the top of the tower."

"Wherefore?" Allouette demanded.

"So that we may discover the length of a shadow at that hour," Gregory said.

Allouette's expression said that she did not understand. Then suddenly it cleared. "The sun will be at the same angle as it is on Midsummer's Eve, and will cast the same length of shadow!"

"That is it." Gregory nodded vigorously. "Then we have only to strike the path it would have traced on Midsummer's Eve—unless we wish to wait a week and see."

"I shall manage with the estimate, thank you."

They had not long to wait, only a quarter of an hour. When the sun was level with the top of the tower, Gregory looked down at his shadow and asked, "How long is it?"

Allouette gave him an odd look but stepped off the length of his shadow, heel to toe. "Nine feet."

"I am just six feet tall," Gregory told her. "How tall is your average oak?"

"Sixty-four feet." She smiled, eyes bright. "If a six-foot-tall man casts a shadow nine feet long, a sixty-four-foot oak would cast a shadow ninety-six feet long."

"Well calculated, and instantly!"

Gregory thrilled to know she was learning the concepts so quickly and thoroughly. He sketched out the problem so that Allouette could calculate the angle of the evening sun from her average oak height, then the location of the fallen tree's shadow. She jumped to her feet, pink with excitement. "Come, wizard! We must discover if we have calculated aright!"

Gregory rose and hurried after her, protesting, "Do not expect too much. We only knew the average height, after all. We may need to probe ten square yards to find it."

"Ten square yards instead of an acre?" Allouette called back over her shoulder. "A good bargain indeed!"

The widow followed with her children, wide-eyed and wondering.

Allouette whirled at the tree stump, setting the back of her heel against it, then paced off the distance and stopped, pointing at the ground. "There! Will you move the earth, wizard, or shall I?"

"You may have the honor of the first excavation," Gregory said with a smile. "If you tire, I shall take it up."

Allouette gave him a strange little frown as though wondering if he were mocking her, but turned to glare at the earth. It burst into a fountain of loam, dirt shooting up into the air in a tightly controlled spray that fell neatly to the north in a growing mound.

The children cried out in fear and clung to their mother, who, sadly, was in little better condition than they.

The last scatter of dirt fell on the heap, and Allouette scowled down. "Three feet. That should be enough."

"Should." Gregory looked down into a neat cylinder a foot in diameter. "Let us widen it to three feet."

She eyed him askance, wondering if that was really admiration in his voice. "It took small enough skill, you know."

"I know just the opposite. Nevertheless, stand away from the spray and let us see if I can perform in as tidy a fashion as yourself."

Allouette stepped back beside him and the earth erupted again, as though a giant mole were trying to claw his way back into his lightless home. It rose in a nearly solid column for minutes as Gregory stared at it with a knit brow, digging by telekinesis and trying to equal Allouette's skill. Abruptly he relaxed and the flow stopped. "Boy," he said to the widow's eldest, "go look in that hole and tell me what you see."

The lad glanced up at his mother for reassurance, but she took firm hold of his hand, took his sib's too, and went with him. All three of them peered down into the excavation—a very ragged circle, to Gregory's chagrin—and exclaimed with wonder.

"I see a chest, sir!" the lad cried. " 'Tis a wooden chest,

banded with brass and fastened with a huge lock.''

Allouette gave a shriek of joy and threw her arms around Gregory in triumph. ''We have found it!''

He stood rigid for a moment, wondering what Geoffrey would have done in this situation, then clasped his arms around her waist and whirled her about, grinning. ''You have calculated marvelously.''

''Liar!'' She pushed away from him but looked up with glowing eyes. ''It is you who did the calculations, but I shall be able to when next I need. . . . Ho! Leave be! It is too heavy for you!''

Turning, Gregory saw the eldest boy standing in the hole, heaving at the little chest. He grinned and stepped over to the lad. ''Is it so weighty, then? That is good news. Let me help.''

The boy gave a shout of fright as the box floated upward in his grip. He let go as if it were hot metal, but it kept on rising of its own accord—or Gregory's.

He let it float to the ground. ''Dame Musgrave, have you the key?''

''That, at least, my husband did leave me.'' The widow came forward, pulling out a key and fitting it to the lock. She tried to turn it and frowned with the effort. ''It moves, but scarcely.''

''It has lain long in the damp with no oil,'' Gregory explained, then turned to Allouette. ''Will you aid?''

''Why not you?'' Allouette retorted. ''I have never seen a telekinetic warlock before. Surely you can manage!''

''My father seems to have had a skill Gramarye telepaths lack,'' Gregory acknowledged, ''but you seem to have it in greater measure than I—or at least have it under greater control.''

''Well, then, if I must.'' Allouette didn't really seem to be upset at the news. She glared at the lock, saying, ''Turn, good dame.''

The widow's lips pressed thin with effort and the lock groaned, then gave and fell open.

''Well done,'' Gregory said softly.

Allouette shrugged impatiently. ''A bagatelle.''

''Not to them.''

Dame Musgrave yanked the lock loose from the hasp, opened the chest, and gasped.

"Is it gold, then?" Gregory asked. "I had thought that might be the reason for its weight."

"It is indeed gold, sir, and surely enough to pay our rent and pay for food till the children are grown." She turned to Allouette, tears in her eyes. "Oh, thank you, kind lady, a thousand times—and you, good sir."

Allouette stood stiff, staring with surprise at the elation the thanks gave her. Then she thawed and nodded. "It was our pleasure, good woman. Take the gold from the chest and hide it about you, all three of you, that you may take it to a safe place. Then have your children fill in the hole."

"We shall, we shall!" Dame Musgrave seized her hand and kissed it. "So much for they who say the witches are evil! Ever shall I sing your praises, sir and *demoiselle*."

Allouette managed to escape without too many more praises, though the children's did move her, especially since they were lisped through tears.

When she and Gregory were back in the greenwood, he said softly, "You need not be so surprised, you know. You are truly a good woman."

"Stuff and nonsense!" Allouette said angrily. "I am a wicked woman who has done one good deed, and you would be wise to remember that, sir!"

"I shall remember that you said it," Gregory temporized.

Allouette looked daggers at him but couldn't ignore the elation in her heart. "You have the advantage of me, sir— you know far more of mathematics than I. I shall require that you share that knowledge with me."

"Gladly," Gregory said, and began to explain the rest of plane geometry. She listened intently, drinking the concepts directly from his mind before he could put them into words and breathed, "Fascinating!"

Gregory broke off, realizing what she had done and staring in surprise. Then his eyes began to glow and he said, "You are truly the most wondrous of women, lustrous as a pearl and brilliant as a diamond."

Allouette turned away, feeling her face grow hot again. "I

was speaking not of my face and form, sir, but of things of the mind!"

"So was I," Gregory said.

She darted a puzzled glance at him. Surely he could not mean that mathematics meant more to him than the pleasures of the senses.

"You are the most beautiful woman I have ever seen," Gregory said frankly, "but the glory of your mind exceeds even that of your face and form."

Now she blushed indeed, blushed beet-red and lowered her gaze, feeling the thrill of his admiration warring against her old cynicism. "I had rather speak of geometry than of my beauty, sir."

"If you must," Gregory sighed, "but there is a beauty to mathematics, too. Contemplation of its orders can lift the mind to an elevation matched only by the finest music or the most excellent poetry. I have never met another who could share that delight."

"Nor have you now, I suspect," Allouette said tartly. She turned away, chin high as she rode the forest pathway—but found herself remembering his arms around her. *Foolish girl!* she scolded herself. His embrace had felt as good as any other man's, no more and no less. Wrenching her mind back to the poor and weak, she proclaimed, "Thus it begins."

"Thus indeed." Gregory's voice was a caress.

She steeled herself against it. "I meant aiding the weak and desperate, wizard."

"I understood that."

She cast him a doubtful glance, then quickly looked away from his beaming smile. "I shall do more to make amends, much more."

"I rejoice to hear it," Gregory said, "but with whom must you make amends?"

"With myself, of course," Allouette snapped. "My victims are either dead or far too wary of me to accept any aid I might offer—and it was unkind of you to remind me of that, sir."

"My apologies, lady," Gregory said with contrition.

"Accepted," Allouette grumbled. "Who else needs assistance, wizard?"

"Why, I do not know," Gregory said. "Let us ride and seek."

They didn't find anyone else in need that day, of course—they were in a forest, not a city. But after dinner, Allouette found time to practice meditation again and considered Gregory's advice first with contempt, then with growing seriousness. Trying to imagine the sound one hand would make trying to clap was nonsense, of course, but merely thinking about it did seem to be leading her deeper into her trance.

The next day, they came to a village whose well had gone dry. Allouette attempted dousing and pronounced the water table still full but lower than when the well had been dug. The villagers were ready to start digging on the instant, but Gregory asked them what they would do if the well went dry the next year. "Dig again," they answered, but Allouette watched Gregory's speculative gaze and told them, "There might be a better way."

Gregory showed the blacksmith how to build a giant auger, then set the villagers to building a stand for it. They ran a pole through the top of the earth auger and harnessed two mules to it, then sent them plodding around and around in a circle.

"Why not let me dig as I did yesterday?" Allouette demanded.

"Because you might not be here next year, when the well fails again," Gregory told her.

When the auger came up wet, the townsfolk cheered, then fell silent, frowning. The elders asked, "How are we to draw up the water? Your hole is too small for a bucket!"

But Gregory had already set the village smith to making the first brazen pipe the town had seen. They forced it into the hole, section by section, while Allouette showed the town potter how to make a stout earthenware spout. It was fired and ready by the time the pipe was in place and, remembering the basic physics she had learned in school, she harnessed a plunger to it, clad in leather to make it airtight. Then she poured in a little water to prime it and began working the handle. The villagers began to growl about wasted labor as she pushed it up and down, up and down, then, wearied, turned it over to another woman. When the water began to flow, the villagers exclaimed in awe, as though they had witnessed magic—which, as far as they were concerned, they had.

"It works!" Allouette said, pink with pleasure.

They accepted the villagers' profusive thanks, then rode off into the forest, discussing ways of calculating air pressure. They expanded the discussion into the peregrinations of air masses and weather. When the trees shielded them from the villagers' sight, though, Gregory added his own thanks, telling Allouette that to the villagers, she had been a fountain in the desert. "To myself, too," he told her. "I never understood what all this nonsense about love and beauty was. Now all the verses of the love-crazed poets seem only common sense to me, for I have met you."

CHAPTER
-25-

Allouette turned away, blushing again. "Be not so effusive, sir! I know you well enough by now, well enough to see that you would have felt only kindliness toward me if I had not shown them how to craft a pump and wished to discuss with you how its partial vacuum brought water up."

"That is so," Gregory confessed.

He was the most maddening man she had ever met.

Another village was beset by invisible monsters; Allouette realized that it had to be something in their food. When Gregory found that their only bread was rye, he examined it closely and identified the little black specks as a fungus that, he said, induced hallucinations. Allouette saw to importing barley from the next county and, with Gregory's smiling but hard-eyed support, talked the baron into paying for it. As they rode away, the two discussed how the fungus had induced hallucinations, which led to a discussion of the nervous system. Gregory listened to her with shining eyes, then said, "So it is not only a matter of your working upon people's minds by manipulating images into symbols—you have actually understood how their brains worked."

"Well, as much as anyone can," Allouette demurred.

"You are the only esper in all the land who has done so by herself," Gregory told her. "Who else would care? Who else could guess? You are an empath as well as a telepath, and the brilliance of your mind is alloyed by tenderness!"

Allouette squirmed, eyes downcast. "You do me too much honor, sir."

"My words cannot do enough." For a moment Gregory dropped his mind shield and she caught a glimpse of herself as he saw her—a shining, ethereal vision. It lasted only a moment before he raised his shield again, but that was enough to make her tremble. "Sir! You do me far too much credit! Besides, I am nowhere nearly as beautiful as you think."

"No, you are more beautiful than even my thoughts can show," Gregory said. "Still, does the fact of your beauty matter so much as my perception of it?"

"Does it exist at all, except in your perception?" Allouette retorted, but she rode on, shaken.

Understanding that, Gregory shrugged. "You might as well ask whether the falling of a tree would make a sound if it fell in the depths of the forest with no living creature near."

"Of course it would!" Allouette frowned at him, relieved to be back on safe ground. "A sound wave is a sound wave."

"It may be a wave in the air, but if there is no ear for it to strike, is it truly sound?"

They rode on, companionably (and safely) wrangling about philosophy. The discussion produced no concrete results, of course, but it served Allouette remarkably well that evening as an aid to meditation.

She needed it. She had begun to imagine Gregory in bed holding her in his arms and had need to banish the vision.

Gregory managed to keep the conversation philosophical the next day, but Allouette gave it frequent tangents, goading him into talking about the arts and the social sciences. She listened with rapt attention. When she knew something he didn't— the anarchists had given her a firm but biased grounding in history—she told it to him. They compared notes on different versions of the same events with hilarious results.

That evening, as they cleaned their bowls, Gregory remarked, "You seem to be completely recovered from the ordeal of your healing—at least, in being rested and restored to full energy."

"In that respect, perhaps," Allouette said, frowning, "though in others, I doubt that I ever will."

"Surely you will recover from the healing." Gregory reached out to touch her hand.

His touch was light, ever so light, but it sent a thrill through her whole body. She shivered but forced her hand to hold its place. "Recover from the healing, yes—but will I ever truly be healed?"

"You shall," Gregory said with full conviction. "You have only to believe in your own inborn goodness and your own worth." His hand opened to cover hers and his eyes seemed to expand, filling her vision. "*I* believe in it," he said softly. "I believe you are a woman of immense talents and intelligence, born good and loving and generous. That goodness cannot be eradicated, only covered up, hidden even from yourself—but it is still there and is the true source of your beauty."

She shivered again, but the thrill had centered within her and begun to glow. "Surely you do not mean that you would fail to see beauty in me if I were wicked!"

"I mean exactly that," Gregory said, and his hand caressed hers. "Never before have I failed to shake off the effect of a woman's loveliness. Only you are so outstanding, so vibrant and brilliant, yet so warm and tender that I cannot resist your allure."

She could not stop trembling, so her voice turned harsh. "What a heap of nonsense! If you so believed that, sir, you would have attempted to ravish me even as I woke!"

"Never," Gregory said, with total sincerity. "Never could I seek to hurt you, and such would be hurt."

Allouette shrugged impatiently, as though the word itself made no difference. "Seduce, then. You would have sought to seduce me any of these past few nights if you truly could not resist my charms."

"It is your mind I cannot resist, not your body. Then, too, I have been reared to respect women and would never seek to force upon you attentions you might not want—fully and freely, of your own will."

"What good is it to me if you love only my mind?" she challenged, then spoke from a surge of anger. "These past days you have spoken a lover's words, sir, flirting shamelessly but never following your words with actions. I tire of such teasing. Make love to me here and now or be done with your blandishments and honeyed words."

Christopher Stasheff

Alarm shadowed Gregory's eyes. "Do you challenge me? Surely love cannot come thus!"

"Surely it can—if you have the courage for it. I think you fear the act itself, sirrah. You are willing to speak of it all day, to versify and make poetry of it, but poets only sing about the things they cannot do. If you mean what you say, give me proof in a kiss!" She leaned forward, eyelids growing heavy, lips moist and parting just a little.

Gregory hesitated, then seemed to hear Geoffrey's voice inside his head commanding, *Take the cash and let the credit go!* Suddenly he understood Allouette's misgivings and leaned forward, brushing her lips with his own.

What began as a brushing deepened most amazingly and most quickly. She gasped, then responded with ardor equal to his own, and in minutes he was lost in the wonder of her kiss.

After ten minutes of this, with only quick gasps of air, though, Allouette grew impatient. Would he never reach out to caress?

It seemed he would not. She reached out instead, finding his hand by touch and guiding it to the curve of her breast. He froze, then thawed and drew his fingers lightly over the swelling, and Allouette gasped with surprise at the exquisite sensations his touch evoked. Never since Orly's first caress had she felt such. How could this be?

Still, he seemed quite content to tickle and caress the cloth that covered her. She reached out for his hand again and, step by step and with a few whispered directions, guided him into deeper and deeper intimacies. She was amazed at his skill, for though he was undoubtedly completely new to the game, he seemed to know exactly where to touch, where to tickle, and how to use his lips to best effect; he was the strangest combination of virgin and experienced lover that she had ever discovered. Any presence of mind, or notions she might have had of planning, vanished into a jumble of sheer sensation as he touched here, caressed there, matching her thrill for thrill until they lay naked on a bed of fragrant bracken, touching and marvelling at the sensations they evoked in one another, sensations that spiralled upward and farther upward until their minds mingled in ecstasy and the world went away, stripping their souls bare and leaving them joined for a timeless moment as the essence that was the innate Allouette regained the ecstasy she had known with Orly and went past it, so far past that they seemed to reach the sun coupled, a sun that filled them and surrounded them, then burst into fragments that fell and faded, leaving them separate but paired again, and Allouette knew in her heart that she had regained herself, that her cure was complete.

Then they lay in one another's arms, gasping in amazement and, yes, even a little in fright, quivering and holding each to the other for dear life as their pulses slowed and the world began to come back. They lay embracing, catching their breaths, and began to become aware of tiny thoughts, sharp thoughts, larger and rapacious thoughts all around them, as though the whole world had fallen to copulating with them.

At last Allouette looked up at the stunned, disbelieving, and awed face that hovered over hers and whispered, "You had better intend to stay near me for a long time, sir, for I shall want many more such moments!"

"I shall stay," Gregory whispered, then smiled as his voice turned to a purr. "Oh, be sure I shall stay, most lovely of women, for as long as you will have me!"

She eyed him askance, her cynicism returning. "You should be careful what you promise, sir."

"Promise?" asked Gregory. "I thought it was a demand."

Then he kissed her again, and it was a while before she thought coherently.

They celebrated the sunrise in much the same manner, then dressed and breakfasted, their gazes locked so completely it was amazing their hands found their mouths. Then Gregory sighed with regret that he must tear his gaze away from her and went to bring the horses.

They rode for some while in silence, only looking into one another's eyes now and then and smiling. At last Gregory said, "Does it not seem to you that the whole world must be in love today?"

"It seems so indeed," Allouette said with a tender smile.

Then her eyes widened in shock and she stiffened. "It seems so in cold fact! Listen a moment and see! Every living creature near us has copulated last night and this morning, even though most of them were far from their seasons!"

Gregory lost his smile. He gazed off into space a few moments, listening to deer and foxes and even earthworms. Then, with a feeling of dread, he reached farther and listened to the thoughts of the people in the nearest village, only now going out and about their daily rounds though the sun had been up for an hour and more, and the plowman should have been in the fields long since. He turned to Allouette, words of dismay on his lips—and saw her smiling at him with a dreamy, lazy, satiated look. "It would seem, sir, that we must forfend, or the birth rate of the whole kingdom will soar as the overflow of our lovemaking stimulates all living creatures around us."

"We shall have to find some way to block our unwitting projections, then," Gregory said, "for I do not mean to deny myself your desires, whenever and wherever they may occur!"

Allouette gave a low, exulting cry and leaned forward from her saddle to kiss him.

All around them, birds began to bill and coo.

Allouette broke the kiss with a laugh of delight. "You see, sir? Even our kisses are infectious!"

"May the world catch a plague of love, then," Gregory said fervently and reached out for her.

She held him off with a teasing smile. "We must be careful, sir, or folk who are not in love will copulate with whomever is near, simply because the one they love is not." Then Allouette's eyes brightened with inspiration. "Your house! What great good luck that you have begun to build walls that absorb telepathic energy!"

"What great good fortune indeed!" Gregory said fervently and reined his horse up against hers, catching her about the waist and holding her tightly against him. "I cannot wait to finish it! Come!"

There was a strange double booming and a moment of dizziness; then Allouette looked around to see the clearing with Gregory's wall of pale blocks at its center. "So that is what it is like to teleport," she said in a shaky voice. "I think I shall prefer to fly in the future, sir, if it is all the same to you."

"Only if I may share your broomstick."

Allouette turned to give him a smile and a kiss, then slid off her horse, calling, "Come! For we must have four walls about us ere nightfall!"

"Even at that, it will be hard to wait." But Gregory slid from his horse and glared at the underbrush, which began to form itself into rectangular blocks.

Allouette watched him craft the first block, then float it into place, face twisted with the effort. Having learned the process, she pitched in herself, forming the blocks with her mind, matching the molecular structure he had fashioned, then floating them into place by telekinesis. Gregory watched her with more than agreeable surprise; in fact, she turned from placing the first block to see him gazing raptly at her with an expression that should have been censored. "I had known you learned quickly, but not as quickly as that—and from observation alone! How did you know the structure of the molecules?"

"Why, I probed into it with my mind, foolish man, and felt out which atom had bonded to which!" But the tone she had meant to be scornful turned teasing and she couldn't help a smile. "If so minor a feat as that is apt to kindle desire in you, I shall never dare learn anything."

"Then school is out." Gregory caught her hand.

She gave it a squeeze as she gave him a look that was half promise and half feigned irritation. "Finish your walls first, scholar. Then mayhap I shall give you another lesson in life."

Gregory spun away, calling, "A hundred blocks, quickly!"

Allouette laughed, but inside her triumph was mixed with a rejoicing that she had thought she would never regain—indeed, that she had unknowingly come to think wrong.

They worked all that day and the underbrush in the vicinity disappeared, transmogrified into the blocks that fitted into a wall that grew amazingly. When the outline of the building was clear, though, her old ambitions for grandeur and luxury reawakened. "If you intend for me to dwell here with you, male, you shall have to make me a building such as I have ever dreamed of holding—not simply a cottage or even a small manor, but a tower!"

"Why, a tower let it be, then," Gregory said, and the blocks all lifted into the air, sorted themselves out, and came down in a circle sixty feet across.

"Why do you stare so?" Gregory asked softly. "Do you not know that love lends a man the strength of ten?"

"I had thought that came from a pure heart." Inwardly, Allouette both trembled and rejoiced, for he had said the word "love." Oh, he was scarcely the first to have spoken thus— but he was the only one since Orly whom she had not purposely compelled by her projections, and the first since Orly whose love she had wanted for her own sake, not as a means to an assigned end.

By evening, the ground was clear for a hundred feet around and the wall was ten feet high. Gregory turned to her, weary but hopeful. "Have I crafted enough of my dwelling to prove my earnestness?"

"You have." Allouette stepped close to him, and closer still as she said, "There are walls enough to protect the countryside from the effects of our delight. It lacks a roof, of course, but it will cause little trouble if the songbirds couple like turtledoves."

Gregory made a cooing noise. She laughed and pressed against him to stop the cooing with her lips. When they broke apart, she gave a little shriek as he swung her into his arms, then clung to his neck laughing as he carried her through the empty doorway and into the ring of blocks.

She had spoken truly—any birds who did fly over them that evening behaved most outrageously, even allowing for the fact that it was early summer. So, for that matter, did the bats, and the insects had a reprieve that evening. It was just as well, for they were behaving insanely, too.

As she lay wrapped in the arms of the first man she had ever begun to really trust, weakened and dazed in the afterglow, Allouette trembled, for she had to admit to herself that she was truly in love again at last, and the vulnerability that created frightened her.

Gregory felt her shivering. "What troubles you, love?" he said tenderly. "Tell me the wound, and I shall heal it."

"Only I can do that," Allouette said into his chest, not meeting his gaze. "I feel so horribly guilty, Gregory."

Gregory was still, then said sadly, "I had thought you were healed of that."

"Of thinking sex evil? Oh, be sure that I am, and what your mother did not mend, you now have!" She felt his lips on her forehead but resisted the diversion and explained. "Naetheless, I am supposed to be seeking penance, and I have found only ecstasy!"

"Ah," Gregory purred, and there was a wealth of understanding and reassurance in the sound. "Take what comfort you can, love, for you have already saved a widow and her children, not to mention two whole villages. Take what strength I can lend, for I am sure you will find yourself weary work to do."

"Well," Allouette said, "if you put it that way, I suppose . . ." She let the sentence trail off and tilted her head back to accept his full kiss, letting the energy it gave tingle through her.

As they labored the next day, a doubt surfaced in Allouette's mind. She told herself to accept the most complimentary interpretation, but felt the determination to face the facts instead. "Gregory," she said, "your walls of this strange psi-proof substance serve most excellently for shielding the villagers round about from the danger of our projections, but I cannot think you intended that when you began your building."

"Intended to craft a love nest into which to entice you?" Gregory looked up, shocked, and a hundred-pound block fell to the ground. "I would not have had such audacity! Never think that I have taken you for granted!"

Well, that put a different light on the matter—and a flow of warmth within her. "Never do," Allouette advised him.

"Therefore, if you did not craft it as a means of inducement, why did you begin it?"

"It is my site of power, love," Gregory explained. "When I found it, I knew. . . ."

"Not that it would increase the force of our lovemaking!"

"No, though it seems to have served that function as well." Gregory's gaze warmed. "Still, I intended to research the ramifications of psionic powers here, and am well aware that I may make mistakes that could have drastic side effects—as the animal life in this area has shown."

Allouette frowned, intent on the other implications of his words. "But some side effects could be harmful?"

"Aye, and with the power of this site to fuel them, they could be most harmful indeed. Therefore do I wish to craft walls about me that will contain any such, so that my research will not contaminate the countryside."

Allouette kept her frown. "What manner of researches could these be?"

"Ways to keep weeds from sprouting while crops grow faster," Gregory told her, "so that fewer people will go hungry. Ways to cure diseases, even to prevent them from beginning. Perhaps, though I doubt any study can achieve it—ways for noblemen to resolve their differences and ways to limit their ambitions, so that we need never again see war stalk the land."

He took a breath to go on, but Allouette cried, "Enough!" She stood vibrant, eyes shining. "If these researches can yield so much good as that, there is some small chance they may redeem me from the evil I've done! To work, wizard! Let us be done building this tower so that we can begin with research! I shall aid you, I shall study by your side, and you shall have to grind away most slavishly if you do not wish me to surpass you!"

Gregory stepped close to embrace her with shining eyes. "There is just so much that labor can do in this work, my love, and that is the testing of an idea. The idea itself comes when it will come, and there is no way to force it; one must needs wait until it occurs of its own accord. Will you be my inspiration, then?"

Allouette's breath caught in her throat, but she managed to say, "Aye, and your slave driver, too!" before his lips cut off her words.

At last she pushed him away, saying, "To work!" and stalked off to find another mound of brush.

Gregory gazed after her with shining eyes.

At the end of the day, the tower was thirty feet tall but still had no roof. The birds and the bees were quite busy that night, too.

But the next day, as they worked, Gregory became less and less talkative, seeming absentminded, saddening. Allouette became indignant that he seemed to pay so little attention to her, then noticed that he stole glances at her when he thought she wasn't watching—but they were furtive glances, and guilty.

As she melded the molecules of the underbrush into a new and crystalline structure, she began to seethe within. So he was no better than the others after all! He yearned for her until he had what he wanted, and when he was satiated, he gave way to postcoital depression, to the puritanical imperatives of his religion, took the excuse of sinner's guilt to turn away from her, to spurn her!

Well, let him go if he wished! Allouette would finish this tower and undertake her researches without him! She built blocks and stacked them at a furious rate, burning with rage at the perfidy of men.

Thus it was that when Cordelia and Gwen stopped by to visit, they found two people working at building a tower, neither of them talking, and the air charged with both the tension of anger and the miasma of despair.

CHAPTER
-26-

Cordelia shuddered as they landed. "What manner of lovers' quarrel is *this*?"

"There is more to it than passion worked into a knot," Gwen said, frowning. "Do you draw out the woman, daughter, and I shall worm the truth of this out of my son."

Cordelia nodded and went over to Allouette.

The closer she came to the great pale structure, the more awed she became by its scale. Allouette looked up, irritated by the company, then quickly looked away, feelings of guilt rising as she remembered that she had tried to kill this woman, to rob her of the life of discovery and wonder that lay before her, and she no older than Allouette herself.

"The grandeur of this structure is astounding!" Cordelia said. "For what purpose do you build it?"

"To contain *his* researches." Allouette jerked her head toward Gregory. "He thought to make a mere house, but to live here with him and only him, I shall surely deserve a few luxuries to make my stay bearable!"

"Will you stay with him, then, only the two of you in isolation from the rest of humanity?" Cordelia asked in disbelief.

"So I had meant," Allouette said, thin-lipped, "and he seemed to welcome the thought of my company while he labored at finding solutions to the problems of the world. He seems to be having second thoughts, though."

"Does he truly!" Cordelia felt a woman's indignation toward false promises. "Has he taken what you offered, then, with no sign of recompense or devotion?"

That gave Allouette pause. "No . . . until today, he gave every sign of craving my presence."

"Craving, perhaps." Cordelia could feel the anger at her brother increasing. "But did he say he loved you?"

Allouette was silent for a minute, then admitted, "Several times."

Cordelia's eyes widened. "I am glad to hear it, for he certainly told it to us, and with great pain, because he thought it unrequited. Surely you do not think that you have requited only to have that love withdrawn!"

"It would seem so," Allouette said grimly.

"Have you told him you love *him*?"

Allouette thought back. "Well, no . . . but I have given him every sign of my love! Surely that would be enough for any man."

"Not one who thinks his only worth is as a scholar," Cordelia said, "and who has absolutely no opinion of himself as a man."

"Oh, but he is a most splendid lover! I mean . . ." Allouette blushed flame-hot—"I had not meant to say . . ."

"It does not shock me," Cordelia said with a smile, "nor am I jealous of my little brother. In fact, I am relieved and rejoice to hear it." Then the smile vanished. "Still, I know Gregory well enough to think that he could never suffer so strongly from love as I have seen him languishing over you, and be sorry for it the next day. There is more to this than he speaks of. Come, let us confront him."

Allouette looked up at her in alarm, but Cordelia was already striding away. Allouette ran after her. "No! We must not! What if he should say he does not want me here?"

"Then we had best know it at once," Cordelia said with iron determination.

"But if he says it, I can no longer ignore it!"

Cordelia couldn't believe this was the same woman who had tried to ensnare and steal Alain if she could and, if she couldn't, slay Cordelia herself—both without the slightest trace of remorse. "Best to know the worst," she called over her shoulder as she bore down upon her brother.

Gwen, meanwhile, had come up to her son, who finished placing a block and turned to her with a courteous but miserable attempt at a smile. Gwen's heart twisted at the sight, but she looked up at the sixty-foot wall before her and said, "An amazing accomplishment, my son."

"Oh—not when I have had such excellent assistance." But Gregory's face crumpled at the thought, though he smoothed it again quickly enough.

Gwen probed the wall with her thoughts, found it telepathically opaque, and drew her own conclusions. In a low tone she said, "Rejoice therefore, Gregory. You have found true love, you have found your life's work, and Allouette has found her way to come to terms with herself for her past deeds."

Surprise came slowly over Gregory's face. "That is all true. I had not summarized it so."

"Then do." Gently, Gwen asked, "Why are you troubled, when an embarrassment of riches lies before you?"

"That is so," Gregory said slowly, "though Allouette has never said she loves me . . ."

"You know that she does, though, and that her love will grow if you are true to her."

"Yes . . . but . . ." Gregory's composure broke. "But by that very love, I shall hold her prisoner! What manner of lover am I, Mother, to doom my darling to life imprisonment, here where she shall have no society but me, no human contact but my poor self?"

Gwen studied him for a minute, smiling slowly. "I think she will not notice the lack, my son, not for a long time— and if she does, be sure she will journey where she wants. Will you go with her if she does?"

"Of course! But still, Mother, what manner of life could it be for a gentle and loving woman to be bound to a bookish recluse all her days? Oh, aye, there shall be the occasional festival, and I have no doubt the Crown will summon us for dire tasks now and again—but when all is said and done, we shall live alone more years than not! How can I claim to love her when I do this to her?"

"Have you thought, my son, that after all she has suffered at the hands of other people, she might well choose such isolation with the one man she can trust?"

Gregory was silent awhile, considering the matter.

Gwen matched his silence, letting him work it out. When she thought that consideration was turning into brooding, she said, "You have doomed himself to the same isolation, my son."

"Well, surely—but I have chosen it!"

"So has she," Gwen reminded him.

"What has she?"

Gregory looked up in alarm to see his sister looming, with Allouette fluttering after her in distress.

Cordelia came to stand foursquare, glaring at her brother, hands on her hips. "What has she done?"

"She has been foolish enough to choose me," Gregory said through wooden lips.

"Foolish!" Allouette cried, staring.

"Do you believe me now?" Cordelia asked over her shoulder though she kept her gaze on Gregory. Still, her voice was softer as she asked, "There is nothing foolish in that choice, my sib!"

"But there is!" Gregory cried. "She chooses life imprisonment if she chooses me! She chooses exile, isolation, and one so lovely and so graceful deserves neither! She deserves only to be cosseted, cherished, admired. . . ."

Allouette's eyes glowed as she stepped close to him. "Cosset me, then. Cherish me. Admire me!"

"Oh, I shall," Gregory said fervently, "but you merit far better than me, and you deserve the envy of every woman, the adoration of multitudes!"

"I have had all that and found it worthless." Allouette twined her arms about his neck. "What I have not had is the sincere devotion of one good man—and if you think that, having found it, I shall ever cast it away, you are witless!"

"I do not doubt it," Gregory said, numb but thawing by her nearness. "Still, there is the isolation—"

"Solitude," Allouette corrected, "and I welcome it. Oh, it may be that in a year's time, or two years or three, I may desire to go among people again—and will you not escort me if I do?"

"With great delight," Gregory said fervently.

"Then what need have you to feel guilty, my love?"

Gregory stared, struck by the word "love" more than by the question—and while he was frozen, Allouette kissed him.

Gwen and Cordelia exchanged a conspiratorial glance and a smile.

When they came apart, Gregory gasped, "But you shall lose your freedom if you stay with me!"

"I had not really noticed," Allouette said. "If staying alone with you is my desire, after all, have I not exercised that very freedom of which you speak?"

"How can you be so free to go as not to go?" Gregory protested.

Allouette laughed. "Is that not something a sage once said?"

"No," said Cordelia, "it was a poet speaking about a sage." She turned to her brother. "Do you not intend losing your freedom, too, in your own manner, brother?"

Gregory sighed. "I suppose that all who commit their hearts to something greater than themselves indeed yield up their freedom in large measure, sister, whether that 'something greater' be marriage and family, building an empire, hoarding money, creating great art, or discovering new knowledge."

"There is some truth in that," Gwen said judiciously, with a lifetime's experience. "The great mistake is to think you can commit yourself to two vocations at once. Still, there is no real happiness without one—only the loneliness and aimlessness that sooner or later drive one to distraction, and the pleasures that fail to produce happiness."

"So to which must people devote themselves, Mother?" Gregory asked, very low.

"In that, son, a man must read his weird," Gwen answered. "Go where you find your bliss."

"Why, then, I have found it." Gregory held both Allouette's hands and looked into her eyes.

After a few minutes' silence, the two of them merely standing there and glowing, Gwen cleared her throat. When it produced no reaction she said, "Well, enough delay. We must be up and about, daughter."

"We must indeed," Cordelia agreed. "Farewell, you two.

We shall send a priest to wander this way, if we see one."

"We shall be glad to see him," Gregory said automatically, never taking his eyes from Allouette. "Fare you well, Mother, Cordelia."

"Farewell," Cordelia replied as she hopped on her broomstick.

From the air, circling to gain height, she noted that as soon as they had departed, the lovers had begun kissing again. As she passed her mother in the gyre, she said, "I think we need no longer worry about him."

"It will be the first time since he was thirteen," Gwen said, "and is very welcome."

Below them, Allouette broke the kiss and commanded, "Back to work, ardent lover! We may finish this stronghold tonight and have a roof to cover us!"

"Shall have need of it, then?" Gregory asked.

"Aye, great need," Allouette promised. "To work, now!"

Gregory stole one last kiss. Then, still holding hands, they turned back to building their ivory tower.

Turn the page for a preview of

A Phule and His Money

by Robert Asprin, with Peter J. Heck.

Coming in October from Ace Books.

CHAPTER
-1-

JOURNAL #278

Even the most fortunate circumstances contain the seeds of their own destruction. So it was with the tenure of Phule's Company on Lorelei.

At first glance, a posh gambling resort like Lorelei would appear a plum assignment for a Space Legion company that until recently had been the laughingstock of the Legion. Omega Company had long been the Legion's dumping ground for incompetents and malcontents. My employer, Willard Phule (or ''Captain Jester,'' to use his Legion name), was given command of Omega Company as punishment for a small indiscretion of his own, namely ordering a peace conference strafed. He was lucky—only his status as a wealthy munitions heir kept him from being expelled outright. The generals meant to so overload him with frustration and embarrassment that he would resign. A spoiled rich kid could find plenty of more pleasant ways to misspend his youth, they thought.

Instead he had decided to make the company the best in the Legion, and by applying unorthodox methods had come a long way toward that goal. But he had powerful enemies, and Lorelei appeared a perfect trap for the unwary. Dominated by gangsters, and given over to every sort of sybaritic entertainment, it would have destroyed most military units. That Phule's company had succeeded beyond all hopes confounded those enemies— but they were determined to find new ways to destroy him.

*Now, the company was about to receive new troops—
the first significant additions to its ranks since he took
command. In such a tight-knit unit, any change of personnel has an impact. When the new troops have been
selected by one's enemies, the impact is likely to be
disastrous . . .*

"They'll be docking any minute, now," said Phule, con-
sulting his chronometer. It was the third time he'd checked it
in the last five minutes. Since there were numerous time dis-
plays on view throughout the space station's arrival lounge,
an observer might have concluded that Phule's preoccupation
with the time—combined with his pacing and nonstop talking—was a sign of nervousness. That observer would have
been right.

"A few minutes one way or the other won't make much
difference, Captain," said Sgt. Brandy, who had come with
her commanding officer to greet the new troops assigned to
Phule's Company. "They're coming, and we'll deal with it.
All of us will. I've been through this enough times before."

"Oh, I know you have," said Phule, nodding apprecia-
tively to his Top Sergeant. "And I know you'll do everything
you can to make them fit in smoothly. I've seen what you
can do, Brandy. But this isn't just any new batch of recruits.
It's a completely unique situation."

"You mean the Gambolts, sir?" said Lt. Armstrong, the
third in the greeting party. He stood ramrod straight, almost
managing to look comfortable despite the exaggerated precision of his uniform and posture. "I don't see where they'll
be a problem. They're among the finest fighters in the galaxy.
It's an honor to have them in our unit."

"Yes, I appreciate that," said Phule. "But Gambolts have
never served in mixed units with humans before—and these
three specifically requested to be assigned to us. It's a tribute
to the good work we've done. But I can't help wonder . . ."
His voice trailed off.

Brandy shook her head firmly. "Whether the troops will
accept them? Don't worry about that, Captain. This outfit may
be the most tolerant bunch in the Legion. When you've had

to live down the reputation we've been saddled with, you don't have room to get snooty about your barracksmates."

"Losers can't be choosers, in other words," said Phule. "I suppose that's been true in the past. Most of the company have had to accept whatever hand the Legion dealt them. But we've been changing that."

"*You've* been changing that, sir," said Lt. Armstrong. "If not for you, we'd still be back on Haskin's Planet, slogging through the swamps. Now we're among the elite companies of the Legion—all thanks to your efforts."

"I can't take all the credit," said Phule. "It's been a team effort, and every member has contributed. That's why I'm anxious about the new troops, to tell you the truth. The Gambolts have always had their own elite unit in the Regular Army. Now three of them are coming to us—and I have to wonder why. Will they fit into the team? Will they hold themselves apart from the rest of the unit? Will they—"

Whatever he was about to say was interrupted by the blare of a klaxon and a red-lit sign flashing on and off by the arrival door. The sign now read, SHUTTLE DOCKING: PREPARE FOR DEBARKING PASSENGERS. Phule and his subordinates turned to face the door. Some of their questions were about to be answered.

One advantage of building a casino on a space station is that it can be a true twenty-four-hour operation. With no local cycle of day and night, there is no need for visitors to adjust to the local clock, or to go through what in prespace days used to be called "jet lag." So the Fat Chance Casino was likely to have an eager crowd of gamblers at any hour. This, in turn, meant that Phule's Company had to be alert for trouble at any hour.

But Moustache, who was in charge of "daytime" security at the casino, wasn't expecting any real trouble. The tall non-com with a balding head and a bright red moustache sat at the bar sipping a brisk "cuppa" tea, scanning the early afternoon crowd with detached interest. He knew he wouldn't spot everything—it wasn't really his job, after all. Other members of the Omega Mob, disguised as waiters, croupiers, or fellow-customers, mingled with the crowd, probing for the myriad signs that someone was trying to cheat. Behind the elegant-looking facade, other vigilant eyes performed the same task, aided by state-of-the-art surveillance equipment.

Of course, since the showdown with Maxine Pruett's hoodlums, there had been even less trouble. Word had quickly gone out on the gamblers' grapevine to forget about trying to beat the Fat Chance. Still, there was always a handful of small-time grifters who thought they could outsmart the house security staff. Most of these were quickly spotted and quietly removed from the casino floor to a private lounge to await deportation on the next ship off-station. It was all handled very professionally—and unsuccessful grifters usually accepted their fate with a stoical shrug. After all, it was one of the risks of doing business.

So it came as a surprise when a voice spoke quietly in Moustache's earphone. It was Rose—"Mother" to the Company—the voice of Comm Central, the vital glue that bound the company together. "Wake up, you old buzzard," she said teasingly. "We're about to get some rough trade. I know you senior citizens need your afternoon naps, but it'd be a shame for you to doze through the entertainment."

"Where?" said Moustache, instantly alert. He spoke under his breath, knowing that the super-sensitive directional microphone on his wrist communicator could pick up a whisper inaudible to someone at the next table.

"Blackjack tables, darlin'," said Mother. "We've got a mom and pop team palming and passing cards at Number Five. I've already tipped the dealer, and she's stalling."

"Good," said Moustache, standing up from the bar. "Who's covering that sector?"

"The dealer's a civilian employee. Her orders are to stay clear if trouble starts and let security handle it. We've got a couple of actors playing legionnaires stationed around the room, and they may be all we really need. But Gabriel's on the nearest exit in case they try to run. And if *he* needs help, we've got Sushi and Do-Wop undercover in that area— they're already closing in on Number Five. You might dodder over, yourself, grandpa—just to see how it all comes out. The grifters might accept you as a father figure.''

"Well, Mother, perhaps I'll introduce them to you, as well," said Moustache, smiling to himself. Of course he wouldn't follow through on that threat; there was no reason to let anyone know how thoroughly the gambling tables were monitored. It might inhibit the free-spending attitude the casino wanted to encourage in its legitimate customers. And to give professional gamblers a behind-the-scenes look at security might give them ideas how to beat it.

Moustache had perfected the art of moving quickly without appearing to be in any particular hurry. If a noncom looked flustered or rushed, the troops might decide there was something for *them* to worry about. Moustache had been a career noncom in the regular Army before forced retirement made him join the Space Legion. His crisp military bearing and his carefully polished "British Sergeant-Major" air made him the perfect front man for Phule's undercover surveillance operation in the Fat Chance. While all eyes were on him and his troop of uniformed actors (with a salting of genuine legionnaires to handle any rough stuff), the real security team could work unobserved, ready to respond to any threat before the opposition was aware of them.

That was exactly what was happening as Moustache rounded a bank of quantum slot machines and entered the Blackjack area of the casino. Do-Wop had slouched into a vacant seat at table Number Five, within an arm's length of a pudgy gray-haired man wearing a well-broken-in business suit over a brightly colored shirt. Beside him sat a woman of similar age, in a slightly-too-tight dress and a too-elaborate, blatantly dyed hairdo. A travelling salesman on vacation with his wife, or so it appeared at first glance. But if Mother was correct—and she probably was—the outfits were sheep's clothing, camouflage to make a team of card cheats look like innocent tourists. At the far end of the table stood Sushi, looking for all the world as if he were trying to decide how the cards were running at this table before sitting down to play.

The dealer glanced up as Moustache came into view, and

he winked at her. It was time to put an end to this incident. He stepped forward and put a hand lightly on the man's shoulder. "Excuse me, sir," he said. His voice was very polite but carried an unmistakable stamp of authority.

The man glanced over his shoulder, barely long enough for him to register much more than Moustache's black Legion uniform. What happened next took everyone by surprise. Both the man and the woman abruptly shoved back their chairs, knocking Moustache off balance. In the split second before he could recover, the woman had spun around and begun to throw punches, concentrating on his midsection—which, given the difference of their heights, was her most convenient target.

The woman was stronger than Moustache had expected. He had to call on all his training to fight off a middle-aged tourist. Using his superior reach, he grabbed the chair she had vacated and shoved her back against the table with it, trying to keep her pinned out of lethal range. Do-Wop was already stepping forward to help subdue her, and there were black-uniformed figures closing in from a distance, so all Moustache had to do was keep her at bay and hope the man didn't come to her assistance. With luck, he'd have nothing more serious than bruises to show for this episode.

But the woman's companion had ideas of his own. Instead of helping her break free, he leaped up on the table and launched himself in a flying kick at Sushi.

Sushi had held back from the altercation, ready to cut off either of the pair who tried to escape. So while he was caught by surprise, his reflexes and training got him out of trouble. Instead of trying to duck under the kick, he leaned backward far enough to make the attacker's flailing feet miss him, then gave the flying body a hard shove in the ribs as he went past, trying to spoil the attacker's balance. To that extent Sushi succeeded, and the tourist landed ignominiously on a chair that toppled with a loud *crack* as the back legs gave way.

But the shove transferred enough momentum to Sushi to knock him off balance, as well. He spun around, bounced off the table behind him, and landed on hands and knees on the floor a short distance from his assailant. Almost at once, he sprang up, ready for action. Sushi expected the man to be halfway to the exit, or more likely, lying dazed on the floor. Instead, he was surprised to find the man already in a compact fighting stance. That made no sense at all. The man must have known he was surrounded by the legionnaires. If he wasn't going to try to escape, he should have given up quietly as soon as his cheating was discovered. Unless . . .

Sushi looked more closely at his opponent. Under the baggy suit and graying hair—which upon closer inspection appeared to have been dyed—was a man close to his prime, solidly built and obviously trained in the martial arts. His facial features showed Asian ancestry. Suddenly Sushi understood.

Sushi rose to his feet and bowed, slowly. "I have been expecting you," he said to the man. He kept his voice low, speaking in Japanese. "We have business to tend to, but we should not discuss it in front of outsiders."

The other man snarled. "My family does not dicker with impostors. Our only business today is your death."

"Do not judge too quickly," said Sushi. "Look!" He made a surreptitious motion with his left hand and then dropped both arms to his sides, leaving himself open to the other man's attack.

The other man's face changed in an instant, and he too adopted a more relaxed stance. "Ah! I did not know! Perhaps there is something to discuss after all. But you are right— outsiders should not hear what we have to say, though I think there are few here who would understand us."

"One moment, please," said Sushi. "I will tell the others you have surrendered to me for questioning, and then we will go someplace where we may talk freely. They will not question me, because they believe I am loyal to their captain. Your woman will be taken to a safe place and not harmed, and you may retrieve her at your convenience."

"That is good. I will tell her so," said the Yakuza. The two turned to the rest of the group. Moustache had one hand on the woman's arm—she had stopped fighting when Sushi had begun talking to his opponent in Japanese; presumably she understood that language.

"I need to talk to this man," Sushi said. "She'll go with you to the holding lounge, and I don't think she'll cause any trouble now. I'll take responsibility."

Moustache looked to Do-Wop, who nodded. "Cool with me if you know what you're doing," said Do-Wop. "But be careful—just because you know that cat's lingo don't mean you want to turn your back on him."

"Don't worry, it's under control," said Sushi. He gestured to the Yakuza and together they walked out of the casino. Even before they were gone the normal sounds of gambling had resumed.

"There they are," said Brandy, and there was no question what she meant. Three human-sized cats in Space Legion uniforms would have stood out in any crowd. And while the Gambolts were famed for their ability to infiltrate an enemy position without being seen or heard, there was no need for stealth here. They bounced into the entry lounge, three over-sized balls of feline energy, eyes darting in every direction. Behind them, a group of humans in similar uniform slouched into the lounge—the rest of the recruits.

The Gambolts immediately spotted the three black-uniformed humans standing together. They glided over and drew up in front of Phule, coming to attention. One of them turned on a translator and said, "New recruits reporting for duty, Sir!" The Gambolt vocal equipment could make a limited range of human sounds, but communication was far smoother with a translator in place.

"Welcome to Omega Company," said Phule, stepping forward. He waited until all the recruits had moved up to join them, in a ragged semblance of a line. "I am Captain Jester, and this is Lieutenant Armstrong. Sergeant Brandy here will be in charge of your training. You'll meet the rest of your comrades and officers back at the hotel. We're pleased to have you as part of our outfit." He turned to Armstrong, who had brought out a clipboard. "Carry on, Lieutenant."

"Yes, sir!" said Armstrong, giving his usual crisp salute. He turned to face the new arrivals. "Attention! Sergeant Brandy will call roll."

Brandy stepped forward and took the clipboard from Armstrong. She inspected the new arrivals. While she'd never seen Gambolts up close, these three looked to be in excellent physical condition, and their spanking new uniforms effectively set off their lithe forms. If the Gambolts were as deadly fighters as rumor said, this trio would be a strong addition to the company. The rest of the recruits looked like a perfect match for the assorted misfits and malcontents of Omega Company.

But there would be time enough to sort that out. She looked down at the clipboard and began reading names.

"Dukes?"

"Here, Sergeant." The biggest of the three Gambolts answered, a tawny six-footer, with light green eyes and a nick out of its left ear. (Was this a male or a female? Brandy wondered idly. The Gambolts' sexual differences weren't immediately evident to the untrained human eye, and both sexes were known to choose military careers. It would probably make more difference to the Gambolts than it ever would to her.)

"Welcome aboard, Dukes. Garbo?"

"Here, Sergeant," said another Gambolt. The translator made this one's voice sound lighter and perhaps more feminine—as the choice of name also suggested—though the only outward physical distinction between this one and the other Gambolts was a slightly lighter build. Garbo had darker fur, nearly black, with a hint of a lighter colored undercoat.

"Welcome to the company, Garbo. Rube?"

"Right here, Sarge," said the third Gambolt, perhaps a few inches shorter than Dukes but even more imposingly built. Rube had gray fur, with slightly longer tufts on the cheeks, and its eyes seemed bigger than the others'. Its voice sounded a touch more jovial than the others', too, though that could easily be an artifact of the translator.

"Welcome aboard," Brandy said again. "Slayer?"

"Yo," said a scrawny human with a shaved head and a bone through its nose—again, it was difficult to determine its gender.

This was the kind of recruit Brandy was used to. "That's *Yo, Sergeant* to you, Slayer," she barked. The recruit flinched, and muttered something that sounded like an appropriate response. Brandy nodded—she'd have plenty of time to get into the fine points of Legion discipline, such as it was. For now, it was sufficient to establish who was in charge. She turned to the next name on the list. "Brick?"

There were a dozen more recruits, all present, though none looked anywhere near as promising as the Gambolts. She finished the list, then turned to Armstrong and said, "All new troops present and accounted for, Lieutenant."

"Very good," said Armstrong, but before he could say more he was interrupted by a new voice.

"I'm a-gonna hafta take exception to that, Sarge," said a deep resonant voice. "I'm as much a member of this here company as anybody, and by the captain's own personal request, as it happens."

Brandy turned to see a pudgy human, with long dark slicked-back hair and even darker sunglasses. Like the others in the formation, the newcomer was dressed in black, although his jumpsuit was even more flamboyant than the version of the Legion uniform Phule's Company wore. And there was nothing at all military about the stranger's hipshot stance and half-sneering expression.

It was Lt. Armstrong who broke the awkward silence. He pulled himself up to his full height and snapped, "If you're assigned to Omega Company, then fall in with the rest of the troops and report. This is the Legion, if you know what that means."

"Lordy, do I ever," said the newcomer. He sauntered up next to the Gambolts, drew himself more or less upright, and gave a passible imitation of a salute. "Reverend Jordan Ayres reportin' for duty, suh. But y'all can call me Rev."

"What the hell . . ." began Brandy, gearing up to give the new man a demonstration of how an angry Top Sergeant looked and sounded.

But Phule said, "Wait a minute, Brandy. Reverend . . ." Phule's puzzled expression suddenly transformed itself into a broad smile and the captain reached out a hand for Ayres to shake. "Of course! You're the chaplain I requested from headquarters. Welcome to Omega Company." He shot a quizzical look at Armstrong.

"A chaplain?" said Armstrong, staring at the newcomer. "I'd almost forgotten you'd asked. There wasn't anything about it in the dispatches from headquarters. I'm afraid you find us not properly prepared to greet you, Reverend Ayres. My apologies."

"Think nothin' of it," said the chaplain, falling back into his former posture. "And jes' call me Rev, Lieutenant. Why, the less fuss y'all make about me, the better. I'm jes' here to do a job, same as everybody else."

"Yes, that's the spirit," said Phule. "Now, I think it's time for us to get back to the Fat Chance where you people can meet your new comrades and get started on your duties. I can promise you a very interesting tour of duty with us."

"That's why we're here," said one of the Gambolts— Dukes, the biggest of the trio. His expression could have passed for a grin, although the large and very sharp canine (or were they more properly *feline*?) teeth made it far more ferocious than an equivalent expression from a human.

"Good, then let's go," said Brandy. "Follow me, on the double!"

The new members of Phule's Company shouldered their bags, and followed Brandy and their officers past the line of curious tourists at the Immigration desk out to a waiting hoverbus that would take them back to the Fat Chance Hotel and their new assignment. They quickly stowed their bags and boarded, and the bus nosed out into the light traffic and headed away.

Neither they nor the tourists (who were after all most interested in getting to the casinos and spending their money) noticed the small figure in black that surreptitiously followed the legionnaires to the bus, and then set off on foot behind it, sticking carefully to the edge of the road and doing its best to avoid observation.